Taken at Dusk

ALSO BY C. C. HUNTER

Born at Midnight

Awake at Dawn

Taken at Dusk

• a shadow falls novel •

c. c. hunter

ST. MARTIN'S GRIFFIN ⚔ NEW YORK

TAKEN AT DUSK. Copyright © 2012 by Christie Craig. All rights reserved. Printed in the United States of America. For information, address St. Martin's Press, 175 Fifth Avenue, New York, N.Y. 10010.

www.stmartins.com

Library of Congress Cataloging-in-Publication Data

Hunter, C. C.
  Taken at dusk / C.C. Hunter.—1st ed.
    p. cm.
  ISBN 978-0-312-62469-9 (trade paperback)
  ISBN 978-1-4299-3844-0 (e-book)
  1. Supernatural—Fiction. 2. Ghosts—Fiction. 3. Camps—Fiction.
4. Love—Fiction. 5. Juvenile fiction / fantasy and magic. I. Title.

PZ7.H916565Tak 2012
[Fic]—dc23

                                        2011045137

First Edition: April 2012

10 9 8 7 6 5 4 3 2 1

There's always a person in your life who you know helped make you who you are. A person who, without them, you wouldn't have taken the same journey. A person who didn't just make a difference, they were the springboard for all you've achieved. Thank you hubby, Steve Craig, for all you have done to help me become who I am. Thank you for the love, for the years, and for the endless laughter you share with me. We make a hell of a team, don't you think?

Acknowledgments

To my agent, whose support and guidance is just what this writer needs. To Rose Hilliard, an angel of an editor. To Faye Hughes, my first reader, who isn't afraid of my scary first drafts. Thanks for the help, but mostly thanks for the friendship. To Susan Muller, Teri Thackston, and Suzan Harden: thank y'all for the support, the friendship, the critiques, and a heck of a lot of laughter. You will never know how much you mean to me. To Jody Payne, a woman whose courage and strength inspires me, whose writing support and friendship is invaluable.

To Rosa Brand, aka R. M. Brand, whose brilliance as a graphic artist stuns me. Thanks for your support, for your fabulous videos, and for the newfound friendship. Thanks to Kathleen Adey for the editing and support with publicity; you make meeting my deadlines an easier task.

Taken at Dusk

Chapter One

They were here. Really here.

Kylie Galen stepped out of the crowded dining hall into the bright sunlight. She looked over at the Shadow Falls office. Gone was the chatter of the other campers. Birds chirped in the distance and a rush of wind rustled the trees. Mostly she heard the sound of her own heart thudding in her chest.

Thump. Thump. Thump.

They were here.

Her pulse raced at the thought of meeting the Brightens, the couple who had adopted and raised her real father. A father she'd never known in life but had grown to love in his short visits from the afterlife.

She took one step and then another, unsure of the emotional storm brewing inside her.

Excitement.

Curiosity.

Fear. Yes, a lot of fear.

But of what?

A drip of sweat, more from nerves than Texas's mid-August heat index, rolled down her brow.

Go and uncover your past so you may discover your destiny. The death angels' mystical words replayed in her head. She took another step forward, then stopped. Even as her heart ached to solve the mystery of who her father was—of who she was and, hopefully, what she was—her instincts screamed for her to run and hide.

Was this what she feared? Learning the truth?

Before coming to Shadow Falls a few months ago, she'd been certain she was just a confused teen, that her feelings of being different were normal. Now she knew better.

She wasn't normal.

She wasn't even human. At least not all human.

And figuring out her nonhuman side was a puzzle.

A puzzle the Brightens could help her solve.

She took another step. The wind, as if it were as eager to escape as she was, whisked past. It picked up a few wayward strands of her blond hair and scattered them across her face.

She blinked, and when she opened her eyes, the brightness of the sun had evaporated. Glancing up, she saw a huge, angry-looking cloud hanging directly overhead. It cast a shadow around her and the woodsy terrain. Unsure if this was an omen or just a summer storm, she froze, her heart dancing faster. Taking a deep breath that smelled of rain, she was poised to move when a hand clasped her elbow. Memories of another hand grabbing her sent panic shooting through her veins.

She swung around.

"Whoa. You okay?" Lucas lightened his clasp around her arm.

Kylie caught her breath and stared up at the werewolf's blue eyes. "Yeah. You just . . . surprised me. You always surprise me. You need to whistle when you come up on me." She shoved down the memories of Mario and his rogue vampire grandson, Red.

"Sorry." He grinned and his thumb moved in soft little circles over the crease in her elbow. Somehow that light brush of his thumb felt . . . intimate. How did he make a simple touch feel like a sweet

sin? A gust of wind, now smelling like a storm, stirred his black hair
and tossed it over his brow.

He continued to stare at her, his blue eyes warming her and chas-
ing away her darkest fears. "You don't look okay. What's wrong?" He
reached up and tucked a wayward strand of hair behind her right
ear.

She looked away from him to the cabin that housed the office.
"My grandparents . . . the adopted parents of my real dad are here."

He must have picked up on her reluctance to be here. "I thought
you wanted to meet them. That's why you asked them to come, right?"

"I do. I'm just . . ."

"Scared?" he finished for her.

She didn't like admitting it, but since werewolves could smell fear,
lying was pointless. "Yeah." She looked back at Lucas and saw humor
in his eyes. "What's so funny?"

"You," he said. "I'm still trying to figure you out. When you were
kidnapped by a rogue vampire, you weren't this scared. In fact, you
were . . . amazing."

Kylie smiled. No, Lucas had been the amazing one. He'd risked
his life to save her from Mario and Red, and she'd never forget that.

"Seriously, Kylie, if this is the same couple I saw walking in here
a few minutes ago, then they're old and just humans. I think you can
take them with both hands tied behind your back."

"I'm not scared like that. I just . . ." She closed her eyes, unsure how
to explain something she wasn't clear on herself. Then the words just
came. "What am I going to say to them? 'I know you never told my
father he was adopted, but he figured it out after he died. And he
came to see me. Oh, yeah, he wasn't human. So could you please tell
me who his real parents are? So I can figure out what I am?' "

He must have heard the angst in her voice because his smile vanished. "You'll find a way."

"Yeah." But she wasn't that confident. She started walking, feeling his presence, his warmth, as he accompanied her up the steps to the cabin. The walk was easier with him beside her.

He stopped at the door and brushed a hand down her arm. "You want me to come inside with you?"

She almost told him yes, but this was one thing she needed to do on her own.

She thought she heard voices and glanced back at the door. Well, she wouldn't exactly be alone. No doubt Holiday, the camp leader, waited for her inside, prepared to offer moral support and a calming touch. Normally, Kylie objected to her emotions being manipulated, but right now might be an exception.

"Thanks, but I'm sure Holiday is in there."

He nodded. His gaze moved to her mouth, and his lips came dangerously close to hers. But before his mouth claimed hers, that bone-cold chill that came with the dead descended on her. She pressed two fingers to his lips. Kissing was something she preferred to do without an audience—even one from the other side.

Or maybe it wasn't just the audience. Was she totally ready to give herself over to his kisses? It was a good question, and one she needed to answer, but one problem at a time. Right now she had the Brightens to worry about.

"I should go." She motioned to the door. The cold washed over her again. Okay, she had the Brightens and a ghost to worry about.

Disappointment flashed in Lucas's eyes. Then he shifted uncomfortably and looked around as if he sensed they weren't alone.

"Good luck." He hesitated and then walked away.

She watched him leave and then looked around for the spirit. Goose bumps danced up her spine. Her ability to see ghosts had been the first clue that she wasn't normal.

"Can this wait until later?" she whispered.

A cloud of condensation appeared beside the white rocking chairs on the edge of the porch. The spirit obviously lacked the power or the knowledge to complete the manifestation. But it was enough to send the chairs rocking back and forth. The creaking of wood on wood sounded haunted . . . which it was.

She waited, thinking it was the female spirit who had appeared earlier today in her mother's car as they drove past the Fallen Cemetery on their way to camp. Who was she? What did she need Kylie to do? There were never any easy answers when dealing with ghosts.

"Now's not a good time." Not that saying so would do any good. Spirits believed in the open door policy.

The smear of fog took on more form, and Kylie's chest swelled with emotion.

It wasn't the woman she'd seen earlier.

"Daniel?" Kylie reached out. The tips of her fingers entered the icy mist as it took on a more familiar form. Hot emotion—a mixture of love and regret—coursed up her arm. She yanked her hand back, but tears filled her eyes.

"Daniel?" She almost called him Daddy. But it still felt awkward. She watched as he struggled to manifest.

He'd once explained that his time to linger on earth was limited. More tears filled her eyes as she realized how limited. Her sense of loss tripled when she considered how hard this must be for him. He wanted to be here when she met his parents. And she needed him here, too—wished he'd told her more about the Brightens—and wished more than anything that he'd never died.

"*No.*" His one word, briskly spoken, sounded urgent.

"No, what?" He didn't—or couldn't—answer. "No, I shouldn't ask them about your real parents? But I have to, Daniel, that's the only way I'll ever find the truth."

"*It's not—*" His voice broke.

"Not what? Not important?" She waited for his answer, but his weak apparition grew paler and his spiritual cold began to ebb. The white chairs slowed their rocking and silence rained down on her.

"It's important to me," Kylie said. "I need . . ." The Texas heat chased away the lingering chill.

He was gone. The thought hit that he might never come back. "Not fair." She swatted at the few tears she'd let fall onto her cheeks.

The need to run and hide hit again. But she'd procrastinated long enough. She grasped the doorknob, still cold from Daniel's spirit, and went to face the Brightens.

Inside, Kylie heard light murmurs coming from one of the back conference rooms. She tried to tune her ear to hear the words. Nothing.

In the last few weeks, she'd unexpectedly been gifted with sensitive hearing. But it came and went. What good was a power if one didn't know how to use it? It only added to the feeling of everything in her life being out of her control.

Biting her lip, she eased down the hall and tried to focus on her main goal: getting answers. Who were Daniel's real parents? What was she?

She heard Holiday say, "I'm sure you're going to love her."

Kylie's footsteps slowed. *Love?*

Wasn't that a little strong? They could just like her. That would be fine. Loving someone was . . . complicated. Even liking someone a whole lot came with a downside, such as a certain good-looking half-fae deciding that being close to her was too hard . . . so he left.

Yup, Derek was definitely an example of the downside of liking someone too much. And he probably was the reason she hesitated to accept Lucas's kisses.

One problem at a time. She pushed that thought away as she stepped into the open door of the conference room.

The elderly man sitting at the table rested his clasped hands on the large oak table. "What kind of trouble did she get into?"

"What do you mean?" Holiday cut her green gaze to the door, and she pushed her long red hair over her shoulder.

The old man continued, "We researched Shadow Falls on the Internet and it has a reputation for being a place for troubled teens."

Freaking great! Daniel's parents thought she was a juvenile delinquent.

"You shouldn't believe everything you read online." Only the slightest hint of annoyance sounded in Holiday's tone. "Actually, we're a school for very gifted teens who are trying to find themselves."

"Please tell me it's not drugs," said the silver-haired woman sitting beside the man. "I'm not sure I could deal with that."

"I'm not a druggie," Kylie said, sympathizing with Della, her vampire roommate, who had to deal with this suspicion from her parents. All heads turned toward Kylie, and feeling put on the spot, she held her breath.

"Oh, my," the woman said. "I didn't mean to offend."

Kylie eased into the room. "I'm not offended. I just wanted that cleared up." She met the woman's faded gray eyes and shifted her focus to the old man, searching . . . but for what? A resemblance, perhaps. Why? She knew they weren't Daniel's real parents. But they had raised him, had probably instilled in him their mannerisms and qualities.

Kylie thought of Tom Galen, her stepdad, the man who'd raised her, the man who until recently she'd believed was her real father. Though Kylie had yet to come to terms with his abandonment of his seventeen-year marriage to her mom, she couldn't deny she'd taken on some of his mannerisms. Not that she didn't see more of Daniel in herself—from her supernatural DNA to her physical features.

"We read this was a home for troubled teens." An apology rang in the old man's voice.

She recalled Daniel telling her that his adoptive parents had loved him and would have loved her if they'd known her.

Love. Emotion crowded her chest. Trying to decipher the sensation, Kylie remembered Nana—her mom's mother—and how much she'd adored her, how much she'd missed her when she died. Was it knowing the Brightens were old—that their time was short—that made Kylie want to pull back?

As if the thought of death had somehow caused it, a ghostly chill filled the room. *Daniel?* She called to him with her mind, but the coldness prickling her skin was different.

As frigid air entered Kylie's lungs, the spirit materialized behind Mrs. Brighten. While the apparition appeared feminine, her bald head reflected the light above. Raw-looking stitches ran across her bare scalp and caused Kylie to flinch.

"We're just concerned," said Mr. Brighten. "We didn't know you existed."

"I . . . understand," Kylie answered, unable to look away from the spirit that stared at the elderly couple in puzzlement.

Seeing the spirit's face again, Kylie realized it was the same woman from earlier today. Obviously, her shaved head and stitches were a clue. But a clue to what?

The spirit looked at Kylie. *"I'm so confused."*

Me too, Kylie thought, unsure if the spirit could read her mind the way the others had.

"So many people want me to tell you something."

"Who?" Realizing she'd whispered the word out loud, she bit her lip. Was it Daniel? Nana? *What do they want you to tell me?*

The spirit met Kylie's gaze as if she understood. *"Someone lives. Someone dies."*

More puzzles, Kylie thought, and looked away from the ghost. She saw Holiday glance around, sensing the spirit. Mrs. Brighten looked at the ceiling as if searching for an AC vent to blame for the chill. Luckily the spirit faded, taking the cold with her.

Pushing the ghost from her mind, Kylie looked back at the Brightena. Her gaze took in the mop of thick gray hair on the elderly man. His pale complexion told her that he'd been a redhead in his younger years.

For some reason, Kylie felt compelled to wiggle her eyebrows and check the couple's brain patterns. It was a little supernatural trick she'd only recently learned, one that mostly allowed supernaturals to recognize one another and humans. Mr. and Mrs. Brighten were human.

Normals and probably decent people. So why did Kylie feel so jittery?

She studied the couple as they studied her. She waited for them to make some declaration of how much she looked like Daniel. But it didn't come.

Instead, Mrs. Brighten said, "We're really excited to meet you."

"Me too," Kylie said. *As well as scared to death.* She sat in the chair beside Holiday, opposite the Brightens. Reaching under the table, she sought out Holiday's hand and gave it a squeeze. A welcome calm flowed from the camp leader's touch.

"Can you tell me about my father?" Kylie asked.

"Of course." Mrs. Brighten's expression softened. "He was a very charismatic child. Popular. Smart. Outgoing."

Kylie rested her free hand on the table. "Not like me, then." She bit her lip, not meaning to say it out loud.

Mrs. Brighten frowned. "I wouldn't say that. Your camp leader was just telling us how wonderful you are." She reached across the table to rest her warm hand on Kylie's. "I can't believe we have a granddaughter."

There was something about the woman's touch that stirred Kylie's emotions. Not just the heat of the woman's skin—it was the thinness, the slight tremble of the fingers, and the defined bones that time and arthritis had changed. Kylie remembered Nana—remembered how her grandmother's gentle touch had grown more fragile before she died. Without warning, grief swelled in Kylie's chest. Grief for Nana, and maybe even the forewarning of what she would feel for Daniel's parents when their time came. Considering their age, that time would come too soon.

"When did you learn Daniel was your father?" Mrs. Brighten's hand still rested on Kylie's wrist. It felt oddly comforting.

"Just recently," she said through a knot of emotion. "My parents are divorcing and the truth sort of came out." That wasn't altogether a lie.

"A divorce? You poor child."

The old man nodded in agreement, and Kylie noticed his eyes were blue—like her dad's and hers. "We're glad you chose to find us."

"So very glad." Mrs. Brighten's voice trembled. "We've never stopped missing our son. He died so young." A quiet sensation of loss, of shared grief, entered the room.

Kylie bit her tongue to keep from telling them how she'd come to love Daniel herself. From assuring them that he had loved them. So many things she longed to ask them, to tell them, but couldn't.

"We brought pictures," Mrs. Brighten said.

"Of my dad?" Kylie leaned forward.

Mrs. Brighten nodded and shifted in her chair. Moving with old bones, she pulled a brown envelope from her big white old-lady purse. Kylie's heart raced with eagerness to see the pictures of Daniel. Had he looked like her when he was young?

The woman passed the envelope to Kylie, and she opened it as quickly as she could.

Her throat tightened when she saw the first image—a young Daniel, maybe six, without his front teeth. She could remember the images of her own toothless school pictures, and she could swear the resemblance was amazing.

The photos took her through Daniel's life—from when he was a young teen with long hair and frayed jeans to when he was an adult.

In the adult photo, he was with a group of people. Kylie's throat tightened even more when she realized who was standing beside him. Her mother.

Her gaze shot up. "That's my mom."

Mrs. Brighten nodded. "Yes, we know."

"You do?" Kylie asked, confused. "I didn't think you ever met her."

"We suspected," Mr. Brighten spoke up. "After we learned about you, we suspected that she might have been the one who was in the picture."

"Oh." Kylie looked back down at the images and wondered how they could have gotten all that from one photo. Not that it matttered. "Can I keep these?"

"Of course you may," Mrs. Brighten said. "I made copies. Daniel would have wanted you to have them."

Yes, he would. Kylie recalled him trying to materialize as if he had something important to tell her. "My mom loved him," Kylie added, recalling her mom's concerns that the Brightens might resent her for not attempting to find them earlier. But they didn't seem to harbor any negative feelings.

"I'm sure she did." Mrs. Brighten leaned in and touched Kylie's hand again. Warmth and genuine emotion flowed from the touch. It almost . . . almost felt magical.

A sudden beep of Kylie's phone shattered the fragile silence. She ignored the incoming text, feeling almost mesmerized by Mrs. Brighten's eyes. Then, for reasons Kylie didn't understand, her heart opened up.

Maybe she did want them to love her. Maybe she wanted to love them as well. It didn't matter how little time they had left. Or that they weren't her biological grandparents. They had loved her father and lost him. Just as she had. It only seemed right that they love each other.

Was that what Daniel had wanted to tell her? Kylie glanced

down at the photographs one more time and then slipped them back into the envelope, knowing she would spend hours studying them later.

Kylie's phone rang. She moved to shut it off and saw Derek's name on the screen. Her heart missed a beat. Was he calling to apologize for leaving? Did she want him to apologize?

Another phone rang. This time it was Holiday's cell.

"Excuse me." Holiday rose and started to leave the room as she took the call. She came to an abrupt stop at the door. "Slow down," she said into the phone. The tightness in the camp leader's voice changed the mood in the room. Holiday swung back around and stepped closer to Kylie.

"What is it?" Kylie muttered.

Holiday pressed a hand on Kylie's shoulder, then snapped her phone shut and focused on the Brightens. "There's been an emergency. We'll have to reschedule this meeting."

"What's wrong?" Kylie asked.

Holiday didn't answer. Kylie glanced back at the Brightens' disappointed faces and she felt that same emotion weaving its way through her chest. "Can't we—"

"No," Holiday said. "I'm going to have to ask you folks to leave. *Now.*"

The camp leader's tone was punctuated by the jarring sound of the cabin's front door opening and slamming against the wall. Both of the elderly Brightens flinched and then stared at the door as the sound of thundering footsteps raced toward the conference room.

Chapter Two

Three minutes later, Kylie stood in the parking lot and watched the Brightens' silver Cadillac drive away. She turned to glare at Della and Lucas, who'd stormed into the office and interrupted her meeting with her grandparents. Perry had been with them, too, but he'd wisely disappeared. Holiday, who had followed them outside, was on the phone again.

"Would someone please tell me what's going on?" Kylie asked, feeling as if her chance to discover more about her father were disappearing along with the Cadillac. She suddenly realized she still held the brown envelope of images of Daniel, and she clutched them tighter.

"Don't get your panties in a wad. We're just watching your back." The tips of Della's canines peeked through the corners of her lips. Her dark eyes, with a slight slant, and her straight black hair hinted at her part Asian heritage.

"Watching my back for what?"

"Derek called." Holiday closed her phone and stepped into the circle. "He was worried." Her phone rang again, and after looking at the call log, she held up a finger. "Sorry. One minute."

Patience wearing thin, Kylie looked back at Della and Lucas. "What's up?"

Lucas moved in. "Burnett phoned us and asked us to make our presence known to the visitors." His gaze met hers and, as earlier, concern flickered in his blue eyes.

Burnett, a thirty-something vampire, worked for the FRU—Fallen Research Unit—a branch of the FBI whose job it was to govern the supernaturals. He was also part owner of Shadow Falls. When Burnett gave an order, he expected people to obey. And they usually did.

"Why?" Kylie asked. "I needed to ask them questions." Unexpectedly, the memory of how Mrs. Brighten's hand felt on hers flashed in her mind—gentle, fragile. Emotions came at Kylie from every direction.

"Burnett never gives his reasons," Della said. "He gives orders."

Kylie glanced at Holiday, who was still on the phone. She looked worried, and Kylie felt Holiday's emotions join the others already dancing along her spine.

"I don't understand." She fought the tightness in her throat.

Lucas stepped closer. So close that she could smell his scent—a scent that reminded her of how the dew-kissed woods smelled first thing in the morning.

His hand came up and she thought he was going to reach for her, but he lowered his hand just as quickly. She fought against disappointment.

Holiday hung up the phone. "That was Burnett." She stepped forward and rested a hand on Kylie's shoulder.

She didn't want to be calmed; she wanted answers. So she removed the camp leader's hand. "Just tell me what happened. *Please.*"

"Derek called," Holiday said. "He went to see the P.I. who helped you find your grandparents and found him unconscious in his office. Then Derek discovered the man's phone on the floor outside of his office with blood on it. Bottom line, Derek doesn't think the P.I. sent that text to you about your grandparents. He called Burnett, who's there now."

Kylie tried to understand what Holiday was saying. "But if the P.I. didn't send the text, who did?"

Holiday shrugged. "We don't know."

"Derek could be wrong," Lucas said, his lack of affection for the half-fae deepening the vibration in his voice.

Kylie ignored Lucas and his vibrations and tried to digest what Holiday was implying. "So . . . Derek and Burnett think that Mr. and Mrs. Brighten were impostors?"

Holiday nodded. "If Derek's right and the text was sent by the person who hurt the P.I., then it makes sense that these two could have been sent here for other reasons."

"But they're human," Kylie said. "I checked."

"Definitely human," Della said.

"I know," Holiday explained. "That's the reason I didn't detain or question them. The last thing I need is to bring more suspicion on Shadow Falls. We already have the locals breathing down our necks. But being human doesn't mean they aren't working for someone else. Someone supernatural."

Kylie knew by "someone," Holiday meant Mario Esparza, grandfather to the murdering rogue who'd taken a liking to her.

For a split second, Kylie got a vision of the two teenage girls she'd met in town, the two who'd died at the hands of Red, Mario Esparza's grandson. More frustration and anger wound its way into her emotional bank.

"But they brought me pictures." She held up the envelope.

Holiday took the envelope and quickly glanced through the stack of pictures. For some odd reason, Kylie wanted to jerk them back, as if Holiday's action were somehow irreverent. "There aren't any family pictures in here. You would think there would be one or two of them with their son."

Kylie took the pictures back and slipped them into the envelope, trying to wrap her head around what they were insinuating. Then her thoughts went elsewhere. "But what if they really are my grand-parents and whoever went to the P.I. is going to try to get to them?" She remembered the frailness of the elderly woman's palm on top of hers. What little life the woman had left could easily be yanked away from her.

Kylie's chest ached. Had she put Daniel's parents in danger by finding them? Had that been what Daniel had wanted to tell her? She felt Lucas's gaze on her, as if offering some small amount of comfort.

Holiday spoke up again. "I don't see any reason for someone to involve them. However, Perry is following them. If anyone tries to harm them, he'll take care of things."

"Yeah, Perry could seriously kick ass if he has to," Della said.

"And I'm sure the P.I. is working a hundred different cases," Lucas said. "The P.I. being attacked doesn't mean it's linked to Kylie. It could be one of his other cases. Private investigators piss people off all the time."

"True," Holiday said. "But Burnett was concerned enough to want the Brightens away from the camp. We need to be cautious."

Kylie's mind took a U-turn and parked on the fact that it was Perry, one of the resident shape-shifters, following the Brightens. "What was Perry when he took off after them?"

The last time she'd seen Perry in an alternate form, he'd been some kind of pterodactyl creature that looked as if it had stepped out of the Jurassic age. Of course, Kylie supposed that was better than the SUV-sized lion or the unicorn he'd turned into before that. Oh hell! If he wasn't careful, Perry could end up giving the elderly couple heart attacks.

"Don't worry," Holiday said. "Perry won't do anything ridiculous."

Miranda chose that moment to join the group. "Please, Perry and all things ridiculous go together like toads and warts," she said, and pushed her tricolored dyed hair over her shoulder as if to punctuate her attitude.

Miranda was one of seven witches at Shadow Falls, and she was also Kylie's other roommate. From Miranda's tone, it was clear she wasn't ready to forgive Perry for being cruel to her when he'd found out another shape-shifter had kissed her . . . especially when she'd apologized. The witch's gaze shot around the group.

"What?" Miranda asked. "Is something wrong?" Concern tightened her eyes, proving that while she might not be over being mad, neither was she over caring for the shape-shifter. "Is Perry okay? Is he?" She reached up and caught a strand of pink hair and twirled it around her finger.

"Perry's fine," Holiday and Kylie said at the same time. Then Kylie's mind returned to her concern for the Brightens—if they really were the Brightens.

She looked at Holiday. "What would anyone gain by pretending to be my grandparents?"

"Access to you," Holiday answered.

"But they seemed so genuine." And then Kylie remembered. "No. They couldn't have been impostors. I . . . saw the death angels. They sent me a message."

"Oh, crappers," Della said, and she and Miranda took a step back. While Lucas didn't flinch, his eyes widened. According to legend, death angels were supposed to be the ones who doled out punishment to keep the nonhuman species in line. Almost every supernatural knew of a friend of a friend who'd misbehaved and then gotten fried to a crisp by a vengeful death angel.

While Kylie sensed the power of these angels, she wasn't so sure their harmful reputation wasn't exaggerated. Not that she was eager to test the theory. However, considering she made her share of mistakes and hadn't been burned or turned to ash, she questioned the rumors of those who had.

"What message?" Holiday asked, her tone free of any misgiving. The camp leader, another ghost whisperer, was one of the few who didn't fear the death angels.

"Shadows . . . on the dining hall wall, then . . ."

"When we were in there?" Della asked. "And you didn't tell us?"

Kylie ignored Della. "I heard a voice in my head say to go find my destiny. Why would I get that message if they weren't my grandparents?"

"Good question," Holiday said. "But maybe they just meant this situation is what will lead you to the truth."

"She should have told us," Della muttered to Miranda.

Kylie recalled Daniel showing up, the urgency she'd heard in his tone in what little he'd communicated. Had she totally misunderstood what he'd wanted to tell her? Had he come to warn her that the couple weren't his adoptive parents? Doubt built, and she didn't know what she believed anymore.

Kylie breathed in, and another concern dove right into her worry bank. "Is the P.I. going to be okay?"

"I don't know." Holiday frowned. "Burnett said Derek was at the hospital with him now. Burnett is still investigating the crime scene."

Worry for Derek tightened Kylie's chest. She pulled her phone out of her pocket and dialed his number.

When he didn't answer, she didn't know if it was because he couldn't or if he was back to not talking to her. Back to pushing her out of his life.

Men!

Why was it that boys said girls were so hard to understand, when she hadn't known a single guy who hadn't confused her to the point of screaming?

• • •

As everyone hung out talking, Kylie snuck away and went around
back to sit beside her favorite tree. She opened the envelope and slowly
went through the pictures, noting all the little things about Daniel.
They way his blue eyes lit up when he smiled, the way his hair flipped
up just a bit on the ends when he wore it long. She saw so much of
herself in him, and her heart doubled over with grief at missing him.

When she came across the picture of her mom and him, Kylie
found herself smiling at the way Daniel was looking at her mom, and
the way her mom was looking at him. Love. Part of Kylie wanted to
call her mom right then and tell her about the photo, but considering
what Holiday and the others thought, she supposed it was best to
keep quiet. But hopefully not for long.

"Hey."

Lucas's voice pulled her attention up, and she smiled. "Hi."

"Mind some company?" he asked.

"I'll share my tree with you." She scooted over.

He dropped down beside her and studied her face. His shoulder,
so warm, came against hers, and she savored his closeness. "You look
happy and sad, and confused." He brushed a few strands of her hair
from her face.

"I feel confused," she said. "They were so nice and . . . I don't
know what to believe now. How could they have these pictures if
they aren't really the Brightens?"

"They could have stolen them," he said.

His words hurt, but she knew he could be right. But why would
anyone go that far to convince her they were Daniel's parents? What
could they possibly gain by doing that?

He looked down at the pictures she held in her hand. "Can I see?"

Nodding, she passed him the stack of photos.

He slowly flipped through them. "It must be weird looking at
someone's face who you look so much like and not knowing him."

She gazed up at Lucas. "But I do know him."

His brows arched up. "I mean . . . in person."

She nodded, understanding his inability to grasp the whole ghost thing, but wishing it weren't so hard for him.

"Burnett will get to the bottom of this." His gaze lowered to her mouth. For a second, she thought he was going to kiss her, but he stiffened and looked up toward the woods.

Fredericka, scowling at the two of them, walked out from behind the bushes. "The pack is looking for you."

Lucas frowned. "I'll be right there."

She didn't move. She just continued to stare. "They shouldn't have to wait on their leader."

Lucas growled, "I said I'd be right there."

Fredericka walked away, and Lucas looked down at her. "Sorry. I should go."

"Is something wrong?" Kylie asked, noting the concern filling his eyes.

"Nothing I can't handle." He pressed a quick kiss on her lips and slid the photos back into her hands.

"Are you going to be okay?" Holiday asked when Kylie walked back onto the office porch.

Kylie plopped down in one of the large white rocking chairs. The sticky heat seemed to cling to her skin. "I'll live." She set the envelope on the small patio table between the chairs and pulled her hair back and held it off the back of her neck. "Do you really think they were impostors?"

Holiday sat in the other rocker. Her red hair hung loose around her shoulders. "I don't know. But Burnett won't let it rest until he gets to the bottom of this. He feels guilty that he wasn't more on top of things and let Mario get to you. I imagine after this, he's not going to want to let you out of his sight."

"He had no way of knowing what the creep was up to," Kylie said.

"I know that. You know that. But Burnett has a tendency to be a bit harder on himself."

"Aren't all vampires?" Kylie considered Della and the emotional baggage she carted around.

"Not really," Holiday said. "You'd be amazed how many vamps refuse to take any responsibility for their actions. It's always someone else's fault."

Kylie almost asked if Holiday was referring to a certain vampire who'd broken her heart in the past. But her thoughts went back to the Brightens. "You were there. Didn't you read their emotions? Weren't they sincere? I felt somehow . . . connected to them."

Holiday tilted her head as if thinking. "They were very guarded, almost too much so, but . . . yeah, they read sincere. Especially Mrs. Brighten."

"Then how could they—"

"Reading emotions is never a hundred percent certain," Holiday said. "Emotions can be disguised, hidden, even faked."

"By humans?" Kylie asked.

"Humans are masters at it. Better than supernaturals. I've often thought that since their species lack any superpower to control their worlds, they have worked harder at controlling their emotions."

Kylie listened, while her heart chewed on concern for the Brightens.

"Narcissism, detachment, schizoid personality, sociopath—these things run rampant in the human race in varying degrees. Then you have the actors who can create an emotion within themselves by simply borrowing it from a past experience. I've attended plays and shows where the emotions flowing from the actors were as real as I've ever felt."

Kylie leaned back in her chair. "I'm part human and I can't seem to control anything."

Holiday glanced at her with empathy. "I'm sorry I had to send them away. I know you were hoping to learn something. But I couldn't risk that Derek might be right."

"I understand." And she did. She just didn't like it. "Mrs. Brighten—if she really was Mrs. Brighten—reminded me of my grandmother."

"Nana," Holiday said, and Kylie remembered that Nana's spirit had paid Holiday a visit.

"Yeah."

Holiday sighed. "I know this is difficult for you."

The camp leader's phone rang and Kylie held her breath, hoping it was news on the Brightens, Derek, or the P.I.

The camp leader glanced at the call log. "It's just my mom. I'll call her later."

Kylie pulled one knee up to her chest and wrapped her hand around her leg. The silence that followed called for the truth. "I feel as if nothing in my life makes sense anymore. Everything is changing."

Holiday wrapped her hair into a rope. "Change isn't the worst thing, Kylie. It's when things aren't changing that you have to worry."

"I disagree." Kylie dropped her chin down on her kneecap. "I mean, I know change is necessary for growth and all that stuff. But I'd like one thing in my life to feel . . . grounded. I need a touchstone. Something that feels real."

Holiday raised her brows. "Shadow Falls is real, Kylie. It's your touchstone."

"I know. I know I belong here, it's just that I still don't know *how* I belong. And please don't tell me that I should make this my quest. Because that's been my quest since I've been here and I'm not any closer to figuring it now than I was then."

"That's not true." Holiday pulled her knees up, and in the over-size rocking chair, her petite form looked even smaller. "Look how far you've come. Like you said, you know you belong here. That's a big step. And your gifts are coming in left and right."

"Gifts that I mostly don't know how to control or when they might or might not pop in again. Not that I'm complaining." Kylie dropped her forehead on her kneecap and let go of an exaggerated sigh.

Holiday chuckled.

Kylie glanced up. "I sound pathetic, don't I."

Holiday frowned. "No. You sound frustrated. And to be honest, after what happened to you this weekend, you deserve to be frustrated. You might even deserve to be a little pathetic."

"Nobody has the right to be pathetic," Kylie said.

"I don't know about that. I think I've earned the right a few times in my life." Holiday set her rocking chair into a slow swaying motion.

Kylie stared at the camp leader, and she had a distinct feeling that there were a lot of things Holiday still hadn't told Kylie about herself.

"Did I sense a new spirit earlier?" Holiday asked.

"Yeah." Kylie leaned back in the chair. "She's still not making sense. Says she's confused." Kylie recalled the angry-looking stitches she'd seen on the woman's head. "I think she died of a brain tumor or something. She had a shaved head and scars."

"Hmm," Holiday said.

"And I think she's buried at Fallen Cemetery."

"Really? Did she tell you that?"

"No, but that's where I felt like I picked her up. Driving here this morning, my mom had just passed the cemetery when the spirit popped into the backseat."

"I guess that could be it."

"But you don't think so?" Kylie asked, unsure of Holiday's logic.

"I'm not saying it can't be that simple, but I've found the majority of spirits that come to us have . . . connections more than just our driving by a cemetery. Now, I'm not saying we don't get random ghosts sometimes, because we do. The other day, I got a dripping wet, elderly man, naked as the day he was born. He died in the shower at his nursing home. Wanted me to tell the nurse to please come get him out." Holiday shook her head.

"What did you do?" Kylie asked.

"I called the nursing home and said I was a friend of the family and had tried to call Mr. Banes in his room and he wasn't answering."

"And he went away?"

"Crossed right over."

"I hope this spirit is that easy. I could use a break." Then Kylie remembered what the spirit had said. "You know . . . the spirit said that there were people who wanted her to tell me something."

"Tell you what?"

"I asked, but . . . she said something like, some people live and some people die. It didn't make sense."

"They seldom do at first."

Kylie bit down on her lip. "Could it be my dad trying to tell me something? He tried to appear right before I saw the Brightens—or whoever they were."

Holiday stopped rocking. "What did he say?"

"He couldn't completely manifest. All I got were a few words." Kylie frowned. "Why does he have to stop coming to see me?"

Holiday's expression filled with sympathy. "Death is a new beginning, Kylie. One can't begin the new until they let go of the old. He has held on to the past for a long time. He needs to move forward. Do you understand what I'm saying?"

Kylie stopped her chair's swaying. "Understand it? Maybe. Like it? No." Sighing, she stood up. "I told Miranda and Della I'd meet them back at the cabin."

"Sure." Holiday hesitated a moment. "I thought now might be a good time to chat about your new gifts."

"What's to talk about? Just because I ran through a concrete wall?" Kylie used sarcasm to cover up her unresolved feeling.

Holiday grinned. "And you healed Sara. And Lucas."

Kylie sat back down. "We hope I healed Sara."

"From what you said, I'd be surprised if you hadn't." Holiday continued to stare. "If one of your gifts is that you're a protector, Kylie, this could only be the beginning of your talents. I'm surprised you aren't peppering me with questions."

"Maybe I'd like a few answers before I start asking more questions. And I don't even mean about what I am, but about who the Brightens are. And what my dad wanted to tell me."

Holiday's eyes filled with understanding. "It's all happening very fast, isn't it?"

"Yes, and talking about it's not going to change anything." Her chest swelled with emotion.

"It could. Sometimes things don't feel real until we talk about them. "

Kylie released a breath. "I'm not sure I want it to feel any more real right now."

"Perhaps we should take a walk up to the falls?"

"No," Kylie said, unsure she could go there and not get upset if all she got from those magical waters was a voice telling her to be patient. Hadn't she been patient long enough? "Can we just talk later?"

"Fine." Holiday started to touch her and then pulled back. "But only a temporary postponement. We really need to talk."

"Yeah, I know." Kylie popped back up and reached for the envelope.

"Can I keep these for a while?" Holiday asked.

Kylie's heart clutched. "I . . ."

"Just for a few days. I'm sure Burnett is going to want to check and see if they are originals or copies."

Kylie nodded. "They're important to me."

Holiday smiled with honest understanding. "I know."

Kylie took one step off the porch and turned back around. "You will let me know the instant you hear something from Burnett or Derek, right?"

"The instant," Holiday assured her.

Kylie started to leave and then turned back, walked over to Holiday, and hugged her. Hugged her really tight.

"Thank you," Kylie said.

"For what?" Holiday sounded confused, but it didn't stop her from hugging Kylie back.

"For being here. For being you. For putting up with me."

Holiday snickered. "You're beginning to sound melodramatic, and that's just a hair away from pathetic."

Kylie broke the embrace, smiled back at Holiday, and took off down the trail to her cabin.

She hadn't gotten halfway there when the hair on the back of her neck seemed to dance and she felt the unmistakable sense of being watched. She glanced to the woods on her left but saw nothing but trees and underbrush. She fixed her stare to the right and found the overgrown terrain to be equally empty. But she still felt it—even stronger.

Glancing up at the cloudless blue sky, she blinked. A bird soared high overhead. The broad wingspan, the hooked beak, and the white splash of coloring on his chest identified him as an eagle. She studied the creature, slowly gliding as if taking his sweet time, as if he were transfixed by . . . the view?

What view?

Did he watch her? Was the feeling she got from the bird? Was it just your average eagle? Or was it like Perry, who could change his form into anything he desired? She continued to watch him, feeling uneasy.

Without warning, the eagle changed course. His movements quickened as he charged. Close. Closer. She met his eyes. The fierceness made her shudder. Or was it his thick talons held out as if prepared to attack?

The *whoosh* of air from his wings hit her face, and she slammed her eyes shut.

Chapter Three

Kylie threw up her arm to protect her face, but she felt nothing, no claws cutting into her flesh. Not on her face or her arm.

She heard rustling at her feet, accompanied by a rattling noise. Uncovering her face, she looked down. Her breath caught. She lurched back as the eagle used his sharp beak and talons to attack the snake that lay a few inches from her feet. The rattling noise hit again. She noticed the diamondlike shapes on the back of the brown-and-tan snake, then her gaze followed the coiled reptile to the dry, tan appendage growing from its tail.

A rattlesnake.

She lunged back. The bird buried his talons into the round, thick flesh of the snake. The eagle's wings worked overtime as he carried the squirming snake a few feet off the ground. The flapping of wings, the *whoosh*ing of air, and the distinctive rattle of the reptile filled her ears. The eagle hung a few feet above the ground, his wings slapping against the air.

She stood in the middle of the path and watched as the huge bird flew away with his prey. Looking back at her feet, she saw dusty marks in the path where the snake had fought for its life and lost. Beside the marks, a pair of shoe prints pressed into the ground. Her shoes. Had the eagle not charged, would she have seen the snake? Or would she now have the rattler's venom running up her leg?

Was she just lucky, or had this meant something? She considered turning around and finding Holiday, but logic intervened. She was in the woods in the Texas Hill Country. Her father—stepfather— had warned her constantly about snakes.

Convincing herself that this was just an uncanny moment that she'd gotten to experience nature at its scariest, she took another step forward. She did glance up one more time, though. The eagle, with the snake still tightly in his clutches, circled above. She stared, her breath caught in her throat. And as crazy as it seemed, she could swear the eagle stared back.

She stood, hand shadowing her eyes, and watched him until he was a dark speck fading into the massive blue sky. A thought hit that she should be grateful to the eagle, but the cold look in the bird's eyes flashed in her mind and sent a shiver down her spine.

Moving her hand away from her brow, she started for her cabin when her gaze clashed with another cold pair of eyes. Fredericka. Kylie remembered how angry Fredericka had been when she'd caught her and Lucas behind the office. Not that they'd been doing any- thing but looking at pictures of Daniel and talking.

"How does it feel to be a play toy?" Fredericka's voice sounded tight with anger, the kind of anger that could bring out the claws. And the hint of orange in the girl's dark eyes said the claws were defi- nitely an option.

Kylie inhaled and reminded herself not to show any fear. "Jealousy isn't becoming on you."

"I'm not jealous." Fredericka flashed a smug smile. "Especially now."

Now what? Kylie wanted to ask, but to do so would have given the bully credence, and Kylie refused to do that. Instead, she started walking away. She told herself to forget about Fredericka, that she had other problems to chew on right now. Kylie pulled out her phone to see if Derek had ever returned her call about the detective. He hadn't.

"Lucas's bloodline is pure, he values that," Fredericka spouted from behind Kylie. "The forefathers value that, too. They've made that clear. So when it comes time for him to seek his true mate, he won't dirty up his bloodline with the likes of you."

Nonsense, Kylie told herself, and kept walking. Fredericka was just talking nonsense. She had grandparents or pretend grandparents to worry about, so she wouldn't let this she-wolf upset her. Then the memory of the eagle filled her mind. Maybe she should worry about that, too.

Less than an hour later, still not hearing from Derek, Perry, or Burnett, Kylie sat at the kitchen table in her cabin with Miranda and Della. She'd told them about the snake and eagle and her thoughts that the incident was somehow more than it appeared.

"I would have smelled it if we had intruders," Della assured her.

"And I would have felt it if magic was being used to cover someone's tracks," Miranda said.

"See, that's why I need you guys," Kylie said. "You keep me from losing it." She leaned back in her chair, wishing their confirmation had chased away all her doubts. Then again, maybe it wasn't the doubts bothering her, but everything else on her plate.

Kylie's pet, Socks Jr.—the kitten Miranda had accidentally turned into a skunk—leapt up and landed in her lap. While Kylie still felt caught in the tailspin of the emotional storm, doing something as commonplace as their diet soda roundtable discussions brought some solace.

Miranda, up first in the discussion of their weekend woes and whines, retold everything about her witches' competition, in which she'd placed second. "I was excited that I placed so high," she said. "I thought my mom would be happy. But no." Miranda hesitated. "Second just means you're the first loser," she recounted her mother's words. The tone in Miranda's voice told Kylie how much her friend was hurting. "I wanted to impress her, and for a minute there, I thought I'd actually, finally done it. I'll never make that woman happy."

Della rolled her eyes. "Why would you want to make her happy?"

"Because she's my mom." Miranda answered with so much honesty that sadness tugged at Kylie's heart. She remembered feeling much the same way about her own mom before they found their peace.

"News flash," Della said, waving her hand. "Your mom's the biggest b . . . witch I've ever heard of. At least my parents' attitude is because they're worried I'm hurting myself by doing drugs and not because they aren't happy with me." Tears brightened Miranda's eyes and anger tightened her expression as she stared at Della.

Kylie felt tension thickening in the air. "I think what Della means is—"

"I'm sorry," Della interrupted Kylie. The smartass look on Della's face quickly faded into a frown. "That sounded mean, and I . . . Truth is if my parents knew the truth, they'd probably rather me be a drug addict than a vampire." Della studied Miranda and sighed. "It just makes me furious at your mom. I know how hard you worked to impress her. And you took friggin' second place, which is fabulous."

"Thanks," Miranda said, her anger dissolving but her eyes getting wetter.

"For what?" Della flopped back into the chair, as if aware she'd shown a softer side of her personality. Della seldom let that side show. Not that Kylie and Miranda didn't see it. Well, Kylie saw it. Miranda had a harder time seeing through Della's guarded front.

Miranda brushed her hand over her cheek again and sat up taller.

"Enough about that. I've got other news. Todd Freeman, a warlock, came over and asked if he could have my cell number. He's like the hottest guy in my old school. So at least someone noticed I did good in the competition." She grinned. "Not that I think it was my trophy he was interested in. I caught him at least three times checking out my girls."

"Jerk," Della said. "I hope the only thing you gave him was your middle finger."

"Duh, didn't you hear me? Cutest guy in school. Besides, big boobs are natural guy magnets—that's just the way it is. Why wouldn't I give my number to him?"

"Oh, I don't know. Maybe because you still want to suck face with a certain shape-shifter?"

"Please, I'm so over Perry," Miranda snapped.

Della tapped the end of her nose. "Pheromones don't lie."

"No arguing on the first day back," Kylie said. "Tomorrow you two can threaten to tear each other's limbs off, but today . . . just give me a little peace today." She picked up Socks from her lap and placed him on the table. "Besides . . . you're gonna upset Socks and then we're all gonna end up getting skunked."

Della and Miranda looked at Socks. The little skunk/cat, uncomfortable being the center of attention, scurried closer to Kylie.

"Truce?" Kylie asked, stroking the scared animal's trembling body.

Thankfully, Miranda and Della nodded.

Miranda leaned closer. "I think I've figured out how to turn our little stinker back into a kitten. But I need the first rays of sunshine to do it." She reached over to pet Socks, but he backed away from her touch and then jumped back into Kylie's lap.

"Smart skunk," Della said, grinning. "No telling what you'll accidentally turn him into next time."

Miranda frowned. "Maybe I'll turn *you* into a skunk."

"And maybe I'll rip your heart out and feed it to our resident pet."

"What happened to the truce?" Kylie whined. Socks's nose nudged deeper into her armpit.

"Fine." Miranda huffed and then looked at Della. "Your turn. Give us the lowdown on your weekend."

"You mean besides constantly being told to go pee on a stick? They tested me four times. I think one was a pregnancy test. Like I've been doing the dirty with anyone." Della picked up her cup of blood and gave it a hard look. "The only thing we did all weekend was go see a movie, some old classic my mother loved. Boring. At least I got to sleep without having to explain why I seemed so tired in the middle of the day." She exhaled rather loudly. "So that's my weekend. Nothing exciting to tell. Nothing." She stared back into her cup.

It wasn't her avoiding direct eye contact that gave it away, more like the emphasis on the second "nothing" that hinted at the truth. Miranda shot Kylie a quick look that said she'd heard it, too. The little vamp was holding back . . . as usual.

While Kylie debated the wisdom of trying to push Della into giving more, Miranda, who spoke first and seldom thought things through, knocked wisdom out the window and went for it.

"Liar," Miranda accused. "If I could hear your heartbeat right now, I bet it would prove it, too. What happened? What are you not telling us?"

Della snarled at Miranda. Kylie could feel the fragile truce shattering.

"Chan didn't show up, did he?" Miranda asked.

Kylie hadn't thought about that. "Did he show up?" Kylie seconded Miranda's question—not out of curiosity, but out of concern.

Chan, Della's cousin, was also a vampire and had helped Della through the turn. However, Chan was also under suspicion of murder by the FRU. After meeting the wild-eyed Chan when he'd broken school policy and dropped by for a visit several weeks earlier,

Kylie wasn't completely sure he wasn't guilty of the crime. Not that Kylie would tell Della that.

"No, he didn't show up," Della said. "But he e-mailed me."

Miranda made a funny noise. Kylie looked at her.

"Frog in my throat," Miranda said, and returned to glaring at Della.

When no one said anything, Della looked at Kylie. "Your turn. It's much more exciting than what happened to me."

"What do you mean by 'what happened to you'?" Kylie asked.

"I knew it!" Miranda leaned forward. "Something did happen. 'Fess up. Did it involve a boy? Tell us! Spill your guts, vamp."

Chapter Four

"No, it's my turn." Kylie, regretting her inquiry, held up her hand, hoping to prevent an out-and-out war between her two best friends. She took a deep breath. "I already told you most of it when we talked on the phone. But what I still can't get over is that I healed both Lucas and Sara. Which means another ability you can add to my hodgepodge of gifts. Any idea what it could mean? Because I'd really like to figure out what I am."

"We can't figure you out," Miranda said. "You're just a weirdo." She snickered, and even Della cut a quick smile.

Kylie frowned.

Miranda wiped the humor off her face. "Just joking. But seriously, you are . . . different. Just the fact that no one can see deep into your pattern, and that it changes, well, it's not normal." She squinted her eyes and stared at Kylie's forehead. "I've never seen a brain pattern shift like that, unless it was a shape-shifter during a shift."

Kylie bit into her lip and considered the wisdom of asking the question now needling her brain. But if she couldn't ask her two best friends, whom could she ask? "What do you know about protectors?"

Silence filled the room. Then Miranda exchanged a quick glance with Della.

"Why?" Miranda asked.

"Shit!" Della said. "Oh, my friggin' God! You're a protector? I mean, I've never met one, but from what I heard they are like . . . super, super rare."

Kylie held up her hand to stop Della from jumping to conclusions. "I don't know anything for sure, but Holiday seems to think it's possible. She said that would explain how Daniel died—because he couldn't protect himself. And it would also explain why I couldn't help myself with the vampire."

"You did help. You broke down a concrete wall," Miranda said.

"Only after I heard the rogue beating Lucas."

Miranda's eyes widened. "And you were only able to take on Selynn when you thought she'd hurt your mom. Holy shit, I'm rooming with a protector. I mean, nobody will mess with me anymore because you'll kick their ass." Her voice rose. "I'm friends with a protector. Do you know how cool that makes me?"

Miranda and Della gave each other a high five.

Kylie stared at them. "Do you know how much more uncool it makes me?"

"That doesn't make you uncool," Della said. "It makes you amazing. You wouldn't believe all I've heard about protectors. It would mean that when you get all your powers, you would be even stronger than I am." A frown appeared in her dark, slightly slanted eyes. "I don't know if I like that, but it's still amazing."

"But I don't want to be amazing. I just want to figure out what I am and then go through my hybrid supernatural life with my not-so-grand gifts. Help a ghost out here and there and, yeah, it will be neat to heal a few people. I'd be fine with that. Because . . ." Kylie hesitated, unsure about being completely honest, but then decided what the hell. "Maybe it's not so much that I don't want to be amazing, it's that I'm not so sure I can live up to . . . amazing. I'm not like you." She pointed to Della. "I'm not fearless and I'm certainly not brave. I like things easy, low or no risk."

Miranda cleared her throat as if waiting for Kylie to add her to the declaration.

"I'm not like you either," Kylie said. "I'm not—"

"Don't worry," Miranda said. "I know I'm not a kick-ass girl."

"You're still braver than I am. And you're never afraid to speak your mind. You don't care what people think. I wouldn't ever dye my hair out of fear that people wouldn't like it."

"But the day you kicked Selynn's ass, you weren't afraid," Della jumped in. "You just acted. And eventually, you'll get used to putting yourself out there. It's not a big deal."

It felt like a big deal to Kylie. "Are most protectors a certain species?" If so, she hoped this might lead her to discovering what she was.

"No," Miranda said. "They can be anything, but they're known to be good and pure. Sort of the Mother Teresa of supernaturals."

"Which I'm *so* not," Kylie said.

Della and Miranda looked at each other and then back at Kylie. "Yeah, you are," they said at the same time.

"Am not! I'm not any better of a person than you two. I mean, look what I did to Selynn and Fredericka."

"Because you were protecting someone else. And that's exactly what protectors do." Miranda shrugged as if in apology when she spotted Kylie's frown.

"But . . . I'm not a saint. The other day I practically shoved Socks off the bed for waking me up. And . . . I ran over a squirrel once."

"On purpose?" Della asked.

"No."

"Then there you go," Della said. "I'll bet you even cried and felt guilty."

Kylie's frown grew tighter.

Della arched a knowing brow. "See? That's what makes you so good. You hardly ever get mad."

"I get mad. I get furious at you guys all the time. Remember—"

"Wait, something doesn't make sense," Miranda said. "I've never heard of a protector being anything but a hundred percent supernatural."

"See? That proves it." Kylie slapped her hands on the table, wanting to believe it. "I'm not that nice of a person, and I know I'm my mother's daughter. So I'm not a protector."

"Or maybe you're just the first hybrid protector to exist," Miranda said. "I mean, usually there's only one protector born every hundred or two hundred years. But, hey, enough about that. Let's get to the good part about what happened that night." She waved her hands through the air as if to push that thought to the side.

"What good part?" Kylie asked.

Miranda's grin spread into the perfect smile—one that could be used to sell teeth-whitening strips. "Pleeeassse. You were there, in the dark, late at night, for several hours, and alone with Lucas. Who happens to be the hottest werewolf alive. I mean, I'm so not into werewolves, but even I can see it. He's like a god. So . . ." She held out her two palms. "What happened? And don't you dare tell me nothing. Because I will totally, completely lose faith in romance if nothing happened."

Kylie opened her mouth to answer and then saw Della leaning forward, turning her head slightly, as if to listen to Kylie's heartbeat to see if she attempted to lie.

"The little witch has a point," Della said. "This might be the good part."

Kylie frowned at Della. For a girl who always kept secrets, she sure didn't give anyone else a break. Then Kylie looked at Miranda, who held her breath in anticipation of Kylie baring her soul.

"Sorry," she said. "Nothing happened."

"Ugh." Miranda dropped her arms on the table and sank into them.

Della stared, and Kylie knew the vamp was listening to her heartbeat and checking for lies again. Frankly, Kylie wasn't sure what Della would hear. It wasn't actually a lie. Nothing happened. Except . . . She'd felt so safe when Lucas had held her, except that she'd turned into Wonder Woman when she'd heard the rogue hurting Lucas. What did that mean? Kylie wasn't sure. So how could she explain it?

Miranda lifted her head off the table. "See what I mean? You're Mother Teresa. Pure. Without lust."

"No," Kylie snapped, not wanting to be viewed as a saint. "I . . . lust."

Della and Miranda shared a pensive stare. "Sorry," Della said. "When it walks like a saint, and quacks like saint—it's a quacking saint."

"He held me," Kylie said. "Held me close. And I fell asleep on his shoulder. It was nice. And kind of . . . He was hot." Though she meant temperature hot, she didn't mind if they drew their own conclusions.

"Yes!" Miranda smiled extra big again. "Did he kiss you? Like the awesome kiss he gave you at the creek when you first got here?"

"No," Kylie said.

Her two friends met each other's gazes again. "Mother Teresa," they said in unison.

"But he kissed me when I got back here," Kylie blurted out, deciding she'd rather kiss and tell than be considered a saint. "And he almost kissed me when he followed me to the office earlier."

Miranda squealed and Della laughed. "So he planted one on you, huh?"

Kylie looked at the humor on her roommates' faces and didn't find any of this so funny. "I'm so confused." She dropped her head on the table. Socks, now back up on the table, stuck his nose against her head and sniffed her scalp as if he were concerned.

"Confused about what?" Miranda asked.

Kylie lifted her head and rested her chin in her palm. "Confused about what I feel for Lucas. Confused about what I feel for Derek—other than pissed off. I'm really angry at him right now." Socks bumped against her hand, seeking some TLC. Feeling as if she could use some herself, she offered the little guy some affection.

"And you should be pissed!" Della shot Miranda an odd look. "She needs to know."

"Know what?" Watching the two of them exchanging gazes, Kylie got a bad feeling.

They didn't get a chance to answer because she heard a cracking sound and the cabin's front door swung open. Burnett walked inside, and behind him stood Holiday. Behind Holiday stood Perry.

Did they have news about the Brightens? Kylie's heart jolted.

"I told you to knock," Holiday snapped at Burnett.

"I did." He looked back at Holiday.

"Well, usually after you knock, you wait until someone tells you to enter."

Burnett shot Holiday a tight smile. "Guess you need to be more specific next time." He glanced back at Kylie, and she could see concern in his eyes.

"What's going on?" Kylie's gaze went back to Perry, who looked almost guilty. But guilty about what? Oh crap! What had happened?

"I'm sorry." Perry's eyes turned deep green.

Kylie's chest tightened. "Sorry for what?"

Perry looked at Burnett and then at Holiday.

"What happened?" Kylie asked. "Are the Brightens okay? Answer me!"

Perry just stood there looking guilt-ridden.

"I'd answer her," Della said to Perry in her snarky voice. "She might go after your ears again if you don't."

Chapter Five

"I don't know what happened." Perry moved in closer, his eyes brightening to emerald green.

"How could you not know?" Kylie looked to Burnett and then Holiday, waiting for one of them to pipe up. When they didn't, she refocused on Perry. "You were following them." Suddenly, the guilt she spotted on his face did a flying leap and landed right on Kylie's own shoulders. If something really bad had happened to them, it was her fault. She'd been the one wanting to contact them. But damn it, she'd been so sure it was the right thing to do.

"They disappeared," Perry said. "One minute they were driving down the freeway in that silver Cadillac and then, poof." He waved his hands out in front of him. "They were gone. Cadillac and everything. Gone. Poof."

Kylie's chest grew heavy. "People, human people, don't just go poof." She managed to keep her voice low, but her frustration laced the tone with sarcasm.

Then the truth hit. She only thought people didn't go poof. Not too long ago she didn't think people could turn into unicorns, or that vampires and werewolves existed. She wouldn't have thought she could use her dreams to communicate with people or that she could break down a concrete wall. So who the hell knew if people went poof or not? And if they did go poof, did that mean . . . ?

Kylie's stomach knotted. "Are they dead?"

Holiday frowned. "Let's not start assuming—"

"We don't know," Burnett interrupted. "I have agents working on finding out, though. The agency is sending me pictures of the Brightens any minute now. At least then we'll know if they were impostors."

Burnett's phone rang and he snatched it up. "What you got?" His expression hardened. "That can't be. I checked them this morning." He paused and eyed Holiday, who moved closer to Burnett's side.

Della leaned over to Kylie. "The cameras aren't working." Her sensitive hearing had obviously picked up both sides of the conversation.

Footsteps sounded on the cabin porch and Kylie looked up as Lucas stepped through the doorway. His gaze found hers, his concern for her reflecting in his eyes, and he stopped beside her. His arm brushed against hers, and she felt his warmth. The memory of his kiss flashed through her head and she felt a little guilty about sharing it with Miranda and Della.

Kylie saw Lucas glance at her two roommates and nod. It wasn't an overtly friendly nod, either. Kylie had heard that werewolves were pretty standoffish, and she supposed it was true. Other than Lucas, Kylie hadn't really befriended any of them at the camp.

"Did Burnett get the pictures of your grandparents yet?" Lucas looked down at her.

"Don't know." She found herself staring at his blue eyes. For just a second, she wished she didn't question what she felt. Wished he weren't another unanswered part of her life. It would feel so good to just give in. So, why didn't she?

"You okay?" He mouthed the words more than spoke them. She nodded but wasn't so sure how true it was.

"Then someone tampered with them!" Burnett paced across the

living room. "Have you gotten the Brightens' DMV records yet? I want to see a copy of their licenses to determine if they're who they said they were." He tightened his jaw muscles and glanced up at Kylie. Empathy for her flashed in his eyes, but it faded within a flicker of a second. Showing emotion, even a glimmer in his eyes, seemed too much for him.

Everything about the man looked hard and dark. And he seemed to like it that way. He had black hair, olive skin, and a body rippled with muscles that kept most men at a distance and most women his age wishing he'd get closer. Kylie saw Holiday studying Burnett and amended her last thought. In spite of the obvious attraction that ran deep between them, Holiday wouldn't let Burnett get close.

"I don't understand what takes them so long," Burnett snapped at the caller. "It's as simple as pulling records at the DMV. I could have done it myself by now." He released a deep, frustrated sigh. "Just send them as soon as they come in." He hung up, dropped his phone into his shirt pocket, and looked at Holiday.

His eyes tightened with frustration. "Someone tampered with our cameras. I checked this morning and everything was working. Conveniently, they went down about an hour before the Brightens arrived. I think we know what that means."

Burnett glanced at Kylie. She knew he thought the Brightens were impostors. And maybe she should be hoping he was right. Because that would mean that it wasn't Daniel's adoptive parents who'd gone poof on the highway. But Kylie wanted proof. Proof of who'd gone poof.

She pressed a hand to her forehead and fought an oncoming headache. "When do they think they'll get pictures of the Brightens?"

"Any time. If they know what's good for them." Burnett's deep voice sounded sincere.

Kylie found herself praying Daniel's parents were okay. That they weren't the couple who'd visited earlier. But even so, she wasn't sure she was emotionally off the hook. Impostors or not, she wasn't sure the elderly couple deserved to . . . She stopped herself from mentally pronouncing them dead. Poof didn't necessarily equal death.

The back of Lucas's hand brushed against the back of hers. Somehow she knew the touch was deliberate and meant to comfort her. And it did.

Burnett's phone beeped. He yanked it from his pocket, pressed a button, and stared at the screen. Glancing up, he held the phone over to Holiday. "Is that the couple that was here?"

Holiday looked at the screen and then at Kylie. "No. That's not them."

It wasn't that Kylie didn't believe her, but she had to see for herself. She stepped over, took Burnett's phone, and stared at the two images side by side. An elderly, partly balding man and an older, gray-haired woman with bright green eyes gazed back from the phone's screen.

"These are the Brightens?" she asked.

Burnett nodded. "Sent from the DMV records."

"It doesn't even look like them." Kylie couldn't deny the relief that washed over her, yet she remembered the touch of the elderly woman's hand, the grief they had seemed to share, and even the sheen of tears in the woman's eyes. Had it all been an act? Kylie looked at Holiday. "Even you said the woman seemed sincere. How could we both be wrong?"

Holiday frowned. "Like I told you, reading emotions is never a hundred percent accurate."

Kylie swallowed the disappointment at having her emotions toyed with by an elderly couple. At least when Derek or Holiday toyed with her emotions, it had always been to soothe or help her. This was different; it had been meant to deceive. And maybe more.

She fought the anger crowding the other emotions in her chest. Targeting her anger toward the elderly couple still didn't seem right.

"But I don't understand what they were going to accomplish by pretending to be my grandparents."

"Obviously, they weren't here just to pat your cheek and offer you cookies," Burnett stated. "Luckily, Derek got wind of it and whatever they were attempting got foiled."

Kylie met Burnett's gaze. "Is Mario behind this?"

"Who else could it be?"

Kylie still struggled to understand. "But why would he send an elderly couple to do this when he could have gotten someone more powerful?"

"Because he thought it would fool us. And it almost did." Burnett frowned. "From now on, we're going to have to be more careful. I'm assigning you a shadow."

"A what?" Kylie was certain she wasn't going to like this.

"A shadow," Holiday said. "Someone who stays by your side at all times."

Yup, she was right. She didn't like it.

"I'll do it," Lucas said.

"No, I'll do it," another deep voice said from the open doorway.

Derek's voice sent sharp little needles of hurt into Kylie's chest. She looked up and stared into his greenish—almost hazel—eyes.

Her heart jerked as she soaked in his image. His brown hair was a little mussed, as if he ran his hands through it one too many times. His faded T-shirt clung to his wide chest, and his favorite worn jeans hugged his waist and legs. His gaze pulled her attention up again, so much emotion reflected in those eyes. She hadn't realized how much she'd missed him until now.

Right now.

She wanted to go to him, to lean against him. To assure herself he was okay.

The warmth from Lucas's shoulder pressed closer.

She saw the slightest narrowing in Derek's eyes, as if he noted how close Lucas stood. Then Derek frowned.

A storm of emotions swirled inside Kylie. One emotion stood out more than the others. Anger. Derek had no right to be upset about how close Lucas stood to her. He'd walked away, even when she'd begged him not to leave. So why did she feel the urge to add an inch or two between her and Lucas?

"I think you've done enough by getting that P.I. involved." Lucas's blue eyes drilled into Derek.

Derek's posture instantly went defensive. "Mr. Smith isn't behind this."

"Maybe not," Lucas said, his voice tight, "but it was through him that trouble arrived."

The tension in the air thickened so much, it made breathing a chore.

Burnett looked at Lucas. "There's no reason to lay blame."

"Burnett's right," Kylie said. "Besides, I'm the one who contacted Mr. Smith." She felt Lucas tense beside her and suspected he didn't like her standing up for Derek. She wasn't sure she liked doing it, not when her anger toward Derek still bumped around her chest. Nevertheless, she wouldn't let Derek get blamed for trying to help her. She continued to stare at the half-fae, wishing she could read his thoughts—or at least his emotions—the way he could read everyone else's. "Is Mr. Smith okay?"

Derek met her gaze again. Anger flashed in the gold flecks of his eyes. She didn't know if he was reflecting her emotions or if he was angry himself. Probably both. "He's going to live." His gaze left hers, and emptiness swelled in her chest. And something told her it was a feeling she'd have to get used to because nothing had changed between them.

Nothing.

"I can shadow Kylie," Della said.

"Me too," said Miranda.

Burnett looked at the two of them. "Since you are in the cabin with her, you two will have your turns."

"She'll be safer with me," Lucas said.

"Get real!" muttered Della.

"Ditto," Miranda added, and held out her pinky as if pointing out her weapon.

Kylie looked from Miranda to Della and then on to Derek and Lucas. Unreal. They were talking about her as if she weren't even here. Still, she knew they were just trying to help, and she loved them all for it. Well, she would when she stopped feeling pissed off.

Burnett looked back at Lucas and then at Derek. "I'm concerned that both of you might be too close to this."

"Which is why we'd be good at it," Derek said.

"Which is why *I'd* be good at it," countered Lucas.

Derek shot Lucas a dirty look. "You're a real jerk, Parker."

Both guys started slinging insults.

"For cripes' sakes, guys!" Kylie snapped. "This is getting—"

"Stop it!" Burnett ordered. And just like that, Derek and Lucas both fell silent. "This is what I mean. Both of you have other agendas where Kylie is concerned."

Kylie felt her cheeks redden, more from anger than embarrassment. "Here's an idea. Maybe somebody should ask me what I think about—"

"That's ridiculous," snarled Lucas. She blinked at him for a moment until she realized he was referring to Burnett's comment, not hers.

Burnett's shoulders grew tighter and his gaze shot from Lucas to Derek. "Right now, I don't think either of you would be focusing on protecting when you're with her. I'm not saying you won't be asked to help in the future, but right now—"

"Still ridiculous." Lucas stiffened beside Kylie, and she could swear she felt his temperature go up a degree or two. "I would die before—"

"As would I," Derek barked out.

"And my job is to make sure no one dies," Brunett countered.

At least on that point, Kylie could agree with Burnett.

An hour later, after Burnett and Holiday went back to the office to assign Kylie shadows, Kylie lay shivering in her bed, staring at the ceiling, wondering when and how her life had gotten so out of control. Right after Burnett left, Lucas had been summoned again by his pack. With regret in his blue eyes, and maybe even still a little anger at her for standing up for Derek, he told her he would see her as soon as his pack business was handled. Kylie hadn't begrudged him going; she'd kind of needed to be alone. But she couldn't help remembering what Fredericka had said. *Lucas's bloodline is pure, he values that. The forefathers value that, too. They've made that clear.* Were those just words cast out to cause Kylie doubt? Or was there something going on?

Kylie closed her eyes and moaned. Socks burrowed deeper under the covers at her side, while a dead bald woman paced around the room, jabbering about how she couldn't remember shit. Kylie released a deep breath, and steam rose from her lips and slowly snaked up to the ceiling.

"Can't remember," the ghost muttered. *"Nothing but a blank."*

Little did the woman know that Kylie kind of envied her right now. She wished she could forget. Forget that look of anger she'd spotted in Derek's eyes, forget the sudden tension she'd felt in Lucas's body when she stood up for Derek. Forget that she very well might be responsible for killing an elderly couple and getting the P.I., Mr. Smith, sent to the hospital.

"What's it called when you can't remember who you are? Isn't there a word for that?" the spirit asked.

"Amnesia." Kylie considered telling Jane Doe—the spirit needed a name, and Jane Doe was as good as any—that her memory loss might be more about the eight-inch scar running across her head than your average amnesia. Then again, Kylie supposed the reason Jane couldn't remember didn't matter. The fact that she had no memory was the problem. How the hell was Kylie supposed to help a ghost who didn't even know who she was?

Kylie suspected that if she asked Holiday that question, the camp leader would say to start looking for clues in what the woman did and the way she was dressed. The jeans and T-shirt the woman wore didn't give much of a clue. As for the bald head and scar, yeah, that might be a clue. However, when Kylie first met the woman, she'd had hair and looked as if her abdomen had been ripped open. Was that a clue, too?

Heck, Kylie wasn't even sure if the woman knew she was dead. Just coming out and asking her seemed a little rude.

"I just don't get why I can't remember," Jane said.

Kylie pressed her palm to her aching temple. She was so not in the mood to deal with this right now. Not that she had a choice. So far, ghosts didn't seem to respond to rain-check requests.

"Are you listening to me?" the woman asked.

Opening her eyes, Kylie sat up a bit. Socks's fluffy black-and-white tail fell out from under the sheet. "I am, I just—"

"Does your head hurt, too?"

Kylie looked up at the woman's angry scar. "A little." She pulled up her quilt from the end of the bed to ward off the chill. "But I've just got boy troubles."

"Boy troubles?" Jane frowned. *"Be careful. Boys—and men—can really hurt you."* The words sounded heartfelt. Was this another clue?

"Did someone hurt you?" Kylie asked.

The woman stopped moving, and her brow crinkled. *"Maybe. I don't remember."*

"Think hard. I mean, you said it like you remembered something."

The sooner Kylie got the ghost to remember who she was, the sooner she could discover what she needed and help her move on.

The spirit placed her index finger on her forehead. "No. Nothing. It's empty up here." She moved her hand to the side of her scalp and traced a finger over her scar. Kylie wasn't sure if she was just discovering it or not.

"Do you remember what happened? How you got that cut on your head?" *How you died?* Holiday had explained that a lot of the time when a death had been sudden or traumatic, the spirit's ability to recall it was difficult. However, to help them cross over, the details of their deaths might be important.

"No." Jane went back to pacing. *"I hate not knowing."*

After a few more laps around the room, she stopped talking and Kylie went back to thinking about Derek, about how her heart had lurched at the sight of him. She couldn't help but wonder if that meant her feelings for Lucas were not as important as she'd originally worried they might be.

Suddenly the ghost stopped at the end of the bed and stared at Kylie. *"I gave you the message, didn't I?"*

Kylie sat up a bit. "You mentioned it, but what was it again?" Perhaps the message wasn't really a message, but a clue.

"Someone lives; someone dies." Her tone dropped to a whisper and sounded like something out of a scary movie. *"That's what they said to tell you."*

Socks, as if responding to the grim note in the spirit's voice, nestled closer.

"Do you by any chance know what that means?" Reaching under the covers, Kylie gently pushed the skunk's nose away from her ribs. Considering the little fellow was afraid of ghosts, fate had really screwed up by pairing them together.

"I . . ." The spirit rolled her eyes as if trying to think. *"They didn't say."*

"Who are 'they'?" Kylie was concerned by the mention of death, but considering she was dealing with an amnesiac ghost, she wasn't so sure how much stock she could put into the message.

Jane inched closer, moving down the side of the bed, her light green eyes filled with fear. *"You know who it's from."*

"No, I don't know."

The spirit bit down on her lip as if saying the name caused discomfort. Then she leaned down, bringing her slightly blue lips only a few inches from Kylie's face. *"The death angels."* Icy crystals floated from her lips and cascaded down onto Kylie's quilt.

Socks bolted from beneath the covers, onto the floor, and under the bed.

"The death angels?" Kylie wrapped her mind around the answer. "How do you know about them?" It suddenly dawned on her that she hadn't checked to see if the woman was a supernatural.

Staring at the spirit's forehead, Kylie tightened her brows. Nothing. Which had to mean something. Everyone had a brain pattern, didn't they? Even humans. Kylie had seen Daniel's brain pattern, and Holiday had said she'd scanned Nana for one, so Kylie knew ghosts didn't just lose them after death. So why didn't this spirit have a pattern?

Closing her eyes, Kylie squinted harder and refocused. Still nothing. The icy chill of the spirit seemed to grow colder, and it clawed at Kylie's uncovered flesh. Yanking the sheet up to her chin, she shifted back from the spirit and asked the question she hated when people asked it of her.

"What *are* you?"

Chapter Six

An hour later, Kylie paced half-moon circles in her tiny room, making almost the same path as the ghost—the ghost who'd vanished without even trying to answer Kylie's question. But the skittish spirit hadn't faded before Kylie noted the sheer panic on her face.

Not that Kylie didn't empathize with the ghost.

How many times had Kylie heard the same damn question? *What are you?* Or rather, *What the hell are you?* Frankly, she didn't like either version.

But did either question instill panic or fear?

Frustration, maybe, but fear? Okay, maybe in the beginning it had scared her, but only after she'd accepted there was a possibility she wasn't human. Should she assume the spirit suspected she wasn't human? Kylie recalled the look on the spirit's face. It was as if the question sent up a red flag or stirred up some forgotten memory. And not a good memory, either.

An eerie chill filled the air, announcing the return of the ghost, and Kylie hugged herself.

"I'm sorry," Kylie said. "I know you're confused. Believe me, I know how you feel. There's a hell of a lot I'm trying to figure out about myself, too." The cold ebbed away. So the ghost wasn't up to talking. Kylie empathized with her on that point as well.

She had almost run to Holiday with questions about the spirit's lack of a brain pattern. Then, because Kylie suspected Holiday would want to go into all the other issues they needed to discuss, she decided to postpone asking the questions. And by issues, Kylie meant her newly acquired gift of healing, knocking down concrete walls, and the possibility that she was a protector. The healing and the walls, she might be able to handle. The whole protector/Mother Teresa thing? Nope. That could go unhandled for a while longer.

And it wasn't as if she were procrastinating, as Holiday accused her of so often. She was prioritizing. Right now, her top priority was Derek and the on again/off again signals he put out. How could he want to be her shadow when two weeks ago he wouldn't even look at her? Had he experienced a change of heart? Did she want him to have experienced a change of heart?

She considered it. Remembered how close she'd felt to him when they'd snuck off and he'd kissed her senseless. She even missed how he'd made everything look like a fairy tale. What she wouldn't give to be in a fairy tale right now and not have to deal with all this mess.

But did that mean if he said he was sorry, she would forgive him? After she made a few more laps around her small room, she came to the conclusion that her heart was too damn confused to know what she wanted.

As if to drive the point deeper, she had an instant recall of how it had felt when Lucas kissed her. No fairy-tale visions, but she couldn't, wouldn't, deny that it had felt pretty awesome.

Damn!

She slung herself on the bed. She was so friggin' messed up. She gave her pillow one good punch and then screamed into the fluffy down.

One deep breath later, she popped back up. She had to do something. Even if it was the wrong thing. After slipping into her tennis shoes, she grabbed her brush. She gave her blond hair a few swipes, slipped on a clean white tank top, and bolted out of her bedroom.

Della popped up off the sofa. "Hey."

"Hey." Kylie continued moving to the door, not wanting to explain where she was going because hearing herself say it aloud might make her think twice. And she didn't want to think twice; she hadn't really thought it through once yet. But she had to do something. She was tired of being in limbo.

"Where are you going?" Della asked.

"Out." Kylie reached for the doorknob. Instead, however, she ended up grabbing Della's waist, because Della had shot across the room in a flash and now stood blocking the door.

"Excuse me." Kylie tried not to let her mood sound in her voice. As moody as Della was, she had no patience for anyone else's bad mood. And getting into a pissing contest with Della right now wasn't in Kylie's plans.

"Where are *we* going?" Della asked.

"*We* aren't going anywhere. I'm going somewhere."

"I gotta come, too."

"No, you don't."

"Yes, she does." Miranda stepped out of her bedroom. "Kylie Galen, meet your first shadow, Della Tsang."

"At your service." Della's tone dripped with sarcasm. She even gave a little bow.

"Oh, screw this!" Kylie said. "I'm not leaving the camp. I'll be fine."

Della frowned. "You're not leaving the cabin unless I come with you." Her right hand landed on her right hip as if to punctuate her tone.

Kylie inhaled and tried to calm down before this got ugly. "Look,

I want to go talk to Derek, okay? And I'm sorry, but I don't want you with me. This is private."

Della's pissed-off expression vanished into something that looked almost like empathy, and she glanced at Miranda. "You still think keeping this from her is the best thing?"

"Oh hell." Miranda plopped down on the sofa. "Maybe you're right. But don't just tell her, show her."

Kylie looked back at Miranda and instantly recalled her friends acting all secretive right before Burnett had charged into the cabin. "Keep what from me? Show me what?"

Della snatched her phone from her jeans pocket and started keying in something. "I got it from Chan. I wanted to tell you right away, but Miranda said with you being kidnapped and all that you had enough on your plate."

"Got what?" Kylie leaned down almost nose to nose with the vamp. Her patience had been stretched to the max.

"Jeez." Della lunged back. "Patience. You're acting like it's a full moon again." She studied Kylie. "It's not, is it?" Then Della looked back at Miranda, who was still stretched out on the sofa. "Is it time for the wolves to have PMS yet?"

Kylie considered the question, almost afraid Della might be right. Was the moon cycle making her feel out of sorts, or was it everything that had happened the last few days?

"No." Miranda popped up and moved in. "We got another week before we have to deal with lunar PMS."

Kylie frowned. She hadn't morphed into a wolf the last full moon, but it appeared she'd experienced the typical mood swings that affected weres right before their shift. And obviously her two roommates still considered it a possibility that she might wind up being a werewolf. Not that Kylie thought the consideration didn't have merit. At this point, she could turn out to be just about anything.

"Somebody better start talking," Kylie said. "And fast."

"Good Lord!" Della snapped back. "I'm trying to find it. Here it is." She looked up. "You see, my cousin Chan sent me a couple of images and asked if this was one of our campers. You know he lives with that vampire commune in Pennsylvania, right?"

She held out the phone and Kylie looked at the image. "That's Derek." A few seconds passed. "What was Derek doing in Pennsylvania?" Then again, she didn't know where the FRU had sent him or where the half-fae had gone looking for his dad.

"I have a better question." Della pulled back the phone, hit another button, and then held it back out for Kylie to see. "What's Derek doing sucking face with a vampire in Pennsylvania?"

Kylie's heart jolted when she saw Derek lip-locked with a dark-haired girl. And it wasn't just their lips that were locked. The girl's legs were wrapped around his waist, while Derek's hands—obviously holding the brunette up and close—were placed on her cute little jeans-covered butt.

An ache settled in Kylie's chest. "Who . . . how . . . what?"

"I asked the who question," Della said. "Her name is Ellie Mason and she was new to their vampire commune. Chan said someone mentioned Derek was from Shadow Falls and he just wanted to see if his source was telling the truth."

Ellie? Kylie recalled Derek telling her he'd dated a vampire named Ellie. She also recalled he'd told her that he'd given Ellie blood. Odd how she hadn't even known she'd remembered it, but now it seemed carved into her memory bank. "Ellie." The word leaving her lips caused a sharp and painful yank on her heartstrings. The heartstrings must be connected to her emotions, because about a dozen different ones started flapping around her chest like wild birds going after a swarm of moths. Anger, jealousy, betrayal, distrust . . . the list went on.

"I need this." She took Della's phone and tried to push Della out of the way. Not that her effort got her anywhere. Della stood cemented in place.

"Sorry. I still can't let you go alone," Della said. "Seriously, I'm your shadow."

"Fine, come. Just don't get in my way! And stay back. Way back. I need to talk to him alone." Tears prickled Kylie's eyes.

Tears of jealousy, betrayal, and frustration.

Tears of knowing that she had no right to feel any of those emotions. She wouldn't let herself cry. But she still felt those tears. Felt them as she swallowed them down her throat and they burned her chest.

Phone gripped tight, Kylie took off through the woods toward Derek's cabin, hoping that he was there. She didn't have a clue what she'd say when she saw him. She didn't want to think; she just wanted to get there. She leapt over thornbushes, ducked under low-hanging branches, and made darn good speed. Della's footfalls sounded behind her, staying close—her friend took her job as shadow seriously.

Too seriously.

The thud of Kylie's feet hitting the earth echoed, and the smell of rain hung in the air. A summer storm brewed somewhere in the distance. But not too far, because thunder rumbled overhead.

Silence followed one particularly big boom. A flash of lightning sent sprays of sizzling silver light dancing through the leaves to the moist earth. Kylie kept running, kept hurting. She could feel the storm, the energy, the power of it, in the air. More thunder followed.

Suddenly, a loud rustle sounded off to her right, and a large deer—a buck with antlers big enough to decorate a hunter's wall—darted out and jolted to a stop in the middle of her path. Shocked, she came to an abrupt stop, too. A few more inches and she might have impaled herself on the beast's antlers. She hadn't caught her breath when a bolt of lightning shot down and struck the trunk of an old tree buried only a foot past the buck. The light still sizzled when Kylie felt Della slam into her.

"What the hell?" Della said.

The buck reared his head back, the heavy antlers dropped forward almost in a threat, and then he shot off. But not before Kylie felt the beast's cold and somehow evil gaze.

The hair on the back of her neck rose. That calculating gaze meant something. Like the look the eagle gave her earlier. She pulled oxygen into her lungs and hoped it would clear her mind and she might realize she was wrong.

She didn't want to add something else to her list of things to figure out. But the air in her lungs didn't help.

The ground still sizzled and popped as tiny sparks danced around the trunk that had taken the direct hit. The smell of burnt wood and oncoming rain flavored the air. Kylie wasn't sure if she imagined it or not, but she felt a few currents of energy sting the heels of her feet.

"That was creepy," Della said.

"Yeah."

"Damn, it almost hit you!"

"But it didn't." Kylie stared at the phone in her hand and remembered Derek.

"Damn," Della repeated. "If the deer hadn't shown up . . ."

"Doesn't matter." And Kylie wanted it to be so. She heard the sound of driving rain pelting down on the leaves above her before she felt it sting her skin. The day had almost turned to night. The storm had arrived, and it matched her mood. She curled her hand around Della's phone, protecting it from the rain, and took off again at a dead run.

In a few minutes, barely winded but wet, Kylie jogged up onto Derek's porch while Della hung back. Kylie's second step brought back a memory. She'd come here looking for Derek once before and had seen blood on his porch. She'd thought he'd been attacked and had barged in only to find him . . . in the shower.

She'd gotten an eyeful that day, and after he'd gotten dressed, they'd sat here, leaning against the cabin, and talked.

Shared.

Laughed.

She couldn't ever remember feeling closer to anyone. How could things have changed between them so quickly?

She moved to the door and knocked. The door swung open, and Chris—Derek's vampire cabin mate—stood there. "Hey." His eyes widened and lowered. "Wet T-shirt contest?" he teased.

Kylie looked down, sending heavy strands of wet hair dancing around her shoulders. Her white tank and thin bra were almost invisible. She frowned and pulled her hair in front of her breasts.

"Is Derek here?"

"Yup," he said. "If he'll come to the door is another thing. He's been brooding in his room since he got back." He looked over his shoulder and called out, "Derek, you got company."

Not wanting to stand there to be ogled by Chris, Kylie stepped back from the door and waited at the edge of the porch. Still trying to control her heartbeat, she peeled her soaked shirt from her chest and flapped the fabric back and forth, hoping it would dry.

In a few minutes, familiar footsteps moved to the door. She turned around and faced Derek and had to will herself not to run and throw herself into his arms.

She took one step toward him, then stopped herself. If he rejected her, it would hurt so damn much.

Chapter Seven

Derek ran a nervous hand through his hair. Hair that looked longer than when he left. And softer. She could remember brushing it back from his brow then, and she longed to do it again. She wanted to hit the rewind button and go back to the way things were before. When things between them had been so good. But life didn't have a re-wind button.

"Hey." He tucked his hands into his jeans pockets.

"Hey." Her heart raced a little faster and hurt more at the sight of him. She tried not to notice things like the muscles in his arms or how tightly his T-shirt hugged his chest. She inhaled.

While it had stopped raining, the scent of rain still clung to her clothes and hair. It still flavored the air. But it didn't hide the scent that she recognized as Derek.

She felt the phone in her hand and looked down at it.

"Sorry about not calling you back earlier," he said, as if he thought that was why she was here. "I had cut my phone off when I was in the hospital with Brit."

She nodded, not completely sure if she believed him, and felt the rise of emotion in her throat. Her sinuses stung. But she'd be damned if she would cry. At least not now. At least not here.

"Where did you go when you left Shadow Falls?" she asked.

"Just on a job assignment for Burnett." He hesitated. "I'm not really supposed to talk about it."

That hurt. She knew he was probably telling the truth, but there had been a time she hadn't believed they kept secrets from each other.

His gaze met hers and she could see the gold flecks meshing into his green irises. She saw emotion there. Hurt, jealousy, betrayal, anger. It struck her right then that everything he felt was what she, too, was feeling.

For a flicker of a second, she told herself he didn't have a right to feel those things; but she'd never been a great liar, not even when she lied to herself. Lucas had kissed her. She had feelings for Lucas, albeit confused feelings, but she still had them for him. How could she be so mad at Derek right now and not accept that he deserved his own anger?

She blinked, and the moment grew more awkward with each beat of silence. "I came here to ask you about . . ." She held out the phone and then dropped her hand back to her side. "But I suddenly realize you don't owe me an answer. I'm sorry, I . . ." Unable to finish, she turned to go.

He caught her. No sooner had his touch warmed her skin than he jerked away. And that hurt, too. Was touching her so unpleasant that it caused him to flinch?

"Ask me about what?" He frowned. "What has you so upset?"

"It's nothing. I'm fine." She started to walk away again.

"Damn it, Kylie!" He jumped in front of her. "Don't lie to me. I feel it, remember? I feel everything you feel tenfold. You're really upset about something. You came here to say something to me, so say it."

She hesitated and then turned on Della's phone.

He watched her. "What are you—"

"You'll see." She found the picture and held it out.

His expression shot from angry to . . . something different. "Shit." He ran a palm over his face.

"It's okay," Kylie said. "I realize you don't owe me an explanation. Really, I overreacted." She tried to step around him, but he grabbed her again. This time his hand lingered for a few seconds before pulling away.

"Please don't go," he said. "Look, that's Ellie. I told you about her when we first met. I dated her for a while. We ran into each other when I was on the job for Burnett. She was . . . she was just happy to see someone she knew."

"Yeah, she looks happy," Kylie said before she could stop the words, and there was an edge of sarcasm to them.

"It looks worse than it really was," he said, but he couldn't hide the guilt that flashed in his eyes.

"You really don't have to explain," Kylie said, suddenly realizing how unfair it was to confront him about this. The last thing she'd want right now was him confronting her about Lucas. She closed the phone and tucked it in her pocket. "You don't—"

"Yes, I do have to explain," Derek snapped. He drew in a pound of oxygen and hesitated before starting again. "Look, I was going to tell you anyway."

"No, you weren't," she said, finding that impossible to believe. "Not that I blame you. We weren't really going out. You don't have to tell me anything."

"I *was* going to tell you. I don't have a choice."

She studied him, not sure what he meant, and she saw more guilt in his eyes.

"Look," he said. "Ellie's here. I brought her back to the camp."

The bolt of lightning that flashed in front of Kylie a few minutes ago had shocked her less than Derek's admission. But she was pretty damn proud of herself for not letting it show. Then again, she didn't have to let it show. He could read her, but it didn't stop her from pretending. And if she pretended long enough, she might even believe it herself.

"That's good." She forced a smile.

"I had to, Kylie. She'd run away from home and was living in some hellhole of a commune. She needed help."

"I'm glad you were there for her," she said.

"Christ, Kylie! Quit friggin' pretending like I can't read you. It's me, damn it."

"Then stop reading me." Kylie's throat knotted instantly. Tears threatened, but she held them back.

"I wish I could. It would solve all our problems. I wish to God I could stop it!" He swung an angry hand through the air.

"What do you mean?" she asked.

He shook his head. "You still don't get it, do you? Being close to you is like sticking my finger into an emotional socket. I don't know why. It wasn't like that in the beginning. I mean, I could feel you more than other people, but this last month, it increased tenfold. When I'm with you, it's like being bombarded . . . attacked with emotions. I can't think straight, I can't rationalize. And if Lucas's name came up, I could feel your emotions connected to him and . . ."

He took another breath. "Maybe what I was feeling was even more than what you were feeling, but . . . I just couldn't handle it. And it wasn't just Lucas. If you were upset at your dad, I would feel the hurt you felt and I wanted to kill the bastard. I couldn't handle it anymore."

She stepped back, hoping a few inches away from her would help him. "Why didn't you tell me?"

"I did, or I tried to. You just didn't hear me. Oh, hell, I probably didn't make it clear because I didn't understand it. I still don't . . . understand it. I just know that being close to you makes me crazy." He did another pass of his fingers through his hair. "I hoped when I got back it would have changed."

"But it hasn't?"

He shook his head. "No."

"Have you asked Holiday about it?" A breeze stirred her wet hair, but it brought with it the smell of sunshine, as if the storm had passed. If only the storm inside her had done the same.

"No. I don't want to . . ."

"Ask her for help," she finished for him. A spray of bright sunlight snuck behind a low-hanging cloud and caused her to blink.

"It's not just that. I don't want her trying to get inside my head to read my emotions. I've seen things in other people's minds that they don't want me to see. I prefer to keep mine private. It's sort of like seeing someone naked." He half smiled.

She tried to respond with a smile, but she couldn't quite do it. First, because this meant his pride was more important to him than trying to fix the problem. And second, because she couldn't help wondering how many of those naked emotions were about her and how many of them were about Ellie.

"We're really mostly just friends, now," Derek said, obviously picking up on her jealousy.

Mostly? She wondered how one defined "mostly" friends? The kiss must have happened in one of the "unmostly" moments. Then she recalled the kiss she'd shared with Lucas, and guilt ran through her for judging Derek.

She met his gaze again. "You don't have to explain it."

He studied her, and God help her, because she knew he was picking apart her emotions. Reading her jealousy, followed by her thread of guilt, and then her feelings of being unfair to him. And he was probably figuring out what had happened, too.

He frowned and stepped back as if standing too close to her caused him pain. "So you and Lucas . . . ?"

The thread she'd tried to push back suddenly tied itself in a big knot in her chest. She searched for the right way to answer, then decided to borrow his. "Mostly friends."

Hurt flashed in his eyes, and she knew he understood exactly what she meant. Though she hadn't really said it to hurt him, she tried again. "I'm still trying to sort through things," she offered, hoping to soften the blow, because damn it, she knew exactly how he felt. Unknowingly, they had done the same thing to each other.

He nodded and met her gaze. "This is killing me."

The pain in his eyes echoed his words, and the knot in her chest tightened. The tears she vowed not to cry stung her eyes again.

"Same here." Her tonsils seemed to swell in her throat. "I should go." She stepped back.

"Wait. Aren't you supposed to have a shadow with you?"

For some reason, his question reminded her of the bolt of lightning. "Della's close by."

"And listening." He frowned.

"I told her not to."

"Right." Cynicism filled his voice.

Kylie took another step back, but the question slipped out before she could stop it. "Why did you offer to shadow me if it's so hard to be close to me?"

He scrubbed his tennis shoe on the wooden planks of the porch. "Because keeping you safe is more important than anything else." He inhaled. "But maybe Burnett's right. I'm too close to this. The fact that someone wants to hurt you makes me feel crazy." He looked down and then up again. "Besides, you have . . . others who claim to feel the same way." Jealousy sounded in his voice.

She wasn't sure how to answer, so she didn't.

"You do know that Brit, the P.I., isn't behind this. I don't know how anyone got to him."

Kylie recalled that Lucas had accused the P.I. of being part of the problem. "I'm not blaming him. I'm sorry he got hurt. Is he really okay?"

Derek nodded. "Yeah."

"Does he remember anything?" she asked, hoping all this could be solved that easily.

"No. And that's strange. It's almost as if he's had his memory erased. And there aren't many people who can do that."

"Maybe it's just a concussion."

"That's what the doctor thinks and what Burnett believes, but . . ." He ran another hand through his hair. "Be careful, Kylie. I heard about what happened—about that Mario guy and his grandson." His gaze dropped. "I'm sorry I wasn't there to help you."

"You had to do what Burnett wanted," she said, even though she clearly remembered begging him not to go.

"I'm serious about you being careful. I just think there could be more to all this than meets the eye."

"More like what?" she asked.

He shook his head. "I can't explain it. I just remember fighting with that rogue at the Wild Life Park that night, and he seemed different. Eerie different."

"I got the same feeling," she confessed.

"Be careful." He reached out as if to touch her, then pulled back.

"I will." She watched him stick his hands into his pockets. Their gazes met again, and it took everything Kylie had not to insist he talk to Holiday and try to fix the problem with reading her emotions too strongly. Instead she walked away. Something told her it was the right thing.

But could someone please tell her why doing the right thing hurt so damn much?

The moment Kylie hit the edge of the woods, she started running, wanting to outrun the living, breathing ache in her chest. In a few seconds, Della was beside her.

"You okay?" Her feet thudded in rhythm with Kylie's own footfalls.

"No," Kylie answered, and ducked beneath a tree limb.

"Where are we going?" Della asked a few minutes later when Kylie turned and headed in the opposite direction of their cabin.

"I want to run," Kylie said.

"Okay." Della stayed beside her.

They ran and ran. When Kylie spotted the fence at the end of the Shadow Falls property line, she stopped and dropped to the ground. Curling her arms around her bent legs, she rested her forehead on her knees. Her lungs worked overtime as she fed them wood-scented air that still carried the scent of rain.

Della, not even winded, sat beside her. The sounds of the forest surrounded them—a bird stirred in the trees, some unnamed creature shuffled in some underbrush not far away. But mostly Kylie heard her own heart racing, sending gushing sounds through her ears.

"Your heart's still beating fast," Della said.

"I know." Kylie kept her face down.

"He was telling the truth."

Kylie knew Della was talking about Derek. "I know."

"I tried not to listen, but it was impossible. I considered moving farther away, but then I wouldn't be doing my job as shadow."

Kylie raised her head. Her gaze went to the fence and she realized where they were. Just through the barbed wire were the dinosaur tracks. And the creek where Lucas had kissed her. She let herself think about it for a second, because thinking about Derek hurt.

Then she looked back at Della. "You listen in on my private conversations, but then you don't share."

"Share what?" Della sounded clueless.

Kylie raised an eyebrow. "What happened while you were at home? I know you were lying. So does Miranda."

"Oh, that." She pulled a long blade of grass from the ground and started tying it around her finger.

Kylie thought Della wasn't going to answer, and then . . . "I went to see Lee."

Kylie suspected that Della hadn't stopped caring for her ex. Not that Della had admitted to it. "And?"

"He's practically engaged to another girl. His parents are pushing him to make it official. They like her." The pain in Della's voice matched the pain Kylie felt for Derek.

Kylie hugged her knees. "I'm so sorry."

"Don't be," Della said. "It's for the best. He could have never accepted me being a vampire."

"Doesn't mean it doesn't hurt." And damn if Kylie didn't know that for a fact.

Della hesitated. "She's a hundred percent Asian. Not a mishmosh like me."

"He said that?" Kylie really disliked this guy.

"Not exactly, but he said his parents had pushed him to date her. And I know they didn't like me because I'm half white."

"You need to move on," Kylie said.

"I already have." Della tossed the grass back to the ground.

It was a lie, but Kylie didn't think calling Della on it would do any good. Kylie leaned back and stared up at the trees. The moisture from the recent rain soaked into her clothes, but she didn't care. The coolness felt good in the Texas heat. A blue jay flitted from one limb to another in the tree. Kylie's emotions seemed to be doing the same.

She studied the bird, so happy, so innocent and trouble-free. Della released an exaggerated breath, as if she were still thinking about Lee.

"Steve likes you," Kylie said.

"No, he doesn't."

"Yes, he does." Kylie glanced at Della. "I saw him looking for you today when we were in the dining hall. You should go for it."

"If he likes me, he'll come to me."

"I don't mean throw yourself at him. Just be nice. Make yourself more approachable."

"I'm approachable," Della said.

About as much as a rattlesnake, Kylie thought.

Della picked up another blade of grass and then lay back on the ground beside Kylie. Their shoulders almost touched. "It's not easy."

"Believe me," Kylie said. "I know."

They lay stretched out on the damp ground for several long minutes without talking. The sun leaked light through the trees and created shimmering golden shadows throughout the woods. Through the leaves, Kylie saw the sky painted in an array of stormy-looking clouds in a variety of colors. Her mind went round and round and somehow landed back on Derek.

"I can't believe he brought Ellie with him." The idea of having to see Derek with Ellie made Kylie's chest tighten.

"Yeah, that'll be tough. I mean, if I had to see Lee with his girl-friend, I'd end up killing someone."

"No, you wouldn't." Kylie sat up, pulled her hair over one shoulder, and removed a few clinging twigs. "You'd do exactly what I'm going to do."

"What's that?" Della sat up.

"Pretend it doesn't hurt, and hope like hell that one day it doesn't anymore."

"Nope. I'd rather kill someone." Della stood and dusted off the wet grass that clung to her backside. Then she looked down at Kylie. "So does this mean you're actually going to give Lucas a real chance?"

Kylie stood up and gave her own butt a few swipes to dislodge most of the grass. "Maybe. If it's what he wants, too."

"If? Didn't you hear him getting pissy with Burnett about shadowing you? He's got it bad for you. I mean, I know you're hurting over Derek, but he doesn't deserve you angsting over him. You have an opportunity with Lucas. Go for it."

She hesitated to say anything, but it spilled out. "Fredericka said something that made it sound like his pack doesn't want us seeing each other."

"Don't listen to anything that b with an itch says. She'll say anything to come between you and Lucas."

Kylie nodded, knowing that Della was right. Or at least she hoped she was.

The bird in the tree called out. Kylie looked up and wondered if that was a mating call. Did birds experience romance? Did they ever suffer from broken hearts? She had to admit it looked awfully lonely up in the tree alone. Almost as lonely as it was where she stood.

"Let's make a deal," Della said. "You give Lucas a chance and I'll give Steve a chance."

Kylie smiled. "Are you that worried about me, or do you just need an excuse to go after the good-looking shape-shifter?"

"Maybe both." Della grinned. "We got a deal?"

Kylie considered it, and mentally she stopped trying to hang on, stopped trying to fix something that didn't seem fixable, and opened herself up to other possibilities. "Yeah."

Della started walking, and Kylie took a step. Then the cold grabbed her. She turned and watched Jane Doe's spirit materialize in the beam of sunlight.

The woman met Kylie's gaze. *"Do you know?"*

"Know what?" Kylie asked.

Della turned around. "What?" She stared at Kylie for a second and then said, "Oh shit. Not again." She backed up. "I'm not freaking out. I'm not. Really, I'm not freaking out."

Kylie held up a hand to silence Della and stared at the spirit as she edged closer.

"Do you know what I am?" Jane spoke in a hushed tone that

seemed to whisper through the trees. The blue jay in the tree chirped extra loud.

"No," Kylie said. "I don't." Then the bird chirped oddly and fell from the tree and landed with a lifeless thud at the spirit's feet.

Chapter Eight

"What was that?" Della demanded.

Kylie stared at the bird. It didn't move. Didn't make a noise. Was it . . . ? Her heart squeezed.

"Screw this! It's raining dead birds. *Now* I'm freaking out. Can we leave, *please*?"

The spirit looked from the blue jay to Kylie. *"Is it dead?"* She knelt and stared at it. When she looked up, she had tears in her eyes. *"It's dead. Just like me. Just like the death angels warned. Someone lives and someone dies."*

"No one is going to die."

Kylie picked up the limp bird. Its neck flopped to one side. She remembered seeing the bird so full of life just moments before. What happened? She looked back at the spirit. "Did you kill it?"

"No, I didn't kill it," Della said. "Wait, you aren't talking to me, are you? Is this a death angel or just a ghost?"

"No." Jane looked around as if she were as frightened as Della. She moved closer. *"The others did. They're not nice."*

Kylie shivered from the ghostly cold. "What others?"

"Shh." The spirit lifted her finger to her lips. *"They're coming."* She faded away.

Della stood back and continued to stare. Kylie cupped her hands around the blue jay. She'd healed Sara. Was it possible that she might be able to . . . ?

Kylie closed her eyes and tried to think healing thoughts.

The bird started quivering. Kylie opened her hands and its wings spread. Its feathers, a bright royal blue and white, caught a spray of sunshine and shimmered in the light, then the bird lunged to its feet and flew away. Kylie watched it disappear into the tops of the trees, her emotions ambivalent. On the one hand, she'd given something life, and that was cool. On the other . . . Well, it was just too freaky.

"Did you do what I think you did?" Della asked. "Did you just bring that dead bird back to life?"

Kylie looked up. "I'm not sure." Suddenly silence filled the forest. The spirit's words echoed in Kylie's head. *They're coming.*

The lack of noise seemed ominous.

She looked at Della. "Can you sense anyone here?"

Della sniffed the air. "No. But it's too damn quiet."

"We should go," Kylie whispered.

"You don't have to ask me twice." Della tore out.

Kylie was right behind her, hoping to outrun the silence, the feeling of danger, and another startling realization about her powers.

"You sure it was dead?" Holiday asked.

"I didn't listen to its heartbeat." Kylie paced the small office. "But do birds regularly fall out of trees unconscious?"

Holiday bit back a smile. "I don't think so."

For some reason, this news didn't seem near as startling to her camp leader as it did to Kylie.

Kylie, still winded from her run, had left the woods and come straight to find Holiday. Della, who took the job of shadowing seriously, waited outside.

"The ghost was there. Do you think her presence did this? Maybe it had nothing to do with me. The bird came back to life when she left. So maybe it was just her."

"It could be. However, I've never heard of a ghost's presence killing wildlife, even temporarily. Maybe the bird was just stunned. Maybe all this is a clue."

"To what?" Kylie asked, frustrated.

"Her identity, maybe."

Kylie stopped in front of the desk. "How is a bird dying going to tell me who she is?"

"Sometimes the spirits have crazy ways of communicating."

Kylie rolled a few things around her already confused mind, and then she remembered. "Jane Doe has no brain pattern. Nothing. It's blank."

"Blank?" This time Holiday appeared genuinely puzzled.

"Yeah. I kept trying to refocus, thinking I was . . . just not seeing it right. Because I thought we all had brain patterns, like fingerprints." Kylie dropped in the chair across from the camp leader.

"I've never seen one that's blank, but . . ."

"I think she's supernatural." Kylie chewed on the side of her lip.

"Why would you think that?"

"Because she knew about the death angels."

Holiday appeared to consider it. "She probably heard you talking about them."

"Maybe. But . . . she's really scared of something."

"Dying can be scary if you're not ready."

"I think it's more," Kylie said.

"More like what?"

"I don't know yet. But it's . . . something."

"Wait." Holiday pressed a hand on the desk. "Didn't you tell me she had some kind of brain operation?"

"Yes." Kylie touched her temple. "She has stitches and her head is shaved."

"It's probably a tumor. I've never seen anyone with one, but I've heard tumors can make one's brain pattern do strange things."

"But can a tumor make it disappear?" Kylie asked. "And what about her getting freaked out when I asked her what she was? I really think she's supernatural."

"I'm not saying she isn't one of us, but . . . rarely do we supernaturals hang around long after we pass. In all my years of dealing with ghosts, I've only had three supernaturals."

"But my dad hung around."

"But he had a very big reason to hang on. To check in on you."

Kylie pulled her leg up in the chair and hugged her shin. Her mind zipped from the ghost to her dad to the ghost again. "I don't know . . . There's something about her that's . . . different. Remember, she told me she had messages from others."

"That's not unusual. I often get spirits who tell me something for someone else." Holiday rolled a pencil between her hands.

"But from the death angels?" Kylie asked.

"No, but like I said, she could have heard you mention the death angels and simply be confusing things. Has she mentioned the message again?"

"Yeah. Every time, like it's important." Kylie frowned. "She keeps saying that someone lives and someone dies. And I don't like the die part." She hugged her knee tighter.

"Me either," Holiday said. "But as you've learned, ghosts aren't the best communicators. So don't panic. Just keep asking questions and watching for clues."

"Is it possible that the only reason she's here is to give me this message?"

"Rarely. She's probably here for something else."

Kylie frowned. "Then how the heck am I going to help her if she doesn't even remember who she is?"

Holiday dropped her chin in the palm of her hand. "I think this might be a difficult one."

"As if any that I've had have been easy." Kylie tightened her hold on her leg. "There's one thing I want to check out."

"What's that?"

"Fallen Cemetery. I know you said she could have come from anywhere, but I still find it odd that this is where she popped into my mom's car."

Holiday pinched her brows together. "I'm not going to tell you not to go, but cemeteries aren't the best place for a ghost whisperer. By now you should be able to see more than just one ghost, and a lot of ghosts hang around the cemeteries for a long time."

Kylie remembered. "At Nana's funeral I got a terrible headache."

"That was probably them trying to get through to you. And that was before you could see them. Sometimes they can come at you all at once and it gets . . . difficult."

"But if that's the only lead I have, I have to try."

"You don't have to," Holiday argued. "In the beginning, I wouldn't have ever refused to help a spirit. But I learned that sometimes you have to say no for your own sanity."

"But they'll just keep coming back."

Holiday tilted her head a bit. "Don't you remember us talking about how to shut them out?"

Kylie frowned. "I remember, but I haven't mastered that so well."

"We could go over it again, but . . ." Holiday looked at her watch. "I have an appointment—"

"I want to help her. There's something about her." Kylie might not have amnesia, but there was so much about her life she didn't know, things she wanted to know.

Holiday nodded. "I understand. And I'll support whatever you feel is right. But just make sure you check with me before going, and . . . as Burnett said earlier, you're not to go anywhere without a shadow."

"I'm not too keen on the whole shadow thing," she said.

"Just until we see how things go."

Kylie bit down on her lip, remembering the other things she needed to discuss with Holiday. The whole healing and protector issues. Not to mention the questions she had about her sudden overpowering effect on Derek's emotions.

Then there was . . . She would never get rid of the shadows if she confessed her other concerns. But to not discuss them was stupid. And Kylie wasn't stupid. "Are our security cameras set for . . . shape-shifters?"

Holiday leaned forward. "I'm sure they are. Why?"

"It's probably nothing, but a couple of things happened. They could be nothing, but they didn't feel like nothing."

Holiday stopped rolling the pencil in her hands. "What kind of things?"

"When I left to go back to the cabins, I came across a rattlesnake, but I didn't see it until an eagle swooped down and snatched it up. It was freaky."

"Did it go after you?" Concern darkened her green eyes.

"No, it never got the chance. But the whole thing was just strange."

"Strange like how?"

"The eagle just swooped down." Kylie suddenly felt as if she were overreacting.

Holiday added, "Rattlesnakes are prevalent this time of year, and I admit seeing an eagle swoop down might be—"

Kylie didn't wait for Holiday to continue. "And then when I went to . . . run in the woods, a deer—a big buck—came hurtling onto my path. I stopped and, not a split second later, lightning struck right past the deer. If the deer hadn't stopped me, I might have been hit."

Holiday frowned. "I don't like the sound of this."

"And the deer and the eagle, they . . . looked right at me as if they were trying to tell me something."

Holiday's brow wrinkled. "You think you can communicate with animals?"

"No. I don't think that. They looked evil."

Holiday tilted her head to the side. "The deer and the eagle appeared evil?" When Kylie nodded, Holiday looked even more perplexed and worried. "With two of these strange things happening, I can't believe they are accidents. However, if I'm understanding you, both the eagle and the deer saved you from getting hurt. How could they have been evil? If anything, they were protecting you."

Kylie pulled a handful of hair over her shoulder and twisted it. "I know it doesn't make sense, but it felt that way."

Holiday set the pencil on her desk and reached for her phone. "We'd better let Burnett . . . Wait." She put down her phone. "Burnett left to have a meeting with the FRU. I don't want to disturb him now, but I'll tell him about this as soon as he gets back."

Kylie heard the front door of the cabin open.

Holiday looked at her watch and frowned. "I have another meeting, but we need to talk more about this. Can you wait until I finish so we can continue this?"

"I can come back later," Kylie said, not really wanting to hang out at the office. It would make her feel like a kid sent to the principal's office. "Oh, does Burnett still need the pictures of my dad? If not, I'd like to have them back."

"He's having them tested to see if they are originals or copies. It shouldn't be more than a few days."

"Hi," came an unfamiliar female voice from behind Kylie. "I'm sorry. I didn't know you had someone in here. I can wait in the—"

"It's fine," Holiday said.

Kylie's heart did a little tumble when she recognized the brunette as the one who'd been plastered to Derek in the picture on Della's phone.

"Kylie," Holiday said, "this is Ellie Mason. She's signing up for Shadow Falls."

Showtime, Kylie thought. Time to pretend it didn't hurt. She forced a smile. "Hi."

"Are you Kylie Galen?"

Kylie nodded, unsure what to expect.

"Derek told me about you." She smiled, then tightened her brows to check out Kylie's brain pattern. "Wow. You do have an odd pattern." She made a funny face as if embarrassed.

"Yeah," Kylie said. "Everyone tells me that." Her forced smile melted.

"I'm sorry," Ellie said. "I didn't mean to be rude. Derek has nothing but great things to say about you."

"Don't believe everything he says." Kylie attempted to soften her tone because she felt like a bitch for not liking her. But how could she like Ellie when all Kylie could think about was how Ellie was most likely one of the four girls Derek had slept with? Then she wondered if a kiss was all they'd shared in Pennsylvania.

"I always believe Derek. Especially about people." Ellie took another step inside.

Kylie hated to admit it, but Ellie was pretty. Blue eyes, thick brown hair, and dimples.

Ellie's sincere smile widened. "Derek doesn't tend to exaggerate. And being half-fae, he's a good judge of character. If he likes someone, they deserve it."

Kylie wished she could have disagreed. Not so much because she didn't want to be considered deserving. But because Derek obviously cared for Ellie enough to bring her back here, which meant Ellie was a deserving person.

The being-a-bitch feeling hit again, and Kylie tried to push it back.

"Maybe I caught him on an off day." She attempted to put some teasing in her voice and stood up. "I should go."

"Kylie, why don't I drop by your cabin in about half an hour?" Holiday asked, concern deepening her tone.

Kylie nodded.

"And be careful," Holiday said.

"I will." Kylie stopped when she neared Ellie. "Welcome to Shadow Falls." And she tried to mean it.

"Thank you," Ellie said.

"Is my vampire hearing off? Did you actually say, 'Welcome to Shadow Falls'?" Della asked sarcastically when Kylie got outside. "I would have bitch-slapped her."

"No, you wouldn't have." Kylie noticed the stormy weather had passed.

"Maybe not, but I would have wanted to." Concern shaded Della's eyes.

"And you think I didn't?" Insecurities rained down on Kylie. "She's pretty, isn't she?"

"No," Della said, but Kylie knew it was a lie. Ellie was pretty and nice and she'd probably had sex with Derek.

Kylie's chest swelled with unwanted jealousy, and her mind created an image of Ellie and Derek together. Of them kissing . . . of them . . .

She started walking toward her cabin. Walking fast. Della stayed with her, but somehow she must have sensed Kylie's mood, because she didn't say anything else.

Kylie got to their cabin without speaking, but once she stepped up onto the porch, she faced Della. "Do you think they had sex?"

"I . . ." Della made an odd face.

"I know I shouldn't care. But I guess I do. And damn it, why does it seem that it all goes back to sex? I'm beginning to hate sex and I haven't had it yet. I've got these images flashing in my head. It's like a porn movie and I just keep seeing them—"

Della pressed her hand over Kylie's mouth and shifted her gaze to a point over Kylie's shoulder.

Kylie reached up and peeled Della's hand from her lips. "Is someone standing behind me?" She prayed the answer was no.

Della's sassy smile told Kylie her prayer hadn't been answered.

Swallowing a lump of embarrassment, she tried to imagine the worst person possible standing behind her. Ellie? Derek? No. She met Della's eyes again and mouthed the word *Lucas*.

Please. Please. Please don't let it be Lucas.

Della nodded. Kylie bit back a moan. Not quite ready to face him, she stared out at the woods. Through a maze of trees, she saw the sun slip lower in the horizon. She wished she could follow it and disappear.

"Can you give us a minute?" Lucas's voice came right over her shoulder.

Knowing it was inevitable, Kylie turned. Her face burned when she recalled what she'd said about a porn movie and her whole "I hate sex" conversation. Great!

"Can't," Della answered. "I'm her shadow."

"Well, I'm taking over," he said, almost growling.

"It's okay," Kylie said to Della.

Della frowned. "If something happens to her on my shift, I swear I'll be all over your wolf ass."

"Nothing's going to happen." His blue eyes grew darker, and around the edges, Kylie saw flecks of burnt orange, which meant anger.

Kylie couldn't help wondering if that was targeted at Della or—

"Fine." Della stormed inside. But not without slamming the door so hard, the porch shook.

Kylie met Lucas's gaze. He still looked half-pissed.

"Let's take a walk," he said.

Kylie recalled how he'd stiffened earlier when she'd taken up for Derek. Was he angry at her, too? The thought of hurting him when he'd risked his life to save her made her stomach clutch. He didn't deserve that, not that she'd meant to hurt him. But neither did Derek deserve to be blamed for trying to help her.

He started off the porch and looked back.

His eyes were a brighter orange now. Kylie remembered a time she would have freaked out at seeing an angry werewolf. Heck, she remembered a time when she hadn't believed werewolves existed, angry or not.

"You coming?" Lucas asked.

Chapter Nine

She could say no, but she didn't want to. She followed him. The sun hung low, but its light clung to the sky. However, once they moved into the woods and under the umbrella of the trees, the remnants of daylight faded into dusk. They walked without talking.

She remembered the dead bird and the ghost's announcement that someone else was out there. Fear brushed against Kylie's neck. Almost as if she could feel the hot breath of something evil on her nape, she reached up and tried to brush away the sensation. Everything seemed to grow darker.

"Should we be going into the woods?" She heard a rustle and looked to her left. And she walked right into Lucas's back, unaware that he'd stopped. He turned and she saw him lift up his face as if to sniff the air.

"You're scared of me?" he asked.

Even through the dimness she could see anger in his expression.

"No. I'm scared of . . . other things." She didn't know what to call them.

"Scared Derek will hear you went off with me?" His tone came with accusation.

"No."

He swung back around and commenced walking again. She matched his steps. He stopped abruptly and faced her again.

"I said I'd be patient and I will, but I won't be made a fool of."

"I didn't make a fool of you," she insisted.

"You stood up for Derek."

"I just stated the facts. You were wrong to blame Derek." Her throat tightened again. She'd been fighting tears all day, and this time when they crawled up her throat, she was helpless.

She turned away, hoping to stop them before he saw. But when she reached up to swipe away the first tear, he caught her hand. How he could have moved in front of her without making a sound was unnerving.

He let go of a deep breath. "I didn't mean to upset you, it's just . . ."

She tried to tell him it wasn't him making her cry, but the concern in his tone had the knot in her throat doubling in size. The next thing she knew she was against his chest, her tears and almost silent sobs being absorbed by his pale blue T-shirt and his extra warm chest.

His arms were around her and she felt his cheek resting on top of her head. She felt safe. Safe and something else. She felt cherished. The way his arms held her, the way every inch of him embraced her—she wanted to stay here. Savor it.

"I'm sorry," she muttered, her face still buried against him. "I shouldn't be sliming up your shirt."

"Is it over?" His words tickled the top of her head.

"Is what over? My crying?" She wasn't ready to give up the wall of muscle or having his arms around her. Nor was she ready to let him see her all red and splotchy.

"No. You and Derek." His tone deepened, and she sensed it was hard for him to even ask the question.

"Yeah." She nodded her head against him.

His arms tightened around her. She almost sighed because it felt so good.

"Then you're welcome to slime my shirt," he said, and the undercurrent of anger vanished. "I don't have a lot of rules, but that's one of them. Only uncommitted girls can slime my shirt."

She chuckled.

"Is that a smile I feel against my chest?" His words stirred her hair.

"A slimy one." She snaked her hand up between their bodies to clear her face before looking up.

"I'll bet it's still beautiful."

He inched back, and in the dark woodsy light, she felt his eyes on her.

"You might lose the bet." She wanted to cover her face but would feel silly doing it.

"You're right, I would have lost." He laughed. "You don't cry pretty."

She thumped his solid chest with her palm. He laughed again.

"Come on." He fitted his hand in hers and started walking again, deeper into the woods. With the night sounds around them, she tuned her ears and waited for it to go silent—for something bad to suddenly appear.

She gave his hand a slight pull. "Let's go back the other way."

He turned and studied her. "What are you afraid of?"

"If we walk out of the woods, I'll tell you." She tried to make light of the dread gnawing at her gut.

A frown pulled at his brows. "I wouldn't let anything hurt you."

"I know, but I'd feel better if we went that way." She nodded back to the clearing.

"Fine." He began walking in that direction. "But start talking. Why are you afraid? Is it still the elderly couple?"

"No." She wished she could see the clearing of the woods ahead, but the night seemed to close in on her.

Suddenly, something dark *whooshed* down from a tree. She lurched back and pulled him with her. Her heart shot up in her throat. She tightened her hand in his, and with everything she had, she started to run. He ran with her, two people moving in one solid, fluid motion, his palm clutched tightly in hers.

Once they reached the clearing, Kylie stopped, bent over, and hungrily sucked oxygen into her lungs.

Finally rising, she looked at him. Out from under the thicket of the trees, night hadn't completely fallen and she could make out his features.

He stood there, watching her. He didn't gasp for air or hold his stomach the way she did. Damn it! He didn't even look winded.

Curiosity filled his eyes. "It was just an eagle."

"It was?" She looked up at the sky, which was painted with only a few lingering colors of sunset, and prayed the bird hadn't followed. Thankfully, only the first few stars of the night twinkled back at her. No eagle. At least she didn't see it.

"Did it follow us?" she asked, remembering he could see better than she could.

"No." He studied her. "Something happened, didn't it."

"Yes. Maybe. Just weird stuff." She realized she still held his hand, and while it was balmy outside, his hand felt nice. It warmed her palm in a good way, like a cup of hot chocolate, a comforting feeling. While his touch didn't hold the magic of the fae to calm one's fear, it did calm her.

"Come on." He went back to running. Fast. Then faster.

Every time she'd push herself to meet his speed, he'd increase it. Then he'd glance at her as if to make sure she wasn't having to work too hard. She got the feeling he was testing her, wanting to see just how fast she could run.

"Where are we going?" she asked, barely able to speak.

"To the creek." His voice sounded even.

His pace kept getting faster. Wanting to impress him, forgetting all about the eagle, she pushed herself to keep going. Finally, he stopped. Not prepared for the halt, she continued forward. She felt the tug on her arm where she still held his hand, and then suddenly his arm swooped around her waist.

Out of energy and off balance, she fell into him and they both went down. Not hard, or at least not for her, because she landed on top of him.

"You okay?" Her heart still pumped, her chest moving up and down as she gasped for air. As her lungs expanded again, she became aware of the intimate way her body rested against his.

He laughed. "Me okay? You're the one who can't breathe." He wrapped his arms around her. His hands rested on the small of her back.

"I can . . . breathe." She laughed. Warm contentment filled her, and she realized she liked being with him. Liked being this close. Maybe too much.

She could feel every inch of his body under hers, and it made her even more breathless. She rolled off of him. The earth and grass beneath her back felt cool, especially considering how warm he had been. The sounds of the night, crickets and a few birds, sang around them. She stared through a curtain of her hair at the midnight blue sky and focused on a star flickering its brightness down from the heavens.

"I'm impressed. I didn't know you could run like that." He rolled to his side, propped up on his elbow, and brushed her hair from her face.

"Yeah." One word was all she could manage. She blinked and stared up at his face. Even in the night, she could see and appreciate the angles and lines of his features. He was so masculine. Always had been, even when he'd been seven. But now, with the light shadow of a beard, he was downright stunning.

The temptation to touch his cheek, to run the tips of her fingers over the stubble, tiptoed through her mind.

She inhaled, her lungs still thirsty for oxygen. Suddenly the sound of water trickling nearby filled her senses. "Are we . . . ?" She raised her head and realized they'd arrived at the creek, the spot she'd brought her mother the day she'd asked about Daniel.

Sadness whispered through her when she remembered she might not see her dad again. She pushed that back and tried not to let the happiness of this moment melt away.

"We made good time." She realized how far they had run.

"How long have you known you could run like that?" he asked.

"Only since I've been here. But I'm getting faster."

He picked up a thick lock of her hair and watched it slide off his palm. His face was only a few inches from hers. She saw him tighten his brows to check out her pattern.

"It's still a mystery," she said.

He met her eyes. "You don't even suspect what you are?"

She frowned. "I wish."

He pulled a long blade of grass from the ground and twirled it in his fingers. Then he looked over his shoulder at the moon, only half-full. "When I was a kid and lived next door to you, when I'd shift, I'd jump the fence into your backyard and watch you through your bedroom window, waiting and hoping I'd see you turn."

"You peeped into my window?"

He smiled. "It's not like you were naked or anything. You mostly wore that Little Mermaid nightshirt." A laugh spilled out of his throat. "You looked like an angel. Sometimes I would stay there half the night thinking you still might turn."

She studied his eyes. "Did you think I was a werewolf?"

"I hoped." He touched the tip of her nose with the grass. Then he slid it over her lips. It tickled and yet somehow felt seductive.

He continued staring as if remembering. "I wanted to run in the woods with you. To show you how fast I could go. To take you to my favorite watering hole so we could chase each other in the spring and play in the moonlight."

"Do you still hope I'm a werewolf?"

He hesitated. "Yeah. I probably shouldn't tell you that, but yeah, I do. It would make everything easier."

"Make what easier?" She thought about what Fredericka had said.

"Everything." He brought the blade of grass back over her lips. "I wouldn't have to be away from you when I shift. We could hunt together. You would be with me when I'm leading the pack."

The thought of hunting and killing wild animals didn't sit well with her, even being with the group of weres that included Fredericka didn't hold a lot of appeal, but she tried not to let it show.

"We'd make a great team."

"And what if I'm not a werewolf?"

He smiled, but for just a second she thought she saw disappointment in his eyes.

"We still make a good team," he said.

"Does everyone feel that way?" she asked, not wanting to mention Fredericka.

"What do you mean?"

"The last couple of times we've been together, someone from the pack sent for you as if they didn't want you with me."

"It's nothing," he said.

"You sure?"

He tickled her cheek with the grass. "Trust me."

"I do trust you."

"You haven't told me what you're afraid of."

She bit down on her lip. He swiped the blade of grass over her mouth.

"Start talking."

She told him about the eagle and the snake and then about the huge buck and the lightning.

He frowned. "Do you think Derek is doing this? He communicates with animals."

"No. Derek wouldn't do that."

"You say that like you trust him." Lucas's tone deepened.

"I do. Please don't take it the wrong way. It's over with us, but I know he wouldn't try to hurt or even scare me. He cares about me."

"And you him?" His eyes went from blue to almost orange.

"Yes. But it's still over." She could tell he didn't like hearing her say that, but he seemed to understand. For a flicker of a second, she wondered how long it would be before she could understand it herself.

He stared back up at the moon. "If it's not him, then who?"

"I think Holiday and Burnett believe Mario and Red are behind it. And they sent the impostors posing as my grandparents. But then Della said that they're vampires, not shape-shifters, so they couldn't be doing it themselves."

"Maybe Mario has a shifter working for him. Though it's uncommon that two species work together like that." He brushed a strand of hair behind her ear. "I won't let that creep lay another finger on you."

She knew he really didn't have the ability to keep that promise, but she liked hearing it.

Then, because it felt good talking about it, she told him about the ghost and the bird falling from the tree.

He looked concerned. "Do you think she's a death angel?" He was obviously more disturbed by the ghost than the fact that Kylie had brought a dead bird back to life.

"No, but I think she's a supernatural."

"Did you check her pattern?"

"That's part of the problem. She doesn't have one."

"Everyone has a pattern," he said.

"But she doesn't. Before she disappeared, she told me the others were out there."

"What others? Like more ghosts?" Lucas looked around.

"I don't think she meant ghosts. She made it sound like they were evil."

"And ghosts aren't evil?" he asked in disbelief.

"Not really. At least none of them that I've met."

He shook his head. "I can't imagine dealing with them."

She hesitated before answering. "It was hard in the beginning. It's still freaky, but not as bad." She met his eyes. "Besides, I can't imagine shifting into a wolf."

He smiled. "It's a piece of cake. I hope you figure that out for yourself, too."

She chewed on the fact that he really wanted her to be werewolf. No disrespect intended, but she wasn't so sure she shared his hope.

"I heard you experienced some of the mood swings last month." His gaze lowered to her breasts. "You also underwent some hormonal changes like female weres do."

Yeah, she'd grown an inch, a cup, and a shoe size—not so strange until you realized it happened overnight. Not that she really liked being reminded of it. Her face heated.

She pushed back the embarrassment. "True, but there's just as much evidence that I'm not a were. According to Holiday, weres are seldom ghost whisperers. They start turning when they're very young and they don't have the ability to dreamscape."

A light smile appeared in his eyes and, blast it, she knew exactly what he was thinking about, too. The dream. The one of them swimming, practically naked and . . .

"Guess we'll have to see in a couple of weeks when the moon is full."

He ran the blade of grass over her lips again and then down past her chin.

Her breath almost caught when it glided across the swell of her breasts above the cut of the tank top. It was just a piece of grass, but it could have been his finger for the sweet sensation pouring into her chest.

He leaned down, his lips inches from hers. "I have a request."

"What's . . . that?" She was barely able to think, much less speak.

He swept the blade of grass up and swirled it around her forehead. "When you close your eyes and get images flashing in your mind . . ."

His words reminded her of what he'd heard her say to Della about the porn movie. Her face grew hot again.

"I want that movie playing in your mind to be of us. Only us."

She felt the warmth of his mouth, then in a flash he pounced over her. He landed in a crouch, then slowly rose, a low growl rumbling from his throat as he stared out at the line of trees.

She scrambled to her feet. "What is it?"

He looked back at her. His eyes glowed that bright burnt orange color. "Someone's coming."

Chapter Ten

Kylie's heart started to pound. "Should we run?"

"No." Lucas's defensive posture relaxed. "It's just—"

"Me," another deep male voice said.

Kylie recognized the voice before she saw Burnett standing behind her. Even in the darkness, she was close enough to recognize the look of discontent on his face. His eyes weren't glowing, so it wasn't about danger, but everything in his expression said he wasn't happy. And he was looking right at her.

What could he be so upset about?

He stepped closer, his presence larger than life. "Holiday is—"

All it took was his two words and Kylie had her answer. "Crap! Holiday was supposed to come by my cabin. I'm sorry."

"Yeah," he said. "And she really got worried when we couldn't find Della, who was supposed to be your shadow." He turned his focus on Lucas, and his grimace deepened.

"Where's Della?" Kylie asked. "Is she okay?"

"She's fine. She and Miranda had gone for a swim. But none of this would have happened if someone hadn't insisted she be relieved of her shadow duties."

"That's my fault," Kylie insisted.

"It's not anyone's fault." Lucas stiffened his shoulders. "I wouldn't have let anything happen to Kylie."

"That's not the point," Burnett growled into the night. "Considering your affiliation with the FRU, you of all people should understand the importance of following protocol. I assigned Della as Kylie's shadow, and it's not your place to change my orders. And by changing them, you caused this situation."

"I wouldn't have had to change it if you'd assigned her to me in the beginning as I asked. And considering my affiliation, you should trust me to protect her."

Kylie looked from Burnett to Lucas and then back again. "I'm the one who forgot about Holiday. If anyone is to blame—"

"I came looking for you," Lucas snapped, as if refusing to let her take any blame. He stared back at Burnett. Lucas's eyes started to change colors.

An owl called out in the woods. The half-moon seemed to grow brighter as the two of them, vampire and werewolf, stood staring at each other.

Burnett was the first to blink, not that it came off as weakness, but rather a sign of reasoning. "Trust is earned. Your overconfidence will not serve you well in the FRU."

"My overconfidence only comes second to yours," Lucas said. "And I think it's part of the reason the FRU is interested in me."

"Perhaps. But there is a fine line between indomitable and supercilious. And the latter character trait is nothing the FRU accepts." Burnett pulled his cell phone out of his pocket and hit a button.

Kylie saw Lucas's jaw tighten, and she knew how hard it was for him to be reprimanded by Burnett, especially in front of her.

Lucas looked away, but not before Kylie saw his eyes glittering with anger. But then he said, "I apologize if I caused a problem." He might be angry, but he was willing to concede.

Burnett nodded and spoke into the phone. "Holiday, I have her.

She's fine. . . . Yes. I will." He hung up and refocused on Lucas. "I'll meet you back in the office in a bit. I need to speak with Kylie."

Lucas met her eyes, as if asking if she was okay with his going. She nodded. "I'll see you later."

He took off and in seconds was nothing more than a speck shifting between the moonlit trees in the woods. Burnett watched him disappear and then he looked back to her.

Kylie spoke before Burnett. "I should have remembered Holiday was coming."

"True. But Lucas shouldn't have requested you leave your shadow without conferring with me."

"He's not supercilious like you said." She frowned.

"Yes, he is." Burnett chuckled. "But so was I when I was his age. He'll grow out of it. I did."

Kylie didn't like Burnett's answer, but she felt better knowing he wasn't holding a grudge against Lucas.

When Burnett didn't automatically go into what it was he wanted to talk with her about, she asked her own question. "Any more news on the people who were pretending to be my grandparents?"

"No, but the car they were driving was found. It was listed as stolen. We're checking for fingerprints."

Kylie nodded and looked back up at the moon as a lacy cloud passed over it, making the night appear darker. When she looked back, Burnett stared and his brow twitched as if he were checking her pattern. Puzzlement filled his eyes.

She should be used to it, but at times she wanted to wear a shield over her forehead.

"Is Holiday mad at me?" Kylie asked.

"More worried than angry. She saves all her hostile emotions to use on me." He shot her a tiny smile.

"But you're still here. That has to mean something."

"It means I'm a glutton for punishment." He hesitated, and while his words came out with humor, his eyes didn't express the same emotion.

"No, I meant the fact that she accepted you being a shareholder of Shadow Falls has to mean something."

He frowned. "She needed my money."

Kylie had to bite her lip not to tell him about the other investor. "You really like her, don't you?" Her heart ached for him. Not that he wanted sympathy. And maybe that's why she felt it. When someone this strong and prideful had a heartache, it made an impression.

"That's not important."

Yes, it is. Kylie saw rejection pass across Burnett's eyes. Somehow, some way, she was going to get Holiday to stop being so stubborn and give the man a chance. It just didn't make sense why she was so hesitant. If he was ugly or obnoxious, Kylie would understand. But Burnett was none of those. And he cared so much about Holiday that Kylie could almost feel it.

"I wouldn't say it wasn't important," Kylie added.

He shrugged. "Tell me about the snake and the deer incident."

Kylie told both stories for what felt like the hundredth time. At least now she could tell it without hyperventilating. When she finished, Burnett just stood there, his dark brow pinched and his lips tight.

"You think I'm overreacting, don't you."

His frown deepened. "No. I agree with Holiday. With two of these instances happening, it can't be a coincidence."

"So the security system isn't working?" she asked.

"No, it's working."

"Then how could—"

"That's what we don't know. A shifter has infiltrated the camp, specifically to target you. And I don't like it one damn bit!"

Kylie felt her stomach drop. He wasn't the only one.

• • •

That night, the dream came on slow. But this one was different from the others. Kylie wasn't moving, she'd just woken up here. She saw Lucas standing by the lake where they'd run to earlier, and just like that, those differences didn't matter. Before she'd gone to bed, he'd tapped on her window. When she opened it, he'd pulled himself up and kissed her quickly on the lips.

"Good night," he'd said, and dropped back to the ground.

She'd grinned as she watched him leave. And she'd gone to bed wishing he hadn't run off so quickly.

Suddenly, the dream became her reality, grounded into the world of the mind where everything felt so real. She stood behind him and enjoyed being this close. Reaching out, she touched his arm and he turned around—not surprised that she was there, but happy to see her. For a second, something didn't feel right, but when he pulled her against him, she nudged away the feeling.

"Have you always been this beautiful, Kylie Galen?" Lucas's hands fell to her waist.

She grinned. "Why don't you tell me? You peeked into my windows when I was five."

"Shame on me." He leaned in closer. Uncertainty nagged at her. There was something off, but she couldn't put her finger on it.

She smiled up at him.

"Tell me what makes you happy," he said.

His statement stirred confusion. "What do you mean?"

"Do you want a mansion? A new car? Do you want to go to Mexico and drink beer on the beach? I can give you that and more."

She shook her head. "I don't want any of that."

"Then what?"

These questions weren't like Lucas, but she felt compelled to answer. "I want everyone to get along. Miranda and Della fought again last night. I want my dad to be able to visit me again. I want the Brightens to be okay. I want to know what I am. And I want to take care of whatever problem it is that this new ghost has."

"I can give you most of that. Just say yes."

"Yes to what?" And that's when it hit her. That's when she realized what was wrong. Lucas wasn't hot.

"You're cold." She took a quick step back, moving out of his arms. "What's going on?"

"I wanted to see you. I knew you would leave if . . ." Suddenly, it wasn't Lucas standing there. It was Red, the rogue vampire who was Mario's grandson, the one who'd killed the girls. The one who'd kidnapped her and beat up Lucas. She started to scream, then realized that this was just a dream and she had the ability to wake up.

"My grandfather and his friends don't think you can be convinced to work with us. I only want to help . . ." His last words faded as Kylie shot up on the bed, gasping for breath. She recalled how her senses had told her in the beginning of the dream that something wasn't right. If she'd only listened to her instincts, this wouldn't have happened. Then she remembered how Holiday had said she could temporarily shut them off. When she was able to think straight, Kylie leaned back on her pillow and did the visualization.

The last thing she wanted was to see him in her dreams.

Or her reality.

The next morning, Kylie felt tiny little skunk paws walking up her chest and then felt a wet pointed nose bump her chin as if summoning her awake.

She lay there for a few seconds, not moving and not opening her eyes, trying to decide why something felt wrong. Her first thought went back to the dream she'd had with Red, but no, this wasn't about that. Then bright light leaked into the corners of her closed eyes. She opened her eyes.

Sitting up cautiously, giving Socks his obligatory morning pat, she looked around. The sun streamed through the blinds and cast horizontal shadows on the floor.

What time was it? She swept her hair from her face.

Her gaze shot to the clock. Seven. Was that what didn't feel right . . . that she hadn't been nudged awake by an impatient spirit? Was her Jane Doe ghost not a morning ghost? Then again, maybe amnesia prevented someone from judging time.

Not that Kylie was complaining. Her last spirit had rarely let Kylie sleep a minute past dawn.

Seeing her phone, Kylie remembered Holiday and snatched up the cell, hoping to find Holiday had called or texted her. Before Kylie and Burnett had gotten back to the office, Holiday had called Burnett and asked if he could take over the camp for a day or so because she had a family emergency and had to leave. The only thing Holiday had told Burnett was that she had to deal with this.

Burnett had been worried, too. Kylie had heard the frustration in his voice when he spoke with Holiday and she wouldn't elaborate on the type of emergency.

Kylie had phoned and texted Holiday but hadn't gotten an answer before she'd gone to bed.

Checking her call log, she found two texts. One from Sara, her old best friend whom Kylie had probably just healed of cancer—please let that be so—and then one from Holiday.

Kylie breathed a sigh of relief as she read Sara's message that she was feeling great, then quickly read Holiday's. It was short and simple. *All is ok. B back soon.*

Wanting more reassurance, Kylie dialed the camp leader's number.

"Hey," Holiday answered. "Is everything okay?"

Kylie almost told her about the dream with the rogue vampire, but her gut said Holiday had something else on her plate. Besides, Holiday had already told her how to deal with this, and if Kylie had listened to her instincts, this wouldn't have happened. "Yeah, just worried about you. Are you back at camp yet?"

"Not yet. I should be there this afternoon." She grew quiet. "I'm sorry I had to bail before we talked. Are you dealing with everything okay? Nothing else has happened, has it?"

"No, I'm fine. We were just concerned about you."

"We?"

"Burnett and me," she said, remembering her promise to herself to play matchmaker. "What happened?" Kylie asked hesitantly, not wanting to overstep her bounds. But her relationship with Holiday felt like more than just camp leader and camper. She truly cared about her.

Holiday was quiet for a moment. "My great-aunt passed away."

"Oh, Holiday, I'm so sorry. Can I do anything?" A cold entered the room. Kylie ignored it and focused on the phone conversation. She'd deal with Jane Doe in a few minutes.

"No. I'm fine," Holiday said. "It was her time. But she didn't get her estate in order and now . . ."

Kylie felt her mattress dip down. She glanced up, and sitting on the foot of her bed was an older woman wearing a yellow housedress and a beautiful pale blue tear-shaped crystal necklace.

"The will is taped to the bottom left drawer of my dresser. But I want her to take all my crystal pieces. Don't let Marty take them, and she'll try. She's a sneaky little twit."

Kylie studied the woman's gray hair hanging down around her shoulders and then noted her eyes were a bright green that looked vaguely familiar.

Kylie's hold on the phone tightened and she shivered. Holiday had told her that she would eventually be able to see more than one

ghost at a time. It looked as if that time had arrived. But could she
handle it?

"Tell her," the ghost said, and that's when Kylie knew why the eyes
were so familiar. She tightened her brows and checked the woman's
pattern.

Holiday started talking. "Dealing with the estate is going to be
such a—"

"Uh, Holiday . . . ?" Kylie said. "What does your great-aunt look
like?"

"Why?".

"Because I think she's sitting on the end of my bed. If it's her, the
will is taped to the bottom left drawer of her dresser."

The ghost started floating up to the ceiling as if something were
pulling her away.

"Long gray hair," Holiday answered. "And green eyes."

"It's her," Kylie answered, now looking at the spirit floating near
the ceiling. "So you'd better check out her dresser."

The ghost smiled. *"Thank you."*

"Thanks, Kylie," Holiday said.

Kylie felt another chill and pulled the covers up a bit. "No problem."

The ghost started to fade into the ceiling, then stopped and slid
back down. *"Almost forgot. They wanted me to tell you something. Someone lives and someone . . ."* She vanished, leaving the sentence unfinished.

But Kylie knew what she meant.

"Dies," Kylie said, and closed her eyes. *Someone lives and someone
dies.* The message wasn't just the mutterings of a crazy amnesia
ghost. But how could Kylie make things right if she didn't know
what to do?

Chapter Eleven

Dressed and still fighting the feeling that something wasn't right, Kylie stepped out of her room an hour later. Either Miranda and Della had already left, or they were still asleep. Either way, Kylie was happy not to have to face them. First, she hoped to find Helen, the half-fae who also had the gift of healing. Kylie wasn't sure if the "someone will live and someone will die" message meant she could prevent a death, but she had to try. Then she planned to talk with Burnett and tell him what she knew about Holiday. Not that Kylie was doing it behind the camp leader's back.

Before they'd hung up, she had asked if she could share their conversation with Burnett. When Holiday had wavered, Kylie asked her how she'd feel if Burnett disappeared on "an emergency" and didn't explain himself.

"Fine," Holiday said.

Although she hadn't sounded happy about it.

A few minutes later, Kylie started out of the cabin, tripped, and landed half on and half off the huge black Lab that was curled up on the welcome rug in front of the door.

"What the heck?" Stunned, she scrambled to get up and, in the process, stepped on the canine's tail. The dog yelped as if in pain, and guilt filled Kylie's lungs. "Sorry."

Was the animal hurt? Once an injured dog had shown up at her doorstep when she'd been a kid. Her mom had her dad take it to the vet and they'd ended up having to put it down.

Kylie had cried and blamed her mom for killing the dog. With the emotional footprints of that memory tugging at her heartstrings, Kylie crouched down.

"Sorry," she told the dog again, and let it sniff her hand before she gave it a gentle pat. "Are you hurt? You get hit by a car or something?"

"No. You stepped on my tail, and of course it hurt," the dog said.

Kylie, still down on her haunches, fell back on her butt and glared at the talking canine.

"What?" the dog asked.

"Don't do that!"

"Do what?"

"Talk!"

Okay, the sparkles now popping all over the place and the changing eye color told her it was Perry, but seeing a dog talk still freaked her out.

She jumped to her feet and continued to scowl at the animal. Basically, she needed a kick-dog to target her frustration, and she'd just found one. A black Lab that at this moment was changing forms.

She waited until Perry was transformed. "Why the hell is your canine butt sleeping on my porch?"

"I was afraid Miranda would come out, and if she knew it was me, she'd wiggle her little pinky at me and give me zits or something."

"Okay." She tightened her gaze. "But that doesn't explain what you're doing on my porch."

"Duh, I was waiting for you," he said matter-of-factly. "I'm your shadow for the day."

"Oh, crap. I forgot about . . . that." She took a deep breath and tried to resign herself to having a tag-along following her around like a . . . lost puppy.

He studied her with his gold eyes. "You're mad at me, aren't you."

"No," she said, biting back her frustration. "You're right. Miranda would have zapped you with zits or something. But you just blow my mind when you're an animal and you talk." She put a hand on each side of her head. "It hurts my brain."

"No, I meant mad about the shit that happened yesterday."

Kylie just stared at him. "You're gonna have to be more specific. Because a lot of shit happened yesterday."

He grinned, but the smile faded quickly. "I mean how I lost track of the old couple who were pretending to be your grandparents." A sincere apology filled his eyes. "I failed."

"That wasn't your fault."

"Yes, it was. Who else are you going to blame it on? I was the one supposed to follow them."

"How about we not blame it on anyone?" She started walking down the path toward the office.

He fell into step beside her. "Sounds good."

They walked a few minutes in silence. Kylie noticed the sky was painted with clouds, the big white fluffy kind, and tried not to think about the elderly couple Perry had followed or exactly what it meant when they went poof.

"Do you think they're dead?" she asked.

"Who's dead?"

"The elderly couple."

His features tightened. "I really don't know. I've never seen humans disappear like that."

They both got quiet again. The morning temperature hadn't risen to the uncomfortable level yet, but she could feel it climbing.

Perry tossed his own question next. "Do you think Miranda is ever going to accept my apology?"

Kylie looked at him. "Did you apologize?"

He looked honestly perplexed. "I spoke to her. That's the same thing."

Kylie shook her head. "Oh no, it's not. Speaking to someone is not an apology, Perry. What you did—kissing her like that, then blowing her off—that was mean."

He frowned and kicked a rock. "She kissed Kevin. I was mad."

"I get that," Kylie said, and remembered seeing the picture of Derek kissing Ellie. "And I know it hurts, but it was really Kevin who kissed her. But even still, two wrongs don't make a right."

She caught him checking out her brain pattern, and she frowned. He continued walking but shifted his gaze to the ground. They didn't talk for a bit, and then Kylie just blurted it out. "Everyone says my pattern moves around like a shape-shifter now. Is it true?"

"Yeah," he said. "But ours only move when we're shifting."

She stopped walking and faced him. "Is there anything else about my pattern that looks like a shape-shifter? I mean, do you see any sign that I might be one?"

He smiled. "You want to be a shape-shifter?"

"No." *Hell, no!* "I mean, not necessarily. I just want to figure out what I am." She bit down on her lip and decided to plunge right into the subject. "How old were you when you started shifting?"

"Oh, I was really young, too young. Five years younger than most shifters. Like barely two years old. Try handling a terrible two tantrum with a shape-shifter. Blew my parents' minds. And their marriage."

Kylie heard the tiniest bit of hurt in his voice. "They split up?"

"Yeah."

"I'm sorry."

"Hey . . . it wasn't my problem."

Oh, yeah, it was. Even his eyes had grown a lonely shade of muted brown. "Who did you live with, your mom or your dad?"

He didn't answer for a minute. "Neither."

She hesitated to ask, but somehow she almost sensed he wanted her to. "Why?"

"Supposedly, I was that hard to handle."

"Where did you go?"

"The FRU has a foster care program. You know, for unwanted strays. I stayed here for a while, and then there for a while."

Kylie felt she understood Perry better than she ever had. And she almost forgave him for being the smartass that he was sometimes.

"Was it terrible?" she asked, and suddenly she knew that she'd lost all her whining rights about how bad her own life had been.

"Nah," he said. "I'm a shape-shifter, I learned to fit in . . . at most places. Of course, I wasn't invited back to some of them." He laughed, but as Kylie had already suspected, Perry hid a lot of pain behind his humor.

She also got a feeling there was a lot he wasn't saying. Not that she blamed him. But damn, she couldn't imagine how it must have been being passed from home to home.

"You know," he said as if he suddenly wanted to change the subject, "some shifters don't start until they're in their teens. Maybe you're one of them."

"Maybe," she said. "But I'd only be half. Do half-breed shifters ever have different gifts? Like healing and stuff?"

"Not that I've heard. I have some cousins who are half-breeds and they're limited on what they can shift into. One can only shift into a bird. I used to turn into a cat and chase him around, and one time—"

"Please don't tell me you ate him," Kylie said.

"I just tortured him a little," he said with a grin. "Hey, when he shifted back, he was fine." He inhaled and almost seemed to get lost in a memory. "You know, I should probably try to find some of my cousins."

Kylie wondered if he ever thought about finding his parents, but not wanting to pry too much, she didn't ask. "Oh yeah," she said, grinning, trying to keep it light. "I'll bet they would love to see you coming."

A few minutes later, they'd reached the end of the path where the cabins that housed the office and the dining hall were located. She glanced around to see if she could spot Helen, the shy half-fae who had checked Kylie for a brain tumor, but Kylie didn't see her.

Because Helen was also a healer, Kylie figured she would be the person to ask about the gift. Questions like "Have you ever brought something back to life?" But Helen wasn't one of the teens hanging out front of the dining hall. However, Kylie did see Burnett walk into the office and she remembered she had things to talk to him about, too.

She turned to Perry. "I need to chat with Burnett for a bit. I'll see you in few—"

"No, you won't," Perry said. "Where you go, I go. It's questionable if you can pee today." He grinned. "And I've got Burnett's permission to morph into a giant anteater and kick ass and ask questions later if anyone tries to take over my job."

Kylie rolled her eyes, knowing Burnett had been talking about Lucas. And thinking of Lucas, she looked around a second time, but he wasn't in the crowd either.

Looking back at Perry, she added, "Yeah, but I'm going to see Burnett. I don't think you have to be there then."

He tightened his shoulders. "Where you go, I go. Until Burnett dismisses me."

"Oh, hell. Come on."

• • •

Breakfast started out awkward. As had walking into Holiday's office, Perry in tow, and seeing Burnett sitting at Holiday's desk for
the second time. Thankfully, Burnett dismissed Perry for their chat.
Kylie asked for any update on the elderly couple who had pretended
to be her grandparents and was told that nothing had come through
yet.

She almost told Burnett about the dream with Red but at the last
moment decided she wanted to be able to handle one thing on her
own. And this was it. If it happened again, she'd talk to Holiday, but
for now, she was flying solo on this mission. As crazy as it sounded, it
felt kind of good, too. She wanted to believe she could take care of
herself.

When she'd told Burnett about Holiday's aunt passing away,
he'd looked shocked and . . . something else. It took her a second,
but she'd recognized the emotion in his eyes. Hurt.

"Why would she not tell me this?" he had asked.

"I'm sure she's just dealing with it in her own way," Kylie had
tried to assure him, but she could tell her efforts were futile. And as
she'd turned to leave, she didn't know what compelled her to do it,
but she'd looked back over her shoulder and said, "Be patient with
her. She's worth it."

Now, in the dining hall, Perry still in tow, Kylie stared at her
breakfast of bacon, eggs, and toast. For a change, the eggs weren't
runny and the bacon wasn't raw or burned. But she'd eaten only a
few bites, and after being painfully aware that everyone was staring
at her forehead again, she decided she must have left her appetite at
the cabin.

A symphony of noise—people jabbering, forks clinking, and trays
being dropped onto the tables—bounced around the large cabin.
Both Miranda and Della were missing in action, and Kylie hadn't
spotted Helen or Lucas either.

Unfortunately, she had spotted Derek and Ellie.

They sat together at a table toward the back. It was only right that Derek sit with her, considering she was the new kid at camp. Last night, staring at the ceiling for a good two hours, Kylie had resigned herself *not* to hate Ellie or Derek, but to accept things—even if it meant seeing them come together as a couple—and move on.

Kylie had also resigned herself to making good on that promise to Della and give Lucas a chance. However, even after all that resigning she'd done, seeing Derek and Ellie whispering to each other stung like a fire ant bite between the toes.

Time, Kylie told herself. In time, it wouldn't hurt. "I need a fast-forward button," she muttered.

"A what?" Perry asked.

"Nothing," Kylie said. "Just muttering to myself." She looked up and caught another three or four people twitching their brows at her. She turned and looked at Perry. "What's it doing now?"

"What's what doing?"

"My friggin' pattern. Everyone's staring again."

Perry twitched. "Oh, shit! It's doing that shifting thing again. Only faster."

Kylie closed her eyes. "I'm so tired of being everyone's entertainment, of being the freak on display."

"You're not a freak," Perry said, sounding concerned. "You're just different." He gave her a nudge with his elbow. "But everyone likes you anyway."

Opening her eyes, she muttered, "Thanks."

"Are you going to eat that piece of bacon?" Perry asked.

"No." She pushed her tray over to him. Miranda came strolling by with her breakfast tray in her hands. Stopping, about to plop down beside Kylie, she spotted Perry.

She froze. "What is *he* doing here?" she asked as if Perry couldn't hear her.

"Eating breakfast," Kylie said, hoping to deter Perry from saying something smartass. Seeing him open his mouth, she gave him a good kick under the table. He flinched but closed his mouth.

"Well, I'll just join my sister witches today and let you enjoy each other's company." Miranda turned to leave.

Kylie grabbed Miranda by the arm, bringing her to a sudden halt that almost had Miranda's eggs taking a flying leap off her tray.

"Sit down. Please," Kylie begged. When Miranda looked about to argue, she added, "I could use the support." She cut her eyes toward Derek and Ellie. And it was true, she could use the support, but neither could she deny that she wanted to get Miranda over her repugnance of Perry. He really wasn't a bad guy.

Miranda relented and dropped down on the bench seat. Kylie mouthed, "Thank you," and then asked, "Where's Della?"

"Off drinking blood with the other vamps," Miranda answered just as she shoved a piece of toast into her mouth.

Kylie grabbed her milk and took a long sip while searching for a topic of conversation that would get Miranda and Perry talking.

"So," Kylie said, dropping the half-empty milk carton. "Does anyone know if Holiday has hired any teachers yet for the school year?"

Perry, as if he'd figured out what Kylie was up to, jumped into the conversation. "When I was at the office last night with Burnett, he got a call from some fae dude that Holiday had supposedly hired. I think he's supposed to show up and move into his cabin next week."

Miranda, as if she'd figured out what Kylie was up to, too, started forking eggs into her mouth.

Kylie and Perry chatted a few minutes about the fae teacher and how it would be odd to actually go to real classes at the camp in the fall. Miranda continued to shove food in her mouth as if needing an excuse not to talk.

Accepting that her last subject had proved to be a failure, Kylie reached for her milk again and went back to brainstorming topics. Finally putting her milk down, she looked at Miranda and said the first thing that came to her mind. "Did you know that Perry nearly ate his cousin when he was two?"

Chapter Twelve

Kylie watched as Miranda dropped her fork to clatter against the tray, leaned forward, and for the first time made eye contact with Perry.

"What?"

Perry smiled. Just having Miranda's gaze on him made the boy's face glow and his eyes turn a nice shade of blue. For just a second, Kylie wondered what his real eye color was.

"I didn't almost eat him," he said. "I just chewed on him a little and spit him out. I was a cat and he was a bird. And he was older than me and always stealing my animal crackers."

Perry continued talking and Miranda continued listening and their eyes met and they both appeared almost mesmerized. Kylie, mentally giving herself high fives, leaned back a bit to make sure not to block the two lovebirds' views of each other. Then Miranda's phone rang. She broke eye contact with Perry and snatched up her phone, which sat beside her food tray.

Checking caller ID, she let out an excited squeal. "It's Todd Freeman. Oh, my God, he's actually calling me!" Miranda's grin brightened her eyes, and she did a little butt-wiggling dance on the bench.

It took Kylie a half second to remember that Todd Freeman was the warlock, aka the best-looking boy in Miranda's old school, who had asked for Miranda's number at the witch competition. It took Kylie the other half of a second to realize this might not be a good thing. Not for Perry, at least.

Miranda's gaze shot back to the blond shape-shifter, and for a flicker of a second, she looked guilty. It wasn't much, but it offered Kylie a bit of hope.

"Excuse me," Miranda said, and then stood up, phone in hand, and zipped out of the dining hall.

Perry watched Miranda go and then looked at Kylie. His eyes were now a bright green color and they were slightly pinched, giving off a hint of anger. And that contented glow on his cheeks from a few seconds ago was gone. Vanished.

"Should I ask who the hell Todd Freeman is, or do I friggin' not want to know?"

Kylie's mind raced as she tried to find the words to answer. "He's just . . ." Just when she thought she knew what to say, something that would soothe him and hopefully not make him angry, she spotted Derek and Ellie walking out of the dining hall. Derek's hand rested against Ellie's lower back. An innocent enough touch, but it didn't look so innocent to Kylie.

"He's just who?" Perry bit out.

Kylie looked back at Perry. Why, Kylie wondered, was she so involved in trying to fix everyone else's love life when she couldn't even fix her own?

"I don't know what to tell you, Perry. Life's hard. Love's harder."

Thirty minutes after breakfast, Kylie—with Perry still dogging her steps—stood in front of the dining hall again, looking for Helen. Kylie suspected Helen would be among the noisy crowd waiting for the names to be called for Meet Your Campmates hour.

She wasn't.

Lucas walked up, trailed by Fredericka. "Hey." He came close enough that his shoulder brushed against hers. His warmth reminded Kylie of the dream last night when he hadn't been warm. She so preferred him warm. She preferred him to be himself and not some psychotic killer vampire.

"Hey," she said, and tried not to look at Fredericka, who ambled slowly past.

"Everything okay?" Lucas asked, and then frowned at Perry, who stood on the other side of her, not that it affected Perry. He just nodded.

Fredericka kept slowing down, and unable to stop herself, Kylie glanced up. The she-wolf shot Kylie a sassy smile, no doubt wanting to rub it in that she'd been with Lucas.

Lucas dipped his head down a bit. "Sorry I missed breakfast. I had some pack business I had to take care of."

Pack business? Kylie couldn't help but wonder if the pack business wasn't all about them keeping her and Lucas apart. Frustration swelled in her chest. It was bad enough to have Fredericka plotting against her, but to think the whole pack was also against her was too much. She looked at Lucas. "I . . . have to go."

"You okay?" He leaned in, concern filling his blue eyes. She wasn't sure if he'd picked up on her flicker of fear from last's night dream or if it was her jealousy for the little she-wolf who followed him around like a lost puppy.

"Yeah," she lied, and started walking.

"Where are we going?" Perry asked, his footsteps matching hers.

"To find Helen," Kylie answered, and stared straight ahead, even as she felt Lucas staring after her. She might not be able to solve her romantic issues, but perhaps Helen could shed some light on the whole healing process and the fact that Kylie had brought a dead bird back to life. With Holiday gone, she needed all the help she could get. A blue jay swooped past and hovered right in front of her for a millisecond before flying away. Could things get any crazier?

Kylie shook her head. Oh hell, what was she thinking? She was at Shadow Falls; things could always get crazier.

As Kylie drew closer to Helen's cabin, she turned to Perry and looked him right in the eyes. "I want to talk to Helen alone."

"No can do," Perry said.

She frowned. "Perry, I'm serious."

"So am I," he said without a touch of sarcasm or humor, and for Perry, that was a rarity. "Look, I know you don't want me hanging around, but Burnett told me what happened with the eagle and snake and then the deer. And on top of not wanting you to get hurt by an evil being of my own kind, I can't mess up again. I've already screwed up by losing that old couple, and I'm not screwing up again. So you'll just have to suck it up."

Kylie frowned, but she did understand. Who wanted to screw up? And as much as she didn't want to accept that she was in danger, she couldn't argue with the probability that Burnett was right. She didn't want to be hurt by an evil being of Perry's kind, either.

She looked Perry right in his yellow eyes and spotted a touch of insecurity. She felt bad.

"It's just that I need to ask Helen some questions and I'm not sure she'll feel comfortable answering with you here."

"How about I transform into something else and hang back?"

Kylie suddenly got an idea. She didn't know if it would work, because she didn't know how the whole transforming thing worked, but it was worth a shot. "How about you change into a male white cat with bright blue eyes."

"The last time I made myself a cat, you got pissed, bruised my ears, and threatened to neuter me."

"Well, don't start playing Peeping Tom in my cabin windows and you won't be in any danger. Just make sure you're white with blue eyes. Oh . . . and you have to be male."

"Like I would ever become a female," he said.

"Then do it already," she said.

"Fine." He waved his hand up and the sparkles started appearing. In just a few seconds, Perry disappeared and a long-haired white cat with a cute piggish little face and beautiful blue eyes stood in his place, swishing its tail back and forth.

The animal was so adorable, she had to stop herself from picking up the little fellow and snuggling with him. "Very cute," Kylie said.

The kitty, aka, Perry, cocked its head to the side as if puzzled. He reached up with his paw and gave his right ear a good scratch.

It worked. Kylie remembered her reasoning for insisting on the specific animal and smiled.

"I can't hear!" Perry said. "How did you do this?"

Kylie had to bite her bottom lip not to smile. "I didn't do it. Most male white cats with blue eyes can't hear." She said the words slowly so he might be able to read her lips. "You can watch." She pointed to her eye. "But you can't hear."

"That was sneaky," Perry said, obviously able to read lips.

Kylie smiled. "No, it was genius. Now stay back."

"But stay where I can see you."

"Fine." She took off to Helen's cabin and kept an eye out for any unwanted shape-shifters.

Helen answered the knock almost immediately. "Hey, you came to see me." She hugged Kylie so tight and had such a big smile on her face that Kylie felt a tad guilty for not visiting sooner. Helen was . . . well, a little quiet and didn't have a lot of friends.

However, some of the guilt faded when she remembered she had asked Helen to come over to the cabin half a dozen times. The half-fae had declined each and every time because she spent all her free time with Jonathon, her newfound love.

"Come on in," Helen said.

Kylie started to step inside and remembered Perry. "I can't."

"Why?" Helen asked, and ran a hand through her sandy brown hair.

"I've got a shadow."

"Oh, yeah." Helen's hazel eyes widened with concern. "Jonathon was telling me what happened. They think some shape-shifters broke through the security. Are you okay? I mean, after your weekend and now this." Helen stepped out and closed her cabin door. She moved over to the edge of the porch and sat on the whitewashed wooden planks.

"Yeah, I'm fine." Kylie answered, which was a bit of a lie, but she didn't need to dump her problems on Helen.

"Did you actually see the intruder?" Helen asked.

Kylie dropped down beside the girl. Their feet dangled off the edge of the porch. "It was an eagle and a snake and then a deer. And we're not even sure that it's anything. It might not even have been shape-shifters." Or at least, Kylie had been telling herself that. And since nothing else had happened today, it was getting easier to believe it—as long as she didn't remember the evil look she'd seen in the eagle's and deer's eyes.

Kylie suddenly became aware of two birds soaring overhead. A shimmer of fear ran down her back, and she looked out toward the patch of trees to see if she could spot Perry.

He didn't seem too worried. He'd found a patch of sunlight spilling through the trees and had stretched out, as if to soak in the warmth. "Who's your shadow?" Helen asked, following Kylie's gaze but obviously not noticing the cat.

"It's Perry. I had him turn himself into a male white cat with blue eyes."

Helen arched a brow with understanding. "So he couldn't hear us. Good one." She brushed an ant off her knee.

They sat there for a few seconds in silence, both of them gently pumping their legs back and forth.

Finally, Kylie spoke. "I was hoping you wouldn't mind answering a few questions about healing?"

"That's right, I heard you healed your friend," Helen said. "And then Lucas, too. Pretty cool."

Kylie bit down on her lip. "Yeah. It's cool. I mean, I'm still trying to wrap my head around it, but I like knowing I did it. That's what I wanted to ask you about. I really don't know how it works."

Suddenly, a thousand questions started running rampant in her head. Could she heal anyone? Could she go to the hospital and just heal everyone?

"Holiday hasn't talked to you about it?" Helen pulled one leg up.

"She tried. I just wasn't ready to hear about it. And then she had to leave. Her aunt died, but she's supposed to be back this afternoon."

"That's sad," Helen said with sincerity, then she added, "Holiday said that we two were going to start meeting with her on occasion to discuss healing as a group. I've read up on a lot of it, but I've barely made a dent in all there is to know about the gift."

"There are books on supernatural healing?" Kylie asked, surprised.

"Yeah, there's a whole library on all different supernatural subjects."

"Really? I never heard about them."

"Oh, yeah. There are tons of books on just about every subject."

Every subject? If that was the case, Kylie couldn't help wondering if there might be some information somewhere about anomalies like herself. "Who . . . ? I mean, where do you get them?"

"From the FRU library. If you can call it a library. More like a vault with books. It took almost a month before I was approved to check out the books I got. Burnett finally went in and got me approved."

"Why would they not want you to read up on healing or . . . any subject concerning supernaturals?"

"Beats me."

Kylie chewed on that for a few minutes and then asked, "So what did you learn about healing?"

"A lot of it's about the homeopathic. But some of it covers the basics like the different kinds of healers."

"There are different kinds?"

Helen nodded. "And different levels."

"Is any of this based on what type of species you are?"

"Yeah, some. The gift is most common to fairies and witches. But it's found in all sorts of half-breeds, too. I even read one book that said some half-breeds can have more healing powers than full-bloods."

Kylie tried to absorb everything Helen was saying. "What are the different kinds?"

"Well, some of us can just ease pain, but not really heal. Some witches can cure things by mixing up brews and performing certain rituals. Then there are those who heal internal diseases like cancer through touch. And then there's a few of those who are like you."

"Like me how?" Kylie asked, confused.

"Who can heal internal issues, like cancer, as well as physical injuries, like you did with your friend Sara's cancer and Lucas's injuries."

"You can't heal physical injuries?" Kylie asked.

"No. I wish. Jonathon fell a while back and cut his hand. I tried several times to heal it, and got nothing."

Kylie tried to absorb the new information. But mostly what she absorbed was the fact that once again, she was an anomaly. For once, couldn't she fit nice and neatly into a niche?

"You look worried," Helen said, looking at her.

"A little," Kylie admitted. "I'm still overwhelmed, I guess."

"Hey, just be glad you're not like the real freaky type."

"What type is that?"

"The kind that can raise the dead. And every time they do it, they give up a piece of their soul in the bargain. That would be off-the-chart weird, don't you think?"

A chill of fear settled around Kylie's heart. "Yeah. That would be super weird."

Kylie got a text from Holiday on her walk back to her cabin. *Problems. Can't make it bk til tomorrow. U ok?*

Am I okay? Kylie nearly laughed out loud. Hell, no, she wasn't okay! She'd given away a piece of her soul to a blue jay and didn't know what it meant.

As soon as Perry's shadow duties ended and he was replaced by Della, Kylie snatched her phone and started out of her cabin, feeling desperate. Holiday wasn't here, but Burnett was. He might not have any answers, but at least she could personally tell him she wanted a library card to the FRU's source of books. If there was even the slightest chance that their library held something that would help her figure out what she was, then Kylie would keep her nose in a book for years.

"Where are we going?" Della asked, following Kylie out.

"To talk to Burnett about my problem."

"What problem?"

"You got a problem?" Miranda asked as she, too, joined them on the cabin porch.

"It's just crazy shit," Kylie said, unsure she wanted to explain it, and started walking.

"What kind of crazy shit?" Miranda asked. "Does it have anything to do with Perry being in love with you?"

"What?" Kylie spouted out, low on patience.

"I saw the way he was hanging around all day."

"Please! He was hanging around me because he was shadowing me." She met Miranda's gaze head-on. "Okay, look, I'm gonna say this once. Perry's in love with you. But if you don't stop playing hard to get, you're gonna lose your shot with him."

"Amen, sister!" Della said.

Miranda's face tightened and she glared first at Della and then at Kylie. "Since when are you two taking his side?"

Kylie closed her eyes in frustration. "Fine, he was wrong when he did that, but you admitted that you were a little wrong in kissing Kevin, too. It's time to get past it or get over him."

"You make it sound easy." Hurt hummed in Miranda's tone.

"It is easy," Della said. "Just kiss and make up."

Miranda ignored Della and stared at Kylie. "Like you don't have issues with Derek." She turned to Della. "And you with Lee."

"That's different!" Della snapped, her eyes growing bright as she immediately took the offensive.

No, it wasn't different, Kylie realized. "Look. Truth is, all three of us are in the same boat. The sucky romance boat. And Della and I made a pact yesterday." She glanced at Della, hoping she didn't look upset that she was sharing this with Miranda. But hey, they were a threesome, right?

Thankfully, the vamp didn't look pissed, and Kylie continued, "We're moving on. I'm gonna get past the whole Ellie and Derek thing and give Lucas a chance. Della's going to try to be nicer to Steve and see what happens. You want to join the pact?"

Miranda frowned. "But Todd Freeman called me this morning. He said he may come up here this weekend for a visit."

"Who's Todd?" Della asked.

"The cute warlock from her old school," Kylie answered, and glanced back at Miranda. "Look, if you don't want to forgive Perry, or can't forgive him, then that's one thing. But you can't stay on the fence."

"Yeah. Shit or get off the pot." Della snickered.

"I'm not on the fence," Miranda insisted. "Or a pot."

"Yes, you are," Kylie countered. "You still care or you wouldn't be jealous." So what did that say about her and Derek? Kylie pushed that question aside.

"But what if I blow Todd off and then Perry goes back to being an ass?"

"There are no guarantees," Kylie countered. "Not with love or with life. But we can't go through life never taking a risk. And that's what we are all agreeing to do. Put our hearts out there. Take a chance with a boy. We might end up hurt, but we might not."

Miranda stood there, her expression pinched as if considering the offer. "Okay, how about I make a pact to talk to Perry and try to figure it out?"

"Talking's a good start," Kylie said.

"Making out would be better." Della grinned.

Kylie started back walking. Miranda and Della followed.

"So what's the crazy shit problem you need to discuss with Burnett?" Miranda asked.

Kylie sighed. "I gave away a piece of my soul and I think I want it back."

Chapter Thirteen

"What's wrong?" Burnett called out from Holiday's office a couple of minutes later when Kylie stepped inside the camp's main offices.

The camp leader had set up an office for Burnett in the back of the cabin, but he apparently preferred using Holiday's office in her absence. Not that Kylie blamed him.

Holiday's office was small but nice. A tan sofa stood against one wall, leaving only enough room for a desk and a couple of file cabinets. Not that Holiday hadn't added her own mark to the tiny space. Plants, different kinds of ferns, and even some herbs were stationed at every corner. The air even smelled like Holiday—a light floral aroma. And on top of the large metal file cabinet were several different-colored crystals. The light from the front window streamed into the room and got pulled into the crystals, reflecting rainbow colors on the walls.

Burnett quickly closed a few files that were on the desk and then leaned back in Holiday's chair. Kylie couldn't help wondering if Burnett wasn't using her office simply because Holiday's presence was so alive in the room.

"What's wrong?" he asked again.

She just blurted it out. "Do you know anything about healing powers?" She dropped into the chair across from the desk.

"Not a lot, but some."

"If I bring something back to life, do I lose a piece of my soul?"

His brow creased deeper. "What happened? Did someone get hurt? Did you have to—"

"Not someone," Kylie answered. "A bird."

"Oh. Holiday told me about that," Burnett answered. He leaned forward. "However, she said you weren't sure it was dead."

"It looked dead," Kylie said. "And I just want to know, did I lose a piece of my soul when I brought it back to life? And what does that mean?"

Burnett folded his arms on the desktop. "I'm not nearly as up on this as I'm sure Holiday is, but she wasn't concerned. So I don't think you have anything to worry about."

Not happy with his answer, Kylie remembered the second thing she wanted to discuss. "I want a library card."

"A what?" he asked.

"I want to be able to read the books that the FRU have in their library."

He frowned. "It's not a library, or not a normal library. Before you are allowed a book, it has to be cleared."

"Why?"

"Because a lot of items in the collection are FRU documents."

"What is the FRU hiding?"

He looked almost annoyed at her question. "We're not hiding anything. But we can't let normals get their hands on the books."

She pressed a finger to her forehead. "Do I look normal to you?"

"We still have to be careful."

"So you're telling me I can't check out the books."

His frown deepened. "I will see about getting you a few books on healing," he added, as if wanting to console her.

"What other kind of books do you have?" she asked.

"It's not a library, Kylie," he said with some firmness, and then settled back and didn't speak. Finally the awkward silence brought Kylie to another question. "Any more news on the elderly couple who pretended to be my grandparents?"

His guarded expression slipped away. "I just got a call. The fingerprints we were able to pull belong to the owners of the car. I'm afraid it's not going to help us. I'm sorry. But I can return these." He handed her the brown envelope that held her father's pictures. "You really resemble your father."

The genuine concern in his eyes and his tone should have made her feel better, but it just validated her suspicions that he hadn't been completely honest about the whole FRU and the library. What was the FRU hiding?

Kylie took the envelope. "Thank you," she said. While she wasn't going to start mistrusting Burnett, she would proceed with caution when dealing with him.

Kylie started to leave when Burnett looked at the door and said, "Come in."

Lucas walked in. He met Burnett's gaze head-on. "I'd like permission to walk Kylie back to her cabin."

"That's up to her," Burnett said.

"Without her shadow," Lucas said.

Kylie could see it cost Lucas a chunk of pride to ask permission. She recalled something Della said about werewolves hating to be submissive. And asking permission was a submissive gesture.

However, from the look on Burnett's face, Lucas's request had won him some respect and hopefully a few minutes to be with her. Burnett looked at Kylie as if to make sure it was okay, and she nodded.

"Just back to the cabin. And stay on the path." Burnett looked toward the window. "Della takes over again when she gets to the cabin. You got that, Della?"

"Yes," came her answer, and Kylie rolled her eyes a bit, wondering if Della was always listening in.

. . .

Della and Miranda were gone when Kylie and Lucas walked out of the office. The afternoon air was warm but tolerable. A few campers hung around the front of the lunchroom. Kylie saw Will, another werewolf, standing to one side, watching them. She also saw Lucas shoot him a frown.

"Come on." Lucas started walking toward the path.

Only after they made the first turn and were out of view did Lucas reach for her hand. Right then, Kylie suspected that Fredericka wasn't just blowing smoke about the pack's disapproval of her.

She started to ask, but Lucas spoke first. "Are you okay?" He stopped and turned to face her. His blue eyes studied her with intensity. "For a second, you were scared of me this morning, and then you just ran off with Perry as if you were mad."

She hesitated to tell him, but she wanted Lucas to be honest with her, so she needed to be honest with him. "It wasn't you I was afraid of. Last night I was pulled into a dreamscape. I wasn't sure what was happening, but you were there."

"No, I wasn't," he said.

"I know it wasn't you now. It was Red, Mario's grandson. He appeared as you in the beginning."

Lucas stood there as if contemplating. "He's vampire. They don't dreamscape."

"Well, he did. I don't know how, but he did."

"Maybe it was a regular dream."

She shook her head. "I know the difference now."

"Did you tell Burnett?"

"No," she said. "I . . . handled it myself. I know how to shut it off. If it happens again, I'll tell him. Or I'll tell Holiday."

He frowned. "What did the freak do in the dream? He didn't . . ."

She understood what he was asking. "He only put his hands on my waist. Then I realized he wasn't hot like you are." For the first time, she wondered why Red hadn't tried to do more. Then again, she should just be happy he hadn't. The thought of kissing him was too much.

Lucas pulled her against him. "I really want to catch that slimy vamp." He wrapped his arms around her. She stood there for a few seconds, her cheek pressed against his chest, absorbing his embrace. Finally, she lifted her face and looked at him.

He pressed his lips against hers. It wasn't the really hot kind of kiss, but it was nice. Nice enough that she let her feelings about how he was always followed by Fredericka slide away.

"So you're not mad at me?" he asked.

"A little," she admitted.

He looked perplexed. "About what?"

She didn't have a clue how to say it but then just blurted it out. "Every time I see you walk up, Fredericka is with you."

He pressed his forehead to hers. "I've told you nothing is happening there."

"I know, and I believe you, but she's so . . . smug."

He half grinned. "She's a werewolf; smugness is instinctual."

"I don't care. I don't like it."

His half smile faded. "She's part of my pack. I can't kick her out without just cause and major consequences for her."

The fact that he cared about Fredericka stung, but then she realized she wouldn't want bad things to happen to Derek. But it wasn't just Fredericka causing this problem.

"Your pack doesn't want you with me, do they."

He looked a little shocked. She almost repeated what Fredericka told her, but she didn't want to come off like a jealous girlfriend.

"It's stupid," he said. "It doesn't matter what they want."

"Doesn't it?"

"No, it doesn't," he said with firmness. "I refuse to let anyone dictate who I like or see. Besides, you might end up being one of us."

"And if I'm not?"

"It still doesn't matter," he said, but the conviction in his voice had lessened.

"What will happen?" she asked.

"Nothing. Because I won't let it happen." He touched her cheek. "This is my issue. Let me deal with it."

Thirty minutes later, Kylie walked into her chilly bedroom—yep, she had a ghostly visitor, but Kylie was determined to ignore her. She had to mull over her conversation and suspicions concerning Burnett and her conversation with Lucas. His pack's attitude was his issue, but it involved her. She also wanted to spend some time looking at her dad's face. As crazy as it sounded, she hoped staring at the pictures would somehow bring him closer to her.

"Someone lives and someone dies."

Kylie frowned. Okay, ignoring the spirit was probably going to be harder than she thought, especially since the so-called message the ghost was delivering was supposedly something the death angels had sent Kylie.

Ditto for Holiday's aunt, when she dropped in the day before.

"Who lives and who dies?" Kylie turned around to see the ghost woman hovering behind her. She had hair again, long dark hair that hung around her shoulders.

"They didn't say. But they did say that it isn't your fault."

"What's not my fault?" Kylie demanded.

The spirit shrugged. *"They never explain anything. They just tell me to give you the message."* She nipped at her bottom lip. *"They scare me."*

Kylie dropped onto the bed, and that's when she noticed something else about the ghost. She was pregnant. The pink maternity shirt clung to her round belly.

Suppressing her frustration, Kylie motioned to the woman's baby bulge. "You're pregnant."

She glanced down and dropped her hands around her middle. *"How did that happen?"*

Kylie shook her head. "If I was at home, I could give you a pamphlet to explain it step by step. A sperm meets an egg and so on. My mom gives me one of those every few months. But basically, it means you had sex with someone."

The spirit's expression grew puzzled. *"Sex?"*

"Please tell me you know what that is, because I'm too young to have to give you the whole sex talk. I haven't even heard it yet. I've just read the pamphlets."

"I know what sex is. I'm just . . . Who did I have sex with?" she asked. *"I can't remember."*

"I wouldn't know that."

The spirit moved closer, and so did her chill. She dropped down on the bed beside Kylie, her palms still stretched across her belly. Closing her eyes, she sat there in silence. Kylie sensed she was searching her mind, trying to remember.

Kylie pulled a throw over her shoulders to ward off the chill. After several silence-filled minutes, the ghost opened her eyes but continued to stare down at her round middle. Her hands started moving tenderly over the child she carried within, as if to show it affection.

Kylie had never seen so much love shown in a simple touch. For a crazy second, she wondered what it would feel like to carry a child inside her own belly.

When the spirit looked up, she had tears in her eyes. *"I think my baby died."*

The grief on the spirit's face and in her voice brought a lump to Kylie's throat. "I'm sorry."

Then the spirit pulled her hands away from her belly, and both her palms were bloody. Kylie's breath caught when she saw the spirit's rounded abdomen was gone and the front of her dress was drenched in blood. *"No."* The deep, painful sob of the spirit filled the tiny room and seemed to bounce around from wall to wall.

Kylie opened her mouth to say something, to ask the spirit if she could remember what happened, to offer more apologies and sympathy. But before she could say anything, the woman disappeared.

The spirit's cold vanished but left a wave of icy sadness and grief so intense that it filled Kylie's chest with pain. And it wasn't just any pain. It was the grief of a mother losing a child. Kylie reached for her pillow and hugged it.

After a few minutes, Kylie pulled the pictures out of the envelope and flipped through them slowly. When she came to the one of her mom and Daniel in a group of other people, Kylie reached for her phone.

"Hi, sweetie." Just hearing her mom's voice brought back some of the empathy Kylie felt for the spirit.

"Hey, Mom."

Odd, how not so long ago, Kylie felt certain her mom didn't love her, didn't even want her. Now, there wasn't a doubt of her mom's devotion to her. Deep down, Kylie wondered if this was a part of growing up. The part where teens stopped seeing their parents as instruments out to destroy their lives and started seeing them as people.

Not perfect, of course. Kylie knew her mom still had flaws—lots of them—but none of them involved her love for Kylie. And none of them prevented Kylie from loving her.

"I'm glad you called," her mom said. "I've missed hearing your voice."

"Me too," Kylie managed to say without choking up, and she wished her mom were here to hug her. She wished she could tell her mom about the pictures, but then she'd have to explain about the Brightens, and she didn't think that whole mess was explainable. Not yet, anyway.

"I was going to call you tonight if I didn't hear from you," her mom said.

"I'm sorry, I've been going a little crazy since I've been back."

"I figured as much. Sara called and said she'd tried to call you and you hadn't returned her call. She sounded so good. She told me it was like a miracle—her cancer up and disappeared."

"I'm sure it was one of the treatments they did on her," Kylie said, biting down on her bottom lip and wondering how she was going to handle the whole Sara issue. Kylie hadn't returned Sara's call because she'd wanted to ask Holiday first. Poor Holiday. When she did return, Kylie had a list of things they needed to discuss.

"I guess," her mom said. "But I would like to believe in miracles."

"Then you should believe," Kylie said, now unsure what to say to her mom about it. Because more than ever, Kylie knew miracles did exist. The fact that she had been the one performing the miracle still had her feeling out of sorts.

"Are you okay?" her mom asked, as if picking up on Kylie's mood.

"I'm fine."

"No, you're not," her mom said. "I hear it in your voice. What's wrong, baby?"

"Just . . . boy trouble," she said.

"What kind of trouble?" her mom asked, the tension in her voice indicating that she worried Kylie's problem concerned sex.

"It's nothing." Searching for a change of subject, Kylie tossed out, "How was work today?"

"It was strange," her mom said. "I got a new client."

"Why is that strange?" Kylie asked. Her mom worked in advertising and she was always getting new clients.

"*He's* strange."

"Strange in what way?" Kylie asked, glad the subject had taken a turn.

"He seemed more interested in me than . . . the campaign." Her mom giggled.

Kylie frowned. "Define 'interested.'"

"Oh, I don't know. It's just the way he acted," her mom said, as if she were trying to make light of the subject. "We're supposed to do lunch tomorrow and discuss his ideas for the special promotion on his new line of vitamins."

"Is it a work lunch or a . . . date lunch?"

"Don't be silly," her mom said. "It's work."

"Are you sure?" Kylie asked. "I mean, if he seemed interested in you . . ."

"I think it's work," she said, no longer sounding so sure. "But . . . if it were a date lunch, how would you feel about it?"

Kylie took a deep breath. An image of her stepfather filled her head. She recalled him sitting on the edge of her bed only a few weeks ago, crying when he told Kylie he'd made a terrible mistake. She knew he wanted to reconcile with her mom, and while Kylie wasn't sure he deserved a second chance after cheating on her, she couldn't deny wanting at least one thing in her world to go back to the way it had been.

"You're not answering," her mom said.

Kylie swallowed a big lump of indecision and stared down at the image of her mom and Daniel. Was it fair of her to want her mom to forgive her stepfather just to bring a sense of normalcy back into Kylie's life, especially when she sensed the man her mom really loved was dead? The question bounced around her head, and Kylie decided to be honest.

"That's because I don't know what to say. I guess part of me was thinking you and Dad might work things out. Don't you love him anymore? Or did you ever really love him?"

It was her mom's time to get quiet. "I loved him. I probably still love him," she finally confessed. "But I'm not sure I can forgive him. Or trust him. And ever since we talked about Daniel, I just . . . I'm not sure that marrying Tom wasn't a mistake. And if that's true, then us getting back together would also be a mistake. But I shouldn't be talking to you about this, Kylie."

"Why not?"

"Because, my darling, you shouldn't have to worry about this."

"You're my mom. I have a right to worry." And Kylie realized she did worry about her mom being alone and being lonely. But did that mean she wanted her mom to start dating? To completely rule out getting back with the man Kylie had loved and considered her real dad all her life?

"No," her mom said. "You've got that backwards. Moms have a right to worry about their kids, not the other way around."

"Then we'll just have to agree to disagree," Kylie said.

"You are way too stubborn, you know that?"

"And I wonder where I got it from," Kylie answered with a chuckle. Kylie's mom's phone beeped with an incoming call. "I'll let you go," Kylie said. "But Mom . . ."

"Yes?"

"Enjoy the lunch. Just be careful. And don't go falling in love or anything. Oh, and no kissing on the first date. That was your rule, remember?"

Her mom chuckled. "I'm sure it's just a business lunch. I'll talk to you tomorrow."

When Kylie hung up she heard a tap at her window. She looked over, expecting Lucas, but instead the blue jay perched on her windowsill. It flapped its wings, hovered right outside her window for a second, and then flew away.

Great. Now she was being stalked by the blue jay she'd brought back to life. What did that mean?

• • •

The melancholy from the ghost and the mixed feelings about her mom—as well as the possibility that she'd given a piece of her soul to the blue jay—hadn't completely faded an hour later when Miranda and Della stormed into her room.

"Get ready," Della said.

"Ready for what?" Kylie asked, lying on the bed, still hugging her pillow and staring holes into the ceiling.

"Burnett agreed to let us have a party tonight," Miranda said. "This is our chance to work on our pact. Steve will be there, so will Lucas and even Perry. We're ordering pizza and playing music. Maybe even dancing. I think I'll wear the new jeans I bought last weekend."

"You didn't tell us you got to go shopping," Della said.

"Yeah, and I also got this brand-new jeans skirt." Miranda looked at Della. "It would look fabulous on you. Why don't you borrow it?"

"Really?" Della said. "You'd loan me your new skirt?"

"Of course. I like you most of the time," Miranda said, and nudged her with her elbow.

Kylie's lips were poised to say, "You two go without me," but she spotted a hint of excitement in Della's eyes. Kylie remembered that since the vamp was assigned as her shadow, if she didn't go, Della didn't go, either.

So Kylie stood up and went to her closet. "I say we get all dressed up and impress the socks off those guys."

Thirty minutes later, the three of them, dressed to kill, walked into the dining hall. Miranda had loaned Della her new jeans skirt, and it looked really good on her, especially paired with the spaghetti-strap top with art deco black-and-red print with flared tiers of fabric hanging down the front. Miranda wore her new jeans with a low-cut pink lacy tank top that showcased her girls. When Kylie had packed to return to camp, she'd brought some more clothes. Her black knit dress wasn't fancy, but it still fit well, especially with her recent growth spurt. The hem of the dress now came a tad higher, and the scooped bustline fit tighter. While she had been faking her enthusiasm in the beginning, somehow getting dressed up had her looking forward to the evening.

The music was already playing and boxes of pizza were stacked on one of the tables that had been pushed against the walls, making room for dancing. Most of the campers were already there, mingling and talking. The smell of pepperoni and zesty tomato sauce filled the air. Then Chris walked in from the kitchen carrying a large pitcher and a bunch of cups.

"Man, that smells good." Della lifted her face into the air, and Kylie caught the wild berry scent of blood. And though she didn't like admitting it, her mouth watered more from that aroma than from the pizza.

Not that she would indulge in it, or had indulged in it since she'd tasted blood at the vampire ceremony. If Kylie ended up being vampire, she'd deal with it. But until then, the idea of drinking blood, even when it tasted like ambrosia, was not her cup of tea.

Miranda must have pushed the door closed a little hard because it slammed shut and the crowd looked up. Kylie felt everyone's eyes on her, or on her forehead, checking to see what her forever changing brain pattern was doing now.

But then she noticed one pair of blue eyes, and they weren't looking at her forehead. They were looking at her.

She knew Lucas liked her dress. Or at least he liked her in it. And wasn't that what she wanted?

The desire to do another visual sweep of the room to see if Derek was there hit strong. She fought it. Tonight was about Lucas. And from the way he stared at her, she had a feeling he wouldn't mind.

Chapter Fourteen

Lucas didn't smile. Well, not with his lips, anyway. His eyes, however, did smile, and their warmth washed over Kylie as he started moving her way. He took slow, even steps, as though he had all the time in the world, but what mattered was that he was coming. When she first saw all the weres clustered together, she worried he might not want to leave them. Somehow Kylie sensed he did it purposely to send a message to her and to his pack. And suddenly she was glad Miranda and Della had pressed her to come to the dance.

Lucas had gotten about halfway across the room when she felt another pair of eyes on her. Pulling her gaze away from Lucas, she spotted Fredericka. Refusing to let the were bully intimidate her or ruin her good mood, Kylie ignored her and refocused on Lucas. He looked good tonight, too. He wore jeans that fit just right and an aqua blue shirt spread across his chest. The color made his blue eyes appear bluer.

When he stopped beside her, his natural scent filled the air and she could feel her pulse flutter from his nearness. He didn't tell her she looked beautiful; he didn't even touch her. But his eyes did both.

"Hey," he said.

She smiled. "Hey."

His gaze moved to Della. "Burnett said I could take over shadowing."

Della nodded.

"Want to get something to drink?" Lucas asked Kylie, and motioned toward the back where the sodas were waiting and the people weren't. Lucas wasn't much with crowds. Tonight, she felt the same way.

She nodded and turned to her two roommates. "I'll see you." Then she leaned in toward them. "Remember the pact."

Miranda smiled and wiggled her eyebrows in excitement. Della, who Kylie knew struggled with the whole romance issue, frowned.

"Yeah, yeah," Della said. "But I'm not making a fool out of myself."

"Just be more approachable," Kylie whispered, and then turned back to Lucas. They moved together across the room, and Kylie could feel people staring at them. She forced herself to ignore them.

Lucas moved in a step closer to her. "What's going on with those two?" he asked, obviously having overheard Kylie's conversation with Della and Miranda.

"Nothing really," Kylie answered.

He grabbed them each a drink and then pushed two folding metal chairs against the wall. When she sat down, he edged his chair closer and sat beside her. His jeans-covered thigh pressed against her bare leg. She could feel his warmth through the cotton material, and it sent a fluttery feeling to her stomach.

He leaned in so his voice could be heard over the music. "I'm glad you came tonight."

"Me too," she said.

"You're not mad at me anymore?" The back of his hand shifted against her forearm and she felt his fingers glide gently up past her elbow.

"I think I'm over it." She smiled.

"Good." His gaze swept over her. "You make my blood race," he said, so low that she could hardly hear him.

She smiled. "Really?"

"Feel for yourself." He took her hand and placed it on the back of his wrist. The flutter—more like a vibration, really—was so rapid that it almost felt electric. Her first instinct was to jerk away, but his steady, tender gaze kept her fingers against his warm skin. And after a second, it wasn't actually scary.

"Is this a werewolf thing?" she asked.

He leaned a bit closer until she felt the warmth of his breath against her ear. "Yeah."

She shivered a little. "So I really didn't cause it?" she asked, feeling a bit disappointed.

A light smile tilted his lips. "Oh, it's all your fault. It only happens when I'm . . . captivated by something or someone."

She returned his smile. "Then I'm glad I captivated you."

The smile in his eyes suddenly vanished, and she could swear she heard a light growl rumble from his throat.

She barely had a chance to wonder what could be wrong when Perry stopped right in front of them.

He nodded at Lucas as if making a point that he wasn't the least bit afraid of him. "You want to dance?" he asked Kylie.

She was so surprised, she wondered if she'd misunderstood his question. Then she felt Lucas tense beside her. "Uh, not now," she said, trying to keep her tone light. "But thanks for asking."

Perry disappeared into a group of campers. When she looked back at Lucas, he scowled into the cluster of people. "Am I going to have to teach a smartass shape-shifter a lesson?"

"No."

"I can't believe he actually hit on you when—"

"He wasn't hitting on me." Kylie looked back at the crowd and found Perry standing away from the others, watching Miranda, who was surrounded by a group of boys. For a second, Kylie felt bad. Perry had probably wanted to ask her something about Miranda and she'd brushed him off.

"I don't buy it," Lucas said, his tone deep.

"He only has eyes for Miranda," she said. "Look at him, he's green with jealousy." And literally, his eyes had changed color to a bright green.

"Yeah, right."

"It's true. Believe me; he's not into me."

He dipped his head closer. "And you're not into him?"

She grinned. "Are you jealous?"

"No." He sat up straighter. "I'm just . . . possessive," he said as if the two traits were somehow different. "And you didn't answer my question."

"I'm not into Perry," she assured him. "We're just friends."

"Fair enough. So, who are you into?" he asked, and those blue eyes captured hers.

"I'm sort of falling for a jealous werewolf at the moment."

He grinned and quickly brushed the back of his hand against her forearm. "Well, don't tell me his name, because I'm likely to whip his jealous ass."

They both laughed and then sat and stared at each other until it got awkward. Not awkward because looking at him felt strange, but it just seemed as if one of them should lean in and finish the moment with a kiss. But neither of them seemed to want to take the initiative. Kylie suspected his reason was the same as hers. Too much of a crowd. She just hoped it wasn't because of his pack.

"I've been meaning to ask, did you get the answers from Holiday about the whole bird thing?"

Remembering the bird's little visit this afternoon, she felt frustration tickle her mind. "No."

She took a sip of soda, focusing on the music, and tried to push all the negative stuff back. Unfortunately, it kept coming at her. "Did you know the FRU has a library of books on everything supernatural?"

"Yeah, I heard about it. Why?"

"Do you know why they don't let us read them?"

"I think some of them contain government documents."

"But why would they need to hide anything?" she asked.

He shrugged. "The same reason the U.S. government hides things. Some things might skirt the ethics line, or if certain information got into the hands of the wrong people, it could be detrimental."

The music changed to a slow song. Kylie looked up and saw several couples moving to the center of the dining hall to dance. Helen and Jonathon, holding hands, were among the first to make their way to the empty floor space. They wrapped their arms around each other and started swaying to the music. They didn't even appear to be dancing, just holding each other and occasionally doing a small side step. Not that it looked dorky; it sort of looked sweet.

A few other couples moved to the dance floor and started to sway to the beat of the music. The lyrics of the song spoke of love, being close, and kisses. Someone turned down the lights, and since Kylie didn't think the lights had a dimmer switch, she suspected it had been one of the witches using a touch of magic.

Maybe they'd even added a bit of romance potion to the air, because Kylie felt it. Suddenly, she wanted to be out on the dance floor, too. She wanted to feel Lucus's hands on her waist while she rested her cheek on his shoulder.

She glanced at Lucas, leaned in, and asked, "Do you want to dance?"

He made a funny face as if she'd asked him to stand on his head or something. "I . . . no. Sorry."

"I guess that might upset the guards too much, huh?" She looked over at the pack of weres watching them.

"It's not that." Lucas released a deep breath. "Come on." He took the plastic cup that held soda from her hand and set it on the floor beside their chairs. He caught her fingers and pulled her up. For a second, she thought he meant to take her out on the dance floor, but instead he headed to the front of the dining hall.

"Where are we going?"

"Outside."

He pulled her through the crowd so fast, Kylie didn't have time to ask his reasons. When he stopped, they stood outdoors and off to the side of the dining hall.

Alone.

The music, while only a distant humming, could still be heard, and it seemed to play along with the night sounds. Crickets and a few birds sang along with the lyrics.

"Isn't this better?" He took her hands and placed them around his neck and then set his hands around her waist as if to dance.

"So the pack won't see us?" she asked, insecure.

"No," he insisted. "Did you see one were out on that dance floor?"

She had to think, but then she shook her head. "No."

"We don't like drawing attention to ourselves in public."

The air was warm, but not as warm as Lucas's hand pressed against her hip. Kylie glanced up and saw a half-moon offering the night a minimum of light. Not that it was all that dark outside; the stars appeared to be working overtime. No clouds hung in the heavens, so the sky seemed sprayed with stars. She could hardly find a piece of sky that didn't have a tiny diamond shape twinkling and adding a silver glow to the night. Slowly, he started moving to the distant music.

"But in private, that's another matter." He didn't just sway but danced. And he obviously knew how, because his steps encouraged her feet to follow the same pattern his were making.

With scents of pizza and blood no longer perfuming the air,

Lucas's own scent stood out and mingled with the woodsy scent of the night air.

She looked up at him again. "Who taught you to dance?"

"My grandmother. She told me it was the way to a woman's heart," he said, his voice a light whisper against her ear. His head dipped down and his lips brushed against her cheek. "I personally believe when two people get this close, it should be in private."

His words made her realize how close they were standing to each other. She gazed again into his eyes, and his mouth met hers. They danced and kissed for what seemed like forever. Not that she was complaining. She felt as if they were floating, lost in a moment. His kiss didn't push for more than she was ready to give. It was just a soft meshing of his mouth on hers, with an occasional slip of his tongue across her bottom lip.

The kiss finally ended. She placed her hand on his warm chest right beside where her head rested and listened to his heartbeat, which was very fast.

"Is your blood still rushing?" She raised her head, rested her chin on his chest, and smiled up at him.

"More than before." His tone rang deeper than it had been. He adjusted his hands on her waist and she could feel the racing of his pulse where his wrist touched the bottom of her rib cage.

"Feel it?" he asked.

"Yeah." Leaning her head back on his chest, she decided she could stay there forever with his breath stirring against her hair. Closing her eyes, she enjoyed the closeness and the sensation of being held, of being cherished.

With her ear again pressed to his chest, she heard a soft humming, almost a purring. The sound filled her head and she felt as if it pulsated inside her. She sensed he'd pulled her closer, his nearness warmed her inside and out, and the floating sensation returned even stronger this time. Leaning into him a bit more, she longed to be closer still.

His fingers pressed against her waist, making tiny little shifts up and down. The light touch tickled and caused a fluttering sensation deep in her belly. Then his hands glided up her sides, almost to her breasts. The slightest warning whispered in her head, but she pushed it back. This felt too good to—

He inhaled, sharply, and she thought she heard him swear, then he yanked his hands from her and stepped away.

Without his support, she almost felt dizzy. She gazed up at him confused. "What . . . ?"

"We should . . . we should go inside."

When she met his eyes, they glowed a brighter blue. "Is something wrong?" she asked.

"No. It's . . . just safer inside."

"Safer from what?" She looked around, thinking he'd seen something. Had the eagle or deer returned? It could even be the blue jay, back to —

"From me," he said, and shoved his hands into his pockets. "I'm low on willpower tonight, Kylie. About a week and a half before the change, I tend to run more on instinct than logic. And right now, my instinct says to pull you in the woods, find a soft spot of grass, and have my way with you."

She moved in and placed a hand on his chest. "I know you well enough to know that you would never force me to do something I didn't want to do."

He pulled her palm from his chest and held her hand gently in his. "I would never force you, Kylie. Never. But I'm not above trying to persuade you. And . . ." He tilted her head back with his other hand as if to make sure she knew he was serious. "Werewolves have a knack for persuading. And that's not how I want this to happen."

She blinked and tried to understand what he was saying. Her insides still felt like liquid, and she missed his warmth against her. She tried to move closer to regain what she missed, but he took another step back.

He pulled her hand to his lips, and after placing a quick kiss to her knuckles, he tightened his grip and gave her a tug back toward the dining hall.

She took a few steps. Then, still trying to process what he'd said, she put on her mental brakes. "What do you mean by a 'knack for persuading'?"

Chapter Fifteen

Lucas didn't answer. Instead he just tugged on her arm, and she let him pull her back inside the dining hall. But the more she thought about what he'd said, the more she wanted answers. For a minute back there, she'd felt almost drunk with . . . passion. Did werewolves, like faes, have the ability to manipulate a girl's feelings so she would . . . give him anything he wanted?

Kylie stared up at Lucas, who was holding her hand and leading her back to the place where they'd sat earlier. Mentally, she sorted through her emotions.

She wasn't angry at Lucas; she didn't even regret their slow dance in the moonlight. On the contrary, she'd loved every second of it. So, what was the problem?

A tiny internal voice answered the question. The problem was she didn't want to think that someone other than herself could persuade her to do something that she might not have done otherwise.

And yet, another little voice whispered, wasn't that what passion and seduction were about? All the magazines talked about how women wanted to be seduced. So was it a bad thing?

Okay, so she was confused. She looked at her hand where Lucas's fingers locked with hers and tugged her along. She followed him through a small crowd of campers to get their seats. Finally settled in their chairs again, she wondered when any of this was going to get any easier.

"You want something else to drink?" he asked, having to raise his voice for her to hear him over the music and the crowd of voices.

"I'm fine."

"Pizza?" he asked.

"Not now." She almost asked for an explanation about what he'd said earlier. Then she realized that the noise and the crowd would make having a lengthy and private conversation impossible. She glanced at Lucas and found him studying her, staring deep into her eyes—almost as if he were trying to read her thoughts.

He leaned in and rested his forehead against hers. "Are you upset with me?"

"No," she said honestly, and meant it. It wasn't anger she felt, just uncertainty, confusion. Because even if Lucas had the ability to seduce her to do certain things, he hadn't done it.

Blinking and offering him a smile, she decided tonight, at least at the party, might not be the time to talk about this. However, before she did any more moonlight dancing or make-out sessions by the creek, she needed answers.

She recalled Holiday's words weeks earlier when they were talking about boys and sex: *What I'm asking is that when you decide to do something, that it's something you've thought about and decided to do. Not a spur-of-the-moment decision that you might regret later.*

Did Holiday's words of wisdom have more meaning to them than Kylie had guessed?

An hour later, they'd indulged in pizza and drunk enough diet soda to drown an Italian fish. The number of couples dancing had dwindled; now, almost everyone was eating and mingling. Even the lights had been brightened. When people started stopping by to chat, Kylie had expected Lucas to disappear, but he hung in there and was even very friendly, which was so out of character for a werewolf. He was doing this for her, and she appreciated his effort.

Both Della and Miranda had stopped by and said hello as they got drinks and pizza. Kylie wanted to ask them if all "pact" things were going well, but she couldn't find a way to do it without being overheard, so she decided to wait until later to get an update.

As soon as the pizza disappeared, someone lowered the lights again and several couples started making their way back to the makeshift dance floor. As Kylie's vision adapted to the change of light, her eyes lit on Della being led to the dance floor by . . . Chris.

Kylie immediately did a sweep of the room for Steve, and she was pretty sure he was the guy in the black T-shirt, standing in the shadowy corner talking to a couple of girls, one of whom was Fredericka. The other looked like . . . Ellie.

Kylie's gaze moved around the room for one quick second, searching for a certain fae. She didn't find him and wondered if he hadn't come because he knew she'd be here.

I'm not thinking about Derek. She closed her eyes and repeated those words to herself as if they were her new mantra.

When she looked back up to find Della, Kylie spotted Miranda moving on the dance floor with Clark. Kylie didn't know Clark that well, except that he was a warlock and known to be a bit of a troublemaker.

What were Miranda and Della doing? What happened to their pact? Why weren't they going after the right guys?

"Something wrong?" Lucas asked.

She glanced over at him and realized she was frowning. "Not really. It's just . . ." She looked back at the crowd, stalling, trying to figure out how much she could tell him. Before she could come up with an appropriate answer, she spotted Perry. Perry, who looked angry enough to chew nails and spit out staples. His gaze met hers, and then he started walking to the door.

"Give me just a minute, please," she told Lucas, and shot up and took off after Perry.

By the time Kylie got outside, Perry was nowhere around. Then she saw him. Well, it had to be him. One of those big prehistoric-looking birds stood in front of the main office.

"Perry!" she called out, and ran to catch him.

His wings, a span of about five feet, were spread open, and he appeared ready to take flight.

"Don't just run away," Kylie snapped.

"I'm not running. I'm flying. And for a damn good reason. If I have to stand there and watch her flirting with all those guys, I'm gonna end up hurting someone."

Kylie watched the bird's beak move up and down as it talked. "First, turn yourself back into human form before you speak to me. Second, you don't have to just stand there. Go ask her to dance."

Diamond-shaped sparkles started appearing around the bird. From where Kylie was standing only a foot from him, the air seemed to get thin. She wasn't exactly sure what happened when Perry shifted, but it had to do some weird stuff to the ozone.

One of the sparkles floated up; on its descent, it brushed against her arm and popped like the blow bubbles she'd played with as child. But instead of a tickling sensation, Kylie felt a jolt of electricity run up her arm.

Suddenly Perry stood there instead of the pterodactyl. His eyes were red, angry. "Ask her to dance so she can reject me in front of everyone? Do I look like an idiot to you?"

"No, right now you look like a coward afraid to take a chance on what you want."

"I'm not a coward!" he growled. "I have more power in my pinky finger than ten of you supernaturals."

"Then prove it by standing up for yourself." He didn't looked convinced, so Kylie added, "I have a feeling she won't reject you."

He just stared at her, disbelief shining in his eyes as they changed from red back to his normal blue.

"Trust me," Kylie added.

She could see he wanted to give in. But then he waved a hand back toward the door. "She's already dancing with someone else."

"Then cut in." Kylie frowned when she saw Lucas standing in the shadows. Then she remembered he was her shadow. He had to follow her.

"Cut in?" Perry asked, as if he weren't familiar with the term.

"Go tap on the guy's shoulder and just say you want to cut in."

"And he'll just step aside and let me dance with her? Where the hell did you get that idea?"

"It's not an idea. It's proper dancing etiquette. When someone wants to dance with someone who's already dancing, you're supposed to tap on the guy's shoulder and just say you're cutting in."

Perry frowned. "And what happens if he says no?"

"He's not supposed to say no."

Perry rolled his eyes. "In the human world, maybe, but—"

"Oh, for Christ's sake." She held up her hands in frustration. "Just try it."

"Fine," he said. "But if he gives me any shit, I might end up hurting him." His eyes turned red again. Blood red.

"No, you can't hurt—"

Before she could finish, Perry shot back inside. She took off after him. Oh, friggin' great. Maybe this hadn't been the best idea.

Lucas called to her, but she didn't slow down.

Kylie had barely made it back inside when she heard the commotion. She took off toward the dance floor.

"I said I'm cutting in!" Perry's voice rose over the music and chatter of the other campers.

Kylie tried elbowing her way through, hoping to get to them in time to prevent things from escalating, but a crowd had already started to circle and her elbows must not have been sharp enough because everyone just grunted and ignored her.

"And I said go to hell!" a voice, obviously Clark's, answered back.

"What about what I want?" Miranda said.

Kylie stood on her tiptoes to get a better view but still couldn't see anything.

The sound of a scuffle filled the room. Most of the female campers started squealing, while the males just started cheering the fight on.

"Stop it!" Kylie yelled, and started jumping up and down, hoping to see what was happening.

"Watch out!" someone screamed, and like a wave, everyone dropped to the ground as a fireball the size of a volleyball shot through the air.

"Crap!" Kylie yelled, and took advantage of everyone's position to move in. By the time she'd stepped over two or three people, apologizing when she felt fingers or feet beneath her step, she spotted Miranda giving Clark hell.

"I said I wanted to dance with him!" Miranda yelled.

Perry stood there watching, listening to Miranda with a big smile on his face.

Miranda continued her rant, and Kylie couldn't make it out because of everyone else's chatter, but she could see Clark's face turning angry red. Miranda poked him in the chest. Clark retaliated by shoving Miranda back and calling her a name.

Miranda hadn't caught her balance when diamond sparkles started popping off like fireworks. A huge green dragon the size of an eighteen-wheeler appeared where Perry had just stood. Smoke billowed up from the dragon's long, bumpy snout. Most of the camp ers started running like cockroaches in a Raid commercial.

Well, everyone but Kylie, Miranda, and Clark. Kylie moved in and grabbed Miranda's arm, hoping to get her out of the way of danger. But the little witch slipped out of Kylie's hold and stood there staring up at the dragon with what looked like admiration.

"Oh my, he's beautiful," Miranda muttered.

Kylie gazed up at the huge green beast, and while she couldn't agree with Miranda, she decided to forgo speaking her mind. Especially when Perry swiped his fifteen-foot tail around the room, knocking down several of the daring onlookers and tossing a few others across the room. The building shook again, and then everyone left standing moved back.

Della swooped in and screamed at Kylie and Miranda to get back. Miranda ignored Della, too. And until Kylie could get Miranda out of harm's way, she wasn't leaving.

"He won't hurt me," Miranda snapped, and then she turned her angry eyes on Clark. She started wiggling her pinky and chanting.

Unfortunately, right then Burnett swooped in, landing directly in front of Clark. He looked mad enough to kill innocent puppies. He opened his mouth, no doubt to give them all hell, but before he spoke a swirl of rainbow colors started swirling around him like ribbons. Then the hard-as-nails vampire vanished into the smoke-filled air and standing in his place was a very pissed-off kangaroo.

"Oh, shit!" Kylie said.

"Oh, shit!" screamed Miranda.

Burnett, now a very unhappy kangaroo, started hopping around like a marsupial on speed. Miranda, shaking and dancing from one foot to the other, had her pinky in the air, muttering out chants so fast that Kylie couldn't catch one word.

Perry, aka the large, out-of-control dragon, took a step toward Clark.

Clark, looking about ready to crap his pants, started tossing more fireballs. One missed and hit the dining hall wall. One slammed into the trash can containing the pizza boxes, which immediately burst into flames. Another went sailing through the air, heading right for . . . Miranda.

Kylie felt her blood fizz and rush to her brain. Without thinking, without even realizing what she planned to do, she jumped into the fireball's path, caught it, and tossed it to the other side of the room.

Perry released an ominous sound, half roar, half cry. Smoke shot out of his nostrils. Clark tossed another fireball. Before Kylie could stop this one, it hit Perry—in dragon form—and singed the green scales on his side.

The smell of burned dragon, along with burning pizza boxes, scented the air. Smoke rose to the ceiling.

Perry reared his head back and roared so loudly that it shook the whole dining hall to its rafters. It wasn't so much a cry of pain as a cry of warning and of complete and utter fury.

Lucas suddenly appeared beside Kylie and caught her hand in his. He looked at her palm. Then, appearing perplexed, he grabbed her by the elbow and started yanking her away. She pulled free and leapt over some turned-over chairs to grab Miranda.

Just as Clark tossed another fireball, Della swooped back in and was hit by a cylindrical flame in the hip. It knocked the little vampire back a good five feet, and she landed in a dead heap on the floor.

Kylie screamed, Miranda chanted louder, Perry snorted more fire, and Kylie bolted back over the chairs to get to Della.

Before Kylie got to her side, Della popped back up, apparently unharmed. But Kylie had never seen her so pissed. Her eyes glowed bright green, her fangs extended past her bottom lip, and if looks could kill, Clark was worm bait. Growling with raw anger, Della shot across the room after Clark. Burnett, in all his kangaroo glory, jumped in front of Della, blocking and preventing her attack.

Perry let loose a breath of fire that shot clear across the room and left black marks on the log walls and the ceiling.

Miranda, pinky still in the air, chanted louder. Then another swirl of rainbow colors flew across the room, and Burnett zapped back to vampire form. Not a happy vampire, either.

With eyes glowing neon red, he let loose a scream that matched Perry's dragon roar. "Everyone stop! Right now!"

The commotion stopped. Even the crowd standing at the front of the building ceased jabbering. Silence reigned.

Burnett looked first at Clark. "Throw another fireball and you'll be expelled from Shadow Falls until the day I die. And I plan to live a very long time." He turned his gaze to Lucas. "Can you please put the garbage fire out before this whole place goes up in flames?" Whirling, he faced a very angry Della. "As much as I'd love to let you rip this guy's head off"—Burnett glared at Clark—"I think Holiday would disapprove. So, go cool off somewhere." He pointed toward the door.

Before he lowered his hand, Della was gone, leaving only an angry blur in the air.

Taking a deep breath, Burnett aimed his angry gaze at the dragon. "Change back this instant!"

Perry let out one roar of protest, but then the sparkles started floating down from the ceiling to the floor. Kylie noted that everyone else knew to avoid the little bubbles of electricity. Funny how people didn't warn her about these things.

A second after it stopped raining charged, diamond-shaped bubbles, the dragon disappeared and Perry stood before Burnett. He didn't look any less angry than Burnett. Then, proving Kylie's assumption, he took a flying leap over Burnett and landed on top of Clark. Fists started swinging.

Burnett reached effortlessly into the scuffle and yanked Perry up by the collar of his shirt and held him a good five inches off the concrete floor. "No more fighting." He dropped Perry on his feet.

Perry glared at Clark and then looked at Burnett. "He pushed Miranda," Perry said, fury in his tone. "You never, ever hurt a female. You taught me that when I was six."

Six? Kylie looked from Burnett to Perry. Did that mean Burnett knew—?

"I know," Burnett said. "And I'll take that up with him later. But you have to learn to deal with things without shifting, or you'll never be able to coexist with humans."

"He was throwing fireballs!" Miranda piped in. "It's logical that Perry would shift into something that could deal with it."

Kylie saw Perry cut his gaze to Miranda. The anger in his eyes faded and he stared at her in something like astonishment. Something told Kylie that Perry wasn't accustomed to people standing up for him. Right then, her heart broke a little bit more for the shape-shifter who'd been abandoned by both his parents.

Burnett let go of a deep breath and his angry gaze went back to Clark. "Go to your cabin. I'll be there shortly to dish out your punishment."

Clark took off, but not without sneering at Miranda. For a second, Kylie thought Perry was going to attack again. So did Burnett, for he reached out and latched on to Perry. "Don't you dare shift."

Again, Kylie noted the familiarity with which Burnett treated Perry. Obviously, Perry's stint with the FRU foster program had brought him into contact with Burnett. And somehow she sensed that Burnett had taken the orphaned shape-shifter under his wing. It weakened Kylie's earlier misgiving about Burnett and the FRU library. Not that she was completely over it, but everything in her said Burnett wasn't the enemy.

Lucas returned, bringing with him a scent of smoke, and stood by Kylie's side. She looked over at the trash can that minutes ago had been shooting flames up to the ceiling. It had been extinguished, and now only a few wisps of smoke floated up from the rim of the can.

Lucas reached for Kylie's hand again, opened her palm, and studied it. Then he leaned down and whispered in her ear, "Are you really okay?"

"Yes," she said, perplexed by his question.

He stared at her hand again and tenderly ran his finger across her palm. "It should have burned you."

She remembered catching one of the fireballs aimed at Miranda. "Well, it didn't." Then she recalled how she'd felt as if her blood had turned into soda and she'd felt it fizz into her brain.

His look of awe changed into a tight frown. "Nevertheless, the next time I try to remove you from a dangerous situation, don't fight me."

She frowned right back at him. "I wasn't fighting you. I just wasn't leaving Miranda or Della."

He shook his head as if she exasperated him. "You really are a protector, aren't you?"

"Maybe I'm just a good friend." For some crazy reason, she sensed he preferred she not be a protector. Why? Did her being a protector mean she had less a chance of being a werewolf?

Burnett looked back at the crowd of campers watching them. "You guys go back to your cabins. Party's over."

As soon as they left, he fixed his gaze on Miranda. "You so much as twitch that finger at me again and I'll . . ."

"Della says she'll rip it off," Miranda said, and giggled, not the least bit intimidated by Burnett. Burnett let go of a growl, not appreciating Miranda's candor.

"She didn't mean to turn you," Kylie and Perry said at the same time.

"It was Clark she was aiming at," Perry added, frowning at Burnett.

"I don't care," Burnett said. "It will never happen again. You understand that?" He glared harder at Miranda.

Miranda nodded. "Understood. I'm sorry."

Kylie could tell she had to work to look reprimanded, but the apology rang sincere. And that was when Kylie knew all the campers had accepted Burnett as one of the leaders. He might not have Holiday's easy, somewhat loving method of connecting with the campers, but he made up for it in other ways.

Burnett folded his arms over his chest. "Now, all of you go back to your cabins."

They all turned to leave. Lucas slipped his hand in Kylie's, letting her know he'd be walking with her.

But then Burnett added, "Everyone but Kylie."

Oh joy. What now? Kylie stopped moving and turned around to face Burnett.

Chapter Sixteen

As soon as the sound of the heavy wooden front door closing echoed in the empty, still smoky dining hall, Kylie decided to confess and get it over with.

"I know, it's my fault. I apologize. I thought I was helping."

Burnett, arms still crossed over his chest, stared down at her. "What's your fault?"

"This," she said, suddenly wishing she hadn't been so gung ho to take the blame. Then again, accepting responsibility was right.

Burnett stared down at her as the seconds passed, which only intensified Kylie's growing need to fill the silence. "Okay, look," she said. "I'm the one who told Perry to cut in on Miranda and Clark."

He nodded. "Yeah, I heard that. I was in the office."

Kylie frowned, wondering if he'd also eavesdropped on her conversation with Lucas.

He dropped his arms to his sides, making him appear less intimidating. "But that doesn't make it your fault."

"So you didn't have me hang back to read me the riot act about starting this mess?"

"No." He reached down and snatched two chairs upright and motioned for her to sit down.

"Am I in trouble for something else?" she asked as she sat down.

He flipped the chair around and straddled it. "No. I just wanted to talk to you." His palms curled around the back of the chair. "Is your hand okay?"

She held out her palm for him to see. "Yeah."

He looked down at her hand, then up at her face again. "Holiday called and was worried about you."

"Why?"

He seemed to struggle to find the right words. "I told her what you'd asked about the bird."

"What did she say?" Kylie leaned in a bit, ready to get at least one answer to her long list of questions.

"She said you shouldn't be worried. If you did bring the bird back to life, it would only cost a very, very small piece of your soul."

"But I did give some of it away?"

"Possibly," Burnett said.

Kylie hesitated to ask, but she needed to know, so she just did it. "Did she say anything about the bird stalking me?"

"Stalking you?"

"Yeah, it was flying around me today, but I wasn't so sure it wasn't just some fluke. But then it came to my window earlier today and tapped on it."

Burnett's eyes widened a little in surprise, and then his inscrutable expression slammed down again. "Are you sure it's the same bird?"

"No, but it's too much of a coincidence not to be, don't you think?"

"Perhaps," he said. "Did you feel any kind of threat from the bird? Like you did with the eagle and the deer?"

"No, nothing. It was all peaceful and serene."

"Good." He stared down at his hands as if he had something else to say and it wasn't going to be easy. "Look, about the FRU library . . ."

"What about it?" she asked, immediately feeling nervous.

"I don't want you to think I was lying earlier. I wasn't. However, considering that I work for the FRU, I'm only allowed to say so much."

"So you did lie to me?" she asked.

"No." He tightened his lips as if frustrated. "I told you as much as I could. The truth is that there are some books there I'm not allowed to see."

She felt suddenly cold, the kind of a chill that came from being afraid of where their conversation was headed. Of being afraid to discover the truth about herself.

"There are books about . . . others like me, aren't there?" she asked. "Others who don't know what they are."

He hesitated again and laced his fingers together in a tight ball. "I don't even know what all is there, but if they were there, I doubt very seriously that I could obtain permission to allow you to read them."

"Why?"

"The FRU considers ninety percent of what they have collected as classified."

Frustration built in her chest. "What's the big secret? I mean, the key to understanding what I am could be in that library. And you're locking me out—it's so frustrating. It's like you're deliberately trying to keep me in the dark about my powers, my identity."

"You're not being kept in the dark, and the key to understanding what you are is much more likely to be elsewhere—here in the outside world—than in that library. There's a lot of classified information at stake, but there's nothing we're trying to hide from you."

"It sure as hell feels that way," she said. "Tell me the truth, please. Do you know what I am?"

"No," he said again, and her instincts told her he wasn't lying. "Look," he said. "The only reason I brought this up is that I don't want you to stop trusting me. I'm as perplexed by you as . . . well, as you are."

Kylie slumped in her chair, resigned to the fact that he wouldn't, and maybe even couldn't, give her anything more. "Fine."

He nodded and then looked around the dining hall. "You think we might convince everyone not to tell Holiday about this disaster?"

Kylie looked up at the singed wood, which had been marked by the dragon's breath and Clark's fireballs. "It might be difficult."

He looked around and frowned. "I guess so. But damn, I wanted to prove to her that I could run the show without screwing up."

"You didn't screw up," Kylie said. "All's well that ends well. No one's hurt."

He let out a deep gulp of air. "I got myself turned into a kangaroo."

Kylie couldn't help but snicker. Then Burnett laughed. Kylie couldn't swear by it, but she thought it was the first time she'd ever heard him do that. "Holiday is going to enjoy that one, isn't she?"

Kylie continued to grin. "Oh, yeah. Can I be the one to tell her?"

"Afraid not." Then he flashed her what she could have sworn was a smile. "If it involves making her laugh, I'll keep that pleasure for myself."

She studied him for a few moments, again feeling his devotion to Holiday. Thinking of devotion and Burnett, she decided to ask another question that had been pulling at her mind. "You and Perry have a history, right?"

He paused for a second and then said, "Sort of. Why?"

"The way you two relate to each other."

He nodded but didn't offer any details.

"It was through the foster program, right?" she asked. "Were you like a caseworker or something there at one time?"

Burnett's expression stayed stoic. "He told you about the foster program?"

"Yeah."

Burnett nodded. "Yes. We crossed paths through the program."

He didn't seem eager to share anything else about his past, so Kylie decided to drop it, or at least drop part of it. "Perry's not going to get in too much trouble for this, is he?" She frowned. "I mean, I was the one that sort of caused it. He was leaving and I stopped him."

Burnett arched a brow. "Truth be told, he behaved extremely well . . . considering." He looked around again. "You wouldn't believe the kind of messes I've had to clean up because of him."

Kylie imagined Burnett coming to the aid of a younger Perry— a Perry who had no one because his parents abandoned him. Her doubts about Burnett and trusting him practically vanished. Without thinking, she said, "You know, you aren't near as badass as you pretend to be."

Burnett frowned as if he didn't like being considered anything but bad. "I wouldn't bet on it," he said. "Just ask Holiday." He stood up. "Come on, I'll walk you to your cabin. I need to go deal with Clark before it gets any later."

"You don't need to walk me. I think I can manage."

"Nope. You're still under shadow guard."

As they walked out of the dining hall, Kylie welcomed the night air without the scent of smoke. The memory of her dance with Lucas tickled her mind, but she pushed it back, not wanting to think about that with present company. Especially when she half feared that Burnett might have been privy to their entire conversation.

They started down the path to her cabin. A few night creatures rustled the underbrush along their way. Burnett cut his gaze from one side to the other, always aware, always on guard.

"You haven't experienced any more threats, have you?" he asked.

"No."

"It always amazes me what just having a shadow with you can prevent."

Kylie looked up at him through the darkness. "Do you think that's the only reason it hasn't happened again? That someone, more than likely Mario or his grandson, is still waiting to get me alone?" She considered telling him about the dream but didn't see how it would help.

"I think we can't be too careful."

Kylie felt a familiar chill slide past her, slowly, and she knew they had company. She gazed around to see if the spirit had materialized yet, but she saw nothing.

But the sense of grief that seemed to seep into her pores told her it was Jane Doe. Kylie's mind shot back to the spirit and the loss of her child. A need to help the spirit tightened her chest. If Holiday were here, she'd talk to her about it. But she didn't think Burnett would be helpful where ghosts were concerned. Especially when it involved a pregnant ghost.

"Who's shadowing me in the morning?" she asked.

"I believe it's Della," Burnett said, and looked around almost as if he felt the ghostly presence.

"Would you mind if we go to the cemetery in Fallen tomorrow?"

Burnett stopped walking. "Why would you want to go there?"

Kylie rubbed her arms to try to chase away the chill. "It has to do with my latest ghost."

"Which is a good reason not to go," he said.

Kylie frowned at the thought that she and Holiday were the only ones who weren't antighost. "The spirit can't remember who she is, and because the first time she appeared to me was when my mom and I were driving past the cemetery, I think she might be buried there. I asked Holiday about going and she said it would be okay as long as I had someone with me and if you guys knew where I was."

His expression didn't change, but something about the way he held his shoulders told her he'd given in. "Let me check with Holiday. If she says it's okay, I'll . . . I'll go with you."

"You shouldn't have to go. I'm sure Della and I would—"

"No." From his tone she knew he wouldn't budge. "Until we

know the threat against you is over, you won't leave the camp without me." His stern gaze punctuated his words, and then he continued, "I'm serious about this, Kylie. I don't want to scare you, but if this is Mario or Red, they won't give up. They're waiting for a time that you are at your most vulnerable to attack again. And next time you may not be so lucky."

Kylie, with a cloud of the spirit's cold following her, walked into the cabin a few minutes later. Della and Miranda were sitting at the kitchen table, chatting.

Miranda popped up. "Did you see Perry? Was he not totally off-the-chart awesome? He even fought for me when he was in human form."

"Yeah, I saw that," Kylie said, hanging back a bit, not wanting to ruin the moment by having them sense the spirit. Kylie looked at Della, whose eyes still glowed with anger.

"Is Burnett sending Clark packing?" Della asked. "Because if he doesn't, I'm gonna have to teach that warlock a lesson he'll never forget."

Kylie recalled Della taking a hit with the fireball, and she knew that for a vamp that was probably embarrassing—especially when Kylie had somehow managed to catch one and toss it aside. "I know Burnett is going to see him now, but I don't know what he plans on doing about it."

"He burned Miranda's new skirt!" Della held up the skirt, which had been scorched.

Miranda waved a hand. "I told you it's not a big deal."

"It is a big deal," Della retorted. "If Kylie hadn't been there, he could have hurt you."

"What about you?" Kylie asked, looking at Della. "Did you get burned by the fireball?"

"A bit, but I've already healed." Della's gaze went to Kylie's hand. "You must heal fast, too. "

"Yeah." Kylie decided not to tell them that she'd never been burned by Clark's fireball. Or at least she hadn't gotten the sensation that she'd been burned. She recalled Lucas's remark *You really are a protector.* And again, she wondered why he'd sounded almost unhappy about the possibility.

The spirit's cold drew closer, and Kylie ran her hand over her forearms where goose bumps chased goose bumps over her bare skin. She leaned back against the edge of the sofa.

"How pissed is Burnett at me for turning him into a kangaroo?" Miranda asked.

Kylie grinned. "I think he's over it."

"I'd still avoid him for a few days if I were you," Della suggested. "I mean, did you see how mad he was when you turned him back?" She grinned. "Though not as mad as I'd have been. I swear, if it'd been me, I'd have hopped all over your ass, right after I'd kangaroo-punched Clark out. But damn, it was funny seeing Burnett hopping mad."

"I didn't mean to do it," Miranda said. "I wasn't even going for a kangaroo."

"What were you going for?" Kylie asked.

"A cockatoo. I guess I said it wrong." She pursed her lips as if thinking. "But hey, at least I figured out how to turn him back. I should get some credit for that."

"Credit?" Della snickered. "If you hadn't been able to change him back, I have a feeling you'd be kangaroo food right about now."

Miranda sighed.

Kylie decided to change the subject and looked at Della. "So what happened with the pact?"

Della frowned. "Let's just say it didn't work out as well for us. But forget about us. How did things go with Lucas? I saw you two went outside for a while."

Kylie bit down on her lip, unsure how much she wanted to share. "It went good."

"How good?" asked Miranda, never one to appreciate privacy. The little witch even rubbed her hands together in giddy anticipation.

"Really good," Kylie answered, remembering how it had felt to dance with Lucas—to kiss him as if they had all night. The memory chased away some of the ghostly chill prickling her bare arms. Kylie glanced around again to make sure Jane Doe hadn't manifested.

"Good as in first base? Second base?" Miranda's hazel eyes got big. "Or are we talking third?"

"We just kissed." Remembering their accusation that she was up for sainthood, Kylie added, "And slow danced in the moonlight. It was very romantic."

"Romantic or sexy?" Della asked. "There's a difference, you know."

Kylie frowned. "No, there's not."

"Oh yes, there is," Della smarted off. "Romantic is . . . 'Oh, he's so sweet,' and sexy is . . . 'He's so hot, my panties might just catch fire.' So which was it? Romantic or sexy?"

"Panties catch fire?" Kylie rolled her eyes.

"It's just an expression, but you know what I mean," Della insisted. "So which was it? Romantic?" She held out one hand. "Or sexy?" She held out the other.

Kylie considered the question and then admitted the truth. "It was both."

Miranda squealed. "Was it as hot as the kiss at the creek he gave you?"

Kylie remembered being at the creek with Lucas over a month ago. She'd fallen on top of him and they had kissed. Kissed deeply while the cold, crisp water ran over them and Lucas's hot body pressed against hers. And she decided Della might have a point about the difference between sexy and romantic. The kiss at the creek had been sexy. Tonight had been . . . well, more romantic, but still sexy.

"You know, you guys have to start having your own romantic escapades. I'm tired of being the only one sharing this stuff."

"We're working on it," Miranda said, and shrugged. "So? Give us more details. Was tonight as hot as the famous creek kiss?"

Socks waddled out of her bedroom and came and bumped his pointed nose against her ankle. "Not quite as hot," Kylie said, reaching down to pick him up. She pulled the little skunk close and nuzzled his nose. "But almost."

Remembering just how "almost as hot" tonight had been, Kylie looked at her two best friends and wondered if they might know the answer to the question she planned on asking Lucas later. "How much do you guys know about werewolves and their powers?"

"I know they're not nearly as powerful as vampires," Della piped up.

"I'm not talking physical strength. Other kinds of power."

"What other kinds of power?" asked Della.

Kylie tried to figure out how to put it. "The power to persuade a girl to do things?"

"Things? What kind of things?" Della glanced at Miranda, whose eyes grew round. "Do you mean . . . ?" They both turned back to Kylie.

"Okay, spill it," Della said. "Just what the hell happened out in the moonlight?"

"Yeah," Miranda added. "And don't leave out a single juicy detail."

Chapter Seventeen

Kylie felt her cheeks begin to redden. "Okay, it's not what you think. . . ."

Even as she said the words, she knew she was lying.

"Okay, fine," she said. "It's exactly what you think."

Miranda's mouth dropped open. "You mean . . . Did you—"

"No." Kylie slapped her hand against her chest. "God, no. I mean, like I told you, we just danced and kissed. But . . ."

"But what?" Della demanded.

"Yeah," Miranda said. "But what?"

Kylie took a deep breath. "But . . . he said something that made me think that maybe he had the ability to convince me to, you know." She blushed again.

"Do the horizontal bop?" Della offered. "Do the Humpty dance? Knock boots?"

Kylie rolled her eyes. "Where do you come up with that stuff?"

Della grinned. "I get around."

Miranda giggled.

"Uh-huh." Kylie felt her cheeks grow even hotter. "Anyway, yeah, that's what I mean," she added before the smart-mouthed vamp could come up with some more half-vulgar, half-hilarious terms for sex. "I just want to know if werewolves have any special powers, okay?"

Della leaned back in her chair. "Maybe he just means he'll seduce you by kissing you. Let's face it, he's pretty hot and you said his kisses were out of this world. Hey, he makes my knees weak, and I'm vampire with a natural dislike for weres."

"He is hot," Miranda added.

Kylie tried not to think about her two roommates weak-kneed for Lucas.

"Then you don't believe that power really exists?" she asked instead.

"Yeah, it exists," Miranda said, and her brow pinched as if she were thinking. "I've heard something about it. Nothing specific, but just a few mumblings."

"What have you heard?" Della and Kylie asked at the same time. Kylie put Socks down, moved to the table, and dropped onto a kitchen chair. For some reason, the ghost had decided to move on, which didn't bother her at all. She could use some downtime.

Especially right now.

"I can't remember the details," Miranda said. "Just that it's a little dangerous to date a were. It has something to do with animal pheromones. They're basically animals, and all animals have a natural way of attracting the opposite sex."

"Attracting like how?" Kylie asked.

"Well," Miranda said, "lizards have a brightly colored balloony thing that they blow out from their throats and supposedly girl lizards find that all kinds of sexy."

Kylie shook her head. "Lucas doesn't have a balloon in his throat."

"Hey," Della added. "Have you ever seen those blackbirds—grackles, I think they're called—do the mating dance? They jump around on one foot and ruffle their feathers out. The females supposedly get horny just seeing the male birds do it. I mean, the guy with the better feathers always wins. Or is it the bigger feathers?"

Miranda snickered. "And I heard some male baboons have brightly colored buttocks and they go around mooning the females. Supposedly it's a huge turn-on."

While Kylie was serious about finding answers, she couldn't help but laugh. "I don't think Lucas has colored buttocks, either. Not that I've seen them." She laughed harder.

Before their conversation was over, Della was on the computer looking up strange mating behaviors that included everything from exploding testicles to slinging poop with a tail, and they laughed themselves silly until way past midnight. It was, Kylie decided as she finally slipped into bed, just the type of evening she needed.

Although she still didn't have the answer to her original question: Just what kind of power did Lucas really have?

And could she trust him not to misuse it? Her gut said she could. But was her gut being persuaded by outside influences?

The floating sensation filled Kylie's head several hours after she went to bed that night. Mental alarms went off. Was this Red again? Then she realized the difference: she was floating, which meant she was the one moving.

She considered trying to stop it, but she was too tired, so she just let herself go. Let herself float and zip through the air—moving through clouds of sleep.

The sense of freedom was exhilarating. She didn't have a clue where she was going, and she didn't care. Obviously, her subconscious had a plan. But what?

And then she saw him. He looked so good, lying in his bed, that her breath caught and she put on her flying brakes. He was shirtless, too. The covers came low on his waist, several inches past his belly button. Her gaze moved up and then down his bare torso. There was a lot of skin to appreciate.

Then she studied his face. So peaceful in his slumber. His eyelashes rested against his cheeks. His hair rested against his brow in a ruffled mess, as if he'd run his fingers through it too many times. Her heart spasmed and then she felt herself moving closer, into the room, into the bed, into his . . . head.

No! She stopped herself at the last moment.

She'd vowed to get over Derek. To move past him. Unfortunately, her subconscious hadn't gotten that message. Then, as if gravity, or maybe her own will, started pulling her backward, she let herself sail through the clouds, back through the universe of sleep.

She woke up with a start, as if she'd been slammed back into her body. Catching her breath, she reached for her pillow and hugged it tightly to her chest. The vision of Derek asleep filled her head. *No! No! Don't think about Derek. Think about Lucas.*

Lucas, who'd danced with her in the moonlight. Lucas, who'd kissed her so sweetly. Lucas, whose blood raced every time she was with him.

Closing her eyes, she lost herself again in the oblivion of sleep. The sweet nothingness of slumber. The next thing she knew, she stood in a room of clouds, in front of Lucas. Thoughts of Red hit, but Lucas spoke. "It's me. Feel me. I'm hot." He reached out and took her hand in his. His touch sent warmth through her palm and her heart.

She remembered telling herself to think about Lucas, and she wondered if she was learning to control her dreamscapes. A little thrill ran through her as the sensation of accomplishment filled her chest. With so many unknowns and out-of-control issues happening, it felt great to think she'd mastered something.

He smiled up at her with his sleepy blue eyes. "I was beginning to think you would never visit me in my dreams again."

Suddenly, the clouds evaporated like unwanted fog and they

were back outside where they'd danced earlier that evening. The moon and stars cast lovely shadows around them. Only this time, the night played the music. Crickets and an occasional bird harmonized with the sound of a light breeze stirring through the leaves of shrubbery and the rustle of live oak trees.

"Shall we dance?" He held out his hand.

She started to place her hand in his palm when she realized he didn't have on a shirt. Instead of jeans, he had on a long, loose-fitting pair of boxers. The kind boys slept in—if they didn't sleep nude. The kind the movie stars often wore in those sexy photos.

She swallowed a nervous tickle. He looked really good. Warm and so touchable. And almost naked. As if nothing more than a flick of his thumb could leave him completely bare.

"Uh . . ." She waved her hand up and down. "Shouldn't you get dressed?"

He grinned and then laughed outright—something he didn't do often. "This is your dream, Kylie. You dressed me for the occasion. You're in charge of what I wear. So, the better question is . . . is this how you want me to be dressed?"

She felt her face heat up and wished she could deny it, but Holiday had told her as much during their discussions of dreamscaping. She controlled everything, from the person she visited to what happened during her visit. So what did it mean that she had visited Derek first?

And why had she wanted Lucas half-dressed?

Okay, that was a stupid question.

"Oh . . ." She let her voice fade away, not really sure what else to say. That's when she noticed what she was wearing. The same short pajama set she'd worn to bed—they consisted of a pale blue body-hugging tank top and a pair of tight dark blue boy shorts. A bathing suit would have shown more skin, but she still felt slightly naked.

She wasn't sure how she could change the clothes they were

wearing, but she closed her eyes and concentrated for a couple of seconds. When she opened her eyes again, she saw she was back in her black party dress—much more appropriate. Lucas wore jeans and a white T-shirt with a big yellow smiley face on it.

He looked down at his shirt and then back up at her with a funny frown. "Seriously? This is what you chose?"

"I'm new at this," she said, defending herself. "But it's not that bad."

"A smiley face?" He chuckled again. "Just remind me to never let you buy me clothes."

She laughed, and then he held out his hand again. "Are we here to dance?"

This time, she took it and let him pull her against him.

When his warm arms went around her and his chest melted against hers, it reminded her how it felt to slip into a warm bed on a cold night. She sighed at how comforting it felt to be held by him again. When she rested her cheek on his chest, his hand moved around her waist and his almost electric pulse fluttered against her lower back. That flutter seemed to move inside her and caused her blood to pulse.

She recalled the question she needed to ask him and lifted her head and rested her chin against his chest. He looked down and met her gaze. His blue eyes were hooded with something that looked like passion, and she wondered if her own eyes showed the same emotion.

"Can I ask you something?"

"It's your dream," he whispered. "We can do *anything* you want." There was an emphasis on the word *anything* that caused a ripple of nervousness to move through her.

Anything.

Taking a deep breath, she stopped dancing and slid her hand up his chest to where she felt his heart pumping.

"Tonight, you mentioned that you were good at . . . the art of persuasion."

His lips curled into a smile. "Yeah, I remember that." His voice had a teasing, sensual quality that made her want to shiver and press herself closer to him.

"What . . . what did you mean by that?"

His smile turned ultrasexy. "I'd rather show you."

She nipped at her bottom lip, considering his offer. She was tempted—Lord, how she was tempted. And what would be the harm in saying yes, just this one time? After all, this was just a dream. Anything that happened here would have no effect on her real life. Right?

"Relax, Kylie," he said. "It's just a dream." His words echoed her own thoughts. Then his warm lips brushed against her brow and the ripple of unease increased.

"Maybe it's just a dream," she said. "But it feels real and I'm . . . I prefer you just answered my question the old-fashioned way."

He nodded. For a second, he appeared not to want to continue, but then he said, "It's not like a trick or anything. It's part of what I am. It's instinctual."

"What's instinctual?"

"When a were is with a potential mate, our bodies react in certain ways." He paused as if he knew his explanation wouldn't be enough. "Last night, when you had your head on my chest, you heard the sound . . . the low growl."

"Like a purring or humming," she said, remembering being lulled by the soft noise.

He nodded. "Well, that reverberation is supposed to be somewhat hypnotic. It encourages our potential mate to want to be closer."

Close and naked, Kylie thought, but didn't say it. "It makes one dizzy, too," she said, remembering how she'd felt last night.

He caught her face in his hands. "I guess maybe a little." He brushed his thumb over her cheek. "But it's not a ploy to trick girls into bed. It's just a natural thing male weres do. If that's what you're worried about."

"I'm not exactly worried," she said. And she wasn't. Because as potentially dangerous as the werewolf's purr could be, she didn't think she had to worry about Lucas misusing it. Last night, he'd had a chance to let things escalate between them and he'd put a stop to it.

"Like I told you," she said. "I trust you." And she still did.

He studied her face. "But?"

Okay, there was a but. She hesitated to find the right words. "But knowledge is power. I like knowing what I'm dealing with. And I like being the one in the driver's seat, if you know what I mean."

He frowned slightly as if he didn't like her answer. "It's not like entrapment. A female has to be close, really close, to a male were before she's even aware of it."

Kylie smiled. "So I guess I need to be careful how close I get to you."

"Or not." He leaned in and kissed her softly on the lips. "I really, really like you, Kylie Galen."

"And I you, Lucas Parker." She raised herself up on her tiptoes to press a quick kiss to his lips.

His eyes met hers and he let go of a deep breath. "Okay."

"Okay, what?" she asked, sensing his remark meant something.

"Okay, I'll be a bit more patient. Okay, I'm happy with this. With just being this close to you." He picked her up and twirled her around.

She grinned when he set her back on her feet. "Thanks," she said, and touched his lips with her fingertips.

He caught her hand. "We just have to be a little careful when we're not dreaming."

"Careful about what?"

"Like I told you last night. The closer to the full moon, the more I run on instinct. And sometimes, my instincts are short on patience."

She didn't like the sound of that. "Do you mean we can't see each other when it's time for your change?"

"I didn't say that." He frowned. "We can see each other. But we shouldn't . . . dance in the moonlight for too long. Or roll around on the ground by the creek." He grinned. "Or go skinny-dipping at the swimming hole." His tone seemed to deepen.

"That was just a dream." She felt her face flush.

"A good one, too." He smiled. Then he breathed in as if to sober his thoughts. "But basically, we'll be fine as long as we don't play too close to the fire until after the change." He ran his hand through the curtain of her hair and brought a handful of it to his nose. "Unless you change your mind. You do know that what happens in dreams isn't really real, right? I mean, we could—"

Suddenly, she felt something yanking her from behind and pulling her away from Lucas. Pulling her to someplace she didn't want to go.

Lucas yelled out her name. But a cloud appeared between them. She realized that two men dressed in white lab coats had her in their grips. One on each arm, holding her so tightly that she couldn't get away. The camp had dissolved. Now she was in a building of some kind, and the two men pulled her down a dark, dismal hall. She screamed and tried to pull away, but she was helpless.

Her heart thumped in her chest, and she tasted fear on her tongue. Nothing made sense. Then she remembered—this was a dream. All she had to do was wake up.

She slammed her eyes shut. Tight. Then tighter.

Wake up. Wake up. Wake up.

Suddenly, a bright light shone in her eyes. Everything had changed again. The men who had dragged her away were gone. She felt disoriented, lost, alone. Empty. She felt empty. What was happening to her?

The light shifted from one eye to the other, and she saw a man's face inches from her nose. She realized she was lying in a bed. Not her bed, though. Not the twin one at camp or her full-size mattress at home. This bed felt different. She tried to move but felt numb. No, not numb—she felt paralyzed.

"Is she okay?" a female voice asked. Kylie cut her eyes to the side to see her new captor, but she was out of vision range, and Kylie was unable to turn her neck. Panic started to tighten her throat again.

"She should be," said the man, shining the flashlight into her eyes.

Kylie blinked and when she opened her eyes, she saw his pattern. He was vampire.

Then he turned her chin in his large hands and ran his finger over her head. Oddly enough, Kylie realized he touched her bare scalp. She was missing her hair.

Missing her hair?

She blinked again and remembered her ghost, Jane Doe. Was that what was happening? Was this a vision sent to her by the amnesiac ghost—one of those crazy ones where Kylie actually became the spirit? Fear swelled in her chest. She cut her eyes to the side and stared at the man's eyes until she saw her own reflection. Or saw the ghost's reflection.

It should have calmed her, but the panic built higher. She wanted out of here. She hadn't wanted to be here to start with. She'd already lost everything that mattered. Thoughts, feelings, and emotions collided in her chest and she wasn't sure which ones were her own and which ones belonged to her spirit.

"Wake up. Kylie, wake up!" Kylie could hear voices coming from somewhere far away. But then the voices faded and she felt the vampire's hand on her head again.

"She's healing nicely," he said. "Maybe she'll just take a while longer to come around. Let's do another MRI scan on her." The man stood up and twitched his brows at her. "Then again, it could be more. Her pattern still hasn't emerged." He frowned. "I don't understand that. Something isn't right."

"What do I tell her husband? He woke up several hours ago and is asking for her," the female voice said. Kylie had yet to see the owner of that voice.

Help me! Kylie screamed in her head, because she couldn't make her throat work.

"Tell him she's doing fine. But we're keeping her for observation. Release him if he's ready to go."

"Do you think she's going to live?" asked the woman again.

"I don't know." He slipped his flashlight into his coat pocket. "But I guess it's inevitable that we will lose a few subjects. We just have to remember it's for a good cause."

"I guess," said the female voice.

"Get me the results of the test. However, if she hasn't awakened by tonight, go ahead and extinguish her."

Extinguish her?

Kylie's fear ratcheted up a notch.

Noooooooooooo!

Chapter Eighteen

"Damn it! She's not breathing!" a familiar male voice boomed in Kylie's ears, and she wanted more than anything to answer him. She tried to move but couldn't. She still felt paralyzed.

Help me. Please . . .

"She did this once before." That was Della talking now, but panic filled her voice. Della never showed panic or fear. To the contrary, the vampire was fearless.

"Kylie, wake up!" the deep male voice said, and this time Kylie recognized it as belonging to Lucas.

Suddenly, Kylie's lungs opened up and demanded air. She opened her mouth and gasped and started coughing as if her lungs wanted to reject the oxygen. Rolling over on her side, she continued to cough, certain she was going to blow a lung. Finally, she opened her eyes and realized she was on the kitchen floor in her cabin.

After a few more seconds passed, the coughing stopped and she focused on breathing. Someone grabbed her and pulled her up into their lap and held her. Heat surrounded her. He was hot. So hot. And she was cold. So damn cold.

She focused on the face of the person cradling her so tenderly. So close. So warm. And his eyes were so blue. Lucas.

Then his face faded and she saw a strange woman's face moving close. The feel of Lucas's arms around her seemed like a memory that time was pulling away a little bit each moment.

"She stopped breathing again!" Lucas shouted, and he started rocking her. "What do I do? Someone tell me what to do!"

"Holiday says she'll be okay."

Kylie recognized Burnett's voice, but it seemed to be coming from somewhere else, from someplace far, far away.

"Holiday thinks she's probably having a vision. That sometime . . ." His voice faded into the background.

The vision yanked Kylie back completely, and she watched in horror as a group of women brought something up to her face. Only it wasn't her. She was experiencing Jane Doe's life, but it felt as real as if it were happening to her.

She felt a thick, nubby towel being forced against her mouth. She gasped, tried to move, but couldn't. She—Jane Doe—was paralyzed, and someone was smothering her.

The unfairness of it stung her throat as her lungs begged for air. Everything went black and then she saw the spirit standing over her. She leaned down, her blue lips frosted over. *"They killed me. They really killed me,"* she said. *"You must breathe, though. You must live."*

Kylie's lungs screamed for oxygen, but she felt unable to gasp for the air she needed. Then she became aware that she was back in her kitchen.

Kylie heard Miranda chanting in the distance. She heard Della muttering that Lucas should give Kylie CPR. And Burnett kept asking questions to Holiday over the phone.

"Breathe, damn it!" Lucas yelled.

She pressed her forehead tight against Lucas's bare chest and pulled big swallows of oxygen into her throat. Tears filled her eyes, and she cried for the life that had been so brutally taken. Cried for the woman whose name she didn't know. Cried for the woman who, in addition to losing her life, had lost her child. How unfair was that?

"She's breathing again," Lucas said, cradling her tighter in his arms. "And she's crying." He dipped his head. "Shh," he whispered for her ears only. And then he said to the others, "I'm taking her to her bed. She's so cold."

Kylie felt herself being lifted in his arms. She vaguely recalled that he'd been the one to carry her to the bed that night weeks ago when she'd had the vision of Daniel, and for some reason, it felt right him being here now. It felt right when he lowered her on the bed and then crawled in beside her and held her against his chest, with his arms around her. And being so tired, too emotionally spent to talk to anyone, it especially felt right when she fell asleep with her head pillowed on his warm chest.

Unfortunately, when Kylie stirred awake a short while later, still curled up in Lucas's arms, Burnett, Miranda, Della, and Lucas all stared at her in shock and concern, and it felt a bit like getting caught French kissing a boy in public. It didn't feel so right.

She pushed off his chest, brushed her hair from her face, and gazed at all her onlookers, who stared at her as if her head might start spinning or something. Didn't they know their own abilities and powers were just as weird to those who didn't have them?

The words *You okay?* and a couple different variations of the same question came from all four people.

She nodded. "I'm fine."

"She's awake and says she's fine," Burnett said into his cell phone, which he held to his ear. "Yeah, I'll have her call you as soon as she's able."

Kylie recalled hearing Burnett talking to Holiday. "I'm sorry," she said. She wasn't sure why she felt the need to apologize. What happened wasn't her fault. Though she still wasn't sure exactly what had happened, beyond her getting caught in a vision about Jane Doe's death. Still, she supposed it was a good idea to apologize for causing a scene in the middle of the night.

She looked at Burnett. "How did . . . Why are you . . . ?" Embarrassment fluttered in her stomach. "Was I screaming so loud it woke the whole camp or something?"

"No. You hardly screamed at all this time," Della said. "I woke up when you were walking around the kitchen, muttering and, well, screaming just a bit. When I went to see if you were okay, you were, like, totally out of it. I mean, the lights were on but nobody was home kind of thing. You weren't here."

"Yeah," Miranda said, moving in. "And I woke up when Lucas was trying to bust down our door saying he had to check on you." Miranda looked at Lucas. "How did you know she was having another one of her dreams?"

Lucas didn't answer, and Kylie recalled that she'd been dreamscaping with him when the vision had started. Had he seen it, too? He must have if he ran here.

"I . . . uh . . ."

Kylie figured he didn't tell them they were dreamscaping because he knew she probably wouldn't want him to share that with everyone.

"It wasn't a dream," Kylie answered, hoping to shift the question from Lucas. "It was a vision."

"That's what Holiday says, too," Burnett said, sitting in a chair beside the bed. When Kylie glanced at him, he added, "I was walking the camp when I heard the commotion and I came running."

Kylie nodded and glanced at the clock on her bedside table. It was almost three in the morning. "You guys should all be in bed asleep. You should go."

"Are you sure you're okay?" Burnett asked.

"I'm fine," Kylie said, and she was fine. At least she thought she was, but she needed to figure out what the vision meant without an audience.

"Holiday wants you to call her," Burnett said.

"I will," Kylie said, and the words scratched her raw throat.

Burnett nodded and waved for Lucas to follow him out. But Lucas stayed sitting on the corner of her bed. "I want to talk with her just a second," he said.

Burnett looked at Kylie, and when she nodded, he started out. "Keep it short."

"Do you need us?" Miranda asked, and stifled a yawn.

"No, you two go to bed. I'm okay. Thanks." Kylie watched both Miranda and Della walk out, and then she looked at Lucas. He was frowning, his brow crinkled and his blue eyes filled with all sorts of concern.

He leaned in a bit and spoke low. "Are you sure you're okay? That was freaky."

"You saw it, too?" she asked.

"I saw you being pulled away by two guys. But then all of a sudden it wasn't you. It was some other woman. And then it was like you disappeared in a cloud. I woke up, scared shitless, and I ran over here to make sure you were okay. When I got on your front porch, I heard you walking around and I guess I lost it." Fear flashed across his face. "Does this ghost vision stuff happen all the time?"

She wondered if he knew she was equally frightened of him turning into a wolf. "No. Not all the time."

"What is it? Why does it happen?"

Kylie hesitated. "It's the spirits' way of showing me what happened to them."

"The spirits who are haunting you?" He looked mortified and even glanced around as if thinking they were there.

"Yeah. But you can relax. She's not here now." She settled back

against the pillows. And then, "It's not as bad as it seems." She recalled how helpless she'd felt in the vision. She recalled the horrify-
ing sensation of being smothered to death, and her heart hurt for the
ghost. Okay, maybe it was as bad as it seemed, but if it helped the
spirit pass on, then Kylie would do it.

Kylie's phone rang. It startled her until she remembered she was
supposed to call Holiday. "I should . . . It's probably Holiday," she said.

He leaned down and pressed a quick kiss on her cheek. "Call me
if you need me."

She watched Lucas go and reached for the phone. She didn't check
the caller ID. She just assumed it was Holiday. Who else would be
calling her at three in the morning? But she assumed wrong.

"Are you okay?" Derek's voice filled the line, and the image of him
shirtless in his bed, with the covers pulled to his waist, filled her head.

Her cheeks flushed. "I'm fine. How did you . . . know?"

"You came to me," he said. "In a dream."

"I did?" she asked, and bit down on her lip and stared at her lap.
Had she returned to Derek and not known it? She saw Socks crawl
out from under the bed and leap up to be with her. No doubt he'd
been scared of Lucas.

"You were here for only a second and then you left."

She felt a little better. "Oh yeah. I realized what was happening.
I didn't mean to disturb you."

"I wouldn't have been disturbed," he said, sounding disappointed.
"I thought maybe you'd come to me because you needed something."

"No. I'm still learning how the dreamscaping works. I woke
up . . . there."

He paused. "So you don't need me?"

"No. I'm fine." She closed her eyes and tried not to let the caring
sound of his voice lure her into wanting things she couldn't have. He
was with Ellie now. Or maybe not with Ellie. It didn't matter. What
did matter was that he'd ended their relationship. He hadn't even

wanted to try to fix whatever it was that made it hard for him to be with her.

And she'd moved on. She was with Lucas—maybe not actually going out, but practically. And he'd been here for her. He wanted to be here for her.

"Okay, I just . . . wanted to check on you. I do care about you, Kylie." His voice dropped, and for a moment he sounded like the old Derek. The Derek who'd cared about her. The Derek who'd have done anything to make her happy. "You know that, don't you?"

She swallowed before answering. "Yeah," she said honestly. "I care about you, too." And then she forced herself to ask, "How's Ellie doing?"

He was quiet for a second, as if he knew what she was doing. Reminding him that they were just friends. "She's good. Adapting."

"Good," Kylie said. "I met her briefly the other day. She seems nice." *And very pretty.* She bit down on her lip.

"She is nice," he said.

"Yeah. Well, I'm happy for you." Kylie wasn't sure how true it was, but she wanted it to be true, and for that reason it didn't feel like that big of a lie.

"I told you we're not really together," he said, sounding frustrated.

"Yeah," she said, and when he didn't say anything else, she decided to do the right thing. "I need to go. I'm supposed to call Holiday."

"Okay," he said.

She disconnected the call and pushed away the melancholy. She did need to call Holiday, and then she had to figure out what the ghost had meant her to learn from the vision.

Even though she was sleep-deprived, Kylie called her mom first thing the next morning. She had to know what happened.

"So?" Kylie dropped back on the bed.

"So, what?" Her mom sounded as if she were still sleeping.

"Was it a business lunch or a date lunch?"

"Oh. It was . . ." Her mom's pause told Kylie more than her mom probably wanted to share. "It was fun."

"How fun?" Kylie tried not to let her emotions leak into her voice as she knotted a handful of sheet in her hand.

"Just fun. I enjoyed myself, that's all. I don't mean . . . It's not as if . . . Look, baby, we had a good time, but I'm not sure anything will come of it."

"He didn't ask you out again?" Kylie petted Socks, who had jumped up to get some attention.

"He said he'd call. But you know men always say that. And they never do."

Kylie tightened her hold on her phone. "If he calls, will you go out with him?"

"I don't know," her mom said. "Oh, someone's knocking on the front door. I'd better run." The line went dead.

Kylie sighed. She had a sneaking suspicion nobody was at the door. Her mom just didn't want to talk about it. Not that she could blame her.

Seconds ticked by, but Kylie didn't move. She just lay there, stretched out on her twin mattress, staring up at the ceiling. Ambivalence filled her chest. Did this mean her mom and her stepdad would never get back together?

A quick shower later, Kylie walked out of the bathroom with a towel around her to find Miranda standing attentively in the hall, as if waiting on her.

"What's up?" Kylie asked.

"I'm your shadow," Miranda announced proudly.

"I thought Della—"

"You don't think I can protect you?" She held out her pinky. "I have powers, girlie."

Actually, Kylie had doubts about Miranda's protecting abilities, but she wouldn't dare say that. "No, I just remember Burnett saying it was Della this morning."

"She went to her sunrise ceremony and I'm supposed to get you to the office, where Della will meet us in about five minutes. So let's go."

Kylie looked down at her towel. "Can I get dressed first?"

"Someone's not a morning person this fine day." Miranda made a funny face, and Kylie took off to her room to get dressed.

A few minutes later, they walked out the cabin door. Miranda turned back to the door, waved her arms around, and began to chant. The last time Miranda did that, she felt unwanted visitors; it turned out Mario and Red had been hanging out, watching Kylie.

"What are you doing?" Kylie asked. "Do you sense someone's here again?"

Miranda frowned. "A little." She pinched her right thumb and forefinger together.

"A little?" Annoyance snaked through Kylie. "How can you sense someone here just a little? I mean, they're either here or not, right?"

"Don't wig out on me," Miranda said. "I just got a feeling and I thought it couldn't hurt to do a protection spell."

"Have you told Burnett?" Kylie asked.

"I was going to but I'm kind of scared to talk to him alone after . . ." She flushed. "You know."

The memory of a marsupial Burnett hopping around the dining hall, dodging Clark's fireballs and Perry's dragon breath, flashed across Kylie's mind. Hence, part of the reason Kylie doubted Miranda's ability to protect her.

"Anyway," Miranda went on, "you said Holiday would be back today. So I figure I'll just tell her then."

Kylie rolled her eyes and wanted to point out that if Miranda was right and there were intruders, Burnett needed to know ASAP, but she bit her tongue. A few hours probably wouldn't matter all that much. Besides, Miranda had a point; she was in a bad mood this morning, and it wasn't fair to take it out on Miranda.

As for why Kylie was in a bad mood, well, she figured her bad mood probably hinged on the fact that she was running on only a few hours' sleep. She and Holiday had spent almost an hour on the phone talking last night. They'd discussed everything from Holiday's aunt's passing to Kylie's vision and what it could and couldn't mean. When Kylie asked her about the healing powers and the whole "giving up a piece of her soul" issue, Holiday suggested they wait until they could talk about it when she got back today.

Kylie had almost told Holiday about her misgivings with Burnett over the FRU library card issue but decided to wait and discuss that in person, too.

Miranda did one more wave over the door, pulling Kylie back to the present.

"Do you mind if I tell Burnett?" Kylie asked Miranda.

Miranda made a face but then said, "Fine. But I'm telling you, it's just a feeling. It's not nearly as strong as the last time I had one. It might not be anything."

"Or it could be something," Kylie said. And since that something probably had to do with her, it made her a wee bit nervous. And face it, she had enough to be nervous about.

Kylie stood in front of the heavy, creaky-looking rusted gates of the Fallen Cemetery. Burnett stood to her right—and Della held her spot to her left. Neither vampire looked especially happy to be there.

She couldn't blame them. She wasn't all that thrilled about it herself. But after experiencing the vision sent by Jane Doe, Kylie was more eager than ever to get this spirit sent on her way.

"You sure you want to do this?" Della asked, her voice laced with fear.

Kylie nodded, but in truth she wasn't sure about anything anymore. She took a look around. If Hollywood ever needed a set for a horror film, this was it. As if to prove her point, a gust of wind picked up and the gate swayed and creaked. The eerie sound filled the air.

Air that should have brought with it a sunny mood to match the morning. Above them, blue, cloudless skies promised a picture-perfect day filled with cheer. A vibrant sun beamed down and set the last of the night's dew in a sparkle. And yet nothing felt sunny, vibrant, or cheery.

To the contrary, it felt cold—so cold that Kylie's skin crawled with goose bumps. Della let go of a deep breath and steam billowed from her lips.

"I used to hang out in cemeteries sometimes," Della said. "They never felt like this." She hugged herself against the chill.

"The dead don't disturb humans nearly as much as they do supernaturals," Burnett said. Even his voice sounded hesitant. He looked at Kylie. "If you're at all worried about doing this, just say the word and wait until Holiday is here."

Kylie considered it and then remembered the pain, grief, and confusion the ghost had felt. Jane Doe needed answers as much as Kylie did.

"No. I'm fine."

"You're lying," Della said.

"I know." Kylie looked at her and then over to Burnett. "You guys don't have to come inside."

"We don't?" Hope filled Della's voice.

"The hell we don't," Burnett snapped, and took a step forward. "If you're determined to do this, let's get it over with."

Chapter Nineteen

As soon as they crossed into the grounds of the Fallen Cemetery, a big gust of wind slammed the gate shut behind them.

Kylie started. Della jumped and growled, exposing her elongated canines. Burnett didn't move, but his eyes glowed a bright yellow.

"Don't worry," he muttered. "I can knock the gate down if I have to."

Della looked at Kylie. "I do not see why you feel compelled to do this."

Kylie looked from Della to Burnett. "Can I have some space? I need it to communicate with them."

She hated having to lie, but she hoped the offer of space would alleviate the hardship of their having to accompany her into the graveyard. She knew they didn't want to be here. It seemed crazy, but supernaturals hated all things related to ghosts. At least maybe the coldness she always felt when a ghost was present wouldn't bite into them the way she knew it would take a chomp out of her.

"Yes, go ahead, but don't go so far that we can't see you," said Burnett.

Considering that Kylie had yet to tell Burnett about Miranda's "little feeling," she didn't mind him keeping a close visual on her.

Not that right now she worried about Mario and his grandson. Right now, it was the whispered voices Kylie heard that concerned her.

Looking at the graveled paths between row after row of graves, she let her eyes shift from tombstone to tombstone, hoping one of them would call out to her. Some graves had small concrete or marble markers with just names and dates inscribed on them. Others were ornate statues. Some looked new; others were painted with mold and time. Some had vines clinging to the arms and legs of angel and saintlike figures, as if trying to claim them from deep beneath the earth where only the dead lived.

She couldn't see any of the ghosts yet, but she could hear them. They all talked at once. Chattering. Like two or three radios left on at the same time, but with tons of static. If they were speaking to one another or to her, she wasn't sure.

Some of the voices felt as if they were a block away, others felt as if their owners stood so close that Kylie could touch them if she moved her hand. Not that she wanted to touch them. Their cold already surrounded her, reaching for her like hands trying to warm themselves against a fire.

Kylie realized in a way that was what she was to them. She was like a fire, something that drew them. She was life. Probably the only life that they had been able to feel in a long time. Or maybe the only life that could feel them.

Footsteps sounded and Kylie looked to her right down the opposite path. An old man, his cane in his hand, shuffled between the row of grave sites. For a second, Kylie didn't know to which world he belonged.

But then she noticed Burnett and Della twitching their brows at him. Kylie did the same and was not surprised when his brain pattern revealed he was human. All of a sudden, an elderly woman of the same age appeared behind him. Her gray hair was long and thin and hung without luster at her shoulders. She wore one of those housedresses Kylie's grandmother had always worn. This one was a blue paisley print. On her feet were a pair of baby blue slippers.

It took only a second for Kylie to realize that she was not of this world.

"You're not taking your meds like you should be, are you?" she said to the old man. *"I can tell because your ankles are swollen. You're supposed to take the little red pills twice a day, not the blue ones. What are you trying to do? Kill yourself? You promised me you'd take care of yourself. Why won't you ever listen to me?"*

Then the woman shifted her gaze and stared right at Kylie. Her aged gray eyes widened, then she vanished. Kylie hadn't taken her next breath when the woman materialized inches from her. Her skin was a dead gray color that matched her eyes. Her hair, only a slightly different shade of gray, got caught in the wind, and it swept up and floated almost motionlessly in the air around her head.

"Mother of God, you can see me," the elderly woman said.

The spirit's nearness brought more chills running down Kylie's spine. But the drop in temperature wasn't nearly as disturbing as the sudden silence.

The chattering of spirits had stopped. The only noise in the cemetery was the sound of the old man's footsteps. His shoes scrubbed against the gravel with his faltered steps while his cane tapped down on the earth, searching for a steady spot to rest his thick stick to support himself.

Tap, tap. Shuffle. Tap, tap. Shuffle. Tap, Shuffle.

Kylie sensed more than heard Burnett and Della move back. She'd asked for this space, but now she regretted it. Maybe she didn't want to be alone. But did she regret it enough to admit her fear? She knew someone like Burnett respected courage, and Kylie didn't want to come up short.

"Answer me, girl! You can see me, right?" The old woman waved a hand in front of Kylie's face.

She held her breath. The silence seemed to grow louder. The lack of chatter meant something. It meant the spirits were listening. Waiting for her to answer. Waiting to see if she admitted to being able to see one of their own.

Suddenly the air she pulled into her lungs grew so cold that it hurt. They, the silent spirits, were moving in. She couldn't see them, couldn't even hear them, but she could feel them. The cold increased tenfold.

Fear turned her stomach hard. She felt the thinnest layer of ice form on her lips. For a second, she questioned the wisdom of being here. Could she pretend she hadn't heard the woman? Was it too late to look away from the desperation of the elderly spirit?

"Tell him he needs to take two of the little red pills."

Kylie still didn't speak. Frost formed on the tips of her eyelashes, blurring her vision.

"He's going to get to meet our first great-grandchild. For years, all he's talked about was living until he saw his third generation make it into the world. But if he doesn't start taking his pills right, he'll never make it."

Suddenly, the other spirits started materializing around her. Ten, then twenty. Then more. And when they slowly inched closer, Kylie's heart raced with panic. She considered running, but could she outrun them?

"Can she hear us?" asked an older-sounding male spirit.

"Can she see us?" added a younger female spirit, crowding closer.

"Y'all are being silly," came another male spirit's voice. *"The living can't see us no more."*

"But this one can," argued the younger female spirit. *"Look at her."*

The spirits started to move closer.

"Do you think she can help us?" a female asked.

"Maybe," someone else said.

The older male spirit peered into Kylie's face. *"What is she?"*

The spirits crushed closer. A barrage of new questions started spilling out of their mouths, each talking so rapidly that it was hard to distinguish one voice from the other. The sound was so loud, Kylie fought the need to cover her ears. She couldn't remember what Holiday had said about the rules of shutting out the voices. Was it too late to attempt to shut them out?

"You looking for a particular plot?" The words seeped into Kylie's hearing and bounced around her panicked brain. It took a minute to realize that this male voice was different from the rest. The words were not from the dead, but from the living.

Kylie managed to look over and saw the old man walking toward her between two large tombstones. His cane pushed holes through the green grass into the moist dirt. Each time he pulled the tip of the walking stick from the ground, it created a squishing sound that seemed too loud.

Remembering she wasn't completely alone, Kylie glanced around and spotted Burnett standing at the end of the row, watching, ready to pounce in case the elderly gentleman posed any danger.

Little did Burnett know it wasn't him she feared, but all the others he could not see. The old man continued toward her. His presence brought a wave of calm that lessened the chaos sizzling in her blood. The closer he came, the farther back the spirits moved.

Kylie touched the tip of her tongue to the melting frost across her bottom lip and blinked away the shiny crystals of ice from her lashes.

"You look lost," he said again, coming to a stop a few feet away from her.

Thankful his presence had brought her some reprieve, she tried to smile, but the gesture seemed to fail.

"Cat got your tongue, child?" he asked.

"No," Kylie answered. Realizing she hadn't answered his initial question, she searched for a believable-sounding lie. "Yes, I'm looking . . . for my aunt's grave."

"What's her name? I should be able to point you in the right direction. Lord knows I've walked these grounds enough. I'm here daily, visiting my Ima."

"I'm Ima," said the man's dead wife, and she came closer and peered into Kylie's face.

Kylie hesitated and then glanced to her right and read the tombstone. "Lolita Cannon. That's my aunt's name." She still didn't know if she should acknowledge the dead man's wife or not. Kylie's heart beat around in her chest with indecision. But if she didn't tell the man about his medicine, he could—

"Why, I think that grave is right around here somewhere." He turned and started looking, pointing his cane at the markers as he read.

"Are you sure she can see and hear us?" Another spirit appeared. Kylie glanced at the newcomer briefly, trying not to give away that she could see anyone. This spirit was another woman, younger, late twenties, wearing a dress that looked like something popular in the 1970s.

"I'm pretty sure," answered Ima, and then she leaned so close that her icy presence burned Kylie's arm. *"Tell him about his medicines,"* she pleaded. *"If not, he's gonna pass without ever seeing his third generation."*

"Here, right here." The old man pointed with his cane and waved for Kylie to follow him.

"Thank you," Kylie said, stopping at his side and still wavering on what to do.

"It's a nice marker," the old man said, and had to use his cane to get his balance. "Well, I should be going. Enjoy your time with her." He started to take a step and then paused. "You know, I somehow feel my Ima can hear me, so go ahead and talk to your aunt if you have anything you want to say to her."

The man's wife held up her hands as if frustrated. *"I can hear ya, old man. But it's you that don't listen to a word I say. Don't know why it surprises me."* The woman looked back at Kylie again. *"The ol' fart never listened to me when I was alive. And he's talked to me more since I've been dead than when I was alive. But I love the ol' coot. And you gotta help me help him. Please, missy. I don't know what you are, or how come you can see me, but I'm begging ya."*

Kylie watched the old man take a few steps away from her. If she told him, she knew the barrage of spirits would return, but if she didn't . . . Kylie wouldn't be able to live with herself if something happened to the old guy. "Wait, sir. I . . ."

He turned around.

Crap! How was she going to tell him? "I . . . I couldn't help but notice you're a little shaky. You know, this happened to my aunt and it was caused by a mix-up in her meds. She was taking the wrong pills twice a day. The blue ones instead of the red ones."

The man's dead wife let out a victory yelp. The younger woman beside her stared at Kylie with complete awe. *"She can hear us. Jiminy Cricket. She can. My name's Catherine. What's your name?"*

The same look of amazement flooding across the younger ghost's face now filled the old man's expression. "Why, child, I . . . I swear you might have . . . I mean, Ima was always telling me to be careful. And I have been feeling not so good lately. I think I'll go home and check my prescription." Then he turned and headed toward the gate.

Kylie forced a smile, even though the chatter was now louder than ever since all the spirits knew the truth. Knew she could hear them. Knew she could help them. But could she? So far all the spirits came to her for help, but could she help those she accidentally came into contact with?

Just as the old man turned to leave, another wave of cold landed beside her. Jane Doe's ghost materialized. She looked at Kylie as if confused. *"What are you doing here?"*

"Isn't this where you are buried?" Kylie asked, struggling to ignore the cold and the noise.

"You say something?" The old man turned back around. His words were almost lost in the loud chattering again.

"Just to myself," Kylie answered, and prayed he'd turn around before she . . . A wave of dizziness almost overtook her. She struggled to remain standing.

The spirits had moved in again, surrounded her, all talking at once. Wanting her to do something for them. Asking her questions. Her gaze flipped from one dead face to another. Her heart felt heavy with sadness for them. It made her realize how insignificant she was—one person and so many souls needing something.

The wave of dizziness crashed over her again, only harder this time. Her head started pounding—pain exploded behind her eyes. Hugging herself against the cold, she lowered herself onto the green grass, wrapped her arms around her shins, and dropped her forehead on top of her knees.

"I can't do this," she muttered.

"Move back," Jane Doe said. *"You are hurting her."*

Kylie felt some of the cold begin to ebb, the pain behind her eyelids lessened, and she could only assume the ghost had been talking to the other spirits. The noise level lowered almost to the point where it didn't hurt to listen anymore.

"Are you okay?" Burnett's deep, concerned voice came at her ear.

Kylie raised her head and saw the only spirits remaining were Jane Doe, the old man's wife, and the other younger spirit.

Kylie looked at Burnett. "Yeah. I'm fine. Or getting better," she said.

Burnett nodded and then backed away. Kylie stared at Jane Doe and waited a few more seconds before she asked, "Isn't this where you're buried?"

Jane's brow wrinkled in that confused way of hers. *"I . . . don't know."*

"Oh, phooey!" said the younger woman who'd said her name was Catherine. *"Of course you're buried here. Your grave and marker are right over there. You were put in the ground by the Texas prison system. You'd been given life for killing your own baby."*

Chapter Twenty

Shock filled Kylie's chest. Jane had killed her baby? Was that why Jane had amnesia? The horror of what she'd done had been too much for her to bear?

Jane swerved toward Catherine and held both her fists up in front of her face, her body tight with fury. *"How many times do I have to tell you that I'm not Berta! I did not kill my own child. I would never kill my baby. I loved my baby."*

Catherine looked at Kylie. *"She's confused. I think they gave her a lobotomy. Probably trying to fix her."*

"I'm not Berta!" Jane Doe's scream rang so loud, Kylie flinched. *"And I'm sick to death of hearing you call me that."*

"Then what's your name?" Catherine spouted back.

Jane got tears in her eyes. *"I don't know. I don't know who I am, I don't know what I am, but I know who I'm not. And I'm not Berta Littlemon. I think my baby died, but I didn't kill it. I was somebody's wife. Now I'm just lost. And empty. And dead."* She turned and looked at Kylie as if remembering the vision. *"Somebody killed me."* Tears slipped down the woman's cheek and then she disappeared.

Kylie's chest filled with empathy. She got back to her feet, and while she felt inclined to believe Jane Doe, she'd come here to find answers. And to find them, she had to ask questions. "Why do you think she's Berta Littlemon?"

"*I don't think, I know,*" Catherine said. Then she smiled, "*And I'll tell you all I know if you'll do me a favor.*"

Kylie still stood by the grave of Berta Littlemon when Burnett walked over to join her about thirty minutes later. This time, he didn't inquire if she was okay. But then, he didn't have to ask. Kylie sensed he could guess she wasn't okay by the look of dismay on her face. Placing his hand lightly on her shoulder, he asked, "Was this . . . helpful?"

"I don't know," Kylie said, confused and disturbed by what she'd learned from Catherine O'Connell. Sure, she'd gotten some information, but mostly all the trip to the Fallen Cemetery had accomplished was to underscore how little she knew about Jane Doe and how impossible it would be to help her.

"Are you ready to go?" he asked.

She nodded and they started walking toward the gate where Della stood, looking as ill at ease as she had the moment they'd first arrived. The crowd of spirits followed them, moving close but not crowding her.

"*Will you come back?*" whispered an older-sounding male spirit.

"*Please, say you'll come,*" begged a younger female spirit.

"*It's not fair,*" wailed another female. "*Why does she have to leave now? I didn't get a chance to talk to her!*"

Then all of the spirits began to talk at once, making it hard to understand them and bringing Kylie's headache back in full force. Through the crowd of voices, she was dimly aware of Ima, the old man's wife, walking from one small group of spirits to another and whispering something to them.

Kylie stopped and massaged her temples. "I'm sorry," she said, and she truly was.

Right now, all she wanted to do was run from them, run into the sunlight, ignore the shadows and pretend that they didn't exist. But even as she wanted to run away, she knew she couldn't. How could she when she felt their pain, their heartbreak, as intensely as she did her own? How could she when she knew they all had some kind of unfinished business they wanted resolved and she was their only chance to make that happen?

Still, she had to establish some boundaries or else she'd likely lose her mind the way Jane Doe obviously had.

And then Kylie wouldn't be able to help any of them.

"I have to leave now," she said. "You can't come with me. You need to stay here. But . . . I will come back. I promise." It was a promise she intended to keep, but not one she looked forward to.

"I'm not coming back," Della said, and walked toward the car.

Burnett shot Kylie a worried look and she shook her head, indicating that she was fine. When they stepped out of the cemetery property and the spirits didn't follow, Kylie sighed with relief. She'd never appreciated the blast of Texas heat that swamped her as much as she did right now.

She glanced behind her at the cemetery. The spirits were still there, staring at her wordlessly. She wondered if her promise had been enough to convince them to stay behind, rather than follow her. Or if it had more to do with whatever message Ima had been whispering to them. Kylie felt a shiver move down her spine. She ignored it and walked with Burnett and Della to the car.

The drive back to Shadow Falls was short. They didn't speak. After Burnett parked, Kylie and Della crawled out of his black Mustang. Kylie locked her gaze with Burnett and asked if she could be relieved from camp activities for the rest of the day.

He hesitated and she was frightened he was going to say no, but then he frowned and asked, "Would Holiday say yes?"

Kylie nodded. "Yes," she answered with honesty. Helping ghosts was part of her job as a supernatural. Holiday would understand that, and the toll it took on her. The camp leader was probably the only one who would understand.

Burnett still paused. "Are you okay? Do you need to talk or anything?"

"No," Kylie said.

The relief showing in his face was almost comical. Obviously the idea of having to offer advice or commiserate about spirits didn't appeal to him. Kylie might have teased him about it if she weren't so wrapped up in what she'd learned. "I just want to do some stuff on my computer and check some of the facts I learned."

"Okay," he said, and motioned Della to follow her.

"Please don't ever ask me to go back there again," Della said as they walked away. "That was super weird."

"I'm sorry," Kylie said.

"Did you learn what you needed to know?"

"Not really."

"Didn't they answer your questions? I heard you talking to them."

"It's not that easy."

For a second, Della looked ready to ask more questions; then she lapsed into silence.

Good thing, too. Kylie wasn't feeling up to explaining how communicating with the dead worked. Right now, she needed to focus on what she'd learned from her trip. She hadn't even begun to mull everything over and decide what she believed and didn't believe.

Was Jane, or was she not, a child murderer and all-around evil person? Anxious to prove Catherine O'Connell wrong, Kylie hurried her steps.

She cut through the first bend in the path, where the trees hung over, creating shade. She breathed in the scents of summer, the greenness of the forest, the heady aroma of dry earth. She had almost managed to calm her chaotic mind when the blue bird swooped down and landed right in her path. The blue jay cocked its head and chirped cheerfully as if performing just for her.

"Shoo!" Della said. But the bird, intent on watching Kylie, ignored Della.

"Shit!" Della belted out. "Is that the evil shifter?" When she started to bolt forward—to do God only knew what to the bird—Kylie caught her by her arm.

"Stop. It's just a bird."

Della's eyes widened. "Is that the same bird you . . . brought back to life?"

"I don't know," Kylie said, but she knew it was a lie.

Della waved her arms, trying to scare the bird away. "This is freaky." The bird continued to sing.

"Get out of here before I break your neck!" Della bellowed.

"Just leave it alone." Truth was, the bird scared the crap out of Kylie, too, but it didn't deserve to die. Or to die again.

Besides, Kylie wasn't up to giving it another piece of her soul by bringing it back to life.

The bird finally finished its song, then flapped its wings and rose to hover in front of Kylie's face. A spray of sunshine came through the trees and made the creature's royal blue feathers glow. Then, letting out one more bit of song, it flew away. Kylie took off in a run and didn't slow down until she got to her cabin. Della followed at the same pace. Maybe after Kylie researched Berta Littlemon, she'd research blue jay stalking. Though she doubted Google would have anything on that.

"So you actually spoke to the spirits?" Jonathon asked. The vamp had taken over shadow duty for Della right after they'd arrived back at the cabin. Of course, first Della had given him the blow-by-blow account of what had happened at the cemetery. Kylie looked back at Jonathon, reclining on her sofa.

"Can I do this computer stuff right now, instead of chatting about the ghosts?" She'd been proud of herself. Instead of giving in to the desire to go straight to bed, pull the covers over her head, and have a good long cry, she'd booted up her computer.

Her screen brought up Google, and she typed in the name "Berta Littlemon." As the computer chewed on that information, Kylie looked back at Jonathon again. "I just need to get this done."

"Whatever." His tone told her he thought she was rude.

And maybe she was, but with a possible child-murdering ghost on her hands and a blue jay stalking her, she didn't have time to be polite. "Sorry," she still muttered.

Kylie read the list of Web sites that Google spilled onto her screen: *Famous female murderers in Texas, Mamas who murder, Mean women in the past.* Kylie's heart started to ache. She clicked on the first Web site and prepared herself to be disgusted.

She wasn't disappointed. The only thing she didn't find was a decent picture of Berta Littlemon that was clear enough to identify her.

"Some shadow you are, vampire."

Kylie swung around and found Lucas standing in the doorway, staring at Jonathon sleeping on the sofa.

Jonathon didn't move. He didn't even open his eyes when he spoke. "I heard you a block away. Smelled your wolf ass two blocks away."

Lucas growled.

Kylie rolled her eyes. Ah, the love between vamps and weres was never lost. For a crazy moment, she recalled Lucas's desire that she turn out to be a were. And she wondered what would happen if and when he discovered he was wrong. What would happen if she discovered she was vampire? Would Lucas still care about her? She so wanted to believe that it wouldn't matter to him, that he was above that type of prejudice.

But the truth was, she knew it probably would matter.

And that scared her more than stalking blue jays and amnesiac ghosts who possibly killed their own babies.

Lucas shifted his focus from Jonathon to her. "Are you okay?"

Kylie took a deep breath. She'd felt that hiding her weakness from Burnett had been a necessity. Nor had she felt comfortable sharing anything with Della or Jonathon, but one look at Lucas's caring blue eyes and she felt her throat tighten with the need for a little TLC.

He must have sensed her stress, or maybe it was the tears prickling her eyes, because he moved to her, grabbed her hand, and started walking her into her bedroom.

"I'm supposed to keep an eye on her," Jonathon called out from his still reclined position on the sofa.

"Why don't you just check out the back of your eyelids like you were doing when I came in," Lucas countered, and slammed her bedroom door shut. The cabin shook from the force.

Once they were alone, Lucas's gaze went back to her. "What happened?" He moved in, cupped his hand around her neck, and pulled her against him.

She rested her forehead on his warm chest and fought the need to cry. The need for TLC was one thing, but tears were too much.

"It was awful," she said, and swallowed hard.

"What was awful?" he asked.

"They were everywhere. And then—"

"Who were everywhere?" His hand moved to her back, consoling and offering just the comforting touch she needed.

Her heart hurt with the need to have someone help her understand the experience. She lifted her head and looked at him, but she didn't pull away. "The spirits. But that wasn't the worst part. I—"

He let go of another frustrated growl, cutting her off. Then he studied her for a second as if weighing his words with care. "Didn't you expect them to be everywhere at a cemetery, Kylie? After what happened in that vision, why you would even go there is beyond me."

Okay, so Lucas was like the others; he didn't understand what she did. She couldn't really blame him, though. Just as Della had pointed out this morning, ghost whispering pretty much made her a freak. Still, it hurt.

She wanted him to understand, to be able to sense how important this was to her. But he couldn't. He wasn't . . . fae. He wasn't Derek. Not wanting to go there, she pushed that thought away, far away.

"I had to," she said, though she didn't think it would make a difference to Lucas. "That's what I'm supposed to do. That's why they come to me for help."

He frowned. "But at what cost? I don't like seeing you upset like this. I sure as hell don't like thinking you're putting yourself in danger to help someone who's already dead. For all we know, they're dead because they did something stupid and now they're gonna try to make you do something stupid and you could end up getting hurt as a result."

His tone, his expression, and even his body posture told Kylie that telling him that her ghost very well may be a murderer of small children might not be a brilliant idea. So she resigned herself to her current reality. She'd just have to bundle up the rest of the story until Holiday arrived. Which Kylie hoped would be soon.

"Damn, I hate seeing you upset," he muttered through gritted teeth, and then tugged her closer.

She bit down on her lip, remembering how it had felt when it had been coated with ice. "It was a little scary, but nothing happened."

He lifted her chin and gazed into her eyes. "You sure?"

Not wanting to lie to him, she rose up on tiptoes and kissed him. He tasted so good—a little like toothpaste and a bit like chocolate. She'd always been fond of chocolate mint, so she opened her mouth wider and he accepted the invitation and the kiss went from sweet to passionate in a heartbeat.

When his tongue slipped inside her mouth, she melted against him even closer, and any remnants of worry in her heart faded. All Kylie could think about was the wonder of this moment. The wonder of passion.

She loved having him this close to her. The silky feel of his mouth against hers was so perfect. The slight stubble on his cheeks tickled her, and his hard chest pressed against hers as though it were made to fit. She savored the tight feel of his strong hands on her waist. A voice deep within said she could deal with anything, stalking blue jays, a barrage of ghosts, even the amnesiac spirit of a child murderer. She could take it all on as long as she had Lucas's arms and kisses waiting for her when it was over. She could survive as long as she had the wonderment of his closeness to help her cope.

"Someone lives and someone dies."

The voice came at the same time as the chill crawling up and then down her spine. Kylie pulled away from the hot kiss and buried her face on Lucas's warm chest, not wanting to feel this cold. Not now. Not so soon after the visit to the cemetery and the haunting memory of all those lost souls who needed her help. Not when she'd just read the terrible things this woman had done.

"They keep insisting that I tell you," Jane, aka Berta, said.

Who dies? Kylie asked the question in her mind.

"Maybe they meant me," the spirit said, sounding confused again.

Somehow Kylie knew that wasn't right. *Someone lives and someone dies.* The words flowed again through her head. Perhaps there was one thing Lucas's kisses couldn't fix. The idea of losing someone she cared about was too much to bear.

Lifting her cheek from Lucas's warm chest, she opened her eyes and tried to focus on Jane Doe.

Staring at the spirit's face, Kylie recalled bits of the story she'd read about Berta Littlemon. She hadn't killed just her own child, but that of a neighbor, too.

The spirit gazed back at Kylie without reservation. No worries.

No shame. Had the woman forgotten about what happened at the cemetery, that Catherine had ratted her out—that Kylie now knew everything?

But even now, as Kylie looked deep into the spirit's eyes, she didn't see the soul of a killer. She saw the soul of a woman who was lost, forgotten, and needed her help.

What, if anything, did this mean? Kylie wondered.

Chapter Twenty-one

An hour later, Lucas left to go to a hiking class and Kylie continued her online research. She'd read most of the articles on the Web sites containing information about Berta Littlemon. She'd also done a quick search on Catherine O'Connell, the woman who'd ratted on Jane. Not just because Kylie intended to keep her promise to her—a deal was a deal—but because she wanted to know if the woman was honest.

Kylie's quick search on the information Catherine had given her proved to be true. But did that also mean she was right about Jane Doe?

So far, she'd found one other site that had a picture of Berta Littlemon, but it too had been so fuzzy that Kylie couldn't swear it was her Jane Doe. Sure, she had brown hair and it appeared to have been long at one time, and the facial features were similar, but . . . there was still hope.

A lot more hope when Kylie vaguely remembered something that Holiday had told her about spirits who were overall bad.

Almost as if thinking the woman's name had worked magic, Kylie heard Holiday's voice.

"Can I come in?"

Kylie saw Jonathon jerk from a dead sleep, then she bolted from her chair, ran across the living room, and threw her arms around Holiday.

"I'm so glad you're home," Kylie said, releasing the camp leader only after a good long hug. She'd missed talking with Holiday, missed having her around. But Kylie probably missed Holiday's hugs most of all. "I have so many things to ask you, to tell you." She was about to dump her emotional trauma on the woman when Kylie suddenly remembered the reason Holiday had been away. Her aunt had died. And the death had rocked Holiday's world to its core.

Maybe, Kylie realized, Holiday already had enough on her plate and didn't need Kylie to add more.

Kylie paused a moment to catch her breath. "Are you okay? I'm so sorry about your aunt. Did you get things settled?"

"I'm fine." Holiday gripped Kylie's shoulders as if she understood Kylie's thoughts. "And yes, I think I managed to get everything in order. The important question is if you're okay. Are you?"

Jonathon sat up on the sofa, looking half-asleep. Holiday must not have seen him earlier because she jumped a little at the sound of him shifting.

"Oh, Jonathon. You startled me." Holiday stared at the sleepy vampire.

"Do I need to stay here now that you're here?" he asked.

Holiday looked at her watch. "I should be here for an hour, and Della will be back before that, so if you want to go, you can." They watched Jonathon leave, then Holiday draped an arm around Kylie's shoulder. "Now, tell me what's going on with you."

Kylie met her gaze. "Are you sure you can handle this?"

"Is it that bad?" Holiday's brows creased with worry.

"No. Well, yeah, it is, but I mean, can you handle my problems right now with your own?" Kylie looked at Holiday with empathy. "I know what it feels like to lose someone. When my grandmother died, I could hardly breathe."

Holiday smiled. "I'm fine. I'm still grieving a bit," she added honestly. "But let's just say I'm using the Kylie Galen method of dealing with my problems."

"Which is what?" Kylie asked, puzzled.

Holiday grinned. "Concentrating on everyone else's problems, so I don't have time to think about mine." She looked Kylie right in the eye. "Seriously, I'm fine. Now, tell me what you learned at the cemetery. And then we have a lot of things to discuss."

Kylie started walking over to the kitchen table and then remembered the imminent question she'd wanted to ask Holiday. She swung back around.

"One thing first. Didn't you tell me one time that really bad souls don't hang around, that hell claims them pretty quickly?"

"In most cases, that's right. But there are some that . . ." Worry pinched Holiday's brows together. "Why?"

Kylie frowned, and just like that, all the frustration from earlier landed on her shoulders with a big thump. "Why does everything have to have exceptions? It would be so nice to ask a question and get a definite yes or no. It's either black or white." She dropped into a kitchen chair. "Life would be so much easier."

"Easier, yes. But realistic . . . no. Few things are ever black or white." Holiday tilted her head to one side and studied Kylie for a moment, then frowned. "Please tell me you haven't gotten mixed up with a hell-bound spirit."

Fifteen minutes later, Kylie sat beside Holiday as she read the different articles about Berta Littlemon on the computer screen.

"That's it. I can't read any more!" Holiday reached over and turned off the computer "You shouldn't even being reading this. You are not to deal with this spirit anymore." Something about Holiday's tone, so maternal, so un-negotiating, sent up warning flags all over the place.

"We don't know it's even her," Kylie said. "I can't just assume she—"

"Yes, you can! You said the other ghost told you that your Jane Doe rose from the grave of Berta Littlemon. That's good enough for me."

Kylie frowned. "Yeah, but maybe she's lying. And you saw the pictures of Berta. They are fuzzy. I mean, yes, they sort of resemble my Jane Doe, but they're not clear enough for me to be sure."

"Okay, but why would the ghost lie?"

Kylie shrugged. "Because if she didn't have information that sounded useful, she might have been afraid I wouldn't have agreed to help her."

"Wait—help who? The old man's wife?"

Kylie realized she'd obviously left out that part of the story when she'd explained everything to Holiday. "No, the other ghost. Catherine O'Connell. I agreed to help her if she'd tell me what she knows about Jane Doe."

"No," Holiday said, and put her palms over her face.

"No, what?"

Holiday moved her hands. "You never make a deal with a spirit, Kylie. Never!"

"Why?" Kylie asked.

"Because it can be as bad as making a deal with the devil. What they want is sometimes impossible, and they can be relentless about making us pay up. If they think you haven't delivered on your promise, things can get ugly."

Kylie felt her throat tighten. She had looked forward to Holiday's return so much, and now it seemed all Kylie was going to get were reprimands. "I didn't know," she muttered.

Holiday released a deep sigh. "I'm sorry," she said, and dropped her hands on top of Kylie's. "I didn't mean to snap at you. This is my fault. All of it. I knew that your going to the cemetery was a bad idea. I should have vetoed it right off the bat."

Kylie swallowed the tightness down her throat, which had seemed to lessen somewhat with Holiday's touch. "It wasn't a bad idea. And maybe I shouldn't have made a deal with Catherine, but even that doesn't seem so bad. I mean, what she wants is doable and for a good cause."

Holiday shook her head, still looking too unrelenting. "It's still not a good idea to make a deal with a spirit."

"Yeah, but all she wants is for me to send some family history stuff to her kids. She's Jewish and she lied to them and her own husband all her life because back then, being a Jew wasn't so cool. Her parents died in the concentration camps and her grandparents managed to bring her to the U.S. She changed her name. And now, it feels like a lie."

Holiday shook her head. "Kylie, I'm sorry, but I can't let you do this."

"No." Kylie stood up, and although she kept her voice low, even she heard the determination in her tone. "I'm sorry, but I'm not going to stop any of this because you're afraid I'm in over my head. Because you don't think I can handle it. I'm helping Jane Doe, and I'm sorry, but I don't believe she's this murderer, and I'm also going to help Catherine O'Connell. It's the right thing to do."

Holiday closed her eyes in frustration. "Kylie, you don't understand how dangerous this could be for you. There are things about dealing with evil spirits that . . . that will put you at risk. There is so much you still don't know."

Kylie shook her head. "Then explain it to me. But I'm telling you, Holiday, I don't think she's evil. How many times have you told me to follow my heart—that if I do that, I'll figure out the right thing to do? Well, my heart is telling me to do this, and I'm doing it."

When Holiday opened her mouth, presumably to argue again, Kylie added, "Besides, I wasn't asking you for permission. I was asking for advice."

Chapter Twenty-two

As soon as she'd let the words out of her mouth, Kylie wished she could get them back. Not because she hadn't meant them. She did. She just regretted the way she'd said them.

Holiday sat there for a long moment, staring at Kylie as if she were thinking about what to say. Kylie returned her gaze with an equal amount of vigor. Regretting her tone didn't mean she was going to back down on this. She couldn't. Maybe it was because she emphathized with Jane Doe and her identity crisis, but it felt like more. Kylie knew she had to help the amnesiac ghost. And she would help her, with or without Holiday's blessing.

"Good Lord, when did I become my mom and you become a younger version of myself?" Holiday asked, and smiled.

Kylie saw and heard the lessening of resolve in the camp leader's voice and posture. Then the tension in Kylie's shoulders dissolved and a wave of relief filled her chest. Tears stung her eyes. "I don't know."

"Okay," Holiday said. "Sit down and let's figure out how we're going to work this so I can live with it and you can, too."

Kylie gave Holliday a quick hug of thanks and then settled in to talk. They discussed how Kylie was to go to the library to e-mail the family of Catherine O'Connell. Then Holiday went over and over and over how Kylie could shut out an unwanted ghost . . . or unwanted groups of ghosts. And then she made Kylie promise that if she did discover that Jane Doe was a child murderer, she would immediately pull back.

Kylie hesitated to give her word about the last one, but after searching her heart, she realized she didn't believe Jane was a murderer, and so she promised.

When Kylie asked Holiday for an explanation of how evil spirits could hurt her, the camp leader hesitated. Kylie quickly added, "It's not for Jane Doe, but in case I ever run into any." When Holiday still didn't start talking, Kylie added, "Keeping me ignorant is not a good way of protecting me. Don't you think I need to know?"

Holiday released a deep breath and nodded. "It's as much about protecting you as it is about . . . It's about knowing you're capable of handling this."

"I'm capable," Kylie said. "It can't be much worse than . . ." She pointed to the computer, where the story of Berta Littlemon had been posted a short time ago.

Holiday nodded. "You're right about that. But before I tell you, let me say again that most evil spirits don't hang around. They are yanked away quickly, but it has and it will happen."

"What do they do?" Kylie asked.

"You've had visions from the other ghosts, so you know how real they feel. Well, these evil spirits can make you relive some of their lives, and believe me, it can rip your heart out. Being that close to evil isn't something you can forget easily."

The way Holiday said it, Kylie knew the camp leader had suffered through it herself. The thought that Kylie, too, might have to deal with it one day sent a sharp shiver racing down her spine.

"They mess with your head, Kylie. They . . ." She inhaled again. "To put it bluntly, they mentally rape you, try to break your spirit, and if you show the least bit of weakness, they can possess you. It's also believed, mostly with bad supernatural spirits, that they can take you with them to hell when they go. Legend says that they think if they can bring something good with them, they stand a chance of alleviating their own punishment."

"So how do I avoid meeting one?" Kylie asked, certain only that she didn't want to experience any of the things Holliday had just described.

"That's the thing. They are just like other ghosts. Some you might just stumble across, shortly after their demise. Others, if their powers are strong enough, will seek you out for a purpose."

Holiday must have sensed Kylie's fear, because she dropped her hand on top of Kylie's again. "If you ever find yourself in their presence, you have to remain strong."

"How?" Kylie asked, feeling her fear ebb with Holiday's calming touch.

"It's the same as shutting out the ghosts. Mentally, you need to put yourself in a different place, a place where you feel love and good things, where you experience life at its best. And hold tight to your faith, because they will try to convince you that all things good are frivolous, that they don't matter."

"Oh my gosh, you're back!" Miranda screamed at the doorway, and came rushing inside the cabin. The moment her vibrant spirit entered the room, it chased away the dismal cloud of emotion hovering over Kylie.

Miranda embraced Holiday, nearly turning over the chair in the process. "I'm so glad you're back. We need you here. I mean . . . Burnett's okay, but . . . he's not you."

Holiday arched a brow. "I hear he wasn't even himself for a while there."

Miranda frowned. "He told you about the whole kangaroo thing, didn't he."

"Yeah," Holiday said, and her brows tightened. "And I must say,

I'm very disappointed with you, Miranda." She reached out and gripped Miranda's hand. "The next time you turn him into anything, do it when I'm here to enjoy It."

They all started laughing.

It was thirty minutes before Kylie and Holiday were able to pull away from Miranda to continue their private conversation. Especially when Miranda told Holiday about her sort of/kind of feeling that they had another mystical stalker in the camp. Kylie wondered if the stalker wasn't her little blue jay friend.

Now, Kylie and Holiday sat out on the front porch. The five o'clock sun, touched with a bit more golden hue, brushed against their faces. Kylie dangled her legs off its edge. Holiday did the same.

Kylie, barefoot, swayed her feet back and forth, and the longer blades of grass tickled the bottoms of her feet. Her mind went to the things she needed to talk to Holiday about.

"Did Burnett tell you about my asking about the FRU library?"

Holiday frowned.

Not a good sign.

"Yeah, he mentioned it."

"Why would they not let me see information about other super-naturals like myself if they had that information on file?" Frustration sounded in Kylie's tone. She hoped Holiday knew it wasn't targeted at her.

"I don't know," Holiday said, and Kylie believed her. "But I do know that the FRU is like any other government organization: they have skeletons in their own closet. Why, years ago, before I was born, most supernaturals considered all werewolves basically animals. They used to hurt them."

"Why?" Kylie asked, completely insulted on behalf of Lucas and the rest of his kind.

"Ignorance. Stupidity. Take your pick. It's the same thing that happened to a lot of minority groups. Supernaturals can act a lot more like humans than you'd think."

Holiday reached for Kylie's right hand and opened her palm. "I heard you caught a fireball that would have hit Miranda."

Kylie nodded and then asked the question she'd been wanting to ask since the night of the party. "Do you think this proves I'm a protector?"

Holiday shrugged as if she didn't think Kylie would like the answer. "Probably."

Holiday was right. She didn't like the answer. Especially when it just brought on more questions. "What does it really mean to be a protector? I've heard some of it. But . . . okay, here's the thing. Miranda said that every protector she's ever heard of had been a full-blooded paranormal. And I'm not."

"I know." Holiday looked as confused as Kylie felt.

"What could that mean?"

"I don't know, but I could guess it means what I've known all along. Kylie Galen is special." She held up her hand. "I know you don't like hearing that, Kylie, but I think you better start getting used to the idea."

Fear, insecurity, and probably a dozen other negative emotions all washed over her. "What if I don't measure up?" she asked in a low whisper. "What if I'm too afraid to do what I have to do and I turn out to be one lousy protector?"

Holiday pulled one leg up on the porch, rested her chin on her knee, and gazed at Kylie as if she'd said something really stupid, like calling the earth square. "Were you scared when you caught that fireball?"

"No, but I didn't have time to be scared. If I'd known I was going to catch the fireball and had time to think about it, I'd probably have needed to carry an extra pair of panties with me, because I'd have probably pissed myself."

Holiday smiled. "Maybe, but you'd have still done it."

"I wouldn't be so sure about that," Kylie said.

"Please. Look at this whole Berta Littlemon/Catherine O'Connell issue. I'm scared for you to continue investigating this. I told you it's dangerous, but you refuse to drop it. You put the welfare of others before yourself."

Kylie hadn't looked at it like that, and she guessed Holiday had a point, but . . . "I'm not a saint," she insisted. "I sin all the time."

Holiday lifted one eyebrow. "Say what?"

Kylie stared down at her toes for a second. Her pink nail polish was chipping, and so was her courage. Then she looked back up at Holiday's eyes and decided to confess. "Miranda said that protectors are like saints. Not only am I not a saint, I don't even want to be a saint. I want to live a normal life. I want to have fun." She thought of how it felt to kiss Lucas and blushed. "Maybe even sin a little."

Holiday started to grin.

Kylie frowned. "You know what I mean. I want to live my life like every other sixteen-year-old girl. I want to tell dirty jokes with my friends, maybe drink some cool alcohol drink every now and then— that doesn't taste like dog piss—and get tipsy. Not that I'll drive afterward or anything."

Holiday chuckled and Kylie expected the fae had probably picked up on Kylie's emotions and knew what else she wanted to do.

And with whom she wanted to do it.

"Being a protector doesn't make you a saint," Holiday said. "It makes you a caring person. You don't have to give up boys."

Kylie felt her face burn a little hotter. She put her palms down behind her and leaned back. "Well, that's the best news I've had all day."

Holiday laughed again. "How are things going in the 'boy' department?"

"Better. Not perfect," Kylie answered, and she thought about Lucas's reaction to the ghosts and the whole issue with his pack.

"Better is good," Holiday said. "Derek has already called me since I've been back, asking me how you were. He said he heard about what happened at the cemetery. Have you seen him?"

"Not much." Kylie swallowed. She didn't want to talk about him, because then she'd be tempted to ask about the reason for Derek's sudden overcharged reaction to her emotions. If anyone would know that answer, it would be Holiday. But frankly, Kylie didn't think she should care. Not when Derek didn't care enough to put his pride aside and ask for the guidance himself.

The next hour rolled past and they just sat there on the porch, enjoying the breeze that wasn't exactly cool, but not terribly hot either, and they talked about everything but Lucas and Derek. Kylie asked if Burnett had told her anything about the Brightens that he hadn't shared with her.

Holiday assured her that Burnett wasn't keeping anything from her.

"Have you spoken with your stepdad?" Holiday asked a few minutes later.

"Not since I've been back," Kylie confessed. "But I have an e-mail from him and I'll bet he's planning on coming for Parents Day."

"But you don't want him to come?"

"I don't know," Kylie admitted. "I was almost ready to forgive him. But when he tried to use me to get to my mom by saying, 'Kylie would love for us all to go out for lunch,' that's when I remembered how mad I still was at him for leaving us."

"So you haven't forgiven him yet?"

"Maybe I've forgiven him, but I just haven't forgotten."

"Thing is, those two sort of go hand in hand. Not that you'll ever really forget, but you accept that it happened and move on. You accept that all people make mistakes. No one is perfect."

"And what if you can't?" Kylie watched a bee buzz past her. "What if I can't ever really forgive him?"

"Then you let go," she said.

Kylie remembered how she'd hugged her father when he'd come to see her and told her he was sorry. While it had been hard, even painful, hugging him had felt right. She wasn't ready to let go of what they'd had. It would hurt too much.

Even more than accepting the truth.

She couldn't help wondering if that was how one made the decision to forgive or not. If letting go hurt more than accepting someone's mistakes. She could only hope that in time, accepting would come easier for her.

"Are you going to e-mail and tell him to come up for Parents Day?"

"Probably. But he and Mom will have to take shifts again. I don't think they can be in the same room together. Maybe not even on the same block."

"That could change," Holiday said, and brushed an insect away.

Kylie decided to tell Holiday her fear about her mom. "I think my mom is ready to start dating."

"Yikes! I remember when my parents did that. Talk about awkward."

"Yeah. She's ready, but I'm not sure I am." Kylie bit down on her lip. "I guess down deep I was always hoping they would get back together. And I could have one thing that was like it used to be. A little bit of normal would be good, ya know?"

"Yeah, but normal is overrated, too." She grinned. "So tell me about this blue jay."

Kylie wrapped her arms around her legs tight and told her the story. Then she decided to ask the big question. "How much of my soul did I give away?"

"If you gave any of it away, it was very, very little. You won't even miss it."

"But what happens when I give it away? Do I die earlier? Am I more likely to go to hell? What's the price of a piece of my soul?"

Holiday shrugged. "Well, if you do indeed have the ability to raise the dead, the price varies. If it's ordained by the gods, then its cost to you is nothing. It even adds to your soul."

"How do you know if it's ordained?" Kylie asked.

"You'll just know. The powers that be will make it very clear."

Kylie shivered a bit at the mention of the powers that be. She hesitated to ask her next question, but as she'd told Holiday earlier, ignorance was a lousy form of protection. "And if it's not ordained?"

"Then the price is based on the quality of life that the person goes on to live. If they live a good life, the price is very low. Practically moot. If they abuse life, or the lives of others, then it can nip at your soul. Their sins, in a small way, become your sins. I'm not sure how accountable one is held for these sins, but I've heard emotionally it can leave you feeling empty. And yes, the less soul you have, the shorter the life you usually live."

Kylie frowned. "Kind of makes you not want to bring anyone back."

"Well, I'm sure it was designed that way so it gives people pause. As hard as it is, death is a part of life. But we're probably discussing this for nothing, Kylie. Just because you think you might have brought a bird back to life doesn't mean you have this gift."

Kylie wanted to believe what Holiday was saying was true, but she wasn't sure she did. "Does healing someone take a part of my soul? I mean, if bringing someone to life does, it makes sense that healing them might, too."

"Not like it does raising the dead," Holiday said. "It does drain you, though."

Kylie remembered how tired she'd felt after healing Sara and then Lucas.

"I'd like for you and Helen to work together on this," Holiday said. "Maybe even meet regularly like a species group."

Kylie raised an eyebrow and suspected she knew what Holiday was up to. "Because I don't belong to a group, right? That's why you're doing this?"

Holiday rolled her eyes. "You belong here at Shadow Falls. Just because you don't belong to a certain group doesn't mean anything."

Kylie nodded. "I like Helen."

After a few minutes of just listening to nature, she told Holiday all about the blue jay's little dog-and-pony shows. Holiday didn't have an explanation for the bird's pop-in visits, except to say that maybe the bird was only a fledgling and it sort of imprinted on her, meaning it thought Kylie was his mother.

"God, I hope not. Because I'm not chewing up worms and barfing into its mouth. I mean, I know that's what mama birds do."

Holiday laughed.

Kylie looked at her friend and counselor, and the most important question of all popped out. "Does any of this give you any clue as to what I am?"

Holiday frowned. "I wish it did."

"What if I never find out? What if I go through my life never knowing?"

"That's not likely," Holiday said. "Almost every week, we discover something else about you. Sooner or later, something is going to point you in the right direction."

Kylie looked down and watched an ant move across the porch. "I think Lucas wants me to be werewolf."

"Yes, but what Lucas wants isn't important."

Something told Kylie that Holiday understood the reason Lucas wanted this. She almost asked, but she wasn't sure she was ready to talk about it.

"You will be what you are, and whatever it is, you will be fine. Everyone has to accept that and love you for who you are; it doesn't really matter where your heritage comes from."

For some reason, Kylie remembered Derek saying pretty much the same thing.

Holiday's phone rang. She looked at the number and then glanced at Kylie.

"Who is it?" Kylie asked, sensing it was about her.

"Derek again."

Kylie sighed. Why did just hearing his name still sting?

Chapter Twenty-three

Kylie nibbled, without appetite, at her hamburger and fries at dinner that night while sitting between Della and Miranda at the dining hall. When asked, Miranda confessed she hadn't yet spoken to Perry about the dance/dragon thing from last night.

Miranda said that she'd gotten another phone call from the cute warlock back home and he'd arranged to pick her up Friday evening and take her out to dinner. "What am I going to say to Perry?" she asked. "'Hey, I'd like to just talk to you to see if we might have a chance, but first I'd like to go out on a date with another guy and see if I like him better'?"

Both Kylie and Della agreed it would be a difficult conversation. But they suggested Miranda at least thank Perry for standing up for her against Clark.

In truth, Kylie hoped Miranda would talk to Perry and cancel her date with the cute warlock. Kylie had nothing against cute warlocks, but Perry was one of their own.

Kylie placed a greasy fry in her mouth and tried to pretend she was hungry. When she glanced up, she noticed Lucas sitting with his pack of weres; their eyes met across the rows of hungry teens munching on burgers. He smiled, and Kylie returned the smile. He'd asked her to sit with him at the weres' table. She would have, even knowing it would be uncomfortable sitting with a group of his friends who didn't want him to see her. She would have done it because if Lucas could stand up to them, then so would she. But Della was her shadow, and Kylie knew the little vamp would have had a fit if she'd asked her to sit with the were group. So Kylie had refrained.

Lucas picked up a fry, and as he popped it into his mouth, he winked at her. The small gesture might not have meant anything coming from a different guy, but for Lucas to show anything in the way of public affection was a big deal. She grinned big and winked back. She did it even when she noticed Fredericka sitting two people away from Lucas and snarling as though she wanted to rip out Kylie's throat.

The she-wolf could probably do it, too.

Somebody must have said something funny a few tables over because laughter filled the large room. The smell of burgers mingled with the faint smell of singed wood. Thanks to Burnett, the physical reminders of the big fight were all gone, but the memory still lingered. Everyone at the camp seemed extra cheery tonight, no doubt celebrating Holiday's return. If the camp leader doubted how appreciated she was, the number of squeals, accompanied by "You're back!" and unexpected hugs (even from a few vamps and weres, which were not common) should have done her ego good.

For a moment, Kylie worried it might make Burnett feel like a second fiddle. But more than once Kylie caught the vampire watching the emotional greetings with so much pride in his eyes that it was like watching a romance movie. Kylie could almost hear the sappy music playing in the background. She wished she had a camera so she could show Holiday how Burnett looked at her when she wasn't aware.

The door to the dining room swished open. Derek and Ellie walked in side by side, though they weren't holding hands. Derek immediately started moving his gaze around the room, and Kylie knew he'd been looking for her when his gaze landed on hers. She couldn't help but wonder what he'd wanted to talk to Holiday about. Was it her again? And why? Shouldn't he be giving Ellie his attention?

He nodded slightly. She nodded back and forced herself to eat another bite of her hamburger. It tasted like dead meat. Which it was, but the thought made it even more unappetizing.

When the lump of food took two swallows to get down her throat, she pushed her plate aside. She was so done.

Staring at her glass of tea, she wiped away a trail of condensation and searched for a plausible excuse to escape from the dining hall. Escape before she had to watch Derek and Ellie whispering back and forth and sharing fries or something—not that she cared, of course. At least that's what she told herself. And she would continue to tell herself that until it was true. It would happen, too. How could it not when she enjoyed Lucas's company so much? Enjoyed his kisses. Enjoyed being the girl he would actually wink at with dozens of people around to witness.

Kylie's phone rang, giving her the excuse she needed to skip out. Not even checking to see who it was, she leaned over and whispered to Della that she had to take the call. Della, who'd been interested only in the rare meat on her bun and had already wolfed that down, grabbed her real meal—a tall glass of B positive blood—and followed her out.

Kylie hadn't cleared the dining room door when she looked to see the name on her phone. Oh, crappers! It was Sara, her friend from home.

Sara, whose previous call and texts Kylie hadn't answered.

For a damn good reason, too. Kylie knew Sara wanted to talk about her suspicion that Kylie had done something to make her cancer jump ship.

Problem was, Sara's suspicion was right on target.

A targeted subject that Kylie had neglected to discuss with Holiday.

So what had compelled Kylie to answer this call without checking her caller ID first?

Oh yeah, so she'd have a reason to escape from the dining hall. Putting the phone to her ear, she hit the answer button.

"Hey, Sara," Kylie said, and decided to wing it. Not that it was altogether a good idea. She'd never been a good winger.

"Hi," Sara said.

"What's up?" Kylie asked.

"I'll tell you what's up. I've just managed to baffle every cancer specialist in Texas. I still have to finish my chemo, and do one bout of radiation, but they did tons of CT scans and there's not one tumor in this body! Can you believe it? I'm not gonna die, Kylie!"

There was so much excitement, bounciness, and pure hope in Sara's voice that Kylie's breath caught in her throat and tears filled her eyes. It reminded Kylie of the old Sara. Not the sex-crazed, alcohol-loving party girl who'd replaced her, but the one Kylie had been best friends with since elementary school.

And until this second, Kylie hadn't realized how much she'd missed the old Sara, either. "That's friggin' fabulous, girl!"

"Like you didn't know already," she said.

Think. Think. Think. "I don't know what you mean," Kylie said, deciding to play ignorant. What was the saying? Ignorance is bliss? She could really use a little bliss right now.

Della looked at Kylie and rolled her eyes. Kylie frowned, not so much because Della was listening in—she would have told Della about it anyway—but because Della then mouthed the word *liar*.

"Right," Sara said. "But that's not important. We can talk about that Sunday." She let a long pause linger on the phone, as if it were supposed to mean something. "Come on. Don't you wanna know why we can talk about it on Sunday?" Sara finally asked.

"Because you're not going to church and are going to call me?" Kylie answered, throwing out the first thing that came to her mind, but her gut knotted with a strange suspicion. But a suspicion of what? How bad could it be?

"Because I'm coming to see you on Sunday," Sara said, sounding really happy about it, too.

Okay, having Sara visit Shadow Falls could be phenomenally bad. But maybe that wasn't even what she meant. "Uh, I'm not at home, Sara. I'm at camp," Kylie said. "Remember?" *Please let it be that simple.*

"Of course I remember, silly! I'm coming up there with your mom. I just got off the phone with her."

Kylie's heart, poised to make the leap, did a nosedive right into her stomach. The thought of Sara coming to Shadow Falls sent a wave of shock to her brain.

Sara was from Kylie's old life.

Everything at Shadow Falls was part of her new life.

Old life and new life didn't go together. They were like peanut butter and hot dogs. The two were fine separately, but they should never meet.

Never.

Ever.

"Uh, Sara. You . . . you . . ." She swallowed hard. "You can't just visit Shadow Falls. I mean, you have to . . . have to get permission from the camp leaders, and they are very funny about—"

"Duh, your mom told me that. So I took the bull by the horns and called and spoke with a Mr. Burnett James about twenty minutes ago. He said it would be fine for me to ride up with your mom. I can't wait to see you, Kylie. And I can't wait to meet all those hot guys you told me about. We're going to have such fun. Oh, and what was the name of that really bitchy girl you told me about? DeAnn, no, wait, it was Della. We can tag team her ass."

Della's eyes widened. *Bitchy,* she mouthed.

Kylie's hand wrapped around the phone and started to shake. "Ugh. I never said she was bitchy, I said she was blunt."

"Same thing," Sara said. "And the other one with the weird hair? Tell me, are they the ones who taught you how to heal people?"

"I'm sorry." Kylie's heart started to jump beats. "I have to go. Someone just . . . someone just called me." She punched Della in the arm.

"Hey, Kylie!" Della yelled out, and grinned as if she enjoyed playing a part in the shenanigans. Or not. "Oh, you're on the phone. We can talk later. I wouldn't want to be a bitch or anything," she said in her snarkiest voice.

"I'll call you later," Kylie told Sara. "Yeah . . . later. Sorry." She started to hang up and then said, "But I'm happy about you being okay, Sara. Really happy."

Kylie snapped her phone closed and then looked at Della. Della, who seemed to be immensely enjoying Kylie's discomfort. Della, who looked part pissed off and part amused.

"So," Della said. "We finally get to meet Miss Sara, huh? Your oldest and best friend, who has always sounded like a self-centered bitch, if you ask me. You totally upgraded when you came here. Personally, I'd have let her die. But on second thought . . ." Della flashed her fangs. "Hmm, what type of blood does she have? Think I could talk her into donating a pint or two, maybe more? Tag team my ass!"

"Kill me," Kylie said, and brushed her hair back to expose her neck vein. "Just kill me now and get it over with!"

"So we get to meet Sara. Cool," Miranda said later that night as they sat around the kitchen table.

"Not cool," Kylie said, seriously unhappy about it, and gave a demanding Socks a scratch behind his ear.

"Why not cool?" Miranda asked.

"She doesn't want us to meet her," Della said. "We might find out what the real Kylie Galen is like."

Kylie scowled at Della, and yeah, she could pull off a pretty mean scowl, thanks to living with Della. "It's not that at all. If anything, you guys know the real me. It's just . . . over-the-top weird to have her coming here."

"Why?" Miranda asked. "We've met your mom."

"And your philandering dad," Della added.

"That's different," Kylie said, and frowned at the philandering comment. Though she didn't know why she was offended, because it was true.

"How's it different?" Miranda asked. Before Kylie could answer, Miranda added, "Hey, I hope you two get a chance to meet Todd on Friday night. Will you guys wait with me in the parking lot when he comes to pick me up?"

Both Della and Kylie frowned, but they nodded.

"It's different for you," Kylie said to Miranda, still stuck on Sara coming to visit on Parents Day. "You've known you were supernatural all your life. You don't have a presupernatural life." Socks, still on the tabletop, jumped down to the floor with a catlike elegance. "It's like I was a different person back then. And yeah, you met my parents, but it's almost as if they don't count—not the way your friends count."

"I'm sorry, but I don't understand," Miranda said.

"I do," said Della. And she said it as though she hated to admit it. "Kylie's right. It's different when you had a different life. I tried to imagine how it would be for you guys to meet Lee, or one of my old girlfriends. It would be freaky." She met Kylie's eyes. "I'm sorry I gave you a hard time about this."

"Wow," Miranda said. "You'd better be careful, Della. In the last few days, I think you've used up your vampire quota of apologies for the next ten years."

"Kiss my apologetic ass!" Della snapped.

Later that night, Kylie woke up to the mist forming around her. She didn't know where she was, but for some reason she wasn't afraid. Her gaze stayed on the soft, moist mist. She looked at the trees; the leaves, even in the dark, were a perfect shade of verdant green. Beautiful sprays of moonlight spilled through limbs that seemed to reach up into the heavens with pride. Perfect. Fairy-tale perfect. Even the sounds of the forest at night were like a symphony. She heard the water, like a babbling brook, a peaceful, beautiful sound playing in the background.

She immediately thought of Derek and that crazy thing he did when he was really close to her. How he made everything look like a fairy-tale picture, one meant to capture your imagination—one meant to fill you with awe, like the pages of a children's book.

"Hey . . ." His voice pulled her away from the few stars she saw twinkling above the trees.

He sat beside her on a large rock. Not so close that she would have felt awkward, but near enough that the moonlight allowed her to see him. Then she realized this wasn't just any rock; it was their rock. The spot he'd taken her to after she'd first arrived at Shadow Falls.

She'd done it again.

She'd brought him here through the dreamscape, and that was so wrong.

"I'm sorry," she blurted out. "I didn't mean to do this." She closed her eyes and concentrated on moving back, away from the dream. She concentrated really hard, waited for the floating-flying sensation, but it didn't happen. At least she didn't think it did.

She opened her eyes just a crack. Enough to see if she'd moved.

Nope, she was still sitting on the rock. Derek was still looking at her. Why couldn't she fly away from the dream? She jerked her eyes open all the way.

"I'm sorry," she said again. "I didn't mean to do this. Just a minute and you can go right back to sleep."

She slammed her eyes shut again and tried really, really hard to concentrate. *Back. Go back to sleep. Now!*

"Kylie?" His voice tickled her ears as she tried to fix what she'd done. "Kylie."

She tried to ignore him and concentrate.

"Kylie, you're not doing this. I am. I'm the one dreamscaping."

Kylie jerked open her eyes and her vision filled with him sitting there, looking so real. She recalled how the dreamscape had felt different when Red had come into her dreams. She hadn't been able to fly away, she'd had to wake herself up. So that's what she needed to do. Just wake herself up. She didn't do it.

"You can dreamscape?"

He nodded. "Yeah."

The first thing she did was make sure she had clothes on. Hey . . . she knew her own tendencies with dreams, and from what she'd heard, boys were even worse.

She had on her pink nightshirt. Nothing sexy or showy. Good thing. A fluttering of relief waved through her that he didn't intend for this to be that kind of dream. Then she couldn't help but wonder if it was because he didn't feel that way about her anymore. He had Ellie.

"Why didn't you tell me you could dreamscape?" she asked, not wanting to think too much about him and Ellie.

He hesitated. "I sort of figured out how to turn it off before I ever got to Shadow Falls. I was constantly trying to visit my dad to communicate with him, even when I didn't want to have anything more to do with him."

Kylie knew all about unwanted dreamscapes. Then she remembered

Derek's pain at dealing with his dad, the man who had abandoned him when he was really young. "Do you communicate with him now?" she asked, remembering he'd said he was going to look for his dad when he'd left Shadow Falls. When he'd come back with Ellie, she hadn't thought about Derek's problems, only about feeling betrayed by him. A touch of shame filtered into her chest at her selfishness.

"Not really. But I now know how to work the dreamscape, so I . . ."

"You what?" Kylie asked.

"Started using it again. But that's not important. Look, the other night when you came to me in the dream."

"I'm sorry about that," she said. "I'm just now learning how to control them. But as soon as I realized what I had done, that I had gone to your bedroom, I left."

His frown tightened. "I know. But before you took off, in that second that I saw you, it dawned on me that I didn't feel it here."

"Didn't feel what?" she asked, obviously still half-asleep.

"I didn't feel the surge of your emotions." He smiled. "When we dreamscape, I can talk to you, be this close to you without it making me crazy."

Kylie felt so many mixed emotions sitting on the rock, staring at his smile. She took a deep breath. "I'm not sure this is a good thing."

"Why not? I just want to talk. To see how you're doing. Is that a crime? I thought you said you cared about me? That you wanted to be my friend?"

"Okay, let me put it another way. I don't think Ellie will think this is such a good idea."

He frowned. "I keep telling you that it's not like that with us now. Ellie and I are just friends."

"Really?" Kylie let sarcasm leak into her tone. "Because it's hard to believe after the picture I saw of you two making out."

He hesitated and then said, "Fine, you're right. When I first ran into Ellie, she was so happy to see me and I was hurting. Lucas was back and you cared about him. I was just as confused as Ellie was. We kissed and . . . Look, the important thing is that we both realized it was wrong."

It was that little pause that caught her attention the most. "You kissed and then did what?" Kylie asked.

Obviously in the dream world, she felt braver, able to ask questions she might not ask in real life. "Just exactly what happened between you and Ellie in Pennsylvania?"

Chapter Twenty-four

"Is it important?" Derek asked.

"You had sex with her, didn't you." Somehow Kylie had known this all along. It sucked being right, too.

Guilt filled his eyes. "It didn't mean anything."

She shook her head. "How can it not have meant anything? It's the ultimate form of intimacy between two people."

"Not always," he said. "Sometimes it's just two people searching for something. And a lot of times, they don't find it. We didn't find it, Kylie. Ellie knew it. I knew it. And the romantic relationship is completely over. It was a mistake and we both knew it."

"But you brought her back with you."

He flinched. "She's not a bad person, I couldn't leave her there at the commune. It was awful. She'd have been in a gang in a matter of weeks."

Kylie pulled her legs closer to her chest and tried to sort through the emotions bouncing through her. She felt hurt. She felt justified in her feelings of jealousy. And she felt . . . relieved. The last one didn't make sense, though. Why would she feel relieved that Derek and Ellie had sex?

Then the truth hit. She felt relieved because now there was no reason for her to experience guilt over being with Lucas. Not that the truth still didn't hurt. And if she was completely honest with herself, she still felt a tiny wave of jealousy. But she pushed it away, because now, more than ever, she could accept it. She was Derek's friend. Just his friend.

"We're just friends," she said.

He looked at her. "Yeah," he said, but something about that one word didn't seem as honest as his earlier words.

"All I want to do is talk. To make sure you're okay. Give me ten minutes." He studied her frown. "Five. Hell, give me three minutes, Kylie. Is that too much for a friend to ask?"

She looked at the stream and then up at him. "Three minutes. Then this ends."

"Deal." He looked at his watch, and then, as if competing with the clock, he started talking. "How are you? What happened at the cemetery? I heard about it."

She gave him the really short version. Namely, that she thought the ghost was buried there. And she'd discovered her spirit might be a child killer.

He didn't flinch like the rest of them. "What are you going to do?" he asked instead. "How are you going to get to the truth?"

"I'm waiting for the ghost to come back. She hasn't visited me since then."

"She will," he said. "And don't worry too much. I'm sure you'll figure everything out. You always do."

Kylie gazed up into his gold-flecked green eyes. "How do you know I'm worried?"

"Duh, I can feel it."

"I thought you couldn't feel my emotions here?"

"I can feel them, but they're just at a lower voltage. Normal range."

Normal. That word seemed to be popping into Kylie's mind a lot.

She nodded. "Did you ever find your dad?" When he looked upset by her question, she added, "You told me when you left that you were going to try to find him."

He nodded and then swallowed. "I found him."

She felt his mixed emotions as if they were her own. "It didn't go well?"

"I don't know. I thought I'd see him and it would make it right. It's still not right. I still don't know if I want anything to do with him. I'm pretty sure I don't."

"Why? What happened?" Kylie asked.

"He offered me a hundred different reasons why he had to leave me and Mom. His life was a lie trying to live in the human world with my mom. He told me it hurt too much trying to stay in touch. He said he'd like to get to know me again. He said a lot of things. And not one of them meant a hill of beans to me. Maybe it will in time. I don't know. But right now, it just feels totally awkward."

"I understand awkward," she said, and offered him a bit of a smile. "Sara is supposed to be coming with my mom on Parents Day."

He reached for her and then pulled back. "I'm sure it'll be okay."

There was a moment of silence, then Derek started talking. "So, with your ghost . . . have you figured out what to do? I mean, how can you find out who she is?"

"I don't know for sure. But my gut says that she's remembering more and more each time I see her."

He pondered her words and then said, "You know, I remember reading something years ago about how an old state cemetery was dug up and they found that about five percent of all the caskets had two bodies in them."

"Two bodies?"

"Yeah. The state was burying some of the really poor, homeless folks in with other caskets. Just slipping them in so they didn't have to pay for their own burial."

Kylie thought about it for a second, and it made perfect sense. Catherine O'Connell said she saw Jane Doe rise from the grave of Berta Littlemon. However, if Berta Littlemon was in there, too—and the legends about such things were correct—she would have already been snatched into hell. That meant only one spirit would have risen from the grave.

"I think you might have just solved my problem," she told Derek. "Thank you!" If things had been different between them, she would have hugged him.

He grinned. "You're welcome."

She suddenly realized that they had probably been talking way longer than his negotiated three minutes. She glanced down at his watch.

"Oh, one more thing," he said. "After we talked the other day about Red being strange, I did some checking. You know, just to see what I could find out. Contrary to the weird vibe we both got, he is vampire, or at least that's what everyone thinks. The only other thing I found was . . . about his parents."

"What about them?" she asked.

"Supposedly, his mom was murdered in front of him when he was like seven. The case never was solved. It looked as if even the FRU looked into the case, but never found who did it. Then his dad disappeared less than a year later. That's when he went to live with his grandfather."

Kylie frowned. "Damn, I could almost feel sorry for him."

Derek shrugged. "Unfortunately, most people who commit violent crimes were at one time victims themselves. But one wrong doesn't make a right. And we know he killed those two girls."

"I know." When she looked up and found herself gazing into Derek's eyes again, she said, "I guess I should—"

"Go. I know," he said, and his expression turned sad. "I miss you, Kylie. Can we . . . do this again?"

She almost said yes but realized it probably wasn't a good idea for either one of them. "I don't know," she said. "I've got a lot to figure out."

"Between you and Lucas?" he asked.

"Yes," she said honestly. She wouldn't feel guilty about her feelings anymore. She didn't know what she might have with Lucas. But for the first time since she'd recognized those growing feelings, she didn't feel at fault about them. And there was something between them. But with his pack trying to break them up, and his dislike of her involvement with the ghosts, she just wasn't sure where it was going to lead.

"Okay," he said. "But if you need me . . . or just want to talk . . . you know where I am."

Kylie nodded, and then the next thing she knew, she was awake, staring at her bedroom ceiling. "I miss you, too," she whispered, and then rolled over and hugged her pillow.

Perry met Kylie at the front door the next morning when she stepped out of the cabin.

"Hey," she said, and forced a smile. She wasn't exactly depressed about knowing the truth about Derek and Ellie, but there was an underlying sadness to her mood today.

It reminded Kylie of how she always felt the last day of school before summer vacation. She wanted summer to be here, knew there was no changing it, but a part of her wanted to hold on to life the way it was. She supposed she just wasn't a big fan of change.

Perry, his eyes a bright blue, grinned. "Hey." He looked back at the door, and Kylie knew why.

"Miranda already left," she told him.

"Why?"

Because she didn't want to see you because she's afraid of what you'll say when she tells you she's got a date Friday night with a hot warlock.

"I don't have a clue." *And I'm really glad you're not a vampire who can read my heartbeat and tell when I'm flat-out lying.*

His eyes went from blue to a sad brown. "I thought . . . I guess I just hoped that . . ."

"I know," Kylie said, and bumped him with her shoulder. "And while I can't say anything, all I can tell you is that hope is eternal."

"So I still have a chance?" he asked.

"A little one," she said, not wanting to give him false hope.

They started heading down the trail. "I want to see if Holiday and Burnett are in the office. I need to talk with them before breakfast."

"Just lead the way," Perry said, bowing at the waist. "I'm your personal shadow servant."

Kylie grinned. As they walked, she wondered if someday she could hang out with Derek like this and it would feel this right. Feel completely platonic, with no hint of regret about what could have been. She really hoped so. Although her heart said he would have made an awesome boyfriend, he would also make a hell of a good friend. And she hoped they could get there.

Holiday and Burnett weren't in the office, so Kylie couldn't tell them about Derek's theory that there could have been two bodies in Berta Littlemon's grave.

Or ask Burnett what he'd been smoking when he'd given Sara permission to visit Shadow Falls.

At breakfast, Lucas joined her and Perry at their table. Kylie spotted Miranda eating with the witches, and Della had a vampire thing that morning. So Kylie sat between Lucas and Perry, and much to her surprise, they both behaved. Well, Perry behaved.

Lucas slipped his hand under the table and touched the side of her leg. Then he leaned in and whispered, "Want to go dancing in the moonlight again tonight?"

She couldn't be sure, but she could swear the brush of his lips against her temple had almost been a kiss. She nudged him with her elbow, and as she forked a mouthful of eggs on her utensil, she whispered back, "Careful. People are going to actually know you have a thing for me."

"Good," he said. "Maybe it's time we make it official."

Her heart stopped. The eggs dropped from the prongs of her fork and landed with a splat on her plate.

She turned and looked into his blue eyes. "Are you asking me to go out with you?"

"Are you saying yes?" Hope danced in his eyes.

"What about your pack?"

"I told you I don't care what they say."

Joy danced in her heart. "Well, I think I should hear the question first."

"Okay . . . Will you, Kylie Galen, go out with me?"

Yes. Yes. Yes. The word sat on the tip of her tongue, waiting to be released. She smiled, poised to say it, and—

"Can I borrow Lucas for a minute?" Burnett's deep voice shattered the moment. He stood behind them, six feet plus of solid vampire.

Lucas looked up at Burnett. "Is something wrong?"

"I need a word with you."

Lucas got up and left. Kylie watched them leave, so in shock from Lucas asking her to go out that she completely forgot to give Burnett a large ration of shit for agreeing to let Sara come to the camp.

A bit later, Kylie stood beside Perry while Chris announced names for the Meet Your Campmates hour. Lucas still hadn't come back from his talk with Burnett, and that worried her.

Looking up at Perry, Kylie asked, "How are we going to do this?"

He stared over at Miranda. "I pulled my name from the list."

"So we don't have to stay?" Kylie asked.

"I pulled my name. Not yours. I figured I could just tag along with you on your hour."

"Isn't that against the rules?"

"I'm sure Burnett wouldn't mind."

"Speaking of Burnett," Kylie said. "I didn't know you two knew each other."

"He told you?" Perry seemed surprised.

"No. Well, he sort of did when I asked him about it. But during the whole dragon thing, you said something about him telling you something when you were six."

"Oh," Perry said. "And what did Burnett say?"

"Just that he knew you from before. Was he like your foster contact person or something?"

"Yeah, sort of."

"And Kylie Galen . . ." Chris's voice rose, and so did Kylie's attention. She glanced to the front where Chris stood pulling names out of a hat. Yes, a real-life magician type of hat, too.

Obviously, Chris had decided to jazz up his few minutes in the limelight. "You are spending an hour with . . . Ellie Mason."

"Oh, hell!" All her unresolved feeling about Derek and Ellie came bubbling to the surface.

"Oh, boy," Perry countered. "This should be loads of fun!"

Which only went to show how she and Perry had different definitions of fun.

A minute later, Kylie, Ellie, and Perry took off walking along one of the trails. For the longest time, none of them spoke.

"Where are we going?" Ellie broke the unspoken code of silence.

"Down by the creek bed," Kylie said.

"Okay," Ellie said.

They continued for another ten minutes, walking fast, supernatural fast. No one complained. At least not about the speed.

Ellie piped up again. "I'm new here, but I thought the objective of campmate hour was to talk—to get to know each other."

"So talk," Kylie snapped, and dodged a few limbs that seemed to try to reach out and grab her. She also dodged logic that said she should fake a huge migraine and send the little sex kitten on her way back to camp.

"Okay . . . My name is Ellie Mason and I have a feeling you don't like me."

Kylie stopped and swerved around—she had the script down in her head for faking a sick headache. She wouldn't even have to fake it because now her head was actually throbbing. But when she opened her mouth, her words had nothing to do with migraines.

"Okay, let's get something out in the open. I know you had sex with Derek." Her voice seemed to bounce from tree to tree.

"Damn!" Perry said, and grinned. "This is gonna be better than I thought."

Chapter Twenty-five

Kylie glared at the shape-shifter.

Perry's smile vanished.

Kylie arched a brow. "Do it."

He frowned. "Not the deaf cat again," he pleaded. "I can't hear. My equilibrium is thrown off. It's like I'm in a vacuum."

She didn't look away until the sparkles started popping off like fireworks. Then she turned and faced Ellie, who stared wide-eyed at the cascading sparkles around Perry.

"Holy shit! I've never seen a shape-shifter transform before. I mean, I heard about what happens when they shift, but that is so cool."

"Did you hear what I said?" Kylie crossed her arms over her chest as fury built in the pit of her stomach.

"Did you see him change?" Ellie asked.

Kylie tapped her tennis shoe in the moist, rocky soil. "I said I know you had sex with Derek."

Ellie continued to stare at Perry, who was now a white, blue-eyed feline. There was a sudden silence in the woods. Kylie ignored it and focused on Ellie.

"Yeah, I heard you," Ellie said, still not looking at her. "And I'm purposely stalling, so I can figure out how to answer you." The dark-haired vamp released a deep breath and looked at Kylie. "Derek told you?"

Kylie nodded.

Ellie shook her head. "Just like Derek. He's one of those nice guys who think the truth is the best policy."

"You would have lied to me?" Kylie asked, searching for a reason to really dislike the girl. As if having sex with Derek weren't enough of a reason. But then again, Kylie and Derek hadn't had a commitment; they hadn't even gone out on an official date. And Derek and Ellie shared a past.

"Yup. I'd have lied," Ellie said. "Not for spite or anything. Just because . . . well, what happened between me and Derek didn't mean crap, so what would be the point of letting that cause a bunch of shit?"

Kylie frowned. "If it didn't mean crap, then why did you do it?"

She shrugged. "Because I wanted it to mean something."

"That doesn't make sense," Kylie accused.

Ellie frowned. "Okay, look. I like Derek. A lot. I mean, he's hot, he's sweet, and so damn great. But . . . there are just no sparks. Like before when we were dating. We had a lot of sparkless sex. I'm sure you've dealt with that, right?"

Kylie didn't correct her. Admitting she was a virgin to a stranger didn't sit well with her.

"So when he appears at this party, I'm feeling a tiny bit scared, slightly vulnerable, and he shows up like a knight in shining armor. And he looks hot, and I think maybe this time there'd be sparks." She shook her head. "But no sparks."

Kylie felt the air grow cold around them. Dead cold. *Please not now,* she said in her head.

"If he told you about the sex," Ellie continued, "then he also told you that as soon as it was over, we both were like . . . 'God, that was a mistake.' And five minutes later, he's telling me about some girl he met named Kylie."

Kylie stared down at the ground, and she could swear it had just shifted beneath her feet. She glanced over at Perry, who sat on a tree limb, swatting at a butterfly.

"You do know he really cares about you, right?" Ellie asked.

The ghost materialized right in front of Kylie, and she looked panicked, scared.

Please . . . not now!

Kylie ignored the spirit and studied Ellie. Suddenly the whole conversation seemed silly and totally unnecessary. She had no right to be upset that Derek and Ellie had sex. None. Zilch. Zero.

"I'm sorry," Kylie said. "I shouldn't have—"

"Yeah, you should have. If some chick had sex with a guy I liked, I'd be pissed, too. It's cool that you just spoke your mind. I respect that."

"No," Kylie said. "I mean, it's not like . . . that with me and Derek. Yeah, Derek and I were almost something, but then . . ." *He just ended it.* She stopped herself. She didn't want to go into that. "It's over."

"Right. Over." Ellie rolled her eyes. "Seriously? Every time we walk into a crowd of people, do you know what he does? He looks for you." She chuckled. "Which is silly. And so I asked him about it. I go, 'You say you can feel her a mile away, so you know she's not here, so why do you look for her if you already know?'" Ellie grinned. "You know what he said to me? He said, 'Hope lives eternal.'"

Kylie recognized the words she'd offered Perry a little while ago.

"The guy's got it bad for you," Ellie said.

Kylie shook her head again. "No, it's over. He ended it. I'm going out with someone else now."

"You are?" Shock widened Ellie's blue eyes. "Does Derek know?"

"No. I mean, I'm going to be going out with someone else." Feeling like a dork, she added, "Lucas asked me to go out at breakfast. But I didn't get a chance to say yes."

Ellie raised her eyebrows in suspicion. "So, you didn't say yes."

Kylie frowned, and the dead cold seemed to crawl against her skin. "We were interrupted."

"How long does it take to say yes?" Ellie wrapped her arms around herself as if to fight off the cold and looked around as if confused by the sudden change in temperature.

"What's your point?" Kylie asked, feeling frustrated but not sure if it stemmed from the ghost or from Ellie. Then Kylie saw the ghost pacing back and forth, staring at her as if she needed to tell her something. Something urgent.

Ellie did her shrug thing again. "I'm just saying it sounds like you hesitated. And maybe there's a reason for that. Maybe the reason is—"

"There's no reason. I didn't hesitate."

Jane Doe stopped pacing and stared Kylie dead in the eyes. *"You should run!"*

"You sure?" Ellie asked.

"I'm sure," Kylie said, and she was. Wasn't she? She'd been going to tell him yes before Burnett came over. She would tell Lucas yes the next time she saw him.

"Run!" the ghost screamed.

"Why?" Kylie asked the spirit, and glanced at Perry still in the tree, slowly sneaking up on the butterfly.

"Why what?" Ellie asked.

"Run!" The spirit screamed the word so loud, Kylie thought her eardrums would rupture. She looked up and saw the eagle coming at her full blast with his talons out.

She ducked, barely dodging the bird's sharp claws. Right then, the ground under her feet started moving. Seriously moving. A loud rumble seemed to explode from below her.

"Run!" Kylie screamed at Ellie.

The vamp, her eyes glowing a bright yellow, stared at the ground. "What the hell?"

"Run!" Kylie screamed, and grabbed Ellie's arm and took off, dragging her with her. They had gotten less than a foot when the earth where they'd just stood dropped into a big, dark hole. A hole that kept growing wider, moving closer. Kylie got about another ten feet when she remembered.

Perry. He was stuck in a tree and wouldn't be able to hear what was happening below him.

She swung around. Just as she suspected, he was still in the tree. Still staring at the butterfly.

"We should keep going!" yelled Ellie.

The hole in the ground kept expanding as if someone sucked the earth from below. It got almost to the tree. Almost to Perry. He still hadn't seen it.

And it was her fault. All her fault.

"Perry, run!" she screamed with everything she had.

But Perry couldn't hear.

My equilibrium is thrown off. It's like I'm in a vacuum. His words raked across her mind like cut glass.

She saw the hole begin to pull on the roots of the tree.

She saw Perry the feline lose his footing.

He fought to stay in the tree. She watched in horror as he wrapped his feline limbs around the branch, his claws digging into the bark as he clung for life. But the dark hole, like a monster who didn't give up, sucked the tree down, taking the small, blue-eyed kitten into the dark oblivion.

Someone lives and someone dies.

"No!" Kylie screamed, and bolted forward, taking a flying leap into the dark hole.

Chapter Twenty-six

The darkness surrounded Kylie the second her foot left solid earth, and she tumbled down the pit. She heard screams, tortured screams, coming from below. Or were they just inside her head? It was hard to tell. Then she was struck by a cold so intense that it almost stole her breath. She instantly knew the sounds were coming from hell. Was Holiday right? Had she spent too much time with pure evil and now she was paying the price?

And because of her, so was Perry?

Suddenly, painful little sparks hit her body from beneath her, jolts of what felt like electricity. It took two or three strikes before she realized what it meant.

Perry. Perry was shifting.

Then she slammed against . . . something half-soft, half-prickly.

With a lot of feathers.

She bounced off it, flipped over, and screamed as she continued her descent, falling faster now into oblivion and going headfirst.

Huge, leathery-feeling handcuffs latched on to her right arm and yanked her upward. Her arm felt pulled out of its socket. She muttered a curse at the sharp pain.

"I got you . . ." Perry's voice reverberated through the hole.

It was meant to reassure her, but it didn't. What if he lost his grip on her arm? What if whatever it was that waited for them below suddenly decided to come up for a visit?

"Kylie!"

She jerked her head up to the entrance to the large sinkhole. Bright light spilled in from the opening, making it hard to see. Then she saw a body falling.

No, not just a body. It was Ellie.

"Shit!" Perry screamed, flapping his large bird wings as fast as he could. "I can't catch her. I can't."

An eerie sense of calm settled over Kylie. She reached out with her free hand just as gravity brought Ellie's body past them and latched on to the vampire's forearm. Kylie's hold was weak, though, and her palm started to slip. She tried to tighten her grip, lost it, and finally caught the girl by her wrist.

Ellie screamed and started to fight. Her eyes glowed a bright red in the darkness.

"It's me," Kylie said.

"Everyone, hang on!" Perry's voice bounced off the earthen walls of the pit.

Ellie struggled again, and Kylie pulled her closer. "I've got you."

And she did. Kylie put every ounce of thought and strength into not letting go of Ellie's wrist.

The sound of air *whoosh*ing and huge bird wings flapping filled the darkness, and in a few seconds, Perry lifted all three of them out of the hole. Once they were back in the light, he flew them about a hundred feet up the path before he descended and dropped them carefully on the solid earth.

He landed beside them, talons hitting the earth with a thud. As Kylie suspected, he'd shifted into a prehistoric-looking bird with dark gray feathers. He was about the size of a small plane. Then the rumble beneath the ground started again.

"Run!" he ordered.

He didn't have to tell them twice. Kylie and Ellie took off, flying through the woods, dodging trees, ducking under limbs, and leaping over thick bunches of thornbushes.

Kylie kept glancing up to make sure Perry was okay. He was still following them, gliding easily over the tips of the trees, making sure they were safe.

Once they were out of the trees, Kylie dropped to the ground and gasped for air, her pulse racing. She could hear her blood gushing in her veins. Ellie dropped down beside her, breathing not quite as hard, but still a little shaky.

Perry landed beside them and transformed himself back into human form.

"What the freaking hell were you doing?" he screamed at Kylie, his eyes blood red with fury.

She swallowed another gulp of air. "Trying to save you."

"I didn't need saving!" He flapped his arms up and down almost as if he'd forgotten he was no longer a bird. He turned his anger on Ellie. "And you? What the hell is your excuse?"

She coughed and then said, "I . . . figured if I came back alive and you two didn't, the rest of your group would probably kill me. I didn't have a choice but to go in after you."

Suddenly Burnett, eyes in full protective mode and his fangs exposed, flashed onto the scene. "What happened?" he asked, his voice little more than a deep growl. "It sounded like an explosion."

"Earthquake, maybe," Perry said. "The ground just sank below us."

"But that's—" Burnett shook his head. "Is everyone okay?"

They all nodded. Burnett's gaze locked on Kylie. "You're bleeding. Go to the office and let Holiday check you all out." Kylie looked down at her arm. Ellie's nails must have scratched her when she caught her.

Burnett continued, "I'll check to see how bad the, uh, earthquake is." He turned to go.

"Wait!" Kylie called out, and Burnett returned in a blur of motion.

"What?" he asked, impatience clear in his voice.

"It wasn't an earthquake," she said. With clarity, she recalled seeing the eagle coming straight at her in full-scale attack mode. Now she understood his intention had been to make her run, but it didn't change the fact that it had been evil. She'd seen the darkness in his eyes. "The eagle was there."

And so was Jane Doe, although Kylie saw no reason to mention that.

At least not yet.

Burnett let loose another growl. "Go to the office. I'll see if I can get to the bottom of this."

As Kylie, Ellie, and Perry moved toward the office, Kylie looked at Ellie. "Thanks for going in to try and save us."

Ellie shrugged. "Don't give me too much credit. I really didn't know what would happen to me if I was the only one to survive." She chuckled. "Now that it's over with, that was fun."

"No, it wasn't," Kylie said, remembering how she felt when she saw Perry fall into the hole.

They took a few more steps, and Ellie's gaze, bright probably because of the blood, shot to Kylie's arm where the scratches ran down her arm, and she added, "I'm sorry. I'll bet I did that when I was fighting you. Thanks for saving me. I don't know what would have happened if you hadn't caught me. I couldn't seem to get into flying mode. I owe you. You name it and I'll do it, no questions asked."

"No need. You're welcome," Kylie said.

"And what about me?" Perry asked.

Kylie and Ellie looked at Perry and spoke at the same time. "Thanks."

"Can I name it and you'll do it?" Perry wiggled his brows, his tone filled with humor once again.

"No," Ellie and Kylie said at the same time.

"I know, how about instead you two just tell Miranda how I was your hero."

"I can do that," Ellie said. "Who's Miranda?"

"My girlfriend," Perry said, and he looked at Kylie. "Well, she will be as soon as I convince her."

They took a few more steps and Ellie said, "I'm sorry I slept with Derek."

"Forget it," Kylie said, because she planned on forgetting it herself.

The next couple of hours were a blur of interrogations by Burnett, who questioned all three of them, separately, several times. Kylie realized he wasn't doing it because he thought anyone would lie about what happened. He just didn't want something one person said to influence the memory of the other. Kylie didn't care about that. What she wanted to know was what had happened. Had they really gotten sucked down into a pit that led straight to hell? If so, why? Was it because of Jane Doe? Or was this something conjured up by Mario and his pals to torment her?

More important, would it happen again?

Unfortunately, Burnett had questions of his own and no answers. Holiday was just as clueless. But the look of fear on the camp leaders' faces scared Kylie more than anything else.

The moment the interview was over and Kylie stepped out of Burnett's office, Lucas met her at the door and pulled her into another room. He didn't say a word; he just pulled her against his warm—so warm—chest and held her.

"I was running errands for Burnett." His cheek pressed against the top of her head. "I just got back."

After a good long hug, he set her back and asked, "What happened *this time*?"

It was the last two words that hinted at Lucas's true feelings. Kylie frowned. "You sound like you think this was all my fault."

He shook his head. "I don't think that. But damn it, I'd like to go at least a couple of days where I didn't think I almost lost you."

She smiled. "You didn't almost lose me." And then she gave him the quick version about the sinkhole opening up and their mad tumble down it.

He stared into her eyes. "Were there spirits involved?"

"No. Well, one was there, but . . ."

"But what?" he snapped. He shook his head and growled. "You've got to stop letting them hurt you, Kylie."

"They don't hurt me."

"Bullshit!" His blue eyes turned an anger-filled orange. "I saw part of your vision, remember? I had to stand there and feel completely helpless while those people dragged you away. Do you have any idea how that made me feel?"

Kylie knew Lucas's emotion stemmed partly from his werewolf instincts. Weres were known to have an intense need to protect those they cared about. And she liked knowing he cared about her.

But she had to make him understand that dealing with ghosts was as important to her as shifting into a wolf was to him. It was her destiny, her path.

Kylie put her hand on his chest. "The spirit didn't do this," she said. "It was probably Mario and his grandson again and their shape-shifter buddy. If anything, the spirit probably saved my life."

Okay, so she was guessing that was what had happened. But it made more sense to her than it did that Jane was somehow evil.

He inhaled. "Damn it. What's with that guy? Doesn't he know when to quit?"

"Obviously not."

Lucas pulled her against him again. "The timing of this sucks."

"What timing?" Kylie asked.

"I have to go away for a few days." He touched her face. "If it wasn't an emergency, I wouldn't go."

"What happened?" Even as she asked the question, Kylie worried he wouldn't tell her. Werewolves were also known to keep things to themselves.

"I told you about my half-sister. She was supposed to come here for school when the summer camp ended."

"Yeah?" Kylie said, thrilled he trusted her enough to share.

"Well, now my dad has her with his pack and is refusing to let her come. I'm going to have to go there and change his mind."

"I thought you didn't get along with your dad."

"I don't. But I don't have a choice. I shouldn't be gone more than a few days at most, though. I'm going to have Will keep an eye on you."

Kylie remembered Lucas introducing her to Will, another werewolf, a while back. But as with most of the weres, she hardly knew him and didn't particularly like the idea of having a stranger "keep an eye on her."

"I'll be fine," she told him. "Burnett has assigned me shadows. I don't need—"

"It'll make me feel better. Knowing one of my own kind has your back."

Kylie didn't like being reminded that Lucas trusted his own kind more than he did the others. But she had too much stuff to worry about without taking on another problem to chew on her sanity.

"When are you leaving?" she asked.

"Now. I should be back by Saturday, or Sunday at the latest." He kissed her again. The kiss went on longer than a typical good-bye kiss, and it involved a lot of passion.

When he pulled away, she heard the slight humming sound rumbling from his chest.

She grinned with a hint of warning. "You're humming again."

He arched a brow. "You bring out the wolf in me." Leaning down, he gave her another quick kiss.

Seconds after he'd left, Kylie realized he hadn't said anything about asking her out this morning.

Was he having second thoughts? Closing her eyes, she pushed that worry into the mental closet with all her other worries.

Holiday walked into the room and hugged her. "I think we need a trip to the falls, don't you? How about I set it up with Burnett and tomorrow we make it a date?"

"That would be good," Kylie said. "Really good."

The next day, Kylie and Holiday ran through the cascading water of the falls and dropped down on the rocky bank. Tiny pinpoints of water spilled over from the rush of the falls and splattered against Kylie's face. Her hair, already soaked from the walk through the sheet of water, hung around her shoulders and dripped down onto her legs.

She didn't care. The serene atmosphere seeped into her pores, and for the first time in over a week, she felt at peace. She knew this didn't mean her problems were solved. They were far from it. But for right now, for this moment in time, she felt everything in her world was going to be okay.

Burnett, unhappy about their being here, stood guard outside. He'd been extra concerned about them coming out here because of yesterday's incident. That's how they were referring to the giant hole that nearly swallowed up Perry, Kylie, and Ellie: as the "incident."

The geologist they'd called in to look at the pit was calling it a freak of nature, a sinkhole. Kylie knew better, as did most of the campers at Shadow Falls. Amazingly, the size of the hole had shrunk before the scientist arrived. Magic, bad magic, was involved. This much Kylie knew, and Miranda had confirmed it, too.

Because of the weather and the thicket of trees, the security alarm hadn't picked up on any intruders. Burnett had been over-the-top pissed about that, too. Not at anyone in particular, but at the situation in general. She'd heard him on the phone with the FRU, telling them he needed a better security system ASAP.

But since whatever happened apparently came from underground, Kylie didn't know if a system existed that would detect underground intruders.

Powerful underground intruders who, for reasons Kylie didn't understand, wanted her dead.

Kylie breathed in the serenity of the falls. Amazing. Even the thought of being on someone's hit list couldn't ruin her peaceful mood.

Leaning back on her hands, she studied Holiday, who was doing the same. "You know, we should bring all the campers up here."

Holiday opened her eyes. "I wish it was that easy."

"What do you mean?"

"You don't bring someone to the falls, Kylie. They have to be called. Remember?"

Kylie did remember and was suddenly curious. "So why does the falls call some people and not others?"

"Don't know," Holiday said. "But it's said that they call less than half of one percent of all supernaturals."

"Are all of the ones called ghost whisperers?"

"All of the ones that I know of are. There are legends of the falls that go back thousands of years. The Native Americans called it sacred grounds and decreed that only the chosen could enter."

"Burnett entered," Kylie said.

"I know, and that shocks me."

"Because you don't think he's chosen?" Kylie asked.

"No, because he can't see spirits."

"You should have seen him watching you when everyone was greeting you at dinner the other night," Kylie said, acting on impulse. "I think he loves you, Holiday."

Holiday arched a brow. "Still trying to play matchmaker, huh?"

"Maybe I'm just trying to help out a couple of friends."

"Or maybe you're concentrating on someone else's problems so you don't have to think about your own."

"Perhaps," Kylie said with a shrug, "but right now my problems don't seem very bad." She gazed at the rock ceiling, marveling at the beauty of the rock's patterns.

Holiday chuckled. "It's amazing what happens in here, isn't it?" She inhaled. "I wish I could bottle it up and keep it in my purse to take a shot of when I needed it."

"Too bad we can't live in here," Kylie said.

"Have you seen the ghost since the incident?" Holiday stretched out her feet.

Kylie nodded. "She woke me up last night. I did what you said and asked if there was another body in the casket with her."

"What did she say?"

"Nothing. But she got that look again."

"What look?" Holiday asked.

"Like I'd jogged her memory or something. Whenever that happens, she disappears on me."

"Maybe she doesn't want to remember," Holiday said. Kylie heard the implication in the camp leader's voice: that Jane Doe didn't want to remember because she'd murdered innocent children.

"I think she's scared to remember," Kylie said, "but not for the reasons you believe."

"Then why is she so scared?"

Kylie hesitated. "Maybe it's the same reason I'm scared."

Holiday glanced over at her. "What are you scared of?"

"Of discovering the truth. Discovering what I am."

"Why?" Holiday asked as if confused.

"Because it's the unknown. Because it's been kept a secret from me all this time. Because it will probably change my life forever."

Kylie sat up straighter. "It's not that I don't want to know the truth. I do. I want to know it so bad I can taste it. Sometimes it's all I can think about. But I'm still scared. The day the Brightens, or the people we thought were the Brightens, came here, I was so scared my insides shook. I almost ran away. If Lucas hadn't come along, I probably would have."

Kylie swallowed hard. And that's when she decided to ask the question she'd longed to ask Holiday and hadn't had a chance to. "Have you seen any new spirits? Do you know if the elderly couple that came here that day died?"

"Their spirits haven't come to me, if that's what you're asking," Holiday answered.

Kylie bit down on her lip. "I can still remember how the old lady's hand felt on mine. For some reason, I don't think they were here to hurt me."

"Why else would they have been here, then?"

"I don't know." Kylie closed her eyes. "But just like I know that Jane Doe isn't a murderer, I kind of know that they weren't bad."

Holiday sat up and pulled her knees to her chest. "Maybe this is just your way of refusing to see the bad in people."

Kylie considered the theory for a second. Then she recalled the two times she'd seen the eagle and then the deer. She wasn't blind to evil. She could recognize it when she saw it, and it wasn't there with the faux Brightens. "Nope," she said. "That's not it."

Kylie's mind went back to Jane Doe. "Last night I remembered parts of the vision, and I recalled what the nurse told the doctor. That her husband—Jane Doe's husband—had just woken up and was asking about her."

"And you think that means something?" Holiday asked.

"Berta Littlemon was never married. And the vision makes me believe Jane Doe's husband had the same type of operation she had."

Holiday hesitated and then said, "Sometimes visions are hard to decipher."

"But all the other times I've had this type of vision, where I'm actually the person, they weren't puzzles that I had to piece together in order to figure out what they meant. They were scenes that actually took place."

"But the visions are from their perspective. And if Jane Doe is crazy, then . . ."

Kylie shook her head. "I don't think she's crazy. Or evil."

"I hope you're right," Holiday said.

"Me too."

They sat in silence for a long moment or two, just listening to the rush of water and the sound of calm. Kylie looked at Holiday again and felt the slightest bit of worry whisper across her mind. "What am I going to say to Sara when she comes here on Sunday?"

"You don't tell her anything, except how happy you are that she's well."

"It's going to be so weird having her here. She's from my old world, and my old world shouldn't be in my new world. It's like running into your Sunday school teacher at a kegger."

Holiday chuckled. "Or your gynecologist at the grocery store. I did that once. It was so weird." She reached over and rested her hand on Kylie's.

Normally, Holiday's touch brought nothing but calm, but not this time. This time, everything went black.

Chapter Twenty-seven

For a second, it felt as if someone had turned the lights off. Kylie could feel Holiday's hand on hers, but the cave was pitch black.

Then the lights came back on. Kylie looked around, feeling confused. They were no longer in the falls. Instead, she sat in an uncomfortable folding metal chair outside in a clearing under some kind of dark-colored awning. The wind smelled like rain. It was a cloudy day, and she felt sad. So much sadness.

What happened to the serenity of the falls? What the heck had just happened?

It took her a second to realize this was a vision. She wasn't sure what she was supposed to see this time, but she didn't care. She didn't want to see it.

Kylie tried to pull herself out of it. She wanted to be back, back where everything felt right, where calm was all around her, where the sound of water soothed her mind.

When that didn't work, she tried to figure out where she was. Her breath caught when she saw a casket sitting in front of the enclosure. Quiet tears filled her eyes, and she knew someone she cared about lay in that box.

"No," she whispered. "Please, no."

Someone touched her hand. Kylie recognized Holiday's touch before she looked over to see the camp leader sitting next to her. She wore somber black clothes, no makeup, and unshed tears made her sad green eyes look brighter than usual.

Then someone started talking from up near the casket. Kylie looked up, and Chris, the lead vampire, the one who did the Meet Your Campmates hour, stood beside the coffin. "We lost one of our own today. It's our custom when a vampire dies that . . ."

"No," Kylie whispered again, and suddenly she realized she was standing up, back in the falls. The sadness filling her chest now came with a less painful emotion, one that made it easier to breathe, but it still hurt.

She looked at Holiday, who sat on the rock, her arms holding her knees tight to her chest. The tears in her eyes told Kylie that Holiday hadn't just been in Kylie's vision. She'd actually experienced it herself.

Someone lives and someone dies. The words seemed to flow from the rock themselves and bounce around the stone walls.

Kylie looked at Holiday. "What does this mean?"

Holiday blinked and Kylie saw her attempt to put on a brave face. "Whatever happens, we'll be okay."

"*We* will," Kylie said, fighting the calmer feeling and letting the feeling of grief take the lead. "But someone here isn't going to be okay. We have to do something to save her. Or him."

It's our custom when a vampire dies that . . .

Chris's words tore at her heart. *When a vampire dies . . .* Oh, God. Please say it's not Della, or Burnett.

Holiday shook her head. "There's nothing to be done, Kylie." She inhaled. "Can't you feel it? Acceptance." Tears filled her eyes again. "It breaks my heart, but that's what they are telling us. Someone we love will die, and we have to accept it."

"But I don't want to accept it." Kylie turned and walked through the wall of water to the sunlight.

The instant her gaze landed on Burnett, all the calm from the falls shattered around her. The acceptance she'd felt earlier was little more than a vague memory.

Please not Burnett. Please not Della. Please not Burnett.

She repeated the mantra over and over in her mind, as though wishing would make it so. She wanted to run to him, to grab him by his hands and make him swear to her that he would be careful, that he wouldn't take any unnecessary risks.

But even as she thought those thoughts, she knew in her heart that nothing, and no one, would stop Burnett from being himself. And that meant him taking risks.

Kylie felt Holiday come to a stop beside her. Kylie glanced at the camp leader. Her gaze was locked on Burnett, and Kylie knew she'd been having the same thoughts about his safety that Kylie had.

Someone lives and someone dies. The words repeated themselves in her head.

"Are you guys ready?" Miranda called out on Friday evening from the living room.

Kylie sighed. Miranda was nervous. Tonight was her big date with Todd, the cute warlock, and Kylie and Della were going to go wait with her at the main gate.

"Just about." Kylie grabbed her hairbrush and gave her hair a few strokes, not really caring if her hair looked as though a bird had taken up residence there.

The last few days had passed by her in a haze. Accepting that someone was trying to kill her was bad, but trying to accept that someone she cared about, a vampire, was about to die was impossible.

She and Holiday had butted heads about trying to stop the vision they'd shared from becoming a reality. What if it was Della? Didn't Holiday care that it could be Burnett? Kylie had mentally gone through a list of all the vampires at camp. Some of them she didn't know all that well, but they didn't deserve to die. Kylie had come within a breath of telling Della about the vision, but just as she was about to say it, a wave of knowing passed over her. She couldn't tell.

For reasons Kylie didn't understand, she simply knew it would be wrong.

Holiday kept pointing out that Kylie was forgetting the message came with two parts. Someone lives. But what about the someone who dies? "You can't change Fate," Holiday had insisted.

Kylie still wanted to kick Fate's ass. The acceptance that had filled Kylie at the falls occasionally returned and tried to numb the ache. It helped, but not completely.

"I'm waiting," yelled Miranda again.

So am I. Kylie looked at the ghost sitting on the edge of the bed.

"One more minute," Kylie answered Miranda. The ghost was pregnant again, and she just sat there, holding her round belly as if to protect it.

"We have to talk, you know," Kylie whispered.

The spirit didn't answer.

"If you want me to help you, we have to talk."

She still didn't speak.

"I know the other ghosts think you did horrible things, but I don't really believe it. I'm trying to prove it, but I don't know if I can do it alone. I need your help."

More silence met Kylie's pleas. Then she heard Miranda calling again.

Kylie looked at the ghost. "I have to go now." She reached for her door and inhaled, knowing she needed to put on a front for Miranda, who was excited about her date with Todd. Never mind that the girl had asked Kylie at least ten times to tell her the story about how Perry had saved both her and Ellie from the sinkhole.

Miranda needed to make up her mind. But people who lived in glass houses shouldn't throw rocks. And she'd spent a lot of time in that particular glass house herself, trying to decide between Derek and Lucas.

Not anymore.

And she meant it, too. She did.

She missed Lucas. And when he came back, she was telling him straight out that she wanted to go out with him.

Last night, she'd even tried to find him in her dreams. Had Lucas been awake at the time, or could the pack somehow stop her from reaching him? She didn't know. So this morning, she'd found another way to contact him. Through that all-powerful thing called a cell phone.

He couldn't talk about what was happening there. She couldn't tell him about the issues with Fate. And telling him yes to going out with him just seemed like something she wanted to do in person. But they talked for about twenty minute about other things, like the vacations they'd had as children.

He'd visited about every foreign country Kylie had ever heard of and some that she hadn't. But he hadn't ever been to Disney World or to a real amusement park, for that matter, and she'd told him all about them. They'd decided to make that their first real date.

Just as soon as Kylie was removed from someone's hit list and free of her mandatory shadow.

Walking out of her bedroom, Kylie found Miranda pacing by the door. She looked pretty; she wore her hair swept up, with only a few soft blond strands falling around her neck. The different colors in her hair hardly showed when she wore it up.

She wore a sleeveless yellow sundress that had a few ruffles around the bottom and a pair of matching yellow sandals. The outfit was very feminine without looking too cute, sexy without looking slutty, and dressy without looking overdressed. For just a second, Kylie envied Miranda and her evening out. She wished Lucas were here and they could go somewhere away from the camp.

Somewhere she could forget about Fate snatching away one of her own.

Della stood up from the computer desk. Kylie's heart knotted at the mere possibility that it was her in that casket, and then she remembered bits and pieces of the conversation she'd had with Holiday this morning.

"Everyone is going to die sometime, Kylie."

Kylie could tell that Holiday tried to be brave for her. But if the camp leader's eyes were any indication, she'd cried as much as Kylie had and hadn't slept any more than Kylie, either.

"Fine," Kylie had retaliated. "But why tell us this? Why, if we can't prevent it, just to torture us with knowing it beforehand?"

"For some reason, they thought we needed to be warned."

"Well, they thought wrong!"

"They are seldom wrong, Kylie."

"Well, there's always a first time, isn't there!"

"Earth to Kylie!" Della yelled, bringing Kylie back to the present. "What is it with you? Did your little trip to hell mess up your mind?" Della grinned.

"What are you talking about?" Kylie asked.

"You keep staring at me and going blank. You've done it for almost two days now, and it's freaking me out a bit."

"I'm sorry."

"It's probably because she misses her hunky werewolf." Miranda placed a hand over her heart. "She's heartsick. Her aura is all grayish. She's gone without his kisses for almost two days." Then Miranda opened the front door and waved them out.

"Poor little thing," Della said.

Kylie rolled her eyes and followed them out. Good thing she liked her roommates, or she might really be pissed.

They hadn't stepped off the porch when Ellie, with a couple of other vampires, walked past.

Ellie shot over to Kylie. "How are your scratches?"

"Gone." Kylie held out her arm.

"Good." Just a bit of awkwardness moved in, and Ellie apparently noticed. "I'll see you."

"Yeah," Kylie said, and Ellie turned to go. It dawned on Kylie that in the vision, the person in the casket could have been Ellie. "Ellie?"

She swung around, and Kylie didn't know what she wanted to say; she just didn't want Ellie to leave thinking she'd been rude. "Thanks," Kylie blurted out.

Ellie looked puzzled. "For what?"

"For . . . being considerate enough to ask about my arm." *Okay, that sounded so lame.*

"Oh. You're welcome." Ellie walked backward, waved, then swung around and ran to catch up with her group.

"What was that all about?" Della asked when Ellie was out of hearing range and they were down the porch steps.

"Yeah," Miranda said. "I mean, if I'd found out someone had boinked my boyfriend, I wouldn't be so nice."

"Derek wasn't my boyfriend," Kylie said.

"Yeah, and bears don't do it in the woods, either," Della said.

Kylie held up her hands. "Stop it, okay? I don't care what happened between Ellie and Derek."

Della mouthed the word *liar* and then said, "Truth is, I don't like the chick. I hate the way she's so friendly and nice. Gives my kind a bad name."

Kylie frowned at Della. "Don't mistreat her because of this. I'm serious, Della. She didn't know about me when it happened."

"Okay," Della said. "That means she's not devious. But it still makes her a slut."

Miranda laughed and Kylie moaned. "I don't think she's like

that." Kylie hesitated and then added, "She jumped in the sinkhole, willing to risk her life to save Perry and me."

"Yeah, she did do that," Miranda said. "But it doesn't change the fact that—"

"Damn it! Can we just *not* talk about it," Kylie said.

"Man," Miranda said. "It must be time for your lunar PMS, because Della's right. You haven't been yourself lately. You're like majorly grumpy."

Kylie wished Miranda were right. That her mood hinged on nothing more than her being a werewolf, instead of her other long list of problems.

And if she ended up being a were, Lucas would be happy. Really happy.

"Shit!" Miranda muttered thirty minutes later.

They were still waiting for Todd, who'd gotten lost and had called Miranda and told her he was three minutes away.

"Shit what?" Della asked, but then said, "Oh, shit."

"What?" Kylie asked, obviously the only one in the dark.

Then she saw it, or rather him, and she completely agreed with the assessment. "Oh, shit."

"Hey," Perry said as he moved in. Kylie couldn't help noticing that he'd gotten his hair cut and wore a tighter-fitting shirt and jeans. Something about his haircut made him appear older, more of a man than a young teen. The way his shirt hugged his upper torso accented his broad shoulders. His eyes were blue, and the way they twinkled when he looked at Miranda had Kylie's heart melting. Confidence seemed to ooze from his smile. Even his body posture spoke of a coolness she'd never seen him exude. For the first time, Kylie spotted what it was that Miranda found so attractive about Perry.

"Looking hot," Della said, obviously noticing the same thing.

"Why, thank you." His blue eyes sparkled as he shifted his gaze back to Miranda. "But I'm not the only one looking good tonight. Really good."

"Thanks." Miranda looked at Kylie as if begging her to do something.

Kylie glanced at Della, who just grinned.

"Uh, Perry . . ." Kylie started talking, not sure how she would fix this. "We were just sort of talking, privately, about—"

"About Miranda's date," Perry said.

"Oh, shit," Della said again.

Ditto, Kylie wanted to say.

Perry focused on Miranda. "I know about your date."

Miranda shot Kylie a look as if accusing her of spilling the beans.

Kylie shook her head no and refocused on Perry. His eyes changed from blue to bright green, but if Perry was about to wig out on them and change into some kind of warlock-eating monster, he gave no other indication. "I just wanted to tell you that while I don't like it, I'm hoping you'll give me the same chance you're giving this asswad . . . I mean, this guy."

Della chuckled.

"Go out with me tomorrow night," Perry went on. "Let me prove to you that I'm the guy you want."

Miranda opened her mouth to say something, but nothing came out. Kylie couldn't talk either, because she felt a lump in her throat—a lump of emotion and pride for Perry.

"I . . . I guess I could go out tomorrow night." Miranda sounded shocked and a little swept off her feet.

Then, from the corner of her eyes, Kylie saw something move at the office window. When she looked back, she spotted Burnett and Holiday standing there high-fiving each other. No doubt Burnett was listening to the conversation and sharing the details with Holiday.

Kylie should have guessed someone had helped out Perry. She was a little embarrassed she hadn't tried this herself. He so deserved his shot with Miranda.

Perry nodded, stepped closer, and then pressed a quick kiss on Miranda's cheek. It had to be the most romantic thing Kylie had ever seen.

If only the tan truck, with a personalized license plate that read TODD, hadn't pulled up right then.

"Oh, shit," Della said again.

Ditto.

Chapter Twenty-eight

Todd, a fairly hot-looking guy with sandy-colored hair, jumped out of his truck and frowned. He obviously didn't miss that Perry stood touch-me close to Miranda. From the look on Todd's face, he hadn't missed the kiss, either.

"Someone trying to steal my date?" Todd's words could have been meant in humor, but his tone told another story. He strode forward and dropped a possessive arm around Miranda's shoulders.

Kylie saw Perry's entire body stiffen. His eyes turned a bright red.

Todd, still studying Perry, tightened his brows to check out Perry's pattern.

The teen's jaw dropped a little when he realized exactly what Perry was. Kylie waited for the puddle to appear around the guy's feet.

The office door opened and shut behind them.

"Uh, Perry? Can I see you a minute?" Burnett called.

Kylie moved in close to Perry. "Don't screw it up, now," she whispered.

Perry, anger oozing from his pores, continued to stare at Todd. Kylie could feel the electricity start to buzz and hum around the shape-shifter.

"Don't do it," Kylie repeated in a whisper.

Perry looked back at Burnett, then at Kylie, and then back at Miranda. "I'll see you tomorrow night," he said, but his tone was so tight, Kylie knew what it cost him to keep his composure.

Then he turned around, transformed himself into his favorite bird, and flew up, making tight circles around them.

Della leaned over to Kylie. "He's going to crap on Todd's car, just watch!"

Kylie did watch and hoped Della was wrong. Okay, it would have been really funny, because as big of a bird as Perry was, that would have been a lot of crap, but Kylie didn't think it would impress Miranda. And that, she realized, was what this had been all about.

Still, Kylie didn't relax until Perry changed directions and flew back toward the woods.

"Hey, I know. Why don't we go to the swimming hole tonight?" Della suggested fifteen minutes later on the walk back to their cabin. "A bunch of campers have attached a swing to one of the higher cliffs so we can jump into the water. I'm dying to try it."

It was the word *dying* that had Kylie catching her breath. She'd mostly blocked Jane Doe's warning from her mind and had no idea why she suddenly felt so overwhelmed by emotion. "No." She blurted out the answer so fast that Della made a face.

"Why?"

Because you could die. "Because . . ." Kylie struggled to explain the situation until she remembered she had a real reason. "Because Holiday is bringing Burnett's computer over for me to use."

"Why would you need his computer when we have one?"

"To send an e-mail to . . . It's a ghost thing. I'm sending an e-mail to a deceased woman's family, trying to clear up their heritage, and Burnett has an untraceable e-mail address," Kylie said.

"Oh." Della fell silent. Funny how mentioning the word *ghost* was a conversation killer.

"So, what time is she showing up?" she asked finally. "I might run to the swimming hole while she's with you."

And you could get killed. Nope. Not happening. "But you're my shadow."

"Holiday let Jonathon leave early when she was there."

"But that was before the sinkhole." Her explanation sounded convincing, and the knot in Kylie's stomach relaxed. She might not be able to tell Della about Fate's premonition or whatever it was Holiday called it, but it wouldn't stop her from watching out for Della.

"Okay," Della said, but she didn't look happy about it. Which was fine with Kylie. An unhappy but alive Della was better than the alternative.

A group of campers rounded the corner and walked past them. Kylie felt the cold stare practically slap her, and when she recognized one of the girls as a werewolf, she figured she knew whose cold stare gave her shivers.

Another glance at the group confirmed her suspicions.

Fredericka.

Kylie kept walking past them, hoping to ignore—

"Hey, blondie," Fredericka called out.

Closing her eyes for a second, Kylie willed herself patience. When she turned, she found herself staring Fredericka right in the eyes. The were had silently moved in and stood so close that Kylie could count Fredericka's eyelashes. The were smirked in an unappealing way. And that's when Kylie had an epiphany.

She wasn't afraid.

Fredericka with her I'll-rip-you-to-shreds attitude didn't scare her anymore. She annoyed Kylie to no end, made her feel something akin to jealousy—although she trusted Lucas not to cheat—but nope, there wasn't an ounce of fear.

"What do you need?" Kylie put her hand out to stop Della from getting between them. Della, probably livid at being held back, growled and exposed her canines. Fredericka's eyes turned a bright pissed-off orange.

"I thought you'd like to know that Lucas phoned me and told me he's not returning until late tomorrow night," the were said in a sickly sweet voice. "He's having issues with his dad. Sad stuff. Poor guy. He needed someone to talk to."

Kylie knew the only reason Fredericka told her this was to annoy her.

And it worked.

But Kylie's pride had her smiling and pretending everything was great. But darn if there wasn't a part of her that didn't want to kick Fredericka's ass and worry about the consequences later.

"Thanks for letting me know. I'll look for his call in a bit." She smiled extra sweetly right back at Fredericka and walked away.

Fredericka caught her by the arm. Her fingers dug into Kylie's elbow. Kylie almost attempted to pull away. Then she remembered that if everyone was right about her being a protector, she wouldn't have the power to take on the were.

The only way Kylie could take on Fredericka was if she tried to hurt someone Kylie cared about.

And considering that other person was Della, and there might be a death cloud hanging around her and every other vampire at Shadow Falls, Kylie wasn't about to let Della get involved.

Kylie would have to use her wits to get out of this. Did she have enough?

"Do you want to let go of my arm?" Kylie pretended like it didn't feel as if her bones were about to be crushed under the were's grasp.

"Not really," Fredericka growled.

"Okay, but don't say I didn't warn you. Because I've got this spirit hanging around and she's been in a piss-poor mood for about thirty years." It was a lie. Pure lie. But Kylie wasn't above using what she could. "Ever since she was killed by a rogue werewolf, she's been aching—"

Fredericka's hand dropped. "Go to hell."

Kylie smiled. "Thanks for the invite, but I almost went there yesterday and didn't like it all that much." Kylie then wrinkled her nose. "Is that skunk I smell?"

Fredericka's eyes turned burnt orange and Kylie knew she'd pushed too far. The were's hand clamped down on Kylie's elbow and tightened. Someone darted out of the woods. From the corner of Kylie's eyes, she saw it was Will, Lucas's friend.

He cleared his throat, and the she-wolf didn't even look at him. She just dropped her hold on Kylie and took off with a tail-tucked-between-her-legs kind of look.

Kylie didn't like realizing that Will had been hounding her footsteps, unseen. The fact that neither Kylie nor Della had sensed he'd been hounding them told her he was good at it, too.

Della glared at him, but Kylie did the right thing. "Thanks."

"No problem." He disappeared back into the woods.

"What the hell did you say 'thank you'? We didn't need him intervening. I could have opened a can of whoop ass on that she-wolf and she'd have been whimpering like a hungry pup."

And she might have killed you.

They had gotten only a few feet away when Kylie remembered what Fredericka said about Lucas calling her. Pausing, she pulled out her phone to see if she'd missed his call.

Nope.

The were could have been lying. How could Kylie ever know? Then . . . duh, the obvious hit. Della, like the rest of her kind, was a walking, talking lie detector. She could hear heartbeats and pulse rates and knew when someone was telling a lie.

Kylie looked at Della. "Was Fredericka telling the truth about Lucas calling her?"

Della made a face. "Is lying wrong if you know it's what the person wants to hear?"

"Just tell me!"

Della mouthed the word *sorry*. "She was telling the truth."

After Kylie arrived back at the cabin, Holiday came over with Burnett's laptop and they sent an e-mail to Catherine O'Connell's family. They'd concocted a story about being an old friend of Catherine's and thought her family should know that she had wanted to tell them something right before she'd passed away. It sounded good. Convincing, even. And then they did a cut and paste of all the family tree information that came with photos.

Hopefully, it would do the trick. Not that Kylie suspected she'd ever know for sure. But she felt good about keeping her part of the bargain. Never mind that the information Kylie got from her about Berta Littlemon had yet to give her any answers. And Kylie hoped it didn't. The last thing she wanted to discover was that she was wrong about Jane Doe.

While Holiday and Della chatted at the table, Kylie sent her stepfather an e-mail and told him the shift schedule if he wanted to come on Sunday to Parents Day. She hoped he'd e-mail back and say he couldn't make it so she wouldn't have to deal with Sara and her stepdad on the same day. His e-mail came back superfast. He said he looked forward to seeing her on Sunday.

"Crap," Kylie muttered.

Holiday glanced over at her. "Bad news?"

"No, everything is just friggin' fabulous," Kylie said, and dropped her head on the desk. She didn't know if she would survive.

"Are you okay?" Holiday asked when Kylie walked her outside a few minutes later.

"As good as can be expected, I guess," Kylie lied. Holiday nodded and they said their good-nights.

When Kylie got back inside the cabin, Della was answering e-mails and Kylie sat at the kitchen table. She longed to call it a night, but she wanted to be here when Miranda got back from her date with Todd.

Kylie looked at the clock on the wall. That could be several more hours from now, though. Hours that Kylie had to fret over her own problems.

Della swung around. "That's not good. Or maybe it is."

"What?" Kylie asked.

Della pointed to the door and Miranda walked in. Her face was unreadable. She moved over to the table and dropped into a chair with as much drama as she could muster.

"And?" Kylie asked, and spotted hope in Della's eyes. Kylie knew that Della hoped the same thing Kylie did.

Hoped that the date was a complete bust and Perry still had a shot.

Miranda merely shrugged.

"Don't do this!" Della snapped. "Spill it or I'll reach down your throat for the answer myself."

Miranda spoke up. "He was . . . nice. Dinner was nice. Holding his hand was nice."

"Did he kiss you?" Kylie asked, unsure how Miranda defined "nice." If Kylie worked hard enough, she could believe "nice" meant it wasn't anything special.

Miranda nodded. "The kiss was . . ."

"Let me guess," Della said. "It was nice."

"Right," Miranda said.

Della slapped her hand on the table. " 'Nice' is just another way of saying 'friggin' boring'!"

Miranda frowned. "That's exactly what I thought."

Kylie and Della both squealed with excitement.

"What?" Miranda asked. "You're happy my date wasn't exciting?"

"No," Kylie said. "Let's just say we're more excited about tomorrow night's date."

A bright smile lit up Miranda's face. "Me too. Can you believe Perry did that? I mean, he was so . . ."

"Romantic," Kylie said.

"Hot," Della added.

"Sweet," Miranda whispered. "I couldn't stop thinking about him all night."

And that was the best news Kylie had gotten all day.

That night, Kylie stared at the ceiling forever, craving sleep that didn't come. One hour passed. Then two.

Her mind started naming off her problems. She still didn't know what she was. She couldn't stop Fate from taking someone she cared about. She had someone wanting her dead, probably the rogue underground paranormal gang headed by Mario, who still hadn't forgiven her for not wanting to marry his murdering grandson. Lucas was calling and chatting with Fredericka. Sara was coming to visit on Sunday with Kylie's mom. And her stepdad was going to drop by, too. Kylie still hadn't solved her amnesia spirit's issues, and she wasn't even a hundred percent sure the woman wasn't a killer.

Kylie's sleep-deprived brain chewed on each and every issue and didn't spit out any answers. She'd just fallen asleep when she heard a light *tap-tap* on her bedroom window.

At first, she thought she'd imagined it. Then she thought it was the blue jay again. "I'm not your mama," Kylie muttered.

The tapping stopped.

Kylie lay there, listening. The silence suddenly seemed ominous. She took in a shallow breath, and the sound seemed abnormally loud. The window was locked, right?

She recalled opening it the day before, hoping to invite in a breeze. And no, she couldn't recall locking it afterward.

But hey . . . considering the types of intruders Kylie feared the most, the kind that could create sinkholes and materialize out of thin air, what was the chance a locked window would stop them?

So why, Kylie wondered, did the distinct sound of someone lifting her window send sharp jolts of fear straight to her heart?

Chapter Twenty-nine

Kylie bounced out of bed, and her heart leapt with her. Her gaze shot to the window, where she saw two hands gripping the windowsill.

A scream rose in her throat, but then Della's voice echoed outside the window. "Try to crawl in the window and I'm gonna crawl up your ass! And the position is just about right for me to do it."

The hands disappeared. Someone hit the ground.

Kylie ran to the window to make sure Della didn't engage in a fatal fight. Della, in her loose-fitting blue cotton Mickey Mouse pajamas, had her hands on her hips, standing over someone laid out on the lawn. Her eyes were a bright green.

"Shit!" Ellie said, her own eyes glowing. "I just wanted to talk to Kylie." She looked over at the window to Kylie and grabbed her baseball hat that read, LITTLE VAMP.

"See that?" Della pointed toward the front porch. "It's called a door. And most people use them."

"I didn't want to wake anyone else."

"Then you wait until a decent hour!" Della countered.

Kylie didn't know what Ellie wanted to discuss, but if it had anything to do with Derek, Kylie was willing to hear her out.

"It's okay," Kylie said. "Come on in."

"Oh, right. Reward bad behavior!" Della looked disgusted, but Kylie couldn't help it.

Ellie smirked at Della, then stood and started to climb in the window again.

Della yanked her back. "Use the freaking door!"

When Kylie walked out of her bedroom, Della was gone and Ellie sat on the sofa.

"What's up?" She went over and sat in the chair next to her.

She looked up. "I don't know, I just wanted to talk."

"About what?" Kylie asked.

Ellie pulled one leg up to her chest. "A couple of things. Derek said you might be a good person to talk to about my issues."

Kylie chest tightened. "If this is about you and Derek—"

"No." She rolled her eyes. "I wasn't lying when I said there was nothing between us . . . romantically. I like Derek as a friend. A good friend, but that's all. And that's some of what I wanted to talk about."

"I'm not following you," Kylie said.

"I'm worried about Derek. He's really upset about you two, and I sort of feel it's my fault. And when something's your fault, you feel responsible for fixing it."

Kylie frowned. "It's not your fault. Things weren't going right when he left."

"Yeah, he said that . . . but still . . ."

"It's not your fault." Kylie cupped her knees in her palms. Did Derek really regret everything? The question hung somewhere between her head and her heart. "What's the other thing you needed to talk about?" she asked, not wanting to discuss Derek. She wasn't ready to delve into that Pandora box of emotions. The past was the past.

Ellie shrugged and adjusted her cap again. "I just don't think I belong here. I feel bad that Holiday worked so hard to get me accepted, but . . . I think it's best I go."

Kylie leaned forward. "You want to leave Shadow Falls?"

"Yeah." She frowned. "All of it just doesn't feel right."

Her words didn't make sense, so Kylie just shook her head. "All of what?"

She glanced at Della's bedroom door and scooted over to the end of the sofa, closer to Kylie, and lowered her voice. "The whole supernatural world. Derek said you would probably understand because you felt the same way for a while. I mean, don't you miss it? Don't you miss being normal? Just hanging with your old friends? I want that back. I miss . . . Before I worried about what I wanted to take in college. Now I worry about where I'm going to get my next pint of blood."

"You can't leave, Ellie. I'm not mad at you, if that's what this is about. I mean, at first I was hurt, but . . ."

"It's not that. Really," Ellie said. "Even my own kind here aren't exactly welcoming," she whispered. "But that's not even it. Nothing about being this"—she waved a hand up and down her body—"feels right. I miss . . . being human. I miss my mom, who died a couple of years ago." Her voice shook with emotion. "Maybe if I just lived among humans, I would feel better."

A wave of empathy for Ellie washed over Kylie. Damn if she didn't know exactly how the girl felt. "It's hard," Kylie said. "But you can't leave here. Holiday says that most of the young vampires end up joining gangs just to survive." A question slammed into Kylie's mind. Was Ellie the vampire who was going to die? Was she going to leave Shadow Falls and get mixed up in something terrible?

The question caused Kylie to catch her breath.

Della's bedroom door opened and she flashed across the room and stopped right in front of them, her hair a little in disarray. Kylie got an image of her burying her head under a pillow, trying not to listen. Not that her plan worked.

Both Kylie and Ellie looked at Della.

Ellie scowled. "You've been listening, haven't you? Can't a person have—"

"Yeah, nitwit. I tried not to, but I've been listening," she said in her best smartass tone. "But Kylie's right. You can't leave. Nothing is easy about being us, or trying to fit into a new family of vampires, but it gets easier."

"How?" Ellie asked.

Miranda's door swung open. "You make friends," she said, and stumbled into the room, looking half-asleep.

"Does everyone listen in to everyone else's conversations in this cabin?" Ellie asked, sounding annoyed.

"Pretty much." Miranda came over and dropped on the sofa beside Ellie. "Friends don't keep very many secrets."

"But you guys aren't my friends."

"We could be," Kylie said, and Della and Miranda nodded.

Ellie's gaze widened and she looked away, but not before Kylie saw emotion in her eyes. The warm sensation filling Kylie's chest reminded her of the feeling she got at the falls, and she knew it had been the right thing to say. Then for some crazy reason, she saw a flash of the funeral vision in her mind.

Was that a sign? Did that mean Ellie really was the person in the casket? And had this changed the outcome?

Saturday was about two things. Well, three if you counted Miranda's unending attempt to change Socks back to feline form. The other two things were: emotionally getting ready for Parents Day and getting Miranda ready for her date with Perry.

Holiday had stopped by with a plan for tomorrow. Instead of locking Socks in her closet during Parents Day, she thought it would be a good idea to cart the little stinker over to her cabin for the day. That way, Kylie, Della, and Miranda could bring Kylie's mom and

Sara back to the cabin and hang out, making it hard for Sara to ask too many questions about the whole healing process.

Since Kylie pretty much decided that no amount of effort would prepare her emotionally for seeing Sara here at camp, or for having to face her stepdad again, she put all that out of her mind and focused her energy into getting Miranda ready for her date.

When Miranda, a nervous witch, vetoed everything in her own closet, Della and Kylie gave her carte blanche with their own. Ellie even came over for an hour to help get Miranda ready. It was a little awkward, but . . . Derek was right; Ellie really was a nice person. Besides, Kylie hadn't been able to forget the feeling she'd gotten last night, a sense that Ellie had been the one in the casket in that vision. And maybe, just perhaps, befriending Ellie had saved her life.

After trying on about six outfits, Miranda chose Kylie's LBD, little black dress.

At seven o'clock, Perry showed up on their doorstep, looking as much of a hottie as he had the night before. Burnett had loaned him his Mustang, and supposedly, Perry had a night planned that would knock Miranda's socks off.

When Miranda showed up a little past midnight, she had indeed lost her socks. And her shoes. Of course, she didn't need them because she practically floated through the door.

When Kylie and Della demanded details, Miranda said only, "It was a hell of a lot better than nice." Then she floated into her bedroom and went to bed.

Having done a little celebratory dance with Della, Kylie went to bed and waited to see if Lucas would call her. She almost called him but decided against it. She'd called him last time. It was time he made the next move. As she might have guessed, though, her phone never rang. But the ghost dropped by for another cold, silent visit.

Kylie begged her to talk, and she finally spoke, but not anything helpful. *"It's not your fault. That's what they wanted me to tell you."*

"What's not my fault?" she spouted out. The spirit faded, and the cold ache in the room swelled in Kylie chest and reminded her that she was no closer to solving Jane's problems than she was to solving her own.

Sunday morning, when Kylie, with Della in tow, got back to her cabin after breakfast, Lucas sat on the front porch. The moment his gaze touched hers, her heart started racing. He looked good. Was it her imagination that he looked more masculine and somehow buffer, or was it because of the approaching full moon?

He smiled at her, and she smiled back, feeling herself melt a little inside. She wanted to run into his arms and kiss him. But she knew he wouldn't like that in front of Della.

Then all those warm, gooey feelings faded when she wondered if he'd already visited Fredericka. But damn it, jealousy was such an ugly emotion.

"Don't even ask," Della said as she stepped on the porch. "I'll go inside and let you two make out." She opened the door and looked back over her shoulder. "But if you take her off this porch, I'll hunt you down."

"I won't." He nodded his thanks.

The moment the door closed, Lucas pulled Kylie into his arms. "I missed you," he whispered, and his lips melted against hers.

His kiss was light but still passionate. He held her close and she felt the subtle differences in him that she'd noted earlier—all muscle, all male. Hard in all the places she was soft.

When the kiss ended, she ran her fingers over his shoulders. "Do you get . . . buffer the closer we get to a full moon?"

He smiled and pressed his forehead against hers. "Yes. It's my body's way of preparing for the shift." He swung around and leaned against the front of the cabin. Then he pulled her against him and slid his hand down to rest on her waist.

"Did you miss me?" he asked.

"Of course." She smiled at him, breathing in his scent and loving being close.

"No new ghost disasters since I left?" He arched one dark brow.

"No," she said. "No disasters. Except, I was sort of hoping you'd call me back. It's been two days."

"I'm sorry. My dad was being an ass and I had to stay longer than I'd anticipated. Didn't Fredericka tell you?"

Kylie's annoyance peaked. "Yeah, but it would have been nice if you'd called me yourself."

His gaze tightened as if he were trying to read her. "It's not like . . . The only reason I called her was because Clara wanted to talk to her."

"Clara?" Kylie asked.

"My half-sister. She and Fredericka got to know each other when she went back with me before."

Great! Lucas's sister was friends with Fredericka. Kylie's jealousy inched up another notch.

He stared into her eyes. "I heard Will had to calm down Fredericka. I'll talk to her about it."

Kylie instantly realized she didn't want him talking to Fredericka. She bit down on her lip. Could she tell Lucas he couldn't be friends with Fredericka when she wouldn't want him telling her whom she could, and couldn't, be friends with?

No. She couldn't. So she just said, "Don't worry. I handled it." She stared at his chest for a second, trying to get her wayward jealousy under control.

He tilted her chin up and his blue eyes gazed into hers. "You okay?"

"Yeah," she lied. "Just . . . a little worried about later. Seeing my stepdad and then Sara showing up."

"Can I do anything to help? All you have to do is ask."

Her heart tightened at his concerned tone. Lucas cared about her. She knew that. She believed it. Which meant she couldn't let Fredericka come between them. She just couldn't.

"You just did by being here." She gave him a long hug.

It wasn't until he left that she realized neither of them had said anything about him asking her out.

Kylie and Della went to the dining hall a little early to offer Holiday their help. Miranda had stayed behind to get all dolled up, in case Perry saw her.

Miranda and Della—the vamp in full moody mode, probably because she had to see her parents today—had bickered all morning. Kylie reminded them both to be on their best behavior around her mom and Sara. She honestly didn't care if they argued in front of her stepdad.

Well, maybe she cared a little, but Sara and her mom were more important.

They had just about gotten to the end of the path when someone called, "Wait up." Kylie turned, and Ellie, with a bright smile, came running up to join them.

Ellie grinned and reached over as if to hug Della. The fast embrace knocked Ellie's cap off.

Della backed up. "I'm not a hugger, Ellie. Nothing personal. But most vampires aren't huggers either."

"I'll work on that." Ellie grinned and snagged her hat from the ground. "Della voted me into her circle. I'm officially a member of the Shadow Falls vampire family."

"Cool." Kylie was happy for Ellie, but somewhere deep inside, this stood as another reminder that she didn't belong to any group.

Odd, how she'd helped Ellie do something that she couldn't seem to do for herself.

Della frowned. "It's nothing. Don't make a big deal of it."

"It is a big deal," Ellie said. "I was leaving today, but you guys changed my mind. Heck, you could have saved my life." She looked ahead and saw a couple of other vamps. "I need to run. But seriously, thank you!"

Della stared after her. "I still think she's way too touchy-feely."

Kylie watched Ellie run up and chat with the others. She wasn't sure why she believed Ellie was the vamp the death angels warned would die, but the tiniest bit of hope that she'd saved Ellie offered Kylie a shimmer of reprieve from her own troubles.

Or it did until about thirty minutes later, when Kylie saw the parents start to pour in. Everyone but her dad. Had he forgotten again?

Chapter Thirty

As the room filled with parents, Kylie really began to worry her dad was a no show. Her throat felt tight, her heart started breaking. Wanting to get away from the crowd, she escaped outside and went to sit on the office porch . . . to wait. If he didn't show, it wouldn't matter, she told herself. It wasn't as if he hadn't let her down before.

So why did it hurt so much?

It wasn't until she got settled in her chair that she remembered she was still being shadowed. She wasn't supposed to leave the dining hall without Holiday.

She started to get back up when she heard, "Hello, Miss Galen." The female voice startled her and she yelped.

She turned in the chair and found herself staring at Lucas's grandmother Mrs. Parker. The fact that Lucas's grandmother knew who she was was a surprise.

"I'm sorry, I didn't see you. You startled me," Kylie said, still holding her hand over her heart. "It must run in the family." She smiled. "Lucas is always sneaking up on me."

"It's a werewolf thing." She motioned to the chair. "Do you mind?"

"Of course not." Kylie leaned back in her chair and tried to appear relaxed. But she got the feeling that this wasn't just an accidental encounter. What could Lucas's grandmother want with her?

The woman sauntered across the porch. For someone who moved so slow, it surprised Kylie that she did it so silently and with an amazing amount of grace. She lowered herself into the chair, and even the wood didn't creak. She folded her aged hands in her lap, looking the epitome of propriety. She stared out for a few minutes, whether looking at the sky or the woods, Kylie didn't know.

The silence seemed awkward, but Kylie got the feeling it would be rude to rush her. For a second, she stared at the woman's hands, remembering the hands of the elderly woman who had come into the camp pretending to be her grandmother.

Mrs. Parker glanced at Kylie. "My grandson is quite smitten with you."

Smitten? Kylie didn't know people still used that word. But since the woman was well over a hundred, Kylie supposed it fit her vocabulary.

"Uh, I . . . like Lucas, too."

She nodded and leaned in a bit. "He mentioned that you knew him when you two were young."

"Yes." The concerned look on the woman's face told Kylie what this might be about. Most supernaturals believed that a supernatural raised by rogue parents was unsalvageable—once a rogue, always a rogue. For that reason, Lucas had lied and stated he'd been raised by his grandmother all his life. "But I would never tell anyone that he lived with his parents."

"Good," she said. "He has high hopes of making something of himself. He is being considered in line to be a grand leader of the pack—to sit on the werewolf council—and this news could tarnish his reputation." She tightened her brows and studied Kylie's pattern and frowned.

"I'm sorry," Kylie said, assuming the woman's frown was about Kylie's unwillingness to let her see past her pattern. "I don't mean to be rude. I still don't know how to open up. I'm assuming Lucas explained my situation. That I'm not sure what I am."

"Yes. Lucas enlightened me on the matter." She continued to study Kylie. "Tell me, Miss Galen. Do you think you're werewolf?"

The question hung heavy in the air, reminding Kylie that Lucas had asked much the same question. Kylie's stomach knotted, and instantly she suspected what this conversation was really about. Obviously, his pack weren't the only ones wanting him to stay away from her. "I'm not sure."

Mrs. Parker smiled. "For your sake and my grandson's, I hope so."

"What do you mean?" Kylie asked, even though she suspected.

Leaning forward, she touched Kylie's shoulder. The touch was warm like Lucas's, and while Kylie wanted to pull back, she felt no animosity in the older woman's hand, nor did she see it in her eyes. There was only concern and love for her grandson. "The bloodline running in my grandson's veins is pure. His life mate will have to be one of his own kind."

"And if she's not?" Kylie asked.

"If she is part were, but shows loyalty to her heritage, they may overlook her lacking. But if she is not from our blood, then not only will he be forced to step down from his place, but the pack will no longer accept him as one of them. A were must never put another being who is not of our blood before he puts his own people."

"That sounds like racism," Kylie said.

The woman shrugged. "I cannot speak of what is right or wrong. I only speak of what is. Oddly enough, it is to correct a wrong that Lucas has fueled his long held desire to be a part of the council. Since Lucas was seven and came to live with me, he has been forced to lie to his own people and to the world about his upbringing. His goal has been to make it to that respected place and then change the views of our people about children born to rogues. He aches to show that the mistakes of the parents are not always passed down to the innocent child."

She rose from the chair as silently as she sat.

"Hey, pumpkin! There you are." Tom Galen's voice filled Kylie's ears, but she couldn't look away from Mrs. Parker's face to say hello to her stepdad. Was the woman really telling Kylie that if she wasn't werewolf, then she and Lucas couldn't get married?

Heck, she hadn't even officially agreed to go out with him. Marriage was a long, long way from here.

Footsteps sounded on the porch steps.

"I will go and let you visit with your company," Mrs. Parker said, and she nodded politely at Kylie's stepdad and walked off.

"You okay?" he asked, looking oddly at the elderly woman as he dropped into the chair she'd just vacated. "Is something wrong?"

"No," Kylie answered, and tried to push away her concern about Lucas's grandma so she could deal with her concern about seeing her stepdad again.

The visit with her stepdad wasn't as awkward as Kylie had thought. Then again, maybe it was just that after the extremely awkward visit with Lucas's grandmother, Kylie's awkward meter was malfunctioning.

Before Holiday missed her, Kylie moved her dad into the dining hall. Poor Holiday skirted from one group to another, trying to keep the peace.

As Kylie expected, her stepdad asked about her mom. Kylie didn't tell him about the business lunch/date her mom had gone on. He talked about some of the trips they'd taken on their father/daughter outings. Then he asked if she thought maybe they could go on another one soon.

Kylie hadn't said yes, but she hadn't said no. "I'll have to look at my schedule." For once, telling the truth—that some old vampire either wanted her to marry his grandson or planned to kill her—wasn't for the best.

When the time got close for him to leave, Kylie motioned to Holiday that she was going to walk her dad to his car, and Holiday's gaze shifted to Perry, who then followed them out.

When they reached the car, she hugged her dad. It didn't feel as awkward as the hug she'd given him the last time he'd come out for Parents Day, but there were still undercurrents of sadness to it.

"I love you," he whispered.

"Me too," Kylie said, and it was true. She loved him.

Before she released him, she realized he felt thinner. When she pulled away, she asked, "Are you eating okay?"

"Restaurant food isn't as good as your mom's cooking," he said.

"I miss her pancakes," Kylie said.

"I miss her." He gave her hand a tight squeeze. "If she asks about me, tell her I said that."

The loneliness she saw in his eyes gripped Kylie's chest. But he'd brought this pain on himself. None of this would have happened if he hadn't decided to bang his intern.

Mistakes. People make them. And most of the time, they had to pay for them. Was her stepdad destined to live alone the rest of his life because of his foolish decision to cheat on her mom?

"You okay?" Holiday asked as Kylie walked back inside, followed by Perry. "Did you survive the visit?"

"Yeah. It was sad, but seeing him is getting easier." Kylie looked around to check on Miranda and Della. Both looked miserable sitting like little soldiers with their respective parents.

Then she found Lucas. He sat attentively, hanging on every word his grandmother said. Evidently, the woman held a big influence over his life. But was it big enough that he wouldn't marry someone he loved because they weren't werewolf? Did Lucas even consider that a viable concern? Or was his grandmother just mentally stuck in the 1800s and thought it should be a consideration for Lucas?

Kylie looked at Holiday. It wasn't the place to ask, but the need to know was strong. "Do you think that supernaturals worry about who they'd marry because of bloodlines?"

Holiday's brows arched at Kylie's inquiry. "What brought on that question?"

"Curiosity," she lied.

Suspicion lurked in Holiday's eyes. She looked at Lucas and his grandma. The camp leader hesitated before looking back at Kylie. Kylie could tell Holiday searched for the right way to word her answer.

"I think that it might be more of a concern to some species than others," Holiday finally said.

"Like werewolves?"

She nodded. "They are the ones who have fewer mixed marriages than all the others. But it's changing. Today there are five times as many were mixed marriages than even ten years ago."

She tightened her mouth in a disapproving manner. "But those kinds of worries can wait for another ten years, young lady."

Holiday was right. It was a stupid thing to think about now. Stupid thing for Mrs. Parker to bring up, too. Kylie wasn't even seventeen. She didn't sit around and fantasize about getting married. Her dream with Lucas was a steamy make-out session, not going to a preacher to exchange vows. But stupid or not, Kylie knew she wasn't finished thinking about it.

"There she is!" a feminine voice called out, and without a doubt Kylie knew it was Sara.

Thirty minutes later, while her mom grabbed a soda, Kylie sat with Sara, feeling as if everyone in the dining hall watched and listened.

Because everyone had been talking about her latest superpower gift of healing her old best friend, Kylie knew all the campers were guessing this was Sara. It wasn't that she was ashamed of healing Sara; Kylie just didn't like being the center of attention.

Sara still looked thin, but everything from the shine of her brown hair to her complexion said she was okay. Sara kept glancing around at everyone and asking who was who.

"Is that your roommate?" She pointed to Miranda, sitting with her family.

"Yes," Kylie said. "I'll introduce you to her later."

"Where's the other one? The grumpy one?"

Della, across the room, shot Kylie a smirk. "She's over there," Kylie said, and pointed.

Because Della was still glancing at them, Sara waved. "She looks like a b with an itch."

Kylie's mouth dropped. "She's not. She's one of my . . ." Kylie almost said best friends, but she realized how awkward that might be. Sara used to be Kylie's best friend. "She's one of my good friends here."

"I remember you saying—"

"That was a long time ago," Kylie insisted, and hoped Sara shut up before Della got her feelings hurt.

"So, you're feeling better now?" Kylie tossed out the first thing she could think of to change the subject. But from the sparkle in Sara's eyes, Kylie realized it was the wrong question. Obviously, Sara was dying to bring up the whole "you healed me" topic.

"I think you know the answer to that better than I do," Sara said.

"Know the answer to what?" Her mom sat down next to Kylie.

"Nothing," Kylie said.

Sara let her gaze move around the room again. "Who's the hot black-haired guy who keeps staring at you?"

Kylie looked in the direction that Sara nodded. So did her mom. Lucas was staring at her, and he smiled. His grandmother must have left, because he sat alone. Then, as if he saw their gaze as an invitation to join them, he started over.

No. No. Panic stirred in Kylie's gut. At first, Kylie didn't understand why she didn't want Lucas to meet Sara. Then she remembered that Sara had always been the biggest flirt. Kylie didn't want Sara making a play for Lucas. Not so much because she worried Lucas would respond to it, but because Kylie didn't want Lucas thinking Sara was a party girl.

Old life meets new life, and Kylie didn't want either to look unappealing.

She picked up her glass of water and drank just to have something to do with her hands.

"You must be Sara." Lucas extended his hand.

Sara slipped her hand into Lucas's. "That's me. And you are?"

"Lucas Parker, Kylie's boyfriend."

Boyfriend? Kylie's breath caught. The water slipping down her throat went down the wrong pipe. She started coughing so hard, the sound bounced around the high beams of the dining hall. If that wasn't bad enough, her mom, who'd been sipping on a diet soda, did the same thing.

Crap! If there was one person in the dining hall who hadn't already stared at them, they did now.

Holiday walked over, studying Kylie and her mom as they both worked on getting air into their lungs. "Everything okay?"

"Yeah," Kylie managed to say, and felt some water drip from her nose. Oh, wasn't that just lovely. She wiped it away.

"How about we get some fresh air?" Holiday asked. "Why don't we take Sara and your mom to your cabin?"

"Yeah," Kylie said, and they all stood up.

Lucas seemed to sense he'd done something wrong, and he looked at her in confusion. "Well, I'll let you four go. I'll see you later."

Kylie nodded.

Lucas looked at her mom. "It was a pleasure to see you again, Mrs. Galen."

"You too," her mom said, and looked at Kylie with all kinds of parental concerns that involved boyfriends and the unspoken word . . . sex.

They hadn't gotten out of the dining hall before her mom leaned in. "Boyfriend? What have you not been telling me?"

Just great, Kylie thought. Now her mom would probably start mailing her the sex pamphlets.

Sara leaned in and whispered in her other ear, "He's hot."

"I know," Kylie whispered back.

"Not hot like good-looking. I mean hot like you were that day you touched me."

Kylie didn't know what to say to that. When they got to the door of the dining hall, Kylie reached for the knob, but the door swung open first and nearly knocked her down. She jumped back.

Derek and his mom came inside. Derek's gaze shot to Kylie and his eyes tightened as if her nearness hurt him. Then a look of concern filled his eyes when he noticed Sara.

"Look, Derek! It's Kylie!" Mrs. Lakes almost shouted, and again Kylie felt everyone in the room staring at her.

Without any advance warning, Kylie became locked in an embrace with Mrs. Lakes. Thankfully, she was a fast hugger.

Derek looked at Sara. "You must be Sara."

"That's me," Sara answered with her flirty smile. "Who are you?"

"This is Derek," Kylie said, and made quick introductions, which included her mom.

Mrs. Lakes waved her hand back and forth between Kylie and Derek. "I think they're sweet on each other. Isn't it cute?"

Several gasps came from the crowd behind them, probably the vampires listening in. Kylie felt her cheeks break out in embarrassment.

"Mom!" Derek rolled his eyes.

"I'm just saying the truth, honey. She's all you talk about."

Derek's face turned bright red.

Kylie's mom arched an eyebrow and eyed Kylie as if to say she would be certain to send those sex pamphlets now.

Sara chuckled.

And Kylie just wanted to die. Right there, right then. Especially when she looked back and saw Lucas taking it all in and frowning.

Chapter Thirty-one

"Why don't you girls walk ahead?" Kylie's mom said as soon as they got outside the dining hall. "I know Sara is dying to have some girl talk."

Kylie wasn't fooled. Her mom obviously was dying to discuss something privately with Holiday. Probably about Kylie having two boyfriends.

As Sara and Kylie started walking, Sara squeezed Kylie's arm. "Two guys? You've got two guys in love with you? Start talking, girl."

"Did Kylie's dad come this morning? I'm so worried about their relationship." Her mom's words seemed extra loud.

Kylie stopped and looked back. They were well over a hundred feet away and there was no way she should be hearing this. But she was. The sensitive hearing was back, and this time she was grateful.

"Yes," Holiday answered. *"He did come. They seemed to have a good visit."*

"Kylie?" Sara said. "Come on, tell me what's going on."

Kylie looked back at Sara and started walking again. "I . . . it's hard to explain."

"*Good,*" her mom said. "*I'm a bit concerned about Kylie and, well, the boys. I've read when a girl has issues with her father, they find themselves having . . . acting out with boys.*"

Well, at least Kylie now knew it wasn't just her. Her mom couldn't say the word *sex* to anyone.

"*Do you supervise them and make sure there isn't anything happening that shouldn't be happening?*"

"Well, try," Sara insisted. "Talk to me. I'm dying to know."

"Know what?" Kylie asked, failing miserably at keeping up with two conversations.

"Have you lost it yet?" Sara asked.

"*Your daughter has a good head on her shoulders,*" Holiday answered. "*I don't think you need to worry about Kylie.*"

"Lost what?" Kylie asked Sara, and then suddenly she knew what Sara was asking.

Apparently, the two conversations going on at once were about the same thing. Sex. "No. I haven't lost it." Annoyed at Sara's question, she remembered how close she and Sara had once been. They had told each other everything—no secrets. Sort of like she now did with Della and Miranda.

The awkwardness of having her old life cross paths with her new hit again. And in about fifteen minutes, Della and Miranda would meet them at the cabin. How awkward was that going to be?

Probably very.

"But they're so hot," Sara said.

"Yeah. They are."

"So which one do you really like?"

Both. The truth echoed in her head. Kylie inhaled. "Lucas," she said.

"Yum." Sara grinned, then shrugged. "Now, can you please tell me what you did to heal me?"

Kylie recalled the advice Holiday had given her. Just deny it. "I don't know what you're . . ." She started hearing the conversation between Holiday and her mom heat up again.

"Can I ask you a strange question?" Holiday asked her mom.

"I guess," her mom said.

"Do you have any American Indian blood in your family tree?"

"Why would Holiday ask that?" Kylie muttered.

"Why would who ask what?" Sara looked at her strangely.

Kylie shook her head. "Nothing."

"So start talking," Sara said. "And don't even try to deny it. I remember clearly how you rubbed my temples and how hot your hands got when you did it. And I felt it. I felt something happening inside me."

Sara came to a sudden stop and caught Kylie's hands in hers. "They're not hot now. So do you only get hot when you heal people? But why was . . . What's his name—Lucas—why were his hands hot?"

Kylie pulled her hands free, trying to remember what lie she'd given to Sara about her reasons for rubbing her temples.

"That is a strange question," her mom said. *"Why would you want to know that?"*

Sara let out a frustrated breath. "And don't tell me it's because your mom used to do it. Because I asked her about that on the ride up here, and she denied it. Said she couldn't remember rubbing your temples to help your headaches."

"Shh," Kylie said to Sara, not wanting to miss Holiday's answer.

But Sara didn't get quiet. Instead she let out a bloodcurdling scream that could have awakened the dead.

And she continued to scream. The sound pierced Kylie's eardrums. She went on instant alert, but she didn't know why. Her gaze started flipping from side to side, trying to find the source of danger.

Was it the eagle again? The evil-eyed deer? Was there another sinkhole, or had Perry gone unicorn again? Kylie was prepared for just about anything.

Tense to the max, she didn't know if she should prepare herself to fight or run. Then something butted up against her jeans-covered calf.

She glanced down.

Okay, she was prepared for about anything but Socks. Her skunk/cat was supposed to be locked up at Holiday's cabin. And just to make matters worse, her mom and Holiday came running to see what was wrong.

Within two seconds, her mom started screaming with Sara, while Kylie glanced back at Holiday.

"It's probably rabid," her mom screeched. "Get away from it, Kylie. Get away!"

"It's okay," Holiday spouted, but obviously she wasn't heard over her mom's wailing.

Kylie followed her mother's orders and stepped back. But Socks wasn't having it. He followed and pounced at Kylie's tennis shoe.

Sara squealed and darted across the path and hid behind Kylie's mom. Socks, suddenly frightened by the ruckus, shot back across the path and scampered up Kylie's leg. Unsure what to do, she held the scared pet with caution.

"Drop it! Kylie!" her mom screamed. "Drop that vermin this minute!" Then she bolted forward as if to knock the animal from Kylie's arms.

"Mom, it's okay," she said, though it was anything but.

Socks hissed, then swiveled in Kylie's hold and buried his pointed little nose in her armpit. Kylie didn't completely panic until Socks lifted his black-and-white fluffy tail straight up in the air and aimed it at her mom.

"No!" Kylie swung around and started talking sweetly to Socks. "Don't do it. Don't do it," she whispered.

"Everybody, step back," Holiday said, speaking more forcefully this time. "The skunk's not rabid. He's my pet."

Kylie looked back over her shoulder to see her mom gawk at Holiday in sheer horror. "You have a pet skunk?"

"Yes," Holiday lied, and almost sounded honest. "I know, it sounds kind of strange."

"Kind of?" her mom asked, eyes still wide with shock.

Kylie pulled Socks closer and continued to whisper what she hoped were calming words close to his ear. But who, she wondered, was going to whisper calming words to her? This, was exactly why merging her old life with her new was such a bad, bad idea.

"Well, that went well," Holiday said an hour later as they watched Kylie's mom and Sara drive out of the Shadow Falls parking lot.

Kylie, her chest so tight that she thought a few ribs had cracked, looked at Holiday in shock. "You're kidding me. I'm practically told I'm not good enough for Lucas by his grandma. My dad's miserable. My mom thinks I'm having sex with two boys. And she thinks you're an idiot who keeps a skunk as a pet."

"I had to come up with something," Holiday said. "He must have snuck out when I left and I didn't see him."

"Don't forget that it couldn't have gotten any more awkward between Sara and Miranda and Della. They barely spoke to each other. And . . ." Tears filled Kylie's eyes. "And if I ever wondered if you really kept things from me, I know the truth now. What's this crap about you wanting to know if I'm part American Indian?"

Holiday's face flashed with guilt. "I was going to tell you. Honest. There just hasn't been time."

"Yeah, you're always going to tell me something after the fact." Kylie batted at the tears rolling down her cheeks. "I'm sick and tired of all the secrets around here, Holiday. I'm tired of being kept in the dark. I'm tired of not knowing what I am. It's not fair, and I'm not going to tolerate it anymore."

It was Wednesday night. The last few days had passed by in a blur. Kylie had gone into a frenzy trying to dig up her family tree. Holiday had explained that there was an American Indian legend about certain descendants of an Indian tribe having been touched by the gods. And that these mere humans would carry the gift with them for generations.

If Kylie had that blood running in her veins, it would explain how she could be a protector and still be half human. Kylie didn't know why it was so important to her to find out her heritage. It wasn't as if it would get her any closer to discovering what she was. But it might explain why she seemed to have certain gifts. Then again, maybe it was because it was the only lead she could work on right now.

The ghost showed up three or four times a day but still wasn't talking. Lucas showed up two or three times a day, too. And they weren't doing much talking, either. But on the plus side, they were doing a lot more kissing.

She hadn't said anything about what his grandmother told her. Partly because he already seemed so tense—no doubt because of the approaching full moon. And the other part because she was afraid of his answer.

She was afraid he'd tell her his grandmother was right. That he could never consider marrying her if she wasn't a werewolf.

Yeah, it still seemed stupid that she'd worry about it at this point in their relationship. But then, Kylie kept coming back to the fact that being girlfriend and boyfriend was supposed to be all about finding that one person you'd spend your entire life with.

Should she live for the day or plan for the future? And should she start something when she knew it wouldn't and couldn't last? Could she risk giving her heart to someone who could never truly be hers?

Earlier that night, when Lucas came by, they'd sat on the porch, kissed, and stared up at the moon. "You don't feel anything when you look at it?" he'd asked her.

He no longer tried to hide the fact that he wanted her to be were. And it was getting harder for her to pretend that it didn't bother her. Not that it changed how she felt about him. Everything from his smile to his blue eyes to the way he kissed—it all captivated her. The time she was close to him was about the only time she really felt at peace.

Kylie remembered telling Holiday she needed a touchstone, something that felt completely right. Lucas had become her touchstone. In some ways, he was like the falls. When she was close to him, when she felt his warm touch on her, all her problems seemed so much smaller.

But when he wasn't close, those problems came back to sit on her shoulders and eat away at her sanity. Eventually, Kylie knew they needed to talk about the whole bloodline issue. And even his question about her going out. Although she got the feeling he assumed she'd said yes. Looking back, she realized that considering their conversation that day, he might even have reason to believe it. So she'd let that one slide, but the bloodline issue wasn't that easy to drop.

But for now, she decided to just let it be.

"Hey!" Della's voice snapped Kylie back to the present as she walked out of her room. "Is Miranda back yet from her make-out session with Perry?" She plopped down at the kitchen table behind where Kylie sat at the computer desk.

"Not yet." Kylie glanced back. Della looked bored or depressed. She'd been extra quiet lately. Ever since Parents Day.

"What are you doing?" Della asked.

Worrying. "My mom finally got me my great grandmother's maiden name. I thought I'd put it in the database on that genealogy Web site and see if I get anything."

"Why don't you just put a feather in your hat and call yourself an Indian?"

Kylie frowned. "That's not nice."

"Sorry," she muttered. "I'm in a pissy mood."

"Why?" Kylie stood and grabbed two diet sodas from the fridge and then dropped back down in the kitchen chair.

Della took the drink Kylie slid over to her and popped the top. It fizzed and she pressed her lips to the rim of the can to catch the overspill. When she looked up, she had tears in her eyes.

"What's wrong?" Kylie asked.

Della made a little hiccup noise, and Kylie realized that the vamp was crying. She stopped herself from going over there and hugging Della, because she knew Della hated that.

"Della? Tell me what's wrong." And instantly, Kylie got tears in her eyes, too.

Della swiped at her cheeks. "I miss it. It's just like Ellie said. I miss being normal. I miss living with my family. I know I'm lucky to be here. Lucky to have you and Miranda as my best friends. And I'm happy that you've got Lucas and Miranda has Perry, but it just makes me miss Lee, and it hurts so bad sometimes. And I know I should try to go for Steve, but I'm not ready." She hiccuped again and more tears slipped from her dark lashes onto her cheeks. "I miss it. All of it. I miss being human."

Kylie started crying in earnest now. Not just for Della, but for herself. "I know," she said. "I miss it, too."

The next morning, Kylie woke up staring at the back of Della's head. Because Della was the only one with a full-size bed, they had ended up going to Della's bed and talking until they'd fallen asleep. Something moved at Kylie's back and she quickly rolled over and stared at a yawning Miranda.

"What are you doing here?" Kylie asked.

"I thought it was a spend-the-night party and I wanted to come," she said. Then she popped out her bottom lip. "You two didn't even wait up on me."

"You were late," Kylie said, and yawned.

"I know." Miranda grinned. "We had such a good time. We went swimming at the lake. Just the two of us. It's almost a full moon and it was so romantic."

"You went skinny-dipping?" Della asked, and rolled over, sounding half-asleep.

"No. But he did. Only because he thought I was going to." Miranda giggled. "I wore my bathing suit under my clothes, because he said we were going to the lake. And when I started pulling my jeans off, he thought I was taking it all off and he took his off and dove in really fast."

Kylie and Della started laughing.

"But I didn't see anything. Plus, he made me turn around when he got out and pulled his shorts back on."

The three of them stayed in bed, giggling, until they were almost late for breakfast.

It was a good morning. Not quite as mind-easing as being with Lucas, but Kylie had to admit that Della and Miranda were becoming her touchstones as well. Right now, she felt capable of facing another day of problem solving.

But the good mood took a nosedive when they walked into the dining hall and everyone turned and stared at them.

No, not at all of them. Just at Kylie. Or rather, they gaped at her forehead while tightening their brows. Obviously, her pattern was doing something weird again.

"Damn!" someone said. There were several gasps, a couple of whispers, and a few people even dropped their forks. Then came the dead silence—the kind of silence that screamed disbelief.

Della and Miranda both turned toward her and tightened their brows.

Miranda's eyes widened in shock. "Oh, my!"

"Shit," said Della.

"What is it?" Kylie asked.

Della swallowed and leaned in. "You finally opened up. Your . . . your pattern is readable."

Chapter Thirty-two

"What am I?" Kylie gripped Della's arm. "I need to know." Holy hell, she'd been waiting for the answer to this question for months. "Please, Della!"

"You . . ." Della shook her head. "You're human. One hundred percent human."

"Not funny." Kylie wanted to believe Della was teasing her, but the look on her roommate's face said otherwise. But how could she be human after everything that had happened to her? She remembered crying last night and telling Della she missed being human. Missed being normal. Had she willed it to happen?

Kylie darted out the door and ran as fast as she could to the office. Not even Holiday's closed office door slowed her down. She barged in. Burnett and Holiday jumped apart as if . . . they'd been kissing. Oh, my God. The image of what she'd seen for a flicker of a second played in Kylie's head.

Burnett and Holiday were kissing. Any other time, Kylie might have yelped with joy.

Not now.

"We were . . . we were just . . . ," Holiday stuttered.

Kylie didn't care. Her heart pounded. Her mind tried to make sense of the fact that she was fully human. How was that even possible? What did it mean?

Even as she asked herself the questions, she knew the answer to the last one. Being human meant leaving Shadow Falls. Holiday. Burnett. Miranda. Della. Lucas. Perry. Derek. Jonathon and Helen. All of them. It meant walking away forever from her new life.

Tears filled her eyes.

"What's wrong?" Holiday asked.

It meant never helping another lost soul. It meant going back to her old life, where she never felt as if she belonged.

Okay, she had missed her old life. She had. But right now, she knew with twenty-twenty clarity that she would miss her new life more. These last few months, as hard as they had been, she'd come closer to knowing her true self than she ever had before. Maybe she still didn't know what she was, but in so many ways, she knew more about *who* she was.

"Kylie? What is it?" Holiday insisted.

"What the hell does this mean?" She pointed to her forehead.

Holiday and Burnett looked at her and their eyebrows twitched. The shock she saw in both their eyes didn't help Kylie's confusion. The knot in her throat grew to the size of a large frog.

Thirty minutes later, Kylie still sat on Holiday's sofa, with her legs pulled up to her chest, her forehead against her knees. She was dry—cried out.

The camp leader sat beside her. Holiday's hand rested on Kylie's back and sent waves of calm washing over her, but it didn't chase away the fear that swelled in her chest. She'd caused this herself. Brought this on herself. She'd somehow tapped into a power she didn't know she had and turned herself back into a human. Was it irreversible?

Kylie lifted her head. "I didn't mean to do it."

"Do what?" Holiday asked.

Kylie's throat felt raw. "Della and I were talking about how we wished . . . we wished we were human again. That we missed being normal, and—" Her breath caught. "And I do miss it, but right now it's so clear that I would miss this new life more. I don't want to be human, Holiday."

Empathy filled Holiday's eyes and she smiled. "I don't know what's happening. I don't understand it. But if there is one thing I'm certain about, it's that you are not human, Kylie. Well, not just human."

"But what if the death angels are trying to teach me a lesson? What if they got pissed at me for being ungrateful and this is my punishment?"

Holiday shook her head. "I've never heard of them turning someone into a human for punishment. And believe me, there isn't a supernatural alive who hasn't had moments of wishing they were human. That's perfectly normal."

"Really?"

"Of course. We live in the human world. The grass always looks greener on the other side. Truth is, sometimes it *is* greener. But we can't change what we are simply by wishing it was so."

Kylie nodded. "So you think this is just a fluke?"

"I don't know. But if I were guessing, I'd say it will change just like it's changed numerous other times."

"Will I not have any powers until it changes back?"

The question seemed to stump Holiday. "I . . . Wait. Can you still feel me attempting to alter your emotions?" Holiday rested her hand on Kylie's shoulder.

She felt the warmth leak from Holiday's touch through her shirt and flow into her skin. Then the soft heat seemed to form a bubble that flowed into her chest cavity, where it morphed into a soothing wash of emotion.

"Yes," Kylie said.

"Then I'd say nothing else has changed."

"So humans can't sense your touch?"

"No,"

Kylie inhaled and found a little inner peace. Then she looked at Holiday. "Do you think I'll ever figure out what I am?"

"Of course you will." Holiday paused. "I didn't want to mention it because it's not a sure thing, but Burnett told me that the real Brightens, in Ireland, confirmed their plane reservations back to the States for the middle of September."

Kylie's heart skipped a beat. "Do they know about me?"

"Not that we know of. Burnett did some checking on the phone number for the caller the detective spoke to the day he'd thought he'd been talking to the Brightens. It wasn't their phone. The call was made from a cell phone, a throwaway, they call them. They can't trace it."

"But Burnett knows how to reach the Brightens now? I could call them, couldn't I?"

Holiday frowned. "I don't think this is something you want to talk about over the phone, Kylie."

Holiday was right, but Kylie was just so damn tired of waiting. She reached back and rubbed the tension in her shoulder and wished Burnett were still here. He'd cut out shortly after she'd started to cry. She wasn't sure if he'd been frightened by her tears or frightened by the thought of her asking him about what she'd seen when she'd walked in on them.

Kylie glanced at Holiday. "So . . . you and Burnett?"

Holiday rolled her eyes. "It was just a kiss, Kylie. Don't make it out to be something more."

Kylie let a slight smile work its way to her lips. Right now, she could use any good news at all. "Was it a good kiss?"

"Just a kiss and . . . a mistake. We were talking about Perry and

Miranda, about how sweet it was. The moment got away from us and . . . Definitely a mistake."

"Why, Holiday? Why can't you give the guy a chance?"

Holiday frowned. "The only reason I let this happen was . . . my guard was down because . . ." Kylie saw the shadows of pain in Holiday's eyes.

"You're afraid Burnett's the one in the casket?"

She nodded.

"Which means you care about him. Can't you see that?"

"I care, but caring for someone isn't enough. And we work together. Romance and work never go together."

"It could if you wanted it badly enough."

"Then I guess I don't want it that bad," Holiday said sternly. But Kylie knew that it was a lie.

And she suspected Holiday realized it, too.

They sat silently for a few minutes. "About the whole funeral vision thing . . . ," Kylie said.

"Yeah?"

"I think . . . I mean, there's a chance I fixed it."

Holiday studied her. "Fixed what?"

Kylie didn't feel right telling Holiday that Ellie had been going to run away. "I might have done something that took someone out of danger. So maybe a vampire won't die."

Holiday frowned. "I'd love to think that's true. But you can't change Fate."

Kylie recalled that those had been the words the ghost had whispered, but she refused to believe. "Then maybe it wasn't really Fate," she said.

"I wish I could believe that," Holiday said.

"I do believe it," Kylie said. But there was a part of her that doubted.

And when she let herself think about it, it tore her apart.

Holiday's phone rang. The camp leader picked it up, looked at the caller ID oddly, and then took the call.

"What's up?" Holiday asked, and then glanced over at Kylie. "She's fine." Holiday paused. "I'll tell her." She hung up and met Kylie's eyes. "That was Derek. He wanted to tell you that if you needed to talk, he's here for you. As a friend. He insisted I add that last part."

Kylie nodded and her chest swelled with emotion.

A knock came at the door. Holiday looked at Kylie. "Are you up to company? Derek's not the only one worried."

Kylie nodded.

"Come in," Holiday said. Della and Miranda popped into the office, their gazes filled with concern. Behind them came Lucas, Perry, Helen, and Jonathon.

"I'm fine," Kylie told them, but more tears filled her eyes. Tears because she knew that these people weren't just her friends. They were her family.

"We love you," Miranda said, her eyes tearing up. "And we want you to know that we don't care what you are."

Later that night, Kylie received another sign that her human brain pattern hadn't changed things. At first, she thought it was just a dream. She was watching Jane Doe resting in bed, running her hands over her pregnant belly, and staring at the sleeping man beside her. *"I love you,"* she whispered. *"But I have to do this."*

Then things changed and Kylie was Jane. She slipped quietly out of the bed. Her body felt cumbersome with the round, heavy weight around her middle. Her heart felt broken, heavy. Kylie couldn't ever remember feeling so much sadness, as if she were about to lose something more precious than life.

She moved out of the dark room, looked back one more time at the sleeping man. Whoever he was, Jane loved him.

"I'm sorry." The two little words tumbled out of her mouth. The man rolled over, and Kylie got a quick glimpse of his face. Pale complexion, thick, dark brown—no, not really brown, but auburn hair.

Something about his face made Kylie want to continue to stare at him, but she had no control over what happened in these visions. Reliving Jane Doe's past, she turned and walked out. She moved to a closet, grabbed a long black coat, and slipped it around her body. Then she pulled out a suitcase—an old-fashioned piece of luggage, no wheels. Carrying it made walking while pregnant feel even more awkward.

Why are you leaving if you love him? The question flowed through Kylie's mind, but the vision continued, leaving the question hanging in the air unanswered.

With tears now streaming down her face, she walked out of the small house. A car, with its headlights off, pulled up to the curb. She got inside. Kylie wanted to see who was driving, but Jane was too busy crying, too busy trying to deal with a broken heart, to care about the driver.

"You're doing the best thing," a woman's voice said as the car pulled away. *"He wouldn't understand."*

The vision went black. Kylie tried to wake up but got pulled back in.

And not to a good place, either.

There was light now, but she didn't care. She was in too much pain. Something was ripping her insides apart. It reminded Kylie of the worst menstrual cramp she'd ever had. Her body contorted with pain. Her back arched and she screamed.

"It's not coming," someone said. The pain in her abdomen eased and she became aware of the emotional pain in her chest again.

"Don't let my baby die." She raised up on her elbow.

The man standing between her opened knees met Jane Doe's eyes. *"I'd have to take it by C-section."*

"*Then do it!*" Jane screamed.

"*I'm not prepared for that. I don't have any anesthesia.*"

"*I don't care,*" Jane said. "*Don't let my baby die. I can take it. It's not like I'm human.*"

The man looked at the woman sitting beside him. "*Get me a knife.*"

Chapter Thirty-three

No! Kylie screamed in her head, even as Jane Doe dropped back on the bed and resigned herself to being cut open with nothing to dull the pain.

"Kylie? Wake up!"

Kylie felt someone shake her. Still screaming, she opened her eyes and saw Della and Miranda standing over her. She managed to stop screaming but couldn't stop shaking.

"Should we get Holiday?" Miranda asked, looking worried.

Kylie shook her head no. "I'm okay." She rolled over and dried her tears on the blanket. "Go back to sleep," she muttered. Her heart still carried the panic from the vision, and she could feel the cold. Jane was here.

Della and Miranda looked at each other as if unsure what to do next.

"Go," she repeated.

As soon as they left, Kylie sat up. Jane sat on the edge of the bed. Her abdomen gaped open and blood spilled onto the tops of her bare thighs. *"I didn't kill my baby. I loved him."*

"I know. I saw." Kylie hated to ask, but finding answers was why

Jane had come to her. "Did the baby die? Is that what happened? Did your baby die during childbirth?"

Jane looked at Kylie again. *"No."* She smiled, and instantly the blood on her hands disappeared and she was dressed in a pretty sundress with big yellow sunflowers. *"He lived. My baby lived. I made sure he was okay. And then I went back home."*

"Where was home?" Kylie asked. "Home to who?"

She blinked and then looked up. *"I don't know. I can't remember."*

"I'm a little confused," Kylie said. "Did you die during the birth?"

"No, I already showed you how I died. They killed me." And then she faded.

It took Kylie forever to fall back to sleep, and when she did, another dream had her in its trap. Immediately, she recognized what was going on. She hadn't moved into the dream, someone had come into hers.

She waited just a fraction of a second to make sure it wasn't Derek, then she saw him. Red. He stood by the lake.

"I'm not trying to fool you this time," he said.

"Leave me alone!" she snapped.

"I need to tell you . . ."

Kylie woke up in a panic in her bed. Red was gone. "Don't come back!" she said, and hugged herself, proud of how quickly she'd woken herself up.

The next four or five days at Shadow Falls were all about getting the camp ready to become a full-blown school, and that was fine with Kylie. Holiday was busy interviewing a few more potential teachers while a construction group—all paranormals—built a few large classroom cabins. Another all-paranormal crew put heating units into the cabins.

Kylie was still being shadowed. Because nothing else had happened, she'd started to feel guilty about piling on to everyone's busy schedules. On Friday morning, she took off to Burnett's office to suggest he call a halt to the shadowing. He disagreed.

"If anything, this is the time to be more careful," he insisted.

"Why?" Kylie asked.

He frowned. "For starters, how about because this place is a revolving door right now? I don't like strangers being here."

Kylie felt a shiver run down her spine. "You think someone working here could really be working with Mario?"

If so, that might explain Miranda's growing feeling that someone was lurking around their cabin. She'd started putting protective spells on their cabin every day now and had even gone to Holiday and Burnett with her concerns. Concerns they'd listened to but didn't feel held a huge threat. Or at least Kylie had assumed until now.

Burnett, all two-hundred-plus pounds of muscle, leaned back in his office chair. "I've checked everyone's credentials a dozen times." He reached for a heart-shaped stress ball with the words *Donate Blood* and squeezed it. "Maybe Holiday's right, and I'm being overly cautious, but I'm not taking chances."

Burnett turned his head to the side as if listening to something from outside the cabin. He frowned. "Another were is at it again. I'll be so friggin' glad when tomorrow's full moon is past. Excuse me." He shot out of the room.

Kylie ran out of the cabin after him, afraid Lucas was involved in whatever was happening. While normally she wouldn't consider Lucas getting into trouble, these last few days, he'd been extra tense. Last night when he'd come by her cabin to say good night, he'd barely kissed her.

When she'd asked if something was wrong, he'd reminded her that the closer he got to the full moon, the more he turned to his instinct instead of logic. Then he'd reached out and passed a single finger over her lips. "You are temptation in its purest form, Kylie Galen."

There was a part of Kylie that wanted to give in to that temptation, but another part of her still resisted. And as much as she wished it weren't true, she knew her reason for holding back had to do with Lucas's grandmother.

The moment Kylie hit the edge of the porch steps, Della showed up. "Ellie and Fredericka are going at it."

"Why?" Kylie asked.

"Supposedly, Ellie overheard the she-wolf talking bad about you and decided to teach Fredericka a lesson. You know, I hate to admit it, but Ellie's growing on me."

"Oh, crap. Where are they?"

"By Ellie's cabin."

Kylie took off. By the time they got there, Burnett had Fredericka, and Lucas was holding Ellie back. Ellie was bleeding, and from the glow in her eyes, she wasn't finished fighting.

"Let go of me!" she growled at Lucas. "I'll teach that dog—"

"Calm down," Lucas snapped. His own eyes were a bright orange. "She'll tear you apart. You can't win a fight with a were the day before a full moon."

"Watch me!" Ellie tried again to pull away, her fangs showing.

"Stop! Or I'll teach you a lesson myself," Lucas growled, his body growing tenser and his eyes brighter. Obviously, with his own body feeling the effects of the coming full moon, he shouldn't be the one trying to break up a fight.

"Why?" Ellie countered. "Why are you protecting that she-wolf? You should be helping me kick her ass. I thought Kylie was your girlfriend. Where does your loyalty lie? With that she-wolf, or with Kylie?"

Lucas paused; the question seemed to catch him off guard. "I'm trying to save your life, though I'm not sure it's worth much."

"Because I'm not were?" Ellie spit back.

"Enough!" Burnett roared.

Lucas let go of Ellie. The pissed-off vamp stepped back, but her eyes stayed bright. Then her angry gaze found Kylie. "You have definitely chosen the wrong guy. Derek would never defend someone who said those things about you. Never!"

Kylie's gaze locked with Lucas for a moment, and then she turned and walked away.

That night, Kylie awoke to the smell of roses. Before she opened her eyes, she checked the temperature to make sure it wasn't Jane. Or worse, another vision. But nope. No cold. Just the sweet floral scent.

"Hey, beautiful," said a familiar male voice. She opened her eyes.

Lucas knelt beside her bed, holding a bouquet of roses in his hands. She sat up and saw more roses all around the room. "What did you do, rob a florist?"

He gave her his bad-boy grin, and Kylie felt her heart melt just a little. "No, but let me just say that my grandmother is going to be really pissed when she sees her garden in the morning."

She grinned and then remembered she was mad at him. And yeah, it might not have been fair to be mad when all he'd done was do the right thing by breaking up the fight, but Ellie's words had stung and stung deep. And Kylie had been nursing a bit of a broken heart ever since.

It didn't help that Kylie knew, once he shifted into wolf form, he would run off into the woods with Fredericka fast behind him. So when he'd dropped by earlier that day to see her, she'd told him she'd had a headache and was going to bed.

But he was back now. And this time, he hadn't gotten her permission first to come into her room.

"Scoot over," he said.

Kylie arched a brow, remembering his caution about not getting too close to her before the change. "Is that a good idea?"

"I'll behave. I've made sure of it. I just want to hold you and apologize."

"For what?"

He took a rose and ran it down her nose and over her lips. It felt soft against her skin—a bit like velvet.

"I'm sorry that Fredericka is being such a bitch. Sorry for how things may have looked. I wasn't defending Fredericka. I was trying to keep Ellie from getting hurt."

There it was again. The fact that he'd been doing the right thing. And she knew it was true.

"But . . ." He set the rose beside her pillow. "I got to thinking about how I'd feel if it were you defending Derek. I really wouldn't like that." He scooped her up in his arms and moved her over and then crawled in beside her.

His warmth came against her side, and his lips brushed against her cheek. "You are the most important thing to me, Kylie. There isn't anything about you that doesn't fascinate me. The way your eyes light up when you smile. The sound of your laughter." He picked up the rose and ran it across her mouth again. "The shape of your lips. The way they feel against mine."

The rose moved up. "Your nose. The way it turns up on the end."

"It doesn't turn up that much." She'd always hated her nose.

"Maybe it does just a little." He grinned. "But it's so damn cute. And I love the way you sneeze."

"Now you're taking it too far." She giggled.

"Seriously, I love the sound you make when you sneeze. It sounds more like a puppy than human. A very cute and sexy puppy."

His smile faded and his blue eyes stared right at her. "For the first time in my entire life, I'm not looking forward to shifting. Because . . . then I won't be able to kiss you like this." His lips melted against hers, but he ended the kiss too quickly. "I'll be out there. And you'll be in here. And instead of enjoying the thrill of being free of this body, I'll be missing you."

He kissed her lightly on the lips again. "So, please. Please, don't be angry at me. I didn't mean to make you feel bad, or to make you feel as if anyone else is more important to me than you. Because they aren't. I'd kill for you, Kylie Galen. But more than that, I'd die for you."

She felt a tear roll down her cheek. "You'd better not die on me, Lucas Parker."

He caught the tear and wiped it away. "Am I forgiven?"

"Yes. You're forgiven." She reached up and wrapped her hand around his neck and pulled him in for a kiss. His mouth devoured hers, his tongue swept across her lips. After several long, delicious moments, he kissed his way down to her neck. It tickled, it tingled, and before long, she heard the soft humming sound emanating from him. She liked hearing it. Liked knowing she made it happen. Liked how her inhibitions faded while listening to it.

His hand slid up under her tank top, touching bare skin. Touching the edges of her breasts, and then his hands moved higher. His warm hands felt like sunshine against her skin. She closed her eyes, loving how it felt. She wanted this.

He broke the kiss and jerked his hand away. "Okay, it's time for me to go now."

He jumped out of the bed and frowned down at her. "I'm sorry."

She bit down on her lip to keep from telling him it was okay. To keep from asking him to get back in bed. Instead, she whispered, "I'm *not* sorry."

He gazed down at her. "You are so damn beautiful. And if I don't leave now . . ." He started out.

"Lucas?"

He turned around. "Yeah?"

"Thank you for the roses."

"You're welcome." He looked back at the door. "I should probably go before I run out of time."

"Out of time?" she asked.

He shrugged. "I told Della to kick my ass out if I stayed more than twenty minutes." He looked at his watch. "And knowing her—"

"Time's up!" Della pounded on the door with so much force, Kylie was amazed the door didn't break down.

Lucas grinned. "I knew I could count on her."

Kylie laughed.

Once he'd gone, she leaned back in bed, stared at the ceiling, and just breathed in the scent of roses, trying to remember every word he'd said. She wanted to remember this night forever.

Several days later, with her stomach gnawing on her backbone and Jonathon, her shadow of the day, in tow, Kylie set out to the dining room to get some breakfast.

Life had calmed down. A little, anyway. With the full moon behind them, Lucas was back to his normal, patient self. And he was being amazingly attentive, too. But if Kylie were honest, she sort of missed hearing his hum.

Not that she didn't enjoy his sweet side. He'd even brought her more roses last night. If Mrs. Parker didn't have reason enough to dislike her, Kylie figured the she-wolf's decimated rose garden would seal the deal.

Even Kylie's ghost was calmer. Jane Doe still made regular visits, but the ghost was back to giving Kylie the silent treatment. Which was fine for now.

Kylie ducked under a low-hanging branch on the trail and picked up speed.

"No! And I can't believe you'd even suggest it!"

Holiday's voice rang in Kylie's ear a good three hundred feet from the office. Kylie stopped and looked around to make sure the camp leader wasn't standing nearby.

She wasn't.

It must be the gifted hearing again. It had come and gone several times since her mom and Holiday's little discussion during Parents Day. Curious, Kylie looked at Jonathon to see if he'd heard it, too.

"What is it?" he asked.

"I thought I heard something. Did you hear it?"

"Hear what?" He started looking around. "That damn blue jay isn't back, is it? I'm telling you, it's a sick bird."

The bird had returned three more times. Jonathon had been present for two of them. "No. I thought I heard Holiday."

Jonathon tilted his head to the side as if putting his own sensitive hearing to the test. "I don't hear her."

So, was her hearing stronger than a vampire's? What did that mean? Especially when she still had the brain pattern of a human.

"It's not like I have a choice," Burnett said.

Great. They were fighting again. About what this time? Kylie wondered, and continued on to the dining hall. If she had to guess, Holiday was just finding another excuse to try to put some distance between her and Burnett. Since Kylie had walked in and found them kissing, she hadn't seen the two within fifty feet of each other.

"You have a choice," Holiday said. *"You go back and tell them that I said hell, no."*

"It's a couple of tests. They wouldn't take long and they could clear up everything."

"I said, no!"

"Now I'm hearing Holiday," Jonathon said. "She doesn't sound too happy."

"Don't you think this should be Kylie's decision?"

"What should be my decision?" Kylie muttered, and changed direction and started walking toward the office.

"No!" Holiday said.

"She wants answers. And this could give them to her."

Kylie moved faster. *What answers?* It didn't matter, she realized. She'd take any answers she could get.

"I won't allow it!"

"Won't allow what?" Kylie stormed into the office, leaving Jonathon behind.

Holiday and Burnett swung around. Holiday pointed to the door. "Get out!" she told Burnett.

"No!" Kylie stepped in front of him. "He stays. This is about me, and I need to know."

Holiday looked at Burnett with anger, then she looked at Kylie. "You wouldn't understand this."

"Why don't you try me?" She looked at Burnett. "Start talking."

He cut his gaze to Holiday.

"The FRU wants to run some tests on you," Holiday said. "To see if they can figure out what you are."

Hope rose in Kylie's chest. "I thought there weren't any tests that could tell me this?" She remembered asking Holiday that question before.

"There aren't!" Holiday said. "They just want to play around in your brain to—"

"I'll do it," Kylie said.

"No!" Holiday looked horrified. "I refuse to let them use you as some kind of lab rat. There are no guarantees that these tests are safe, and they may not even work."

Kylie looked at Burnett. "Are they safe?"

Burnett stared at Holiday, his eyes getting a pissed-off amber color. "I wouldn't let them do anything to her that's not safe," he growled. "Do you have that little faith in me?"

"I have that little faith in the FRU. History repeats itself."

"What kind of tests would they be?" Kylie asked.

"Just some CT scans," Burnett said.

"No!" Holiday turned back to Kylie. "They'll use you as a guinea pig."

"They're not going to hurt her," Burnett said.

"I know, because she's not agreeing to it."

The cold came into the room so fast that Kylie's breath sent tiny flakes of ice falling from her lips. Jane materialized, and at the same time, the three light bulbs in the fixture overhead burst. Shards of glass rained through the air.

"What the hell?" Burnett looked up and took a step closer to Kylie.

Holiday's crystals hanging throughout the room started swaying, sending rainbow colors spiraling around them.

The laptop computer on Holiday's desk started beeping, making serious malfunctioning noises.

"*You stay away from her!*" Jane shot across the room to stand between her and Burnett.

"*Run, Kylie!*" Jane yelled in the same tone she'd used to warn Kylie about the sinkhole.

"What's wrong?" Kylie demanded.

"*He's wrong!*" Jane yelled.

Holiday looked around the room. "What's happening, Kylie?"

"I think she thinks Burnett is trying to hurt me."

"Tell her to leave," Holiday insisted.

"Jane, you're going to have to go."

But Jane wasn't listening.

Burnett took another step closer to Kylie. Jane screamed and then jammed her hand inside his chest. Not only could Kylie see

Jane's hand, she saw the inside of Burnett's chest. And she watched in horror as Jane's hand closed around Burnett's heart.

"No!" Kylie screamed.

Burnett's gaze shot to Holiday. He reached for his chest.

"Stop it!" Kylie said.

Burnett dropped to the floor in a dead thud.

Chapter Thirty-four

Thirty minutes later, with Jonathon sitting under a tree a few feet away, Kylie sat on Holiday's porch, swatting away bugs and listening to Holiday, the doctor, and Burnett from inside the office.

"He asked you to take your shirt off," Holiday said.

"I don't need to take my shirt off," Burnett snapped. *"I'm fine."*

His voice was loud and clear, and he did indeed sound fine.

Not that it made Kylie feel any better.

"Maybe. Maybe not," Holiday said. *"We'll know as soon as you disrobe and let the doctor examine you."*

In a few minutes, Holiday came out and plopped on the porch beside Kylie. She had tears in her eyes. "I don't know why I'm worried about him. He's too pigheaded and stubborn to die."

Kylie laced her hands together. "I'm so sorry."

Holiday shook her head. "It wasn't your fault."

"You told me to get rid of her when I first told you about her. I refused, and she could have killed Burnett."

"She didn't want to kill him. She just wanted to get him away from you."

"Maybe I've been wrong all along. Maybe she is evil."

Holiday put her arm around Kylie's shoulder. "She wasn't evil. I felt her presence and her emotions. She was concerned about you. She did this to protect you, Kylie."

"Yeah, but, protect me from what? Did she really think Burnett was going hurt me?"

Holiday sighed. "She probably picked up on what I was feeling. I overreacted." She tightened her arm. "I mean, I refuse to let you be tested by the FRU. But I shouldn't have wigged out like that."

"You don't trust Burnett?" Kylie asked.

She shook her head. "I don't trust the FRU."

"Why? And if you don't trust them, then why are they involved with the camp? Besides, if they can really do some simple tests and tell me what I am, I want to do it."

Holiday closed her eyes for a second. "Don't take this wrong, Kylie. I'm not against the FRU. God knows we need them to keep things right. But they have no business testing people."

"But if they can really—"

"I can't let you do it. If they want to tell me the name of the test they want done, I'll ask our doctor if he can order it. But it will be under his care and his care only."

Kylie heard so much in the camp leader's voice. So much she wasn't saying. "Okay, what is it you're not telling me?"

It took a minute before Holiday finally sighed and started talking. "It was over forty years ago. It involved only one small branch of the FRU that has been shut down, and charges were brought against a lot of people. They were doing scientific tests on supernaturals. Something about figuring out genetics. The subjects were forced into doing it, and some people never completely recovered from the tests. It's not as if I think they're doing it again, but I refuse to have you go there so they can poke and prod you to find answers."

Kylie looked at Holiday. Bits and pieces of Jane's vision started replaying in her mind like an old movie. And everything suddenly made sense. "The FRU killed Jane Doe. They killed her and then they buried her with Berta Littlemon in the Fallen Cemetery."

Holiday's eyes widened. "You can't know this for sure."

"I do," Kylie said. "In the vision, Jane was called a subject. Her husband was one, too. And the doctor was a vampire. They mentioned her not having a pattern."

Kylie pulled her knees up and hugged them, trying to wrap her head around everything as it all came together. She didn't understand how Jane's baby fit in, but on some things she was clear.

"No wonder she went after Burnett," Kylie said. "She thought he was trying to do to me what the FRU had done to her."

Kylie was disappointed that Jane Doe was a no-show the next morning. Kylie had hoped now that she knew about the FRU, she could help Jane remember other things, like her name. That together they could figure out what it was Jane needed in order to cross over.

But dead people, just like the living, rarely did what Kylie wanted them to do.

A knock sounded at her door. "Come in."

The door opened and Miranda and Della both squeezed through the opening and shut the door extra quickly behind them.

"What is it?" Kylie asked.

"There's three guys here working on putting in the heating unit," Della said.

"And they're yummy," Miranda said. The contractors who worked around Shadow Falls had become a popular subject for all the female campers. Especially when they took their shirts off in the afternoons.

"As yummy as Perry?" Kylie teased. Lately, Miranda had been spending almost every free moment with the shape-shifter.

"Not quite as yummy," Miranda said, and then grinned. "But close."

"Well, thanks for the warning. I'll get ready to be awed."

"Just don't come out wearing nothing but a towel," Della said, also grinning. "Unless you're into that."

A few minutes later, Kylie walked out fully dressed, hair combed, and the only thing she'd added in honor of their company was a touch of lip gloss.

Miranda sat at the table, sipping a glass of orange juice, Della had a glass of blood, and two of the guys were down on the floor on their knees, saws at their sides and some kind of heating vent beside them.

As much as Kylie hated to admit it, Miranda was right. They were yummy. Both were in their early twenties, had dark hair, and wore tight T-shirts that showed off their dark tans and lots of muscles.

They looked up and met Kylie's eyes. Kylie tensed when they pinched their eyebrows at her, but she did the same thing. They were both werewolves. She saw the shocked look in their eyes when they saw her brain pattern.

"I'm the token human," she said.

Della and Miranda snickered. The two guys smiled and went back to work. No doubt they had orders from Burnett not to flirt with the female campers.

Kylie went to the fridge to get her own glass of juice. She heard Miranda's door open, and the third contractor joined them. Kylie turned around and peered at him under her lashes. This one was equally hot. Black hair. Wide shoulders. Thin waist.

His gaze met Kylie's and her juice slipped from her fingers and shattered at her feet.

His hair had changed. His name, Red, probably a nickname, no longer fit, but his eyes hadn't changed. The image of him appearing in her dreams, and of him staring at her in the mirror with blood dripping down his chin, filled her head. Then the image flashed, and she saw him plastered on her windshield and ramming his hand through her car window. As if that weren't enough, she saw the image of him staring at her while she was chained to the chair when he and his grandfather abducted her.

"Della?" Kylie said in an even voice, hoping she could warn her before the shit hit the fan.

But Della didn't answer. Kylie turned. The vamp still sat at the table, her glass at her lips. A few drops of blood hung in the air between her lips and the edge of the glass. Della didn't breathe. Didn't move. She looked frozen.

The shit had already hit the fan.

Kylie's gaze shot to Miranda, who was also frozen, a finger at her ear as if to brush back a strand of hair.

Ditto for the two guys on the floor.

"It's just you and me, Kylie," the rogue said.

She refocused on Miranda and Della. "Whatever you've done to my friends, you'd better undo it," she growled, and her blood fizzed with fury.

"Don't get worked up. They are fine. As soon as I release them, they will go back to normal and not remember a thing." He looked back to the table and then to her.

"So do it!" Kylie said.

He sighed. "I've never seen anyone who cared so much about others."

Though she wasn't sure why, Kylie checked his brain pattern. He was a werewolf. But how was that possible? He was a vampire. She tried not to show her surprise, but he saw it.

"What are you?" Kylie went ahead and asked.

"I'm the same thing you are. Just born a few minutes later than midnight." He took a step closer. "That's why we belong together. We're soul mates, Kylie. That's what we are."

She tightened her brows again, and this time he was human. Her heart thudded in her chest. "I'm not your soul mate. I'll die first."

"That's why I'm here." He took another step toward her.

She backed up. "You're here to kill me?"

"No." He stopped moving. Something about his answer and his tone rang true. "I'm here to protect you. Though you don't make it easy."

The sound of thunder rumbled from outside. He glanced out the window, and when his gaze came back to hers, Kylie knew something else.

"You were the eagle," she said. "And the deer. You're a shape-shifter?" And if they were the same, as he said, did that make her a shape-shifter, too?

"No. I mean, yes. I was the deer and the eagle, but I'm not a shape-shifter."

Then another thought hit. "You protected me, but you killed those innocent girls in Fallen. Why?"

He cut his eyes downward. "Would it upset you terribly if I said it was to impress you?"

"Impress me? You're sick."

"But they were mean to you and your friends."

"They didn't deserve to die."

"I know you feel that way now. I didn't really know you then. Now, I do. I wouldn't have done it if—"

"You don't know me now."

He shrugged. "I sometimes don't understand you. But I have watched you. You are an interesting study. I have always wondered what it would have been like . . . to have been born at midnight. Funny how just a few minutes on a clock can make a difference. I sometimes wonder if maybe—" The sound of thunder shook the cabin again.

Kylie could swear she saw regret in his eyes. But maybe not. The light in the cabin had been chased away by dark shadows. Kylie sensed the shadows were there for her.

Lightning flashed from the window. "I don't have a lot of time," he said, "but I wanted to tell you—"

"I will not go with you!" She might not win the battle, but she'd go down fighting.

"No, not this time. I'll come back for you later. Like I said, I'm here to protect you."

"From what?"

He glanced at the two contractors, frozen, not breathing, the same as Della and Miranda. "They want you dead."

Did he mean the two guys? "Who wants me dead?"

"The others. My grandfather and his friends. The others like us."

"Like us how? And why would they want me dead?"

"They are impatient and afraid of what you might be able to accomplish if you don't join us. But I will hold them off until you come around. But you must change your mind, soon."

He pointed to the taller of the guys on the floor, still frozen, as if they were working on the vents in the floor. "This guy, he was sent here to kill you. I had a wizard friend of mine peek into the future, and learned that your other friends would have gotten here in time to save you. But"—he pointed to the table—"the little witch wouldn't have made it. And for some crazy reason, I felt compelled to stop that from happening. I knew how much it would hurt you if she died." His brows creased as if he were confused. "It was an odd feeling, wanting to save her, caring if she died, because it's not like me to care. But . . . because of you, I did. I cared."

The words *Someone lives and someone dies* whispered in Kylie's head again.

"No!" This couldn't be happening. It just couldn't.

Then the sound of footsteps hitting the front porch vibrated the floor beneath her.

"Until later." He disappeared.

The door swung open and hit the back of the wall with a loud whack. Burnett, Lucas, Perry, and Derek rushed in.

"What the hell?" Della leapt out of her chair. Miranda dropped her juice and it splattered to the floor. Kylie's heart sighed when she saw they were okay. And yet . . . somewhere deep down, she'd believed him when he'd said they would be.

But did that mean she also believed him about everything else? Was she like him? She looked at Miranda and considered the possibility that she might have died had the rogue not intervened.

"You two!" Burnett said, pointing to the two men on the floor. "Come with me."

They stood up slowly. Then the taller one, the one the rogue had pointed to, leapt at the closed window. Glass shattered, wood splintered, and then he was outside. Burnett and Lucas went after him.

Chapter Thirty-five

"It doesn't make sense," Burnett growled an hour later as he paced back and forth in Holiday's office. Kylie agreed. Nothing made sense anymore.

They had caught the guy who'd been hired to kill her. But his information offered zero help in finding the person who'd hired him. They were no closer to finding the real culprit now than they'd been before.

Kylie, however, felt closer than ever to finding answers. No, she didn't know what she was, but at least she knew there were others like her. Question was, were they all evil? Was she the only one who'd been born at midnight?

"If he had wanted to take you, why didn't he?" Burnett stopped pacing in front of Holiday and Kylie on the sofa.

"He didn't say . . . exactly," Kylie said. "He said he would eventually convince them that I wasn't a danger to them. As if he thought he could change my mind about going with him."

"That's stupid," Burnett said.

Kylie decided to ask the question that had been bugging her for a while now. "How did he freeze Miranda and Della and the other two?"

Holiday answered, "There are some wizards and very strong witches and warlocks who can stop time."

"Do you think that's what he is? What I am?"

Holiday shrugged. "I've never heard of a witch or a wizard being able to change their brain patterns."

"Because it's impossible," Burnett snapped.

"Not really." Kylie pointed to herself.

Burnett closed his eyes and took a deep breath. "This whole thing is friggin' unbelievable."

Holiday stood up. "Which is why you can't report this to the FRU."

Burnett looked at her as if she'd lost her mind. "They have to be told."

"Why? They know someone is trying to kill her. We tell them about that, not about the changing brain patterns."

"Why would we keep it from them?"

Holiday crossed her arms. "Because it will give them more of a reason to take Kylie and use her as some kind of lab rat."

Kylie's gaze shot from Holiday to Burnett. "Did they ever say if they would allow Dr. Pearson to do the tests?"

Burnett's grimace deepened. "They said regular hospitals don't have the necessary equipment."

"Which is exactly what I thought," Holiday blasted. "We have no idea if those tests are safe."

"They said they were." But Burnett's tone had lost its force, and Kylie wondered if he believed it anymore.

"They killed the spirit I'm helping," Kylie said.

"You don't know that for sure."

"Yes, I do. And if you need proof, dig up the grave. Her body is in there."

Burnett swore. "The FRU is not the enemy, Kylie. I admit they've made mistakes in the past, but that was then."

"Right," Holiday said, her tone still sharp. "But they'll sacrifice one if they think it will benefit the whole." She pointed at Kylie. "One of my teens will not be that sacrifice. And if you can't accept that, then walk out of here right now. Because we can't work together."

His gaze shot to Kylie, then back to Holiday. "Do you realize what you're asking me to do? To betray my oath and keep information from the FRU?"

"It's your choice," Holiday said.

Burnett closed his eyes, shook his head, and walked out of the office. Kylie didn't know if that was his answer, but from the sheer pain on Holiday's face, she certainly believed it.

When Kylie left Holiday's office after their meeting, Lucas was waiting. He'd gotten himself assigned shadow duty. He took her down to the stream and they stretched out on the warm grass and tried to find shapes in the clouds. Between finding everything from George Washington to dinosaurs in the sky, Kylie told him about Burnett and Holiday's argument.

"Burnett wants to tell the FRU, and Holiday thinks that will give them more reason to take me in for tests."

Propping up on his elbow, he stared down at her. "How do you feel about being tested?"

"I don't know. Part of me wants to do it if they really think it would give me answers, but Holiday's adamant that it could be dangerous. And I've always trusted her." And then there was what happened to the ghost.

"More than you trust Burnett?" Lucas asked.

"Maybe a little." Kylie looked into his blue eyes. "Do you think I'm wrong?"

"No. I probably trust Holiday more, too." He traced her lips with his finger.

"I just can't stand the thought of them fighting," she said, loving the feel of his touch, but her heart wouldn't let go of the problems at hand.

"That's between them," Lucas said.

"But it's about me. And I know they care about each other. I don't want to be the reason they gave up."

"You don't know they're giving up. I heard Burnett went back to the FRU offices to interrogate the captured were again. He'll be back."

"I hope so." But her heart wasn't so sure.

He leaned down and gently pressed his lips to hers. It was a soft, warm kiss. When he pulled back, his eyes held touches of amber color and she knew whatever thought had crossed his mind had stirred his anger.

"You know, I won't let that rogue have you. You're mine."

"I know," Kylie told him. What she didn't say was that she was worried no one might be able to prevent the rogue from carrying out his promise. So far, nothing had stopped him. Sure, if he was telling the truth about them being the same type of supernatural, and she believed him—she didn't understand it, but she believed him— then she was equally powerful. But if Holiday was right and she was a protector, then she would be able to use those powers only to protect others. That meant she was completely vulnerable to his whims.

It wasn't a good feeling. But she refused to cater to defeat. And she meant what she'd told the rogue. She would die before she became a part of some evil gang.

But she wasn't dead right now. And the proof was in how alive Lucas made her feel.

"Kiss me again," she said.

He grinned. "Is that a request or an order?"

"Both."

"Well, in that case . . ."

•   •   •

The next day, Burnett still hadn't returned. Holiday was moody, and Kylie had a raging headache. Lucas had found her earlier and told her his grandmother was ill and he was going to check on her. At around four, Kylie gave up and asked for permission to go lie down. Della, on shadowing duty, followed Kylie back to the cabin.

She didn't know how long she'd been asleep when the cold hit. She opened her eyes, feeling the icy mist on her breath. Jane was here.

"Thank God, you're awake," a feminine voice said. But it wasn't Jane's voice.

Kylie shot up. Through a curtain of hair, she saw Ellie standing at the foot of her bed.

"How did you get in here?" she asked.

Elle shrugged. Kylie glanced at the window she'd left open.

Kylie pulled the blanket up closer to her chest and looked around the room for Jane. She hadn't appeared yet, but she was here. Chill bumps climbed up and down her arms. Jane hadn't been here the last few days, and Kylie hoped she was finally ready to talk. "You know what, Ellie. This really isn't a good time. I have some business to take care of."

"But I need you to go to Derek," Ellie said. "He's upset. Not right."

Kylie studied her closer.

Ellie frowned. "You have to go to him." She shook her head. "I'm afraid he's hurt."

Kylie yanked her covers off. "Hurt? Where is he?"

"At the park about a half mile past the stream where the dinosaur tracks are."

"Why's he there?" Kylie asked.

"I don't know, but he needs you."

"Why does he need me?" Kylie slipped her tennis shoes on. "Has something happened?"

"I don't know," Ellie said. "I'm confused."

"Is he hurt?" Kylie's heart gripped in fear for Derek.

"No. I don't think so."

Ellie wasn't making sense. Kylie worried it might be a ploy to get her and Derek together. But something about the panic in Ellie's voice said differently.

"Let's go." Ellie moved toward the window.

"I have to get Della. She's my shadow, remember?"

"Hurry."

Kylie moved to the door and looked back again for Jane. She hadn't manifested, but her deathly cold still chilled the room. *I'll be back shortly*, she told the spirit in her head. *Please don't leave. We need to talk.*

Jane didn't answer. No surprise. Kylie walked out her bedroom door and Della looked up from the computer.

"You're slipping," Kylie said.

"How am I slipping?" Della asked.

"Ellie's here. "

"Shit! I am slipping." She stomped into Kylie's bedroom as if ready to give Ellie hell. Not that Kylie worried too much. Della and Ellie had bonded since Della invited her into her vampire circle.

Della came right back out. "Did she leave?"

"No way!"

Kylie stormed back into the bedroom. But Della was wrong. Ellie stood in the same place she'd been standing when she left. "You have to hurry."

"Maybe you dreamed it," Della said, stepping into the room.

The cold in the room pressed against Kylie's skin again. Kylie stared at Ellie. Her heart rolled over and tears crawled up her throat.

No!

"What happened, Ellie?" Tears slipped onto Kylie's cheeks. "Is Derek okay?"

"I don't remember." Ellie sounded befuddled.

"Kylie? Is this a dream?" Della asked.

More than anything, Kylie wished it were. She looked at Ellie. "What happened?" she asked again.

"You have to hurry. I'm worried about Derek."

Fear suddenly set in. Fear for Derek. Fear she might be too late to save Ellie and Derek. It didn't matter how much of her soul she'd have to give to save them. She'd give it.

"What's going on?" Miranda walked in.

"She's freaking again," Della snapped.

Kylie, with tears in her eyes, looked at Miranda. "I need you to call Holiday. Tell her Della and I are going up to the park past the dinosaur tracks. Derek's there and he might be hurt. Come on," Kylie said, and started to run.

Della caught Kylie by the arm. "What's going on?"

Kylie drew in a shaky breath. "Ellie's dead at some park close to here. And Derek was with her. We have to go before it's too late!"

Miranda let out a sob.

"How? What happened?" Della's eyes widened with emotion.

Kylie didn't have time to explain. Ellie bolted out the door, and Kylie went after her. Della's footsteps thudded against the earth as she came behind her.

Kylie never slowed down. Neither did Ellie or Della. When they got to the dinosaur tracks, they crossed the creek and jumped a fence into the park grounds. The path went uphill quickly, but Kylie kept up with no problem. Her blood fizzed with the strange kind of energy she got when she was protecting someone she loved. She just prayed it wasn't too late.

"It's just around the bend," Ellie said. She'd been quiet during the run. Then she suddenly stopped. Panic filled her gaze. *"Oh, my God. I remember."*

"What?" Kylie stopped beside Ellie.

"What? What?" When Della met Kylie's gaze, she must have realized she hadn't been talking to her, and she simply nodded.

"I followed someone here," Ellie said *"I spotted him running from the camp. I was almost here when I heard someone behind me. It was Derek. That's when the person I'd followed attacked."*

"Who was it?" Kylie's mind went to Red. "Was it a young guy, red or brownish hair?"

"No, it was an old dude. Vampire."

Mario. They never had a chance!

Kylie's chest filled with pain. And guilt. This was all her fault. "Where's Derek? Where's your body?" She had to save them.

Ellie pointed to the side of the mountain. It looked as if it had recently been disturbed. Loose rock lay around the ledge. *"Derek came around the bend and a bolt of lightning struck. He was slammed against the rocks. His head was bleeding, but he was breathing. But then more lightning struck. I picked him up and put him in the small cave and moved the rocks in front of him. I was doing that when . . . everything went blank."*

Kylie ran to the edge of the cliff and started moving the loose boulders.

Della moved in. "What are we doing?" Worry filled her expression.

"He's behind here," Kylie said. They moved the rocks to the side. Rocks that weighted well over four and five hundred pounds. Her strength didn't even surprise her; she thought only of Derek and Ellie.

"Oh God!" Della took a step back.

Kylie saw Ellie's mangled body lying between the rocks. Kylie's breath caught, and her tears started falling faster. She picked up Ellie and moved her to the side and rested her body on the rocky path.

"She's dead," Della said.

"Keep moving the rocks," Kylie ordered Della, and with everything Kylie had she prayed Derek was still alive. Prayed she could bring Ellie back.

She laid her hands on Ellie's battered body and sent up prayers that this worked. She closed her eyes, concentrated, and moved her palms over the injuries, as she had with Lucas and with Sara. Blood, Ellie's blood, coated Kylie's hands. She cried harder and tried harder, but no matter how hard she concentrated, her hands didn't heat up.

Suddenly, Ellie was sitting beside her body. *"It's too late. Look."* Ellie pointed up at the sky. The sun was a big ball of orange. *"I see my mother up there. She's waiting for me."*

"No," Kylie said. "Don't go. I'm trying to bring you back."

"But I want to go with her. I've missed her."

"No!" Kylie screamed again.

Ellie's spirit stood. *"Derek's okay."* She pointed back to Della as she moved the rocks. *"But I have to go. Thank you, Kylie Galen. Thank you for being my friend. Thank you for teaching me to think beyond myself. Thank you for everything."*

"Please don't," Kylie begged. But it was too late. Ellie's spirit started floating up toward the setting sun and Kylie knew it was hopeless.

"I got him," Della yelled. "I got Derek."

Kylie bolted to him. He was unconscious but breathing. She found the wounds on his head and pressed her hand against them. More blood oozed between her fingers, but she didn't care. Her hands grew hot and she felt the heat of her palms sink into Derek's scalp.

"Did you save Ellie?" Della asked.

"No, I'm sorry," Kylie said, and stared at Derek.

"Holiday and the others are coming," Della said, and when Kylie looked up, Della had tears running down her face.

"I tried to save her," Kylie said. "I really tried."

Derek suddenly jolted up. "What happened?"

Kylie stood. Derek looked at her and then pain filled his eyes. "Ellie?"

Kylie put a hand over her mouth and more tears flowed.

Derek ran out and found Ellie's body. He knelt beside her and Kylie saw his eyes fill with tears of rage. "Who did this?"

Guilt swelled in Kylie. "It was the old vampire, the one after me."

Holiday and about a dozen of the others came moving around the bend of the ledge. Kylie looked for Lucas, wishing he were here to hold her, but then she remembered he'd gone to see his grandmother.

She turned and faced the cave, her emotions too raw. She heard several of the campers gasp and some cry. No doubt they were seeing Ellie's body.

Holiday moved in and placed a hand on Kylie's shoulder.

Tears streamed down her face; she held out her bloody hands and gazed at Holiday. "What good is this gift, if I can't save those I want to save?"

Holiday didn't try to answer; she just wrapped Kylie in her arms and held her close.

"We need to go before it gets dark," Holiday finally said.

Derek picked up Ellie's body as though she were a rag doll, then Kylie saw him reach back down for her LITTLE VAMP cap. He tucked the cap under his arm and carried Ellie down the steep path.

They walked for about five minutes; no one spoke. Derek dropped Ellie's cap, and the wind blew it past Kylie. Kylie heard him ask someone to pick it up. At the very back of the single-file line, and feeling numb, Kylie turned to go grab the cap. She saw it only about twenty feet away. She moved in, almost ready to reach for it, when a big gust of wind moved it closer to the edge.

Kylie moved another couple of feet. The wind took the cap to the very edge. It hovered there, half on and half off the ledge.

Only then did Kylie sense the unnaturalness of the breeze.

She wasn't alone.

The sound of a dry branch snapping had never sounded scarier. Someone stood behind her. And less than two feet in front stood . . .

death. She had no idea how deep the cavern went, but she suspected the fall would be fatal.

Breath held, thinking any second she would feel someone give her that fatal push, she turned. The old vampire Mario and two other elderly supernaturals stood there staring at her with cold, calculating gazes. All three were dressed like monks, their dark robes stirring in the wind.

"Kylie Galen," Mario said. His voice sounded as aged as he looked, but the sense of power could not be overlooked. Was this really what she was? She studied Mario; closer, his eyes were black, coal black. She saw only evil, and the idea that she shared anything in common with these people disgusted her. "So we meet again."

She took a small step back, closer to the ledge. "Much to my misfortune," Kylie said, and she felt the heel of her tennis shoe find the edge of the embankment.

"'Tis true, my dear," he said. "Although, if you are so inclined as to save yourself, join us now. Pledge to us your allegiance and you will live. My grandson will make you a good husband."

"What are you?" She tightened her brows and saw into their patterns. Mario was vampire, the bearded one was warlock, and the other carried the pattern of a werewolf. But all three patterns were dark and ominous.

"Join us and you will have your answers."

Kylie swallowed and sent up a little prayer. She prayed for help. Then she prayed for forgiveness for anything and everything she'd ever done wrong. Then she prayed for courage. She took another step back until her feet hit nothing.

Chapter Thirty-six

Gravity grabbed Kylie from below. Her breath caught at the same time a hand caught her arm. Her heart throbbing in her chest, she looked up into the face of her rescuer. Red.

He jerked her back to safety.

She found her footing, beside him. But her mind raced as she realized he'd saved her. "Hello, Kylie," the rogue said.

She just stared at him, not sure what to say.

"She made her choice," said the bearded man standing beside Mario. His dark brown robe fluttered in the wind as he raised his hand and pointed those long, aged fingers at her. She stared in something akin to horror as flames came from the tips of his fingers.

Red jumped in front of her, and the old man's flames stopped. "I told you I would change her mind. Give her time. She's too good to kill."

"She has made her choice," Mario said. "Her time is up. Move out of the way. Let her plummet to her death."

"No," Red said.

Kylie stared at Red, confused by his willingness to protect her. And yet hadn't he been doing it all along?

"You dare to disobey me in front of my peers?" Mario growled.

"I dare," Red said. "I've spent my entire life living by your rules. You murdered my mother. You forced my father to run away. I've accepted that all my life, and I have asked nothing of you but this. Spare her. For me."

"She cannot be spared," said the other old man. "She will bring us down."

"She won't. I'll take care of her," Red said. "I'll change her mind, I'll convince her." There was pleading in his voice.

"The decision is made," the bearded man said.

The second old man raised his hand, and a surge of wind picked her up from the ground and knocked her back toward the edge.

She felt herself falling. Felt the air part as her body descended. Fear made her tense; grief for everyone she loved chased off the fear. She saw faces in her mind's eye that she would miss. Things she would never do. She saw Lucas's face and then Derek's. She saw her friends— new and old. Then she blinked, unable to breathe. She saw the sun setting and found an odd sort of calm settle within her. The colors in the dusk sky filled her mind with a surge of calm. She'd be able to be with Daniel and Nana.

Something or someone caught her again. Her memory shot back to being caught by Perry. The grips around her wrist were not human. The jolt brought air into her lungs. Had Perry come to save her?

"I have you. Hold on!"

But the voice didn't belong to Perry. It was Red.

A bolt of lightning shot past them, so close that Kylie felt the sting of it.

In seconds, the huge bird landed back on the ledge and set her gently on her feet. There were no sparkles as he changed back to human form. He was more than just a shape-shifter.

"You okay?" he asked.

Kylie looked at him through the tears in her eyes and nodded. She remembered him saving her from the snake. From the lightning strike In the woods and then trying to save her from the sinkhole. She'd never said thank you, never considered needing to, because all she saw in him was evil. But then he'd saved Miranda, too.

"I don't even know your real name," she managed to say.

"Roberto." He smiled. "I managed to snag this." He handed her Ellie's cap.

Right then Kylie knew. Red . . . Roberto wasn't all evil.

"Thank you," she said.

He stared at her as if he didn't know how to respond. Then he reached out and brushed a tear from her cheek. "You are even pretty when you cry."

"No, I'm not. I get all red and—" A bolt of lightning shot down from above. Roberto pushed her away. Her back hit the rock wall behind her. He looked prepared to run, but before he did, the lightning struck again. It hit him. The ground beneath her shook at the impact. The smell of burned flesh filled her nose.

Kylie dropped to her knees. Panic clawed at her throat. She didn't want to see it, but she couldn't look away. Roberto's eyes turned blood red, and his body contorted backward; something that looked like smoke billowed out of his mouth, and Kylie knew it was his soul. And then he fell. The sound of his soulless body hitting the hard earth was pure sadness.

She moved to try to save him.

"Don't." The sound of his voice startled her. She looked at him. His spirit stood several feet from his body, gazing toward the dusk-filled sky. *"I don't want to stay."* Purples, shades of bright pinks, golds, and shades of gray now laced the sky.

"Do you see them?" he asked.

For a second, she thought he meant his grandfather and the two other men, but then she did see, and she understood. Angels were dancing in the painted sky; like birds, they moved gracefully in the wind.

Kylie nodded. "I do." But she still had to try. She laid her hands on his body. And concentrated. Nothing happened. Her hands would not heat up. Giving up, she finally gazed up at his spirit.

"Why would you want to save me?" his spirit asked.

"Because you saved me," she said, and looked up.

He gazed back at her, and all hints of evil were gone from his eyes. What she saw was a person who never had a chance. A boy raised into evil, taught evil, and never loved. *"I understand now,"* he said. *"I was wrong, Kylie Galen. You are not my soul mate. But because of you, I have saved my soul."* Then slowly his spirit was taken, pulled up by the sky. He became part of the colors in the dusky sky. Part of the beauty, part of something that was eternal. The death angels took him at the last second of dusk.

Kylie wasn't sure how much time passed, but the colors of the sky had turned black when another *whoosh* of wind hit. What was a flash in the night suddenly became a body, crouched down only a few feet from her. Kylie scooted back and then recognized Burnett.

"Are you okay?" he asked.

Kylie nodded.

"I need to get you out of here, now." He pulled her up.

She looked down at the body near her feet. And realized his eyes, empty, dead, were open. She lowered herself and closed his lids.

When she stood up, she told Burnett, "He died saving me."

"Then maybe hell will be easy on him." Burnett picked her up.

"He didn't go to hell," Kylie said.

She didn't know if he heard her. It didn't matter. She knew.

Burnett carried Kylie back to the main office, where Holiday paced across the front porch. He set Kylie down.

"Thank God!" Holiday ran to Kylie and hugged her.

"Thank you," Holiday said to Burnett, but when she released Kylie, he was already gone.

Her frown deepened, but her expression changed and she met Kylie's eyes. "Are you okay?"

Kylie nodded and tried not to cry. "Is Derek okay?"

"He's resting."

Kylie nodded.

"What happened, Kylie? You were there one minute and then gone the next."

Kylie pulled out Ellie's hat from her jeans pocket. "I went back for this, and . . ." The tears she didn't want to cry came anyway, and she told Holiday the whole story.

Kylie wasn't asleep when she heard the knock on her door several hours later. She heard Della answer it. Then she heard Lucas's voice. He came into her bedroom and pulled her against him, and Kylie held on to him like a life preserver. She needed his strength. Needed to feel his arms around her. They stayed like that for hours, not kissing, not making out, just holding on to each other.

The next morning, the mood at the camp was somber at best. Everyone missed Ellie. They missed Burnett. They missed Derek. He'd left for the weekend to stay with his mom. Kylie was almost afraid to see him. Ellie's funeral was set for next week because the FRU wanted to do an autopsy. Kylie knew that no one at the camp blamed her, but she couldn't quite keep from blaming herself.

Holiday, sensing Kylie's emotion, had taken her to the falls. It was there, behind the wall of water, that Kylie felt most of the ugliness of guilt lift. She asked the question why, why it had to happen. The answer came in a feeling. Fate had called Ellie home. Fate was still pissing Kylie off. But some of the guilt did fade.

Holiday worked like crazy to keep the camp running and do interviews for teachers. It was too much for one person, though. So Kylie got together with a couple of the other campers and assigned jobs. One person oversaw the contractors, while another answered calls at the office.

Holiday almost protested but then threw in the towel and accepted their help.

On Thursday afternoon, when Lucas had her for shadow duty, Kylie asked if he'd seen Burnett.

"No, but he's around," Lucas said. "He's set guards around the camp in case anything else happens."

Kylie hoped nothing else would happen. According to Miranda, whoever had been hanging around was now gone.

Apparently, so was Kylie's ghost, because she hadn't appeared in days.

The next afternoon, Kylie was sitting on the front porch when Derek walked up. He must have returned early.

The lingering guilt she felt at Ellie's death bubbled to the surface. And when she saw that he still had shadows of grief in his eyes, she felt her guilt swell to the point of pain.

He lowered himself beside her. "That's what I came to see you about."

She looked at him, unsure what he meant. "I knew you would feel responsible for this. And I just wanted you to know that Ellie made that choice when she took off after the intruder. I made the choice to follow her. It's not your fault. You would have done the same for anyone in this camp."

Kylie felt a knot form in her throat. "But he was here because of me."

"I know. I'm sure Ellie knew it when she went after him. But it didn't stop her. And she would be so unhappy if she knew you blamed yourself for her death. It would be a dishonor to her memory if I let you keep blaming yourself. She liked you. She liked you a lot."

Kylie felt a few tears roll past her lashes, and Derek put his arm around her. It wasn't a boyfriend kind of hug, just a hug from a friend who was offering a warm touch of comfort. And it felt really good.

When the next day came and Jane was still a no-show, Kylie went to Holiday with a request.

"No." Holiday shoved herself back in her desk chair.

"But I need to see her, and I know she's there."

"Don't you remember what happened the last time you went?"

"I remember I survived," Kylie said. "I also remember I ended up helping another lost soul, and I learned something when I was there. I need to go, Holiday."

Holiday slapped her pen onto the desk. "Someone is trying to kill you."

"*Was* trying," Kylie said. "I think Miranda is right. They're gone right now."

"Why would they leave?"

"I don't know. But I refuse to live my life in a prison."

"This isn't a prison," Holiday said.

"It is if I can't ever leave."

Holiday scowled. "If I say no, you're still going to go, aren't you?"

Kylie gave the question some thought and answered honestly. "Probably."

"Fine. I'll clear an hour after lunch and we'll—"

"I don't think you should go," Kylie said.

"Why?"

"I've been there. They know me, and if you show up, it might confuse things. I think you scared Jane Doe. She might not show herself if you're there."

Holiday's frown deepened. "There is no way in hell that I'm letting you go by yourself."

"Not by myself," Kylie insisted. "You could call Burnett."

Holiday frowned, but Kylie knew she wouldn't say no. Not when it involved someone's safety. And yes, this might have been a bit of a ploy to get them back together again, but it was killing Kylie to see Holiday so miserable.

Besides, Kylie did want to help Jane Doe.

Burnett agreed to the plan. But after Ellie's death, he said he wasn't going in with just the two of them. Lucas wasn't there. He'd driven into Houston to get the contractors their supplies. He wouldn't be back until three. So Burnett recommended Derek and Della.

Derek looked thrilled when she asked if he would go with her. He'd agreed before she told him where they were going.

"It's the cemetery," she said. "And there will be ghosts there."

"No problem."

Della hadn't been so thrilled. But of course, after grumbling, she agreed to go.

When they arrived at the Fallen Cemetery gates, Della grumbled some more. Derek put his warm hand against Kylie's back and whispered, "It's okay. I'm here."

Obviously, he'd read her misgivings about making the trip. Sure, she'd put up a good front with Holiday, but it didn't mean she wasn't scared. She could still remember how terrified she'd felt when the ghosts had charged her all at once.

"Thanks." Then she mentally pulled up her big-girl panties and walked through the gates, with Della on one side of her and Derek and Burnett on the other.

Sun and shadows danced across the graves at the same time the unnatural cold fell upon them like an invisible cloud of fog.

Derek leaned in again. "I need to talk to you . . . when we can steal a minute. It's important. Please."

She nodded.

"It's her. She's back . . ." Kylie heard one voice and then a merge of voices, male and female, young and old.

"She said she'd come back."

"And I thought she was just bullshitting us."

"I told you she wasn't lying."

Tension pulled at her skull, forecasting a headache. But the spirit of the old man's wife manifested and the voices retreated.

"My husband got his medicines right, thanks to you."

"That's good," Kylie said out loud.

"What's good?" Derek asked.

"She not talking to you," Della said. "Freaky, isn't it?"

"It's not that bad," Derek said, but Kylie saw him cutting his green eyes from side to side, as though he wondered where the spirits were. Burnett remained silent, standing stoic. He'd hardly spoken since he'd met them at the front of the camp.

Why haven't you passed over? Kylie asked this question in her head as she ambled down the path between the tombstones.

"I decided to just wait on him," Ima said. "But Catherine passed on. That was the woman you helped. Her kids came here. I heard them say they're planning on changing her tombstone to show her real name. That was nice of you to do that."

Kylie nodded. Have you seen the other one? The one you call Berta Littlemon?

"She was just here. She's been a basket case since they took her away."

"Took her away?" Kylie asked aloud again.

The spirit just shrugged and said, "There she is. Sitting by the grave."

"I'm going to be right over there." Kylie pointed to the grave where Jane sat on the ground.

"As long as we can see you," Burnett said.

Kylie moved over to Jane. The ghost looked up and the sun hit her face. She had tears webbing her dark lashes. She didn't have on any makeup. She looked young. And pregnant.

"Are you okay?" Kylie sat down next to Jane.

The spirit looked back at the grave. *"I want to remember so badly. But my brain doesn't work. Sometimes I feel as if the answers are right there, but I can't reach them. Then I remember something and it disappears. Why doesn't my brain work right?"*

Kylie hesitated. But Jane deserved to know. Just like Kylie deserved to get her own answers. "I don't know everything, but I know some."

"What?" she asked.

"There's an organization called the FRU. They're like the government for supernaturals. According to the leader of our camp, several years ago, the FRU were doing tests, something about genetics. I don't know what kind of tests they ran, but from the vision I had, I think you were one of the ones they tested, and they operated on you. You had your head shaved and had stitches. In the vision, you looked paralyzed. I think something went wrong with the test they did, so . . . they killed you."

Jane put her hand over her trembling lips. *"I remember I showed you that. They put a pillow over my face."*

"Yes," Kylie said.

"I didn't want to do the tests, but . . . my husband. What was his name?" she asked Kylie.

"I don't know."

Jane shook her head. *"He insisted that we do it, so they would leave us alone."*

"Who would leave you alone?" Kylie asked, wanting to make sure they were still talking about the FRU.

"The organization that you said. If we didn't agree to be tested, they'd imprison us."

"Why?"

Jane paused again. *"I can't remember. But I think it was because we were different."* She looked at the grave. The dirt around the tombstone had been disturbed. *"He took me away. He dug me out of the ground."*

"Who did?" Kylie leaned closer.

"That bad man."

"What bad man?"

"The one who wanted you to be tested."

"Burnett?" Kylie asked. "He took you away?"

She nodded. *"I don't like him."*

Kylie stared at the grave, trying to figure out what that meant. "He's not bad," she said. But why would he dig up Jane's body? Was it to prove what the FRU had done? Or was it to protect the FRU from her accusations?

"He looks bad." Jane pointed toward the path.

Kylie looked up. Burnett stopped in front of her. "I can explain it."

Kylie stood. "I hope so."

He frowned but didn't explain, so she decided to start asking questions.

"Why did you take Jane Doe's body?"

He hesitated. "I thought you wanted to know who she was."

Kylie sensed he was speaking only half the truth. "Do you know who she is?"

He nodded. "I was going to tell you, as soon as I had a little more information." He paused again. "But I guess now is fine. Her name is Heidi Summers."

Kylie looked around for the spirit. She didn't see her, but she could still feel the cold. Whether it was from Jane or someone else, Kylie didn't know.

"I have an address, too. She lived a couple of miles from here. I thought you'd want to go there."

"Yes," Kylie said. "Is her family still there?"

Burnett started walking, and Kylie followed him. She saw Derek and Della waiting for them by the gate.

"The house is listed to Malcolm Summers," Burnett said. "So I'm assuming it's her family."

Kylie caught her breath when a hundred or more souls lined up on each side of the path. They all reached out for her and started talking at once. Her head started to pound. The icy feel of their touches stung like thousands of needles.

She felt herself being pulled in a thousand different directions.

"Help me."

"No, help me."

"Stop it!" the spirit of the old man's wife screamed. *"If you're not nice, she won't come back."*

The jabbering stopped. They brought their hands to their sides, but they didn't leave. They stood completely still and watched her with soulless eyes—all wanting, needing her to do something for them so they could cross over.

But there were too many to help. Guilt filled her chest. She breathed in the frigid air and forced herself to concentrate on the one she could help. Jane Doe.

"The Summers family. They're supernaturals, right?" Kylie asked, unsure what she would say to them. But if they were supernaturals, perhaps it wouldn't be so hard.

Burnett frowned. "They aren't registered supernaturals."

"You think they're rogue?"

"Not everyone unregistered is rogue. But they could be."

Derek moved in beside Kylie, appearing concerned. He brushed the top of his hand against hers. She felt the calm he offered and appreciated the assistance.

Burnett turned to Derek and Della as soon as they walked out of the gate. "I called Holiday and asked her to pick you two up. I'll bring Kylie by later."

Kylie and Burnett got into his Mustang. As she watched Della and Derek get smaller in the rearview mirror, the craziest thought struck. What if Burnett took her to the FRU to get tested? What if Jane was right? What if he wasn't a good guy?

Chapter Thirty-seven

Neither of them spoke during the ride. The silence seemed heavy, but not that unusual, or so Kylie reminded herself. Burnett had never been Mr. Chatty.

But with every roll of the tires, Kylie's uncertainty rose. She glanced at Burnett, again sitting silent in the driver's seat.

"You seem nervous," he said.

"Should I be?"

He appeared confused. "I thought you wanted to see them."

She nodded, but the memory of Jane and her surgery hit harder. Oh sure, Kylie's heart told her Burnett was a good guy, but she could also remember Holiday saying that the FRU weren't above sacrificing one person if they thought it was for a good cause.

When Burnett parked his Mustang in front of a small white-framed house, the same house Kylie had seen in her visions, a wave of shame hit for ever doubting Burnett.

"I tried to call them, but no one answered," Burnett said. "Of course, I'm going to go in with you, but I'll let you explain things however you see fit."

Two minutes later, after receiving no answer to their knock, a woman, looking all of ninety years old, stepped out of the house next door.

"Can I help ya?" She came toward them, moving amazingly fast for someone her age.

Kylie, thinking she felt a whisper of cold, immediately checked the woman's pattern. Burnett did the same. The woman was human.

"We're looking for Mr. Summers," Burnett said.

"Well, you're too late. He and his sister-in-law flew out this morning. Went to Ireland."

Ireland? Was it a coincidence that the Brightens were there now? Kylie looked at Burnett and saw the same question in his eyes.

"Why did they go there?" Burnett asked.

The neighbor grinned. "Said he was looking for something he lost a long time ago. Said it was more valuable than gold and he figured it might be there."

"Do you know when he plans to return?" Kylie asked.

"I'm supposed to water the plants and feed the cat for a week."

Burnett started moving back to the car. "Thank you, ma'am."

"Did you want to leave a message?" the neighbor asked.

"We'll come back." Burnett smiled and waved.

Kylie got into the car, sank into the seat, and wanted to kick and scream with frustration. More questions and zero answers. She was friggin' tired of this.

Burnett started the car. "Let's drive over to the next block and come back on foot."

"Come back for what?" Kylie asked.

"I figured you'd like to go inside," he said. "See if we can learn anything."

"Isn't that against the law?" Kylie asked.

His eyes widened. "Only if we get caught."

She bit down on her lip so hard, she tasted blood. "Do you, like, have any 'get out of jail free' cards if we do get caught? I wouldn't look good in prison garb."

He patted his pocket. "I think I brought two with me."

The house smelled like herbs. Rosemary. Maybe a little thyme. The furnishings were old. Lots of antiques, expensive-looking things, but nothing too showy. When Kylie stepped into the hall, she spotted the closet Jane had pulled her suitcase from. Right then, she felt the cold come down on her.

She stopped abruptly. Burnett bumped into her from behind.

"Something wrong?" he asked.

"You mean other than the fact that we just broke into someone's house?" She knew he didn't want to know they had company.

"It's fine," he said.

"Right." She moved into the bedroom. Jane Doe, aka Heidi Summers, sat on the bed, staring at the photos on the bedside table.

Kylie studied the woman's face behind the frame. "It's you."

"What's . . . Never mind, I'll wait out here." Burnett must have realized she wasn't talking to him and wanted nothing to do with the ghost.

Considering what had happened to him the last time, Kylie didn't blame him.

Me and Malcolm. Heidi said the name with so much love. *I remember.*

Kylie picked up the picture. She recalled feeling something odd when she'd seen the man's face in the vision. The same thing hit her again. Then chills shot down her spine. Not from the cold this time, but from the realization.

"Burnett?"

"What?" He barged into the bedroom as if ready to fight.

She held out the picture. "That's him."

He took the picture. "Who?"

"That's the same man who came to the camp. The one who claimed to be my grandfather."

Burnett scanned the photo. "Are you sure?"

"Completely."

Heidi stood up. *"It was him, wasn't it? I remember. And that was my sister, too."*

Her sister? Kylie remembered the woman, remembered feeling a connection. "Why would they come to the camp and pretend to be my adoptive grandparents?" Kylie asked, and she meant the question for both Burnett and Heidi.

"I don't know," Burnett answered.

Heidi stood there as if trying to think. *"Wait. They were from Ireland. And the neighbor said—"*

"Who was from Ireland?" Kylie asked, and saw Burnett leave again.

"The people who adopted my boy. I gave him up for adoption. I went to a doctor who placed children with good parents. The doctor was human, but he knew about supernaturals. I remember there were complications, I had to have a C-section, and the doctor didn't want to do it because he didn't have the supplies to put me under; I made him do it anyway. I couldn't let my baby die. I knew whatever pain I experienced would be better than knowing I'd robbed my son of his chance at life. Then I made sure he would go to a good family." She sat up straighter. *"Malcolm's looking for our son."*

Tears filled Kylie's eyes as the truth swirled around her heart, making her dizzy. Heidi Summers was Daniel's birth mother. She was Kylie's grandmother. And Malcolm Summers, her real grandfather, and her grandmother's sister had posed as Daniel's adoptive parents. Why? Why not just tell her? More questions.

"He's going to find our boy. And they'll be a family, the way we should have been."

The pain of everything her grandmother had endured suddenly swamped her. Knowing she would have to tell Heidi that Daniel was dead cut like a knife.

But she had to tell her, didn't she?

"He won't find him," Kylie said.

"How do you know?"

Kylie wiped the tears from her eyes. "He's not in Ireland."

"Why else would Malcolm have gone to Ireland?"

"He went to find the Brightens."

Heidi sank back on the bed, as if trying to absorb what Kylie said. *"Yes, that was their name. They adopted my boy."*

Kylie nodded. "But your son isn't with them."

"Where is he?" She jumped off the bed. *"Take me to him. I want to see him."*

Kylie's breath caught. "He died a long time ago."

"No!" she yelled. *"He lived. I went to see him right before they forced Malcolm and me to go to that place for tests. It was a few months after I had given birth. My son was fine. So healthy."*

"He didn't die when he was a baby," Kylie said. "He grew up, met a woman whom he fell in love with, and then he joined the army. He died when he was twenty-one while on a mission, trying to save a woman. He was a hero. You should be proud."

Heidi dropped back on the bed. *"Are you sure?"*

"Yes." Another wave of tears filled Kylie's eyes. "I'll bet he's waiting to meet you on the other side, too."

She looked up as if she could see heaven. *"Did you know him?"*

Kylie nodded. "Only his spirit." She felt tears begin to roll down her cheeks. "He's my father."

Heidi's eyes rounded. *"That would mean that you . . ."* She reached out and touched Kylie's cheek. *"I should have known. You look like Malcolm. Blond hair instead of red, but those eyes . . ."* A tear slipped from her cheek. *"I think . . . a part of me did know."*

Kylie blinked. "I have so many questions to ask you, so many things I want to know. First, what are we?"

"What do you mean?"

"We're supernatural, right?"

She hesitated, as if she had to think. *"Yes. That was why they took us in to do those terrible tests."*

"So, what are we?" Kylie held her breath, waiting, hoping for her answer.

Heidi frowned as if trying to think again. *"I . . . can't remember. I'm sorry. But . . ."* She pointed to the picture. *"Malcolm will remember. The man never forgets anything."*

Heidi stood up. *"I have to go to my son now. I need to tell him that I love him. That's why I stayed here. To tell him how sorry I am that I gave him away."*

"Why did you do it?" Kylie asked, hoping something would jog her memory. "Why did you give him away?"

She tilted her head as if to think again. *"Because they wanted the little ones more than they wanted us."*

"Who?" Kylie asked. "The FRU?"

"Yes," she said. *"It was the only way to keep him safe. If I'd run with him, they'd have found me. So I gave him away. I told Malcolm I lost the baby. I had to do it. He trusted them. He said they wouldn't hurt our baby and they would just study him for a little while. But I didn't believe them. So I gave the baby away, I lied to Malcolm, and then I came back because I loved him so much."*

"Why did they want to study the baby?" Kylie asked.

"I don't remember . . . Wait, it was because we were different and they didn't like it."

"How were we different?"

She shook her head. Her brow wrinkled. *"Everything is still so messed up. I remember some things and not others. Malcolm will know."*

She leaned down and pressed a hand to Kylie's cheek. *"I'm going to see my boy. But you, Kylie Galen, are everything I would have wanted in a granddaughter. I must go now."*

Kylie wanted to scream no and beg Heidi to stay, that she had more questions. But it was too late. Heidi had already disappeared.

Fifteen minutes later, Kylie sat silently in the Mustang as Burnett pulled up to the camp. She'd told Burnett everything. About how Jane Doe was really her grandmother, and she'd given Kylie's father away for adoption because the FRU were taking children like them to study. He put the car in park and looked at her. "So you think he went to find the Brightens?"

Kylie nodded.

"I'll see if I can find Malcolm Summers in Ireland. But there's a good chance you might have to wait until he gets back."

Kylie nodded, not liking being this close and still so far away. She reached for the door handle and then looked back at Burnett. "You're not coming in?"

He frowned. "No."

She hesitated to ask but then went for it. "Are you ever coming back?"

He gripped the wheel. "I don't know."

"Why?"

He stared straight ahead. "It's what she wants. She doesn't trust me anymore."

Kylie swallowed. "Neither did I."

He arched a brow at her.

"When you were driving me to the house, I was afraid that you were taking me to be tested."

He frowned. Hurt lingered in his eyes.

"But that's because I saw what the FRU did to my grandmother. I lived bits and pieces of it through her, and when someone lives through something bad, it's hard to trust. I don't know exactly what happened to Holiday with that other vampire, she won't even talk to me about it, but it must have been bad. It scared her and now she's scared to love again. But if you just hang in there . . ."

"I have hung in there. I'm done."

They sat there staring at each other for several long seconds. "I should go," he said finally.

Kylie got out. As she watched Burnett pull away, the emotions playing in her heart were the same as the ones she'd felt the day she watched Tom Galen drive away with his suitcases.

Shadow Falls was her family. They'd already lost Ellie. They didn't need to lose Burnett, too. But for the life of her, she didn't know how she could change this.

Lucas met Kylie at the gate. More than anything, she needed a hug. She wanted to tell him what she'd learned, but what she got was his anger.

"Why didn't you wait on me?" he demanded.

Maybe it was because her emotions were already on the edge, but she just started walking away.

"Damn it!" Lucas said, and moved in step with her. "Why in the hell would you go back to the cemetery, anyway? And why would they allow Derek to go with you?"

"Because I needed answers. And because Derek is my friend. Just like Fredericka is yours!"

He caught her by the arm. "Do you know how worried I've been?"

"Yes," Kylie snapped. "You were as worried about me as I am about you when you run off and play wolf for a night."

He looked stunned. "I can't help what I am, Kylie."

"Neither can I, Lucas." Tears sprang to her eyes. "I don't know what I am, but I know that what I do is deal with ghosts. And if you can't accept that, then maybe you can't accept me."

"I didn't say that," he insisted. "I just want—"

"You want me to be werewolf," she said. "You want me to be werewolf so your family and your pack will accept me. But right now, it's not looking good that you'll get what you want. So maybe you need to think about that, too."

She took off.

He caught up with her. "I'm sorry," he said. "It's just I can't stand the thought of something happening to you. And . . . nothing is going to change between us, no matter what you are." He lifted her chin and met her eyes. "Don't you know how I feel?"

He pulled her against his chest, and Kylie let him. She buried herself in his warmth and tried to believe that he spoke the truth, but she couldn't lie to herself. She knew Lucas wanted to believe it, but she wasn't completely convinced that it would be the case if his grandmother really got involved. Kylie wasn't even sure it was fair of her to ask him to make that choice.

Kylie awoke very early Tuesday morning. Her first thought was that today was Ellie's funeral. She recalled the vision she'd had about it and wondered if it was fair that she had to live through it twice.

She ran a hand over her face. Her alarm hadn't gone off. So why was she awake?

The cold suddenly fell on her like a blanket of ice. "Heidi?" She sat up so fast, her head spun. "Is that you? I have more questions to ask."

No answer came. Kylie sat there, waiting. Through the haze of darkness, she saw a figure appear at the end of her bed. "Heidi?" she asked again.

Kylie turned on the lamp. The light filled the bedroom and illuminated the spirit, who stood with her back to the bed. It wasn't Heidi. Kylie couldn't even tell if this ghost was male or female. Somehow he/she looked . . . deader than the others. Sure, they were all dead, but for some reason even the matted hair looked deader than the hair of other spirits.

"Hello," Kylie whispered.

The spirit turned around, and Kylie stopped breathing. Worms, maggots, and creepy insects crawled in and out of the eye sockets, eating away at what little flesh still clung to the face.

Screaming, Kylie slammed back against the headboard.

"Can you help me?" A stream of worms cascaded from the spirit's lips as she spoke, and they landed on Kylie's blanket.

"I . . ." Kylie kicked the covers to stop the gooey-looking creatures from crawling toward her. "I might, but can you do something about your face? Now!"

Della bolted into the room. "You okay?"

Kylie glanced back at the foot of her bed. The ghost was gone. Relief washed over her. "I'm fine," her voice squeaked out. Remembering the maggots—and not one hundred percent sure the ghost had taken them with her—Kylie leapt up, yanked the covers off the bed, and tossed them on the floor. She backed away from the pile of bedding.

"Yeah. You look just fine," Della said sarcastically.

Kylie jumped from foot to foot and brushed off imaginary maggots that she felt crawling on her skin.

Della stood there in Mickey Mouse pajamas, staring at her as if she didn't know whether to laugh or run.

Kylie stopped dancing and tried to breathe normally. "If I die, promise me I'll be cremated."

Della frowned. "Die?"

"Not that I'm planning to die anytime soon." She gave her arm one more swipe. "But still."

Della shook her head. "I don't know why you pretend you're okay."

Kylie wrapped her arms around herself. "Me either."

Kylie didn't go back to sleep. She wasn't sure if she'd ever sleep in that bed again. Instead, she dressed and waited for Della and Miranda to go to the sunrise service.

The service happened just as it had in the vision. Only the grief felt deeper, especially when Kylie saw Derek, tears in his eyes, holding Ellie's hat.

Holiday kept looking over her shoulder. Kylie knew she was looking for Burnett. It wasn't until Chris started talking that Burnett slid into the chair next to Holiday.

She saw the two of them look at each other. Kylie wasn't sure what kind of look it was—other than sad. Sad seemed to be the mood of the day. Well, for everyone except the blue jay who kept flittering by, spouting out song as if wanting to impress her.

Only she wasn't impressed.

When the ceremony ended, Lucas took her hand to walk her to the dining hall, where they planned to have a celebration of Ellie's life. Everyone was going to tell Ellie stories.

But Burnett stopped her. "I need to talk to you and Holiday a minute."

Lucas said he'd meet her in the dining hall. Then Holiday and Burnett and Kylie walked into the office.

"Is something wrong?" Kylie asked once Burnett closed the door.

He pulled an envelope from his suit jacket and handed it to Kylie.

"What is that?" Holiday asked. From her tone, she seemed to think it had to do with Kylie having tests.

"It's the location of her grandmother's body."

"You had her buried in her own grave?" Kylie asked.

"Not exactly." He paused. "Let's just say that if the FRU try to force you to undergo any tests that you aren't comfortable with, you can use this to . . . insist that you prefer not to participate."

"So you think they'll push for Kylie to be tested?" Holiday asked.

He frowned. "I'm under the impression they will, yes."

"You told them about what happened?"

"I haven't told them anything since you asked me not to."

"So the FRU doesn't know you removed the body?" Holiday asked.

"No." His gaze met Kylie's. "What they did to your grandmother was wrong. And while the agency has admitted to some wrongdoings with some of the testing that went down in the sixties, this is one skeleton they wouldn't want brought forward."

"Why did they do it?" Kylie asked.

He shrugged. "The information I could find was very vague. Supposedly, there were a small number of supernaturals who were genetically different from the rest."

"So we still don't know what I am?"

Burnett's expression tightened. "I'm afraid not."

"Except a genetic freak," she muttered.

Holiday sat beside Kylie on the sofa and reached for her hand. "Don't say—"

"I'm assuming it's just the opposite," Burnett broke in. "They wouldn't be interested in something that wasn't working correctly. Just the fact that you can appear human would be considered an advantage. That could be all there is to it, or it could be more."

"What advantage is there to appearing human?" Kylie asked.

"A lot. Right now, supernaturals aren't allowed to run for any political office."

"That doesn't seem fair," Kylie said.

"It probably isn't. But what they did to your grandmother wasn't fair either. However, I do have some news." His expression seemed to change, but to what Kylie wasn't sure.

"I actually spoke with Malcolm Summers. Your real grandfather," Burnett said. "And before you ask, we didn't discuss any details. I was afraid if I started asking too many questions, I'd scare him off. I told him you wanted to meet him."

"And?" Kylie gripped Holiday's hand. *What if he said he didn't want to meet me?*

Chapter Thirty-eight

Burnett continued, "He said he was getting on the next flight available back to Texas. It may be Thursday before he arrives."

Kylie got tears in her eyes. "It's really going to happen, isn't it? I'm finally going to get my answers." She still felt fear, but less than before. She needed her answers. Deserved them.

"It looks like it," Burnett said.

Kylie jumped up, stopping herself just before she wrapped her arms around him. "May I hug you?"

He grinned and grimaced at the same time. "Make it quick."

She did. When she backed up, Holiday watched with tears in her eyes.

Burnett nodded at Holiday. "And this is for you." He pulled out another envelope and handed it to her.

"What is it?" Holiday asked, sounding unsure.

"It's a donation to help cover future costs for Shadow Falls . . . and my resignation."

Holiday stiffened. "That's what you want?" She sounded so hurt that Kylie's heart gripped.

"It's what you want," he said.

"I didn't ask you to resign."

"The hell you didn't!"

"Should I leave?" Kylie asked.

But no one was listening to her, and Burnett was blocking the door.

"Hello?" Kylie said, but they were too busy staring daggers at each other to pay attention to her.

"I said, if you couldn't understand my not letting Kylie go in for tests by the FRU, then you'd best leave."

"Because you don't need me anymore now that you have other investors lined up, right?" Burnett sounded hurt.

"What investors?" Holiday asked.

"Don't lie to me, Holiday! I saw the file. You have four possible investors waiting in the wings."

"You went through my desk?"

"I wasn't snooping! I had to pay the bills while you were away, remember?"

"Well, next time you go rummaging in my desk, you should read the dates on the paperwork!" She went to her desk, opened her drawer, and tossed the file at him.

"What's that supposed to mean?"

"I didn't find these people just now. I found them before you signed on."

He stared at her in growing confusion. "You said the only reason you chose me was because you didn't have anyone else."

"I didn't say that. You assumed it."

Burnett stared at Holiday. "Are you saying you chose me over these other people?" He moved closer, leaving a slight opening to the office door.

"I'm gonna just slip out now." Kylie took a step forward.

They ignored her. And Kylie hesitated for just a second.

"So you care about me," Burnett grumbled. "Why the hell can't you admit it, Holiday?"

"Hiring you was a business decision, Burnett."

"Bullshit!" Burnett said. "Each one of them has more money than I do."

"A business decision, not a financial one."

"Is that why you kissed me?" he demanded.

"I did no such thing. *You* kissed me."

"And you enjoyed it!"

"I'm out of here." Kylie eased around Burnett and walked out, but she carried with her a smile and a lot of hope. She was pretty sure Burnett wasn't quitting now. And in two days, she would have answers from her grandfather Malcolm. God, she hoped it was true.

"Hey." Derek met her on the porch.

"Hey," she said, still smiling.

He stopped, obviously hearing Burnett and Holiday bickering in the office. "Is everything okay?"

Kylie chuckled. "They're arguing. So it's pretty much back to normal now."

"Better than when they weren't talking to each other."

"My thoughts exactly," Kylie said.

Derek studied her. "Can *we* talk?" He motioned to the two rocking chairs.

"Sure."

She sat in the first chair. He took the other. For a second, she got the image of them here before. Of him moving in and kissing her while she reclined in the chair.

She pushed that image away. They weren't kissing now. They were just talking. Two friends, talking.

He started to speak, but then his eyes widened. "You got good news?"

She grinned, knowing he'd read her mood. "My real grandfather is coming to see me in a few days."

"Damn!" His eyes filled with contentment for her. "You'll finally get your answers. Kylie Galen will know what she is. No more mystery."

"I hope so." An odd thought hit: What would her life be like when her quest changed? A wash of cold moved in behind her. She glanced back and just as quickly turned back around.

"I heard about your grandmother," Derek said. "And the rogue vampire. He really sacrificed himself for you?"

"Yeah." Her emotions took a nosedive. "All I saw in him was evil, Derek. But it wasn't true."

"It wasn't just you," he said. "That's what I saw, too. So I get how that makes you feel."

She sighed. That was the thing about Derek. He always understood her feelings.

"Thanks." Someone walked past, and for a crazy second she thought it was Ellie. But of course, it wasn't.

"I miss her, too," Derek said, reading her again.

Kylie looked up toward the sky. "Sometimes, I just wish heaven wasn't so far away."

Things grew quiet. When she looked back, Derek was staring at her. Staring at her the way the old Derek used to stare. The gold flecks in his eyes brightened against his green irises. She felt the world go fairy tale around her, and she noticed things. Things like how his shoulders looked like a soft place to rest her head.

"You were right, you know."

"Right about what?" she asked.

"Me pushing you away. It was the stupidest thing I've ever done. Then the mistake with Ellie, I . . . messed up, Kylie, and it hurt you. I'm sorry. So damn sorry."

"That's history," she said, and another silence fell upon them.

"I talked to Holiday," he whispered.

His soft-spoken words had Kylie realizing that Holiday and Burnett weren't arguing anymore. Were they busy doing something else?

"Talked to Holiday about what?" she asked.

"About why I was feeling supercharged emotions around you."

Kylie bit down on her lip. She didn't need to know this now, did she?

Derek sensed her feelings. "I'm not expecting you to do anything. I just want you to know."

"Know what?"

He hesitated. "Holiday said that sometimes, when a fae really cares about someone, their emotions can become blown out of proportion. Most times, the problem goes away after they accept their feelings. So that's what I'm doing. Accepting it."

She opened her mouth to speak but didn't have a clue what to say.

He cupped his jeans-covered knees in his hands. They were jeans that fit him really well, too.

"I'm in love with you, Kylie." He looked almost embarrassed by the admission. He jumped up, took one step away, then swung around and faced her again. "I don't expect you to say it back, and I don't think this will change your mind about anything. But you deserved to know. And I needed to tell you because . . . I've never felt this way before—for anyone."

Kylie sat there, his words running around her head, feeling . . . Okay, what did she feel, exactly? First was confusion. Then came fear. Derek loved her. Her heart tightened.

She glanced up into his eyes and saw he was reading her emotions. Every one of them.

"I should leave now," he said, but he leaned down and pressed the quickest of kisses on her cheek. It reminded her of how Perry had kissed Miranda that night in the parking lot. Romantic. Sweet.

She just watched him leave. Then she fell back in the rocker and tried to decipher the emotions swelling in her chest.

"How can everything feel so right and yet wrong at the same time?" she muttered.

"Life's weird like that." The rocker beside her, the one Derek had just left, creaked slightly.

Kylie glanced over at the reclined spirit and frowned. "Things aren't going to get any easier, are they."

The spirit chose not to answer.

"Look," Kylie said, and pulled her knees up in the chair. "I don't have a lot of rules. But I told you, you're gonna have to do something about that face."

The ghost's face magically started healing, becoming normal. Kylie gasped. It wasn't seeing it happen that shocked her; it was the face. She recognized it.

"God, no."

The ghost disappeared. Kylie shot up to go find Holiday when another voice spoke behind her.

"Kylie?"

Recognizing Daniel's voice, she swung around. "Daddy," she said, and hugged him.

His cold arms came around her. When she pulled back, she saw he had tears in his eyes.

"That's the first time you called me that."

"I guess it just took me a while," she said.

He smiled and touched her face. *"I met my real mother for the first time. She sure was proud of her granddaughter."*

"She seemed sweet. She loved you so much."

"I know," he said. Suddenly he faded a bit. *"I don't have much time, Kylie. But I found the answer you wanted."*

"What answer?" she asked, scared to believe.

"What we are. My mother finally remembered."

"And?" Kylie held her breath.

"We're chameleons."

Kylie shook her head as she tried to grasp what he meant. "We're lizards? What does that mean?"

He faded a bit more. *"I don't know."*

"We can change our patterns. Is that what it means?" she asked.

"I have no more answers," he said. *"But soon. Soon we will discover this together."*

"Together?" she asked.

He nodded, and the cold and what vapor was left of his visual spirit faded even more.

"I'm going to die?" she asked as the icy tremors prickled her skin.

He didn't have the chance to answer, but she could swear she saw him shake his head. Or maybe it was just wishful thinking.

She stood there on the porch, trying to breathe, trying to come to terms with what she had learned. She was a chameleon. She might be about to die. And . . . she remembered the face of the ghost—the one who showed up before her father. She might not be the only one who was going to die.

"Holiday?" Kylie called out as she stormed back into the office.

Life really wasn't going to get any easier.

Will Kylie figure out how to harness her new powers?

Find out in **Whispers at Moonrise,**
the fourth book in C. C. Hunter's Shadow Falls series!

Read on for a preview.

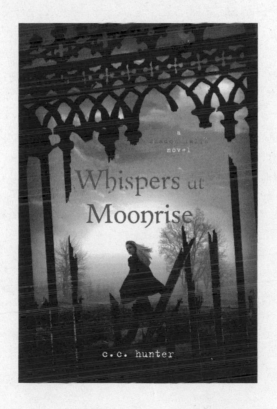

Available from St. Martin's Griffin in October 2012

Kylie Galen stood on the porch outside the Shadow Falls office, panic stabbing at her sanity. A gust of late August wind, still chilled by her father's departing spirit, picked up her long strands of blond hair and scattered them across her face. She didn't brush them away. Nor did she breathe. She just stood there, air trapped in her lungs, while she stared through the wisps of hair at the trees swaying in the breeze.

Why does life have to be so hard? The question rolled around her head like a Ping-Pong ball gone wild. Then the answer spun back just as quick.

Because she wasn't all human. For the last few months, she'd struggled to identify the type of non-human blood she had rushing through her veins. Now she knew.

Or at least, according to her dear ol' dad, she knew. She was . . . a chameleon. As in a lizard, just like the ones she'd seen sunning in her backyard. Okay, so maybe not just like those, but close enough. And here she'd been worried about being a vampire or a werewolf because it would be a little hard to adjust to drinking blood or shape-shifting on full moons. But this . . . this was . . . unfathomable. Her father had to be wrong about that, didn't he?

Her heart pounded against her breastbone as if seeking escape. She finally breathed. In, and then out. Her thoughts shot away from the lizard issue to the other bad stuff.

Yup. In the last five minutes she'd been slapped with not one, not two, not even three, but with four oh-crap eye-opening revelations.

A little voice of reason inside her head spoke up. One of the things—Derek's confession that he loved her—couldn't completely be called bad. But it sure as hell couldn't be called good. Not now. Not when she'd basically considered them history. When she'd spent the last few weeks trying to convince herself that they were just friends.

Her mind juggled all four disclosures. She didn't know which to focus on first. Or maybe her mind did know. *She was a freaking lizard!*

"For real?" she spoke aloud. The Texas wind snatched away her words; she hoped it would take them all the way to her father, wherever the dead who hadn't completely passed over went to wait. "Seriously, Dad? A lizard?"

Of course, Dad didn't answer. After two months of dealing with one spirit or another, the whole ghost-whispering gift and its limitations still managed to piss her off. "Damn!"

She took another step toward the main office's door to unload on Holiday, the camp leader, then stopped. Burnett, the other camp leader and a cold-to-the-touch but hot-to-look-at vampire, was with Holiday. Since Kylie couldn't hear them arguing anymore, she figured that meant they might be doing something else. And yes, by something else, she meant sucking face, swapping spit, and doing the tongue tango. All phrases her bad-attitude vampire roommate Della would use. Which probably meant Kylie was in a bad mood. But didn't she deserve a little attitude after everything that had happened?

Gripping her fists, she stared at the office's front door. She'd inadvertently interrupted Burnett and Holiday's first kiss, and she didn't want to do the same with their second.

Besides, maybe she needed to calm down a little. To chill. To think things through before she ran to Holiday in her bad-attitude hysterics. Her thoughts shifted to her latest ghost issue. How could a ghost of someone who was alive appear to Kylie? A trick, right? It had to be a trick.

She glanced around to make sure the ghost had really gone. It had. Or at least the cold had vanished. All this at one time was just too much.

Turning, she shot down the porch steps and headed around to the back of the office. She started running, wanting to experience the sense of freedom she got when she ran, when she ran fast, ran non-human fast.

The wind picked up her black dress and sent the hem dancing against her thighs. Her feet moved in rhythm, barely missing the Reeboks she usually wore, but when she arrived at the edge of the woods, she came to an abrupt halt— so abrupt that the heels on her black shoes cut deep ruts into the earth.

She couldn't go into the woods. She didn't have a shadow—the mandatory person with her to help ward off the evil Mario and his other rogue buddies if they decided to attack.

Attack again.

So far the old man's attempts had proved futile at ending her life, but two of those times had resulted in the death of someone else.

Guilt fluttered through her already tight chest, followed by fear. Mario had proven how far he'd go to get to her, how evil he was when he'd taken his own grandson's life right in front of her. How could anyone be that wicked?

She stared at the line of trees and watched as their leaves danced in the breeze. It was a completely normal slice of scenery that should have put her at peace.

But she felt no peace. The woods, or rather, something that hid within, almost dared her to enter. Taunted her to move into the thick line of trees. Confused by the strange feeling, she tried to push it away, but the feeling persisted, even intensified.

She inhaled the green scent of the forest, and right then she knew.

Knew with clarity.

Knew with certainty.

Mario wouldn't give up. And she wouldn't, or maybe couldn't, give in. Sooner or later she would face Mario again. And it wouldn't be serene, tranquil, or peaceful. Only one of them would walk away.

You will not be alone. The words echoed deep within her as if to offer her peace. No peace came. The shadows between the trees danced on the ground, calling her, beckoning her. To do what, she didn't know, and along with the unknown came questions. Frightening questions.

Trepidation took another lap around her chest. She dug the heels of her shoes deeper into the hard dirt. The heel of her right shoe cracked—an ominous little sound that seemed to punctuate the silence.

"Crap!" She stared down at her feet. The one word seemed to have been yanked from the air and nothing but a hum of eeriness remained.

And that's when she heard it.

Someone drew in a raspy breath. While the sound came only at a whisper, she knew that the owner of this breath stood behind her. Stood close. And since no chill of death surrounded her, she knew it wasn't from the spirit world.

The sound came again. Someone fed life-giving air into their lungs. Odd how she now feared the living more than she feared the dead.

Her heart thudded to a sudden stop. Much like grooves left in the earth by her three-inch heels, her growing fear left ruts in her courage. Deep, painful ruts that made her shiver inside.

She wasn't ready. If it was Mario, she wasn't ready. Whatever it was she needed to do, whatever plan or fate she was destined to follow, she needed more time.

Welcome to Camp Shadow Falls.
Once you visit, you'll never be the same.

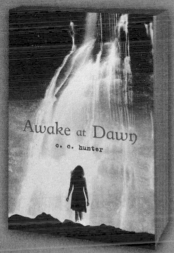

St. Martin's Griffin